TREAT

TERRAWAY
BOOK FIVE

MARY E. TWOMEY

MARY E. TWOMEY, LLC

TREAT

BOOK FIVE IN THE TERRAWAY SERIES

By

Mary E. Twomey

COPYRIGHT

DEDICATION

For Melissa,

The Sister I Chose,
and the sister who always, always chooses me.

TELL ME ABOUT OCTOBER GRACE

The world seemed to be moving in slow motion, taking far too long for the simplest things. The drive from my side of town to Ezra's should have taken only an hour, but the universe bent itself so that the hour felt like seven hundred hours all hooked together, stretching out longer than they should.

Von was gone. We'd had the best kiss of my life, and when we both ran from the intensity of a life neither of us were anticipating, he'd been snatched up by Ekeks – a cannibalistic people from Terraway whose favorite snack was fresh vampire meat.

I tried not to think about all the body parts they might take that could still leave Von alive. I loved every part of Von, even the childish, selfish ones, and wanted him intact.

When we reached Ezra's, Danny had already apprised him of the situation over the phone on the drive. "Where's the stone?" I asked in lieu of a greeting as I marched into the house on a mission.

"It's in a lead-lined safe so it doesn't poison the minds of any humans in my home." When this answer wasn't specific enough for me, he pointed to the basement. "Downstairs, but we're waiting on Sylvia. You remember she's the Queen of Lumipad, and she can port us down and lead us to the main well with less interference from civilians. If all goes without interruption, the whole thing could be done by tomorrow night."

"That's not soon enough!" I was irate, worried that no one was taking this as seriously as they should. "Every minute that ticks by is another that Von's life is in danger. I'm not waiting around for Sylvia to manage her people. Can Lang take us? Finn? Give me a map, and I'll go by myself. No one else has to get hurt."

Ezra wasn't listening. He had Bev swept up in a hug that looked like it hurt them both with the raw emotion they couldn't suppress. "I'm so sorry you were brought in on this. I don't want you worried."

"My children. They're going to do something danger-ous? This is the country filled with cannibals, isn't it?" Her voice was barely recognizable. She wasn't brash or bossy. She sounded afraid. Actually concerned for Ollie and me. Her southern lilt came off as a delicate Belle, and not a brash, demanding woman on the prowl to manipulate men with money. I didn't know who she was, but Ollie was right, this wasn't the Bev I knew.

"I'll be with them. I'll make sure our children come home safe. I won't leave their side." He kissed her lips, and for some reason this made me very squeamish.

"She's so small," Bev whispered. "They'll take her, and I'll never see my daughter again! Then they'll take Ollie and you. I can't sit back while that happens! I'm just starting to see my family for the first time. I can't let you all just go walking straight into danger! We're talking actual cannibals, Ezra!"

I had to get out of there. Bev never referred to me as her daughter unless there was something in it for her. The look on her face was raw, unmakeuped and earnest, and I had no idea what to make of it. I'd never seen her sincere before, and didn't know whether to be overjoyed or very, very afraid.

Ollie had the same reaction, though he'd spent more time with the new Bev. "It's alright, Bev. I'll watch October. I'll make sure we all come home. Like Ezra said, it'll probably be a day of traveling, and then we'll be right back. Easy as that." When Bev made to argue, Ollie held up his hand. "When have I ever not kept October safe?"

Bev left Ezra's embrace to wrap her arms around Ollie, squeezing him tight and shaking in his arms. I'd never seen them hug before. My mouth went dry, and I heard everything as if my ears were stuffed with cotton. Bev shook like a leaf battered by the wind in Ollie's embrace. "I remember the day you were born. I was so scared I would screw you up. Now that you're perfect and I had nothing to do with it? I can't let you die like this. You're my only boy!"

This choked Ollie and I simultaneously, and I knew I had to leave. I ran to the conference room down the hall and shut myself inside to escape land of the body snatchers, lest they come for me next. It was a complete personality change. In passing, I'd heard Bev's old school friends mention that she'd been a real sweetheart, but I never believed it. As soon as she'd run into them, they'd run straight out of our lives when they caught wind of Bev's new deranged personality. This version must've been the one they were expecting to see. The kind of woman who hugs her son and cares if her daughter gets eaten by cannibals.

I barely recognized her.

I waited out the waves of getting everything in order, holing myself up in the conference room, since I knew this was where we would all end up when things were ready to be set in motion. I heard Mason escort Bev toward the stairs to settle her in, but they stopped just outside the conference room door. "Mason, please. You have to see how dangerous this is. A land of starving cannibals? Am I the only person who cares about my children?"

Mason's voice was calm, and I could picture his kind eyes as he remained patient with Bev. "Ezra cares about your children, and he cares about thousands of people's children in Terraway. And all this *is* for October. An Omen needs her Pullers, or she won't live very long. Getting the stone to Lumipad is the only way to keep October safe in the long run. It's a risk, sure, but it's riskier not sending her."

"But why does it have to be her?"

"Because only your family is immune to the stone's magic. Only you, October, Ollie and I suppose Allie can touch it without turning to stone. The tradeoff is that it warps your minds. That's why you were the way you were, and why October is the way she is." Mason was matter of fact about there being something wrong with me, and it made me clench my fists. I was fine. I didn't need Bev knowing my business. It was one of the many reasons I told her next to nothing about my life. That, and she never asked.

Bev's voice was small. "What way is she? I don't know the first thing about her. I'm still sorting things out. For the past who knows however many years, I remember her picking me up and taking me out for the day to make sure I had food, but I don't know anything about her."

"Maybe you should ask her."

"Have you seen the way she looks at me? She won't talk to me. I've lost my chance to know my daughter, and it's killing me! Ollie's giving me a second chance, but I know that look. October Grace won't let me in. Please, Mason. Tell me about my daughter. She trusts you."

"Well, then you already know your daughter has terrible judgment when it comes to trust and that sort of stuff."

"Please. Tell me anything."

"I'm not sure I want to get in the middle of..."

Then Bev cut him off, her voice raising hysterically. "Please, Mason! Tell me about my daughter!"

The sound of her plea shook me up and rattled around the parts of me I assumed were untouchable. I sunk to the carpet, kneeling at the door with my ear pressed to it. I didn't want to see or talk to Bev, but I'd never heard her want to know more about me – or anything about me, really. My fingertips hesitantly fluttered over the door as I let myself consider the painful, confusing and hopeful thought that maybe Bev actually did want me around.

"Okay, alright. Calm down. What do you want to know?"

"Is she happy?"

Mason let out a long and low sigh. "I don't know. She's funny, and she smiles a lot. She's the kind of girl who finds a way to get the things out of life that she wants, and I don't think that kind of person tolerates being unhappy for very long. She'll be glad when this whole mission is over. I know we all will."

"Does she have good friends?"

"No," Mason ruled. "She hides from just about everyone. Made the job so hard in the beginning. Won't let people she doesn't trust help her, so she ends up doing everything herself. Von and I do our best, but she guards herself even from us, not that I can blame her. It was harder in the beginning, but I think we're finding our way."

"Tell me more. I hate that this is all new to me."

"She's kind. Too unselfish sometimes. Not to be disrespectful, but she should've stopped going to see you years ago. She kept it up because she's a good person. The flipside of that coin is that she doesn't care about her own life. A beautiful woman like that working around inmates?"

"Has she ever been attacked by any of them?"

"Do you really think she'd admit that to me? She doesn't work there anymore, so at least that nightmare's over." He paused, and I wondered what his eyes were saying in that moment. If part of him still hated me, if any part of him was capable of forgiving me for all we'd put each other through. "You want to know about your daughter? She's incredible. That's pretty much the sum of it."

I couldn't believe Mason had such lovely things to say about me. He didn't bring up my OCD or how impossible I sometimes made things for him. He was generous with my good parts and politely covered over my ugly ones. He was turning out to be a good friend, despite all we'd been through. A layer of hurt crumbled away, and I felt one degree closer to my constant protector.

"You love her," Bev pointed out.

Mason was thoughtful as he mulled this over. "I do. I love her enough to know that I'm not good for her. Not in the way I want to be, anyway. I was married before, and I think I tried to jump back in too soon. You should know I hurt her in ways I'm too ashamed to mention to her mother."

Bev was quiet, and I feared they'd hear my heart pounding.

Just then, I heard a commanding voice coming from the foyer, calling out for me.

TOGETHER OR NOT AT ALL

"October Grace!" I heard the voice again, bellowing in earnest.

Mason hurried Bev up the stairs, giving me just enough space to sneak out. It was Kabayo, and he was in a state about something. "Where is she? I was sleeping, so I only just saw. Where's the Omen? October!" I opened the door and moved out into the hallway.

Ezra tried to calm down the King of Silo. Kabayo had the body of a man and the head of a horse, which was freaking out Ollie. It's one thing to have a creature explained to you, and quite another when the seven-foot tall half-horse is looming over you, speaking normally and expecting you to understand and not just stare at him like "Oh, holy crap."

Kabayo raised his arm, revealing a glowing blackish-blue X on his forearm. Ezra whipped his head to me when he saw me standing at the base of the stairs. "How did you call Kabayo?"

"I didn't."

"It's a reverse centaur!" Ollie exclaimed, unable to help himself.

Kabayo pounded his fist to his chest. "I felt her fear because I gave her my token." He kept his forearm displayed to Ezra, whose eyes bugged. Kabayo ran to me, his hands gripping my shoulders. "What happened? I felt your panic yesterday, but it dulled quickly. Then today I felt something was very wrong, so I came here as fast as I could make arrangements for someone to handle things in Silo."

"It's Von!" I wanted to cry, but knew I couldn't break down and still be respected by the gruff ruler. "He's gone. The Ekeks kidnapped him to make sure I took the stone to Lumipad next. We're dropping someone off here, picking up the stone and leaving."

Kabayo's wide nostrils flared. "Where's Mason?"

Mason's feet pounded down the steps. "Danny, Bev needed to see you about something. We're ready to go as soon as Sylvia gets here. She'll help us get through the land without interference from civilians."

"How can I help?" Kabayo asked as Danny jogged up the stairs to go see to Bev. It was a steep difference from the last time I'd seen him, where I had to basically bully him into being a decent guy. Now that his head was screwed on straight, he was thinking about the greater good for Terraway.

"Find Von!" I begged. "If we don't make it there fast enough, who knows what'll happen to him!"

Kabayo looked down at my face, taking in the state of things. "I can't exactly go roaming about your world. I don't look like you."

I closed my eyes, nodding in defeat. "Okay. That's fair. Then any way you can help us get the stone to Lumipad's main water source would be great."

Ezra rubbed his temples. "I summoned Sylvia over an hour ago, and she's not answered."

"That's not like her. She's Mrs. By the Book." Kabayo frowned, his arms akimbo. "You want me to go see if I can find some of her spies to check on her?"

"That would be wonderful," Ezra replied, relieved.

Danny's voice was pinched and came from the door to the basement, which was around the corner. "Before you go, I need a word, King Kabayo."

"Sure." Kabayo trotted down into the basement with Danny.

Mariang's arms wrapped around me. "It's alright. We'll find him. King Kabayo's well respected everywhere he goes. Whatever's holding Sylvia up, he can handle it."

I waited until the hug ended and then threw out my arms. "Really? No one's going to state the obvious? No one's going to say it?"

"Say what?" Ollie asked, unsure on the politics of everything.

"Hello, the Ekeks have Von. Sylvia's land is the one with the Ekeks, and she's not answering Ezra's call. She's in on it!"

Ezra shook his head. He was probably expecting something that didn't make him question his belief system that the rulers were good, that he was still in charge, and that Santa Claus was real. "No, dear. Sylvia is the Queen of Lumipad. If she had a problem with the order the stone was to be handed out, she would have simply voiced her concern to me."

"And you would have done what?" I challenged.

"I would have put it before the council again and taken a poll."

"Which would have gotten her exactly nowhere. My point's still valid. I don't think we should wait for her."

"Porting into a land that's riddled with starving Ekeks is dangerous. Sylvia might be able to fly you to the well so you don't have to walk the countryside."

That one took me a second, but then I remembered she had bat wings. I'd never been in an airplane before, and something told me soaring with Sylvia would be even scarier than nervously chomping on airline peanuts in coach.

"No," Mason ruled, his arms crossed over his wide chest. "Out of the question. I'm her Reaper, and I say no.

Sylvia drops her grip on October midflight, and she's dead before anyone can save her."

Ezra leaned against the wall of the foyer, and then realized he had couches a few yards away. "Shall we wait in the living room? Things are getting more complicated than I was prepared for."

"Lang!" I belted out, unable to control my volume or my nerves. "Ezra, can you summon Lang? Maybe he can help Danny and Mariang. They were going to go looking for Von."

"Absolutely not," Ezra replied, sitting on the white leather couch in the living room with too much exhaustion weighing him down. I felt awful for him, and saw the tired lines around his eyes that were usually so good at smiling. "I've already got one daughter running headfirst into danger. I'll not suffer the other to do the same when it's not necessary."

Mariang stood in the archway that separated the living room from the rest of the house. "Dad, I'll be with Danny. If anything, I'll make good bait since they're looking for people close to October. We can draw them out this way."

Ezra pressed his hand to his chest and closed his eyes in sadness. "Not another word, dear. My heart can't take it. No daughter of mine will be bait."

I knew Von would laugh at the irony of that statement, since Bait was my nickname. Something told me Ezra wouldn't be a fan of that if he knew.

Ezra stepped in with a plausible solution. "I can

summon Prince Langgam, if he's not too busy with things in Sakuna. He can at least lend us the use of his minions to help find Von."

"Yes!" I slapped my hand to my forehead. "I was only thinking of Lang in terms of another body to help look. I totally forgot about his minions! You're a genius, Ezra. Dad of the century, right there."

Ezra glanced up at me curiously as I paced the archway next to Mariang. "I'm pleased to hear it. Though I haven't earned that title tonight. I want to keep you here, but the sole plan is for me to let you go into a dangerous country with only Mason and Sylvia for protection."

"And me," Ollie said, his hand on my shoulder to still my pacing. "I'll go. October can stay here. They don't know me, so they won't be expecting I have the stone."

"Obviously not," I ruled, my tone sharp. "You know less about Terraway than I do. This whole thing is my respon-sibility."

"Says who? You did two other lands. It's my turn. I'll do the next two."

"You won't survive this one to make it to the next!"

"And you will?"

I shrugged. "If I don't, then you can take the rest of the stone to the next place, sure."

This was clearly the wrong thing to say. Ollie's nostrils flared and he grabbed my shoulders to shake his brand of sense into me. "I gave up my whole life to make sure you lived! Stop throwing yourself away! You're not garbage!" he shouted, voicing my biggest insecurity. My raw emotion must've been plain on my face, because Ollie crushed me to him in a tight hug I could barely breathe through. "You're not garbage. You're just not. I'm taking the stone down. It's my responsibility."

"Where'd you get that logic?" I asked through wet lashes as we held onto each other.

"Because *you're* my responsibility. I love you, kid. Stop throwing yourself into the dumpster. You're worth more than this!" He shook me at every fourth word, and I felt his anger at our lot in life. "You listen to me, October Grace. You're going to live to be an old woman. You'll get married and go on vacations and have a life better than even *I* could dream for you. You won't go out and die where I can't find you. You think you need me?" He shook his head. "*I* need *you*. I need you to be safe."

We stood in the archway, clinging to each other like the children we were never allowed to be. So much was shifting and rocking our fragile boat. When Allie had left us, we clung that much harder. Now I was telling Ollie I would go somewhere dangerous without him. I'd hidden a good many freak-outs when he'd left for New York, and that was just a plane ride away. I don't know why I expected I'd be able to up and go to another world without pushback. "I'm sorry. You're right. I didn't mean to scare you. We go together or not at all."

Ollie heaved a gust of relief that almost weakened his knees to the point of collapse, but I held him tight.

"Together. Let's get this country done with and move on to the next. Let's finish it, so you can rest."

"Do it to it," I agreed, making Ollie snort and breaking the intensity of the mood.

"And you!" Ollie ramped up his volume again, pointing in Mariang's shocked face. "I don't want to hear anything about you going out looking for cannibals. Using yourself as bait. You're my sister, too, and you're not going to risk your life for this. We're a team, understood? We'll find Von together."

Mariang didn't need the invitation, but Ollie waved her into our hug all the same. He kissed the top of her head and I watched her beam grow for him. It's amazing what a difference a good brother can make. Mariang had a mansion and a good father with a boyfriend who... Well, a boyfriend. I'd had none of those things, but I had Ollie, and most days that was enough to get me through.

3

THE SEARCH PARTY

It was nearing two in the morning when Ezra called down to Kabayo in the basement. "Gentlemen, come on up. Prince Langgam's here, and he wants a rundown from everyone."

Lang had given me a stiff hug as if he had seen the gesture on TV, but wasn't quite sure of its practical mechanics. When our hug ended, he kept his hand on my shoulder. "I haven't seen you in too many weeks," he commented. "It's a shame it's something like this that breaks me out of my kingdom, but it's been a bit chaotic in my nation since Father was taken prisoner. I haven't yet built you the porch swing I promised upon our fake nuptials."

I recalled our little joke that had made him break from his angry and business-like demeanor. "I was going to say.

It's just as I suspected from you. All talk. I bet you're just laying around the castle all day long doing big, fat nothing and eating giant peeled grapes."

"I hope you always picture me doing that. Perhaps one day it'll be real." He looked me over, as if searching for a defect of some kind. "I see you're doing better than when I saw you last."

"That's the thing about not being locked in your dad's dungeon."

"I can't believe Ekeks snatched up Von. They're either getting desperate or they don't fear Ezra anymore. I can't decide which is worse."

"I'm worried how much time is going by. I mean, who knows what they could be doing to Von while we get our acts together in here."

I knew. I knew exactly what they could be doing.

Ruiz leaned on the wall, leaving brown dirt smears on everything he touched. He had a flat nose that was prone to sniffing repeatedly and a small mouth that smiled indulgently at me. "We'll find your Puller, Lady October." He called past Ezra toward the basement. "Get up here, King Kabayo. Claim your victor's kiss straight from my grateful lips. The kingdom's in flux, but it's never been freer than it is now. I want to properly thank the warrior who locked Geon up."

Klark bumped his hip to mine, and I tried not to be bothered by the dirt. "Aranya's an absolute pain, but luckily he's easy to distract. We've got him focusing on a segment of land that couldn't matter less to the kingdom. Meanwhile your husband here's been rebuilding and putting the people in jail who should've been there a long time ago. Our *buhay* crops are finally starting to grow to nearly a foot tall, thanks to you."

"That's awesome. Super happy for you guys." I said the words, but I couldn't smile. Von was in pain. He was probably scared, and there was nothing I could do to help him. "Kabayo! Let's move!" I marched past the others and let myself downstairs to where I'd seen Kabayo disappear with Danny.

I expected to see a half-horse, half-man, but not seeing one was a shock. The lights were on in the concrete basement, shedding enough illumination to every corner so that there was no place to hide. "Kabayo? Danny?" I walked around, flummoxed. "Ezra? They're not down here. Check upstairs?"

"I'll go," Mason offered, jogging up to the second floor.

I could've sworn they'd come down here. I saw them go down and certainly would've noticed Kabayo coming back up. I looked around, seeing something that caught my eye in the corner. The mid-sized black safe was opened. *Why would Ezra leave the safe with the sagrado stone hanging open?* Out of sheer curiosity I went over and peered inside, finding nothing but a note sitting in the dark interior. My eyebrows pulled together when I read my name at the top.

I shivered with the odd feeling that something bad was about to happen.

I gave the letter a skim, dropped it to the ground and screamed. "Ezra!"

4

GIRL TIME CONFESSIONS

"I'm not going to sleep," I protested when Mason finally corralled me into Mariang's room.

Mariang shut the door, her fingers slipping on the lock. "I'm not feeling well," Mariang informed us. Upon closer inspection, the girl looked gaunt, a gray pallor coming over her after reading the note. "Danny's really gone?"

Neither of us could confirm the news again. We'd been over it a jillion times already. Danny had left me a note saying that Bev wanted to take the sagrado stone, so Ollie and I didn't have to. He'd talked Kabayo into porting them down to Lumipad, and they'd be back once it was delivered. It was the weirdest way Bev had ever not listened to me.

Ollie was in a state about it, ranting and losing his temper all over the place. Ezra and I had finally sent him to bed. It was nearing on four in the morning, and we were all tired. Lang sent some of his bug minions throughout the area surrounding my home, hoping to catch wind of Von's location.

Ezra put his foot down about Ollie or me leaving the mansion, and had even gone so far as to make Mason put a protective charm around the house so that no one could leave. He was afraid Mariang might come near a ripe soul and accidentally reap it without Danny there to rip it from her. After much fruitless arguing, Ezra sent us to bed, assigning Mason to pull for both Mariang and I through the night.

Mariang was confused over the simplest things. She chose two pajama bottoms instead of a bottom and a top, and brushed her teeth three times before she realized she'd forgotten to use toothpaste. I had to lead her to the bed, but she grew more nervous the closer she got to it. "I've never slept in a bed with another man," she admitted. "How could Danny do that? We tell each other everything!"

I held her hand and sat her on the edge of the bed. "You're not sleeping in a bed with Mason. You're sleeping with me. Mason? Would you mind being a wolf? She's freaking out about this."

Mason nodded. "Sure. Can I talk to you for a second first?"

I followed Mason out of the room after he pulled a fair

bit of stress off of Mariang. We stood in the hallway, a mixture of worked up and exhausted. "What's up?"

"That Danny, of all people, went off book on this worries me. If you're planning anything crazy you haven't told me about, now's the time to come clean. I mean it. No more surprises. We're down two Reapers, so we can't screw up. If Ezra's on his game, he'll be bringing in another one for Mariang by morning."

"Another Puller? How the crap are we supposed to know if we can trust anyone new?"

"I have no idea. But I'm pulling double duty, so be on my team, here. No surprises."

I held up my hands. "Dude, I've got nothing. I wish I had a plan. I'd give my left set of toes for a solid plan."

Mason scrutinized my face for traces of a lie. "Okay. If you want to strategize, do it with me."

"My plan is to try and get a little sleep so I can stop hating myself for not having a plan to save Von."

Mason let me back into the room, locking us inside with one nervous Mariang. She bit at her fingernails and couldn't look at Mason or the bed. He bowed his head to her and disappeared into the bathroom, coming out a minute later as my favorite wolf. I pulled the covers back and helped Mariang lie down, tucking her pink comforter under her chin. I nearly laughed at her wide eyes when Mason jumped up onto the bed, circling three times before he settled in the center.

I climbed in, petting him and making sure he had a

space under the covers. I ran my hand over his gray fur, and sighed contentedly when his loyal muzzle tucked itself under my chin. "How long have you known Danny?" I asked, searching for girl talk.

"Most of my life. Our parents were friends in high school, and kept in touch over the years. He's been my Reaper for seven years."

"That's a long time. Has he always been so surly?" I kidded.

"He's not surly. Well, he's a little surly, but it's mostly because he's always hungry, always on duty. When it's just us, he's different."

"I may need to install a hidden camera to get some proof."

"Those days you gave us to just be together? They were incredible. I hadn't seen him that relaxed in ages. If he doesn't come back, I'll hold those tight in my heart." Her eyes squinched shut, another tear leaking out the corner.

"Hey, don't talk like that. He knows what he's doing," I lied. "Has Danny let you down before? Has he ever not come through?"

"No, but this is different. He's never gone off without me like this, not when he knew it'd be dangerous and would separate us."

I lifted her hand and twined her fingers through my gloved ones, resting them atop Mason's spine so he could pull from Mariang while she vented. Mason leaned up to give me a kiss in gratitude for helping Mariang warm up to the idea of being pulled from by another Duwende. We petted his fur, sharing quietly as if there wasn't a man in the room. "Danny loves you. He'll be back. Then we can get Von."

"I can see how powerful that kiss must've been. That you saw a vision on your first kiss? We'll get him back, October." I kept my mouth shut, so Mariang continued, lowering her voice. "What was your vision about?"

I looked at the door to make sure it was shut. "It was about Von."

"Well, I gathered that much. Danny and I only ever have visions about each other, unless it's prophetic or something."

"Whoa, you have prophetic dreams?"

"How do you think Dad *really* found your mum? I had a vision of the two of them getting engaged. It happened exactly as I dreamt it. It's why we moved here. You know we're from London originally."

That was worth a jaw-drop. "Are you serious? Is that going to happen to me if I keep kissing Von?" Then a more daunting question popped into my brain. "Have you seen anything else about my family?"

"*Our* family, and no. Nothing all that specific." She looked down and to the side, the lie obvious.

"I can tell you're being evasive. Spill it, sister."

Mariang shrugged. "It's nothing I even understand. I saw you crying. You looked different."

"Different how?"

"Your hair was all done up pretty, and you were in a nice dress. It was black with gold stars scattered all over it. It looked like a special occasion or something. You were crying, but I don't know why." She looked at my hand. "You had… It was fuzzy. Hard to tell."

"Huh. Well I'll be on the lookout for tissues if I ever wear a dress. Weird. How often do you see non-prophetic visions when you and Danny kiss?"

"Every time since they started. Why do you think we don't kiss in public? It's hard to pull out of it on a dime."

"I can understand that. Totally bonkers, though."

"What was your vision about with Von?" she asked with the first hint of a smile in her eyes.

That kind of stuff was private, but the girl had been so wrecked, I didn't want her to feel snubbed. She needed a good distraction. "Um, well we were kissing in the kitchen in real life, and then it all got blurry and we were kissing…" I turned on my back and looked up at the ceiling, not used to talking about this kind of stuff. "Promise not to tell Von?"

Mariang leaned up on her elbow to look down at me, petting our wolf with eager eyes. "Cross my heart."

"He, um…" I blew a raspberry out of my mouth. "I'm not good at this! It's really embarrassing. I swear I don't waste my time thinking about this kind of stuff."

"Spit it out, now. Let's have it." Mariang was smiling now, and I knew I couldn't close myself off when she was so clearly happy for the first time that evening.

"I looked down, and we were in... I mean, he was wearing a tux, and I was in um, a sort of a..." The ending came out of me in a rush. "I was sort of in a wedding dress or something."

Mariang squealed with delight and reached across our pup to squeeze my arm. "Oh, I hope that one's prophetic. Von's like a brother to me. You're so good for him. He's changed and grown so much since he started reaping for you. He's himself again, not lost and trying to waste himself. He used to be the hero to his brothers. Still is to most of them. He just needed to see that the good things about him were still in there."

"That's not the worst of it," I admitted, wanting to clear my conscience at this point more than indulge in girlish gossip. "The vision shifted, and I think we were on our honeymoon. It was... It was pretty detailed."

"You had sex in your vision?"

I nodded, my cheeks pink as I stared up at the ceiling, refusing to look at her. "I didn't mean to. Do you think he had the same vision?"

"I can guarantee it. Von wouldn't have panicked and run out like that if he'd seen nothing. So *if* he had a vision, it would always line up with yours. You would never have two different visions."

I covered my face with my hands. "It was one crazy first kiss."

"I'll say. Danny and I didn't start having visions until a few weeks after our first kiss." When she saw I was clearly distressed about the whole thing, she squeezed my arm again. "It's okay, sister. We'll get him back."

I nodded, staring up at the unmarked white ceiling as I blew out a breath that contained much of my anxiety. "I'm going to try and get some sleep. I can't feel this anymore." I waved my hand over my body.

"Goodnight, sister."

"Goodnight, sister," I echoed, turning on my side and wrapping my arm and leg over Mason to use his furry form like a body pillow. Mariang snuggled up to him, too, and finally fell asleep before the sun rose.

5

THE COLORFUL BLUR OF VON

$\mathcal{M}$y dream was a blur of colors that took no shape at first. I was in some sort of a Crayola windstorm where the different abstract shades kept whipping around me, leafing through my hair and tugging at my clothes. I was dressed in the same peach t-shirt and light green pajama pants I'd worn to bed, my arms still bandaged to ward off my scratching. I'd taken my gloves off before I went to sleep, but I wished for them now, along with a coat and some shoes and socks.

I moved through the cold wind, thinking there must be something more peaceful on the other side of it. Finally, off in the distance, something took shape. A person was huddled in the same windstorm, only it looked less harrowing where he stood. I made my way toward him, if for no other reason than a little camaraderie to pass the time with. As I neared, the man's features became clearer, taking my breath away and pushing my speed up to its peak. "Von?" I cried. "Von!"

Von looked up in confusion, his mouth agape. Then he ran to me at full speed, his eyes focused on the prize.

I was his prize, and he swept me up in his arms as if I was the only thing that belonged in his embrace. My legs wrapped around his waist as we collided in a sea of windswept affection. I kissed his cheeks, but he wasn't interested in playing around. He pressed his lips to mine, and then sucked on the crest of my lower lip. Von pulled back with a heavy moan and sewed succulent kisses into my neck, lighting my body on fire as the storm wrapped us in its cold cocoon. We didn't hallucinate in here. In our dream, we could kiss like normal people. Even without the surreal sensations, I knew that Von was a fantastic kisser, and that we were good together. "Is this real?" he breathed between kisses. "Are you really here? Am I dreaming?"

"Yes to all of it. I'm dreaming, too. And I lied. I had a vision when we kissed. I did hallucinate. I don't know why I didn't fess up. I think I was scared. Did you…" I was afraid to ask, but I had to know.

"Of course I did! You were in a wedding dress, and I was all dashing in a tux. Then the wedding night? How we ever ended that kiss is still beyond me. I love you, November. I'm utterly mad about you."

"I love you, too!" I shouted above the wind and the colors, relieved at the catharsis that came with our confession. "Where are you? Who's got you?"

"I'm still Topside, not far from your house. No more than half an hour or so. It's a handful of random Ekeks and Manas who jumped me. I don't know them. They've got me locked up in a basement somewhere. What do they want? They're not telling me anything."

"They took you to get to me," I told him, letting my legs touch the ground. I stood in Von's arms, and despite the storm of wind and colors in our dream, and the horrors that would greet us when we woke, in that moment of moments, I felt safe. I hadn't experienced a whole lot of that feeling in my life, and knew to cherish every second of it. "They want me to take the stone to Lumipad next, instead of Dagat."

"Finn's not going to like that."

"No one's too thrilled. We're so scared for you, Von. We didn't even know if you were still alive! Lang's got his bug army looking for you, but I can tell him to narrow it down to a circle about half an hour from my house. That helps."

A light shined in Von's black eyes. "On the way here, they stopped for fast food. Blimpo Burgers. We're about five minutes from that."

"That's even more helpful! Oh, that's great. As soon as I wake up, I'll run and come get you."

"No! You stay far away from here." He kissed my face, cherishing the curves and paying homage to each of my few freckles. "I mean it, Peach. I don't want to scare you, but Ekeks and Manas are no joke. The only reason I'm alive is because I'm a bargaining chip. Bring Danny and a whole mess of Duwende fighters. There are at least nine of them that I could count, maybe more that I didn't see."

"Danny's gone!" I cried, burying my face in his chest. Von's body and his arms around my form shielded me from the colorful wind. He was my haven, and I clung to him as such. "Danny took Bev and the stone, and convinced Kabayo to port them down to Lumipad. Danny said it was too dangerous for me to go, so Bev would carry the stone. Said it all in a note after they sneaked off without telling Ezra or anybody. Mariang's freaking out."

"Whoa. How're you doing with that? Bev really took the stone? Why?"

"Because she didn't want me walking into a land filled with starving cannibals. She actually seemed worried for me. I don't recognize her, Von. It scares me how much the stone must've warped her original personality."

"Ollie told me how different she is now." We'd gone too long without kissing, and I knew we were both starting to feel the buildup. "I love your lips. You have no idea how hard it's been to keep things above board with you."

"You love my lips, eh? Prove it, punk. Kiss me like you mean it."

"Oh, sweet November. You don't know what you're playing at."

I shrugged as if I was as of yet unimpressed. It was my best dare to date, and boy did I reap the rewards. My knees turned to jelly after Von's tongue tangoed with mine, but instead of supporting my weight, Von lowered us to the grass. His body pressed down on mine as we made a perfect tangle of limbs, the wind egging us on. It was an amazing feeling to be present for a kiss of this magnitude, instead of the euphoria making my brain check out. This time I didn't miss the details of what made us magical without the use of magic.

I lost track of the time, the day, the year. I lost my mind and my hesitation that had held me back for so long. I shed my OCD that would never have let me roll around on the ground and think it was the sexiest thing ever. In our fantasy life, I was free.

I'd never been free before, but beneath Von's tantalizing and sensual caresses, that's exactly what I was.

I wanted this in real life. As incredible as fantasy Von was, I knew that when we found each other again, it would be the kiss to end all kisses. Our passion began to shift from frantic to a slow, melty love without words. I felt how terrified he was, and how much he needed the comfort we somehow managed to find only in each other. "I'm scared," he admitted in a whisper. I could only hear him above the wind because his lips were brushing my ear. "Tell Ezra to hurry."

The kiss broke as I wrapped my arms and legs around him, trapping his body in a hug that probably looked more like a wrestling hold than anything else. "I will. Tell me anything you can think of. What about smells? Mason's got that wolf sense that's almost as good as your vampire nose."

Von inhaled the scent in the crook of my neck, kissing me into near delirium as he pushed me into guttural moan mode. "I love that I do that to you. To watch you let go after you've bound yourself so tightly?" He stroked the outside of my thigh. "To know only I get to see you like that? I'm mad about you, darling. Solely and completely yours."

"You're scrambling my brains," I admitted, seeking friction when I should've been talking business. "We have to do this in person. Help me find you."

Von rolled off and lay beside me, knowing it was the only way either of us would ever be able to focus. "You're dangerous, love." He rubbed his toned stomach and then linked his fingers through mine as the wind brushed over our bodies, fluttering over our clothes but not whipping at us with its full force, as it had done when we were standing. The wind turned blue, and then lightened with brushstrokes of purple as Von collected his thoughts. "I smell leaves. Leaves and concrete. A little smog, but not enough to be near an industrial plant."

"Good! Keep thinking. Give me anything you've got."

"They're starving me," Von said, matter of fact. "It'll make me too weak to fight back after a few days. I don't feel hungry now, which is odd, since I'm short on blood, but I know I'll feel it soon. When they get word from you that you've delivered the stone, they're going to bleed me dry and leave me locked up here. Then you'll open the door, and I'll attack you." He swallowed hard. "They're counting on me killing you, Peach. That's how they're going to keep the other countries from getting their share of the stone without having any of the blood on their hands."

"Jeez! Why? I don't get why Terraway's so vindictive. It's like, get a life already."

"The Ekeks hate Dagat. Most of us do, but they do in particular. They've had just as bad a drought as Silo, but Finn sent relief to Kabayo and not them. No one likes the Ekeks and the Manas much. They're scavengers who do more harm than good when they visit the neighboring countries. Very few of us try to eat other Terrawayans, but they do when food's scarce."

"Oh good. They sound swell. Totally glad Bev, Danny and Kabayo are risking their lives for them. Do you think they'll get eaten? Do you think they've gone off on a suicide mission?" I knew Von would tell me the truth. He was first and foremost my friend, and I needed a friend that night.

"I certainly hope not. I hope Danny's smart about it. He knows the circuitous routes to take. But it's a risk. The one thing they've got going is Kabayo. He's a face the Ekeks and Manas will recognize, so if they know what's good for them, they'll back off."

My shoulder bumped to his as we stared at the wind while it changed to a rosy red. "Thank you. That actually made me feel a little better. You always know how to do that."

"That's because I'm good for you. I was going absolutely insane down here before you showed up. Tell me we can do this every night."

"I'm pretty sure you'll get sick of me after a few months of this."

"You underestimate the lure of your lips and appeal of your hips." His dreamy face fell into despair. "I made you feel bad about that sexy scar on your thigh. I took Katrina into your room and ruined your carpet! I'm sick about the whole thing."

"Stop. Stop punishing yourself, stop being a d-bag, and stop kissing Katrina. Then we're good."

"You know I wasn't kissing Katrina."

I turned to him. "You know what I mean. I don't want to kiss a guy who's having sex with my friends. I don't want to kiss a guy who's fooling around with anyone, really."

"You want me to only be a fool for you, then?"

"If it's not too much trouble."

Von looked up at the colors swirling and whipping above us. "I'm still not ready for something so serious. You and me? It won't be dates and figuring things out. It'll be forever from the first moment we dive in."

I chewed on my lower lip, not having considered this. "And that's not what you want?"

"That's not what I can give you. It doesn't matter what I want. One day I'll lose control, and I'll be gone. I won't exist as I am now. I'm not eager to attach that weight to you." He kissed my knuckles, closing his eyes as if his words that cut me also pained him. "I know that's not what you want to hear, and I can stop fooling around with your mates easily enough, but a boyfriend/girlfriend arrangement? Give me time. Loads of time. Give me time not chained up in a basement where we can talk about this like proper adults."

I swallowed the hollow feeling his words brushed over me and tried to be cool. "Since when do you consider yourself a proper adult? I only like the improper kind."

He saw through my joke to the slice of a scar beneath. I loved him. I actually went for what I wanted, and got turned down. The worst part about it was that I wasn't all that surprised.

Von's eyes watched my veiled heartbreak with self-loathing. "*Hani*, I'm sorry. I'm temporary, no matter how much I want to stay with you forever."

I pursed my lips as I put on a brave face neither of us believed. "I've never been fond of the word 'boyfriend', so it's fine. You can see whoever you want, minus my pool of friends. You're right. You should do what you like with your life." I hated myself for caving, for not fighting for what I wanted. But I guess the thing I wanted was a man who wouldn't think twice about jumping at the chance to be with me. Maybe that was naïve, but I didn't want to settle for less than that. I wanted a man who didn't have a list of reasons why I wasn't worth the risk. I wanted things to be simple with us. I wanted Mr. Brady.

His voice was gentle, pleading with me for something more, though I'd already given him more than I wanted to.

"I still love you. Just give me time. I gave up on considering all that ages ago. It's a whole new language for me to see if I can learn."

I ignored the lump in my throat, sizing up the very big thing we were discussing for the mountain it was. "I love you too, Von. We can keep things friendly, then, if that's what you want. Do what you like."

"It's what I need. Thank you." He squeezed my hand, clearly pleased as a relaxed smile fluttered over his features, making him, if possible, more stunning as the red wind turned a dusty pink.

6

MASON IN THE NUDE

I awoke when Mariang shook me out of my shared dream with Von, breaking me into the harsh reality of her tearful eyes, with Mason nowhere to be found. "Wake up, honey."

I felt like my lips were swollen, and I checked my clothes to make sure they were decent. "Hey. What time is it?"

"It's eight in the morning, but you looked like you were having a nightmare. You were tossing and turning and mumbling something."

I didn't have the heart to tell her that the things I had been moaning were not for her ears. "Oh. Sorry about that." It took me a solid ten seconds before my two realities caught up with each other. "Von! I can help find him!"

She wiped a tear from her cheek. "They want us to stay here where it's safe."

I ripped the covers off of me and ran for the door. "Screw that. Come on! Von gave me clues to help find him. Mason!" I called through the house, no doubt disturbing everyone who'd barely indulged in half a night's sleep. I bolted down the steps, tripping and righting myself on the wood banister as I called for Ezra, Ollie, Mason and anyone else who was in shouting range. "I found Von, sort of!"

Ezra stepped out from where he'd been eating breakfast in the kitchen, and Lynna came running after him. "You found him?" Lynna asked, her wrinkled face streaked with tears. She looked like she'd been up all night crying. "Where! Where's my boy?"

I relayed everything I knew from the logistics of my dream, bringing about looks of confusion instead of them getting their shoes on to go look for Von. "Well? Let's go! Call Lang and give him the specifics so he knows where to send his minions. Then once they find the house, we can go bust him out."

Ezra put his hand on my shoulder as Mariang came down dressed for the day. "Darling, it was a dream. That's not reality."

"No! It was a psychic dream! We were dreamwalking! Ask Mariang. She can tell you more about it."

Mariang was patient, as if explaining the truths of the universe to a small child. "You know dreamwalking only happens after the Omen and her Reaper make love. You and Von only kissed. What you're suggesting? It's not possible."

A light turned on in my brain. "But we had our honeymoon in our vision when we kissed! I don't know how it happened, but I know it was Von, and I can narrow down where he is!"

Ezra was firm, his chin raised as he laid down the law. "I'm sorry, but no. Lang will find him. We have to be patient."

"Screw your patience!" I spun on my heel and made my way for the stairs. First Von asked me to be patient, and now Ezra was banging that same stupid drum. "You have until I get dressed to lift the spell that keeps me locked inside here. 'Be patient,'" I scoffed. "Their plan is to bleed him dry once they get word I've given them their piece of the stone. Then they're going to give me the location and set him loose on me. They want him to kill me so the other lands that didn't send aid to Lumipad won't get their slice of the stone. Von told me all of it!" I stomped up the stairs, not caring to hear another argument on the subject. I knew what I'd experienced, and I wouldn't question my sanity over it. Not now. Not when Von needed us.

I threw a clean blue t-shirt over my head and tugged on my jeans. I pulled my hair up into a haphazard ponytail and ran back down the stairs to find that the others hadn't moved from the spot I'd left them. "Is the spell lifted?" I asked, miffed.

Ezra was unapologetic. "No. You're staying here. Lang will find Von. Be patient, dear."

I was fuming, my fist clenched at my side. "You call me 'dear' when you're holding me prisoner? Do you think I'd sit down and twiddle my thumbs if it was *you* they were keeping locked up? I'd tear down any stupid enchantment I had to and bust down as many doors as it took to find you. What makes you think I'd do less for my Reaper?"

His stalwart gaze shifted to a softer emotion at my declaration of loyalty to him. "And I appreciate that. But you're acting on a dream, sweetheart. I won't risk your life so easily."

I was desperate. "Fine. You won't let me out the door? I'll break your windows."

"The charm extends to the windows, October Grace."

I shrugged and marched to the kitchen, picking up a stool from the counter and lugging it to the front room's big picture window. "Then I'll bust out your windows for the fun of it. Let me out, Ezra!"

"Dad, do something!" Mariang fretted as I lifted the stool as much like a bat as I could manage.

"Stop her!" Lynna cried, wringing her hands.

It was Mason who came barreling toward me in wolf form, leaping up and knocking me backward just as I started to swing the stool toward the window. He stood over me and growled, his teeth barred as the stool toppled to the floor.

I was furious. "Seriously? You're going to stop me from

trying to find Von? You should be that much more on top of this! Without him, you're stuck with me twenty-four seven until I die. You'll never get to go back to your life without Von! Help me, Mason!"

For a second his slate eyes looked conflicted as he stared down at me. Then he shook it off and maintained his dominant position.

"Oh yeah? Two can play this game. Bite me, you jack-wagon! I friggin' dare you!" I shoved him off of me, ambled to my feet and grabbed up the stool again, aiming it to give the picture window my best assault.

I didn't expect Mason to transform into a man again, and I surely wasn't anticipating him being naked. Though, on second thought it made sense. He hadn't been wearing any clothing as a wolf.

Mason tackled me to the ground, wrestling me into a hold I couldn't get out of as I shrieked at his sudden nudity. "Calm down! Destroying the house won't get you to Von. Think it through, October!"

"Get off me, you d-bag!"

"I will if you'll settle down and have a conversation with me about this whole dreamwalking thing. I'll help you, but I can't let you leave the house. Ezra's right. If the Ekeks catch wind of you not being on the job in Lumipad, who knows what else they'll do to Von to make you obey? We have to make them think you've already gone to Terraway on their mission."

I hated that he made sense even more than I loathed

his hairy mess on display and touching my leg without my permission. I knew he'd transformed on a dime out of desperation to keep from biting me, but dude. Not cool. "Fine! But put on some clothes first. You're freaking me out."

Mason got up when I stopped struggling in his arms, totally unashamed of his nudity as he stood in front of Ezra, me, Mariang and Lynna. The girls turned their eyes, but I saw them both sneaking curious peeks at the painfully obvious point of male pride on Mason.

Ezra glowered at the both of us. "Mason, come back down when you're dressed. October Grace, I hope you've calmed down." He helped me up off the floor and led me to the dining room where he requested breakfast and tea be brought out for Mariang and me while we sorted things out.

I munched on my eggs, not tasting anything but the desire to bust out of here and run to Von. "Please call Lang," I requested. "If I'm wrong, I'll own it. He's out searching already. What's it going to hurt if I give him a more specific place to look?" I asked as Mason joined us, thankfully dressed in a long-sleeved green thermal shirt and jeans.

Mason sat next to me, raising his eyebrow at my glare. "I trust you've become more rational?"

"Keep your pants on and we're good."

Mason chuckled at my chagrin. He leaned into my

body space and took a mouthful of the toast I held in my hand. "It was either that or bite you."

"I think you chose wrong," I groused. "If I can't leave the house, then I need you to send Lang's minions to the areas Von told me he's being held."

"How is Von reaching you in your sleep?" Mason asked, taking a heaping helping of eggs from Lynna after thanking her.

"I don't know *how* it's happened, I just know that it *has* happened, and we have to deal with it." When the men hesitated, I clutched my fork as if preparing to use it as a weapon. "Look, either you do me this favor, or I spend my morning trying to tear your house apart." When Mason cast me a disapproving look, I glared at him. "Do you think I'd let you rot somewhere without doing everything I could to save you? Know me a little bit, Mason. Jeez!"

Mason's shoulders loosened as he rubbed my back in a circular motion, leaning in to kiss my temple. "We can call Lang. But if that doesn't work, you have to write this off as a dream. The charm's meant to keep you inside, but it doesn't help anyone if you break windows because you're angry."

"I'll break as many windows as it takes to get him back," I promised myself and everyone at the table. "Von's scared, guys. I won't sleep until he's home."

7

KEEPING IT ON THE INSIDE

I'd never been a fan of waiting. It went against everything I was raised with. If something broke, Ollie never hesitated to fix it. If we needed money, we all went out that day and did what we could to earn it. I couldn't get Bev and Danny back, but I could sure as Sunday do what I could to help find Von.

Ezra summoned Lang and let me send his minions out to the more specific ring around where I thought he might be after a quick jump on the internet to locate all the Blimpos Burgers I could find half an hour from my home.

When Lang and Ezra shared sympathetic "well, she's a little unbalanced. What did we expect?" looks, I fumed on the inside. Mason was my constant shadow, no doubt expecting I might try to bust out more windows if provoked. He was not wrong.

"They're looking," Ollie assured me, fresh from his

shower and shave. "If Von's there, Lang will find him. Come on, kid. Let's play cards or something to pass the time. It's not going to do you any good to stand here and stare at the door like that."

"No, thanks."

Ollie squinted at me. "You never pass up an opportunity to play poker. We hardly ever let you play, and you're passing on this?"

"Looks like it." I'd been standing in the foyer for too long, waiting for something to happen and thinking through the limited knowledge I had on charms and Terraway spell work. I wished I could somehow bust down Ezra's enforcements. The only thing I could think to do other than that was to try and fall back asleep to communicate with Von again, but I knew I was too keyed up for that.

So I did what I do best. I started cleaning.

Lynna kept a tidy house, but there was always something to do. I started in the basement, sweeping the poured concrete floor and using the broom to reach the cobwebs that had just started to gain traction in the ceiling's corners. I swept out the square-shaped jail cell, shuddering at the memory of Von locked inside, jaws snapping to get at me for all the wrong reasons. He'd been a day without food or blood, which he'd done before. But I knew the days and the hunger would start stacking up if they didn't find him soon.

The bars on the cage were dusty, needing a good

polish. If Von was brought in rabid, I didn't want him to have a disgusting cage to wait it out in. I couldn't imagine a clean cage would make him feel any better, but it was all I could think to do to take care of him.

I couldn't help Bev. I'd never been able to help her, really. As I stood with the dust rag and polish, I realized I hadn't been able to help myself, either. The stone was in Terraway and I was on my medication, but the dirt still called out to me. I wondered when I wouldn't feel the strain of chaos anymore.

"Need some help?" Ezra asked.

"From my warden? No thanks."

Ezra didn't jump back from my bite, but picked up the broom and started sweeping under the steps. "I guess I deserved that."

"Any word from Lang?"

"None yet, but it takes time to infiltrate every home inside the radius you gave us. I do hope your information proves helpful."

I looked up at him, lost. "You don't think I'm crazy?"

Ezra tilted his head at me. "Why on earth would I think you're crazy?"

I swallowed the lump in my throat. He looked on me with such innocent sincerity, I didn't have it in me to tell him that I probably was three marbles shy of a set. "Well, when I explain the whole thing even to myself, it sounds insane."

"Now, now." Ezra's eyes shined for me, and a small

smirk played on his lips. "Don't go second-guessing your-self after almost destroying my front window. I much prefer my daughter has courage in her convictions, even if it costs me a service call from a repairman." He cleared his throat. "I clean when I'm anxious, too. Lynna hates it, so I stick to the basement mostly."

"You must get nervous a lot. It's not too bad down here."

Ezra watched me polish the bars of the cell while he swept the same spot six times without realizing it. "They'll find Von. And Danny will bring your mother back, yeah? I've never known a more stubborn man. Not one to tolerate defeat, that boy."

"I don't really know what to make of the whole Bev situation. Of all the unbelievable things I've had to get used to, that one tips it. I keep waiting for a piano to fall on my head when she says anything nice to me."

"That must be confusing. I've only ever known the more pleasant side of your mother. It's been an eye-opener for me to hear her confess all the ways she neglected being the mother you three deserved. I'd thought her an angel before the stone's effect was known to me. Now? Now she's lost, waking up from a nightmare she has to take full responsibility for. I suppose I don't know either version of her well enough for marriage."

A rock sunk through my lungs and landed in my gut. I'd come so close to having a dad. The kind who loved you when you threatened to bust out his window and somehow talked you down from all the cliffs you wanted to jump from for the greater good. "For what it's worth, either version of her wouldn't have done any better than you. I'm pretty sure that goes for most women out there."

"That's very kind of you." His eyes fell to his broom. "Is Von deserving of someone like you?"

My nose scrunched. "Someone like me?"

"A wonderful, fiery, hardworking young woman."

"Oh. Thank you." I cleared my throat. "I don't think you have to worry about Von and I getting together. He said he's not ready for any sort of commitment. He needs time."

Ezra knuckles stiffened on the broom handle. "I'm very sorry to hear that."

I tried to wave it all off like I wasn't devastated. "It's fine. It barely happened. I mean, we kissed and he's abducted. Not enough time for a full litmus test. I get it. He wants to live before he dies and all that. Doesn't want to be tied down to me, so I'm not a widow when he transitions into a rabid vamp someday."

"I think that's rubbish."

"Yeah. Me, too." I exhaled that someone thought the same thing I'd landed on. "What do you think of Von? Am I being stupid, considering waiting for him to get it together?"

"I think Von's kind when he remembers not to be self-ish. I've watched him rise to the occasion when he stole the job of being your Reaper. I knew him before he was a vampire – I've known his mother for decades – and I've not met many hardworking, smart and caring men such as him. Would I want him dating my daughter?" He shrugged, keeping his eyes on the broom. "I love Von like a son, and you love your son at his best and at his worst. I've seen Von at his worst a few more times than I'd care to mention. But I've only seen him at his best with you."

I didn't miss that he equated me with being his daughter. Maybe I could keep Ezra. Pretending he was my dad wasn't a crime. Even if he never married Bev, I hoped he wouldn't throw me away.

I don't know why I did it, but somehow I managed to put the polish and rag on the floor, parting with them so I could fold myself into Ezra's surprised arms. "I can be a better daughter for you. I'm sorry I threatened to break your window. And you're freaking out about Bev being gone, too. All I'm thinking about is my fear. I'm sorry."

Ezra squeezed me tight, understanding just how rare an unsolicited hug from me was. "There, there. You've no business comforting me when you're just as traumatized by the whole thing, if not more. We're in a sorry state, the two of us." He closed his eyes. "If anything happens to Von, his mother will never forgive me. He was supposed to come out to stay with me to shape up and get his head straight. I didn't realize how much danger would always find its way to him."

"Mariang mentioned you knew his mom from high school. That's a long time to maintain a friendship."

"Lavinia and I stayed close over the years. She was there for me when my wife passed, and I helped her start over when her husband left. When Von was spinning out of control after he was bitten, Lavinia sent him to live with me. Fat lot of good that did him. I adore Von, but I fear I've only managed to wreck his life more by being in it."

I squeezed him through his confession. "You hush that kind of talk, now. It's not true, any of it. Von's still a person, and if not for your kindness and providing a safe place for him to figure things out, he might already be rabid."

"That's very generous of you."

"No, it's logical of me. Have you ever known anyone to resist the transition as long as he has?"

Ezra paused in thought. "Not even close. Von's always been a hard worker. Always tenacious and stubborn. People write him off as a joker, but he's always planning something, always moving chess pieces to take care of what's his. He was the man of the house far too young, and now I fear his youth will be snatched away from him forever."

I could hear the love Ezra had for Von, and adored my father figure even more than I had before. "I don't know how you keep it together. I stop for a minute and I'm screaming on the inside."

His faint smile looked tired, but he managed one for me. "That's the thing about keeping it on the inside. You get to assume I'm holding myself together. I assure you, there's been plenty of screaming and metaphorical breaking of windows in my mind, too."

"Honest?"

He looked down at me when I pulled my head back to read his face. His smile was more genuine now, looking truly happy that I wasn't being so hard to talk to. "I think the two of us are entirely too put together. We deserve a good tantrum or something. Mariang prefers ice cream when she's feeling persecuted. Is that you, too? We might have some upstairs."

"Nah. I'm more of a keep your head down and barrel through kind of girl. You?"

"I used to go running when things grew to be too much. Though my problems are starting to stack up the older I get. I doubt I'm fast enough to outrun them anymore." Ezra's eyes had a note of incurable sadness to them, and I wished there was something that could fix his hurt. He was the in-control one. He had the answers. To live in his world when he didn't have those things to anchor me? Well, that was a scarier thought than Bev meandering through Terraway.

"Maybe I'll tag along on your next run. If our problems start to take us over on the track, I'll bring the stool along just in case something needs a good bashing in."

His chuckle at my violent promise touched my heart. He was starting to get me, and I was beginning to appreciate what a true gift a good dad was.

8

SCRAPS OF TRUST

Ezra and I left the basement cleaning unfinished as we went up the stairs, his arm around me to keep me from putting distance between us too soon. The desire to clean was strong, but my need for a good father was intrinsically more potent. He called Mariang on his phone, drawing her down from her bedroom to join us for tea.

I'd been a pretty boring tea drinker, using tea in a bag and microwaving water on the go. To have a proper tea with legit British people made me sit up straighter and try to recall all the manners Allie had fought to instill in me.

Ollie meandered in as Mason wandered down with Mariang. The five us sat down at the dining room table to assemble as much normalcy as we could, while the world threatened to go up in flames around us.

"I made a few calls yesterday when I learned of Von's abduction." Ezra checked a message on his phone and then set it down with some degree of finality. "Since we don't know who we can trust in the Duwende community, I opted for an inside job, a select team to extract Von who would only operate in our best interest."

Mason shook his head. "There's no one we can trust except the people in this room. Even the ones on the council are suspect."

I blew on my tea. "Hey, Finn's alright. I mean, he risked a lot to help get Silo their stone. If it wasn't for him being Banak's puppet, he'd be a solid option."

Ezra held up his hand. "I agree with you both. When we don't know who to trust, we should look inward. It dawned on me that I have four Duwendes I trust implicitly with Von's life. They're on their way here now. They just landed at the airport, actually."

Ollie handed me the sugar, looking comical sipping from his dainty teacup. "Need me to pick anyone up?"

"No, no. I prefer the family stays in the house. Thank you, son."

Ollie raised his eyebrow at me and inhaled at the familial branding that came easy to the royal family, but might always strike us as strange. Bev only ever called him by his given name, or when she was angry, called Ollie "boy". I knew to either run or duck when that happened.

I shrugged in response, leaning into my brother's side

when he seemed perplexed by Ezra's kindness. Ollie clinked his teacup to mine, neither of us needing to voice the irony of the Reese kids sipping tea out of fine China in a mansion. He smiled at Ezra and worked out a genuine, "Whatever you say, Dad."

Ezra's head snapped over to Ollie, who saluted him with his cup and a modest bow of his chin. Ezra leaned over in his seat on the other side of me and gripped Ollie's hand that was draped around the back of my chair. "Thank you. That meant more than you can imagine." He cleared his throat and straightened. "The team consists of four Duwendes with varying backgrounds, but each of them graduated the Academy and went on to become fine young men." He looked to Mariang, who had a confused twist to her mouth. "Alton, Graham, Bishop and Boston Vandershot are on their way here now." This was met by a gasp and a giddy squeal by Mariang. Even Mason visibly perked up. Ezra smiled at his daughter. "And since Captain Finn's proved he can be trusted with care of the stone, though I don't approve of the sneaking off, of course, Finn will be assisting us as well."

Mariang put her teacup down and stood. "I'm going to get dressed, then." The news sparked new life into her as she scampered up the stairs to her room.

"Uh, am I supposed to know who those four guys are?" Ollie asked.

"Alton, Graham, Bishop and Boston are Von and Danny's younger brothers. I figured that if we could trust anyone to want Von safe and sound at any cost, it would be his family."

"Oh! Wow. Yeah, that's actually a really great idea."

"I have my moments, son. They'll split into two teams. Alton and Graham will be ported down by Captain Finn, who will take them through Lumipad to try and locate Bev, Danny and King Kabayo, offering assistance if necessary. Bishop and Boston will go search for Von the moment Prince Langgam's spies let us know where Von is being held."

I leaned over and wrapped my arms around Ezra's neck. "Thank you. You actually solved it!"

Mason drank his tea as he mulled over the new plan. "Are you sure you don't want to reverse those two teams? Bishop and Boston are slightly more vicious than Alton and Graham."

"Agreed. But I want the twins searching for Von. I want them to send a clear message to the rest of the Ekeks who consider abducting one of mine. They're the right ones to send that sort of unfortunate message."

"I guess that's true. I can help them." When Ezra's hesitation was plain on his face, Mason let out a frustrated groan. "Come on, Ezra. I'm doing nothing here. October barely lets me near her to pull, and Mariang will be fine for a few hours."

"I cherish your list of reasons, but still no. Your job is to protect the national treasures. Be grateful it's an uneventful day inside." Ezra's stomach rumbled. "Excuse me. It seems I can't eat enough today."

"Let me get you something," I offered, standing.

"No, no. I'll not have you waiting on me. I daresay I rivaled Mason this morning for how many eggs I could consume. Must be the nerves. I'll feel better when our boys are home safe."

I went into the kitchen anyway, knowing when to ignore someone and when to listen. I fished through the fridge, offering a sympathetic smile to Lynna, who was crying into her handkerchief at the counter. I poured her a glass of orange juice and set about fixing Ezra a sandwich with probably too much ham, but whatever. Ollie never complained about my sandwich proportions.

I walked back into the dining room and slid the plate onto the long table in front of Ezra. "I'll be in my room if anyone needs me."

"What's this?" Ezra asked, confused at the plate sitting before him.

"A sandwich. I don't know how you like yours, so I just made what Ollie likes. Hope that's okay."

"You made me a sandwich?" Ezra's tone had the ring of wonder to it, making me feel terrible that such a simple thing was seen as a big gesture. I made a mental note to be kinder to Ezra. He'd earned more than the scraps of trust I gave him.

"You said you were hungry. Did you want something else?"

He reached out and held my hand. "That was quite kind of you. Thank you."

"No problem." I made my exit, catching Ollie's fist bump on the way out.

I always wanted a family, and I wouldn't give this one up without a fight, so help me.

LYNNA'S GREATEST HELP

I don't know why I had slight pangs of nerves jumping around in my stomach like ping pong balls when Ezra called me down, announcing the brothers had arrived.

Bishop and Boston were identical twins around my age, wearing almost matching outfits of black long-sleeved t-shirts and jeans with boots. The older two looked to be in their mid-twenties and seemed more subdued than the twins, who kept looking around the mansion as if waiting for someone to pounce. I'd had several conversations with Bishop on Von's phone, and wanted to greet him. I hung back though, since I had no idea which one Bishop was.

Mason barreled past me, pulling the bare minimum amount of anxiety from me on his way down the steps. He was met in a crash of tight hugs and claps on the back, his grin wide at seeing the familiar faces.

Mariang came down in a pink knee-length flowing skirt with a white fitted sweater. I'd pinned her hair up for her, and she looked like a dainty fifties sock hop queen. The oldest brother there in a gray shirt and jeans removed his Newsies cap and held it to his chest as he adjusted his gold wire-rimmed glasses. "Lady Mariang," he greeted her with a slight bow and a modest grin. "Ever good to see you, love."

"Oh, Alton, it's been far too long." I don't know how everything Mariang did looked like a dance, but somehow she flitted from brother to brother, kissing their cheeks. The overly muscular men bent to her whim for their turn at the fair maiden they adored.

Alton had crinkles around his eyes and a grin that split wide across his face like Von's, only Alton didn't have that same smarm to him that served as Von's occasional charm. He more looked like a really built librarian, complete with the circular curve to the frame of his glasses. "I can't believe Danny actually needs help. I made Ezra repeat it three times. Are you alright? Is Mason serving you well in his new post?"

One of the twins elbowed Mason repeatedly until Mason shoved him back. The identical grins spread across the twins' faces, and the wresting match began as Ezra came into the foyer, pocketing his phone. "Gentlemen, into the conference room." He shook Alton's hand, who seemed to be the brother in charge who spoke for the group. "The sooner we get this underway, the better."

"Milady?" The man in the chocolate polo said to Mariang. I'm guessing this one was Graham. His short brown hair matched the hue of his shirt perfectly. A small freckle next to his left eye made him appear playful and kind, despite his humble and subdued deportment. He jutted out his elbow to escort Mariang.

"Thank you, Graham. What a gentleman."

It was Graham. I was right. I'm awesome.

I tried to remind myself of that awesomeness as I silently made my way to the conference room with Ollie, who stuck close while he got the lay of the new guys. Alton turned to me, and I readied myself to be introduced to Von's family, who I prayed would like me. Instead of shaking my hand, Alton said to me, "Could we get some tea in here, Miss? It was a long flight."

I nodded, hoping I'd never asked Lynna for something without a proper please and thank you. "Sure. Are you hungry, too?"

"Always." Then he turned his back to me and moved with the others toward the conference room.

One of the twins sized me up in a way that made me internally roll my eyes. "Well, aren't you a cute little cherry. I'm Boston."

"Good for you." I didn't respond more than that and a raised eyebrow. In my experience, any kind of feedback only spurred guys like that on for more veiled come-ons, and after about a minute, the veil would come off and they'd just be plain old gross. Boston moved along when there was no flirty comeback from my end, which suited me just fine. I knew enough about Boston to hang back. He'd let Von sell himself into sexual slavery to pay off his gambling debts. I didn't so much like Boston.

Ollie's low voice was clipped. "I'll get the tea. That Alton guy only asked you to wait on him because you have a uterus. He has no idea who you are."

"Who am I?"

Ollie blinked down at me. "You're my sister, not their servant."

"Is there shame in bringing someone tea? Is Lynna beneath us?"

"Well, no, but..."

"You raised me to be polite. I don't mind getting them tea, Ollie. I don't need to wave my title around like a snob. If anything, now's the time to serve. Hopefully it'll set a tone for them."

Ollie kissed my forehead. "I love you, you know."

"Love you, too. Play nice."

"I make no promises."

We smiled at each other, and I went into the empty kitchen. I started heating up the kettle and fished through the fridge for something to feed the guys. If they were anything like Danny and Von, they could eat a whole cow without pause.

Lynna came in, her eyes wide. "No, no. I'll get you something. What do you need, October?"

"Not me. Von's brothers want tea and something to eat. Any ideas on what could feed a small army real quick?"

"Darling, I've been doing that my whole life. I know just the thing."

I fished through the cupboard for the canister of tea leaves, and got out the sugar bowl and clotted cream. I hadn't been ready to try the clotted cream yet, but I knew Ezra liked it. "How long have you worked for Ezra?"

"Since before Mariang was born. It's a wonderful family to work for."

"I'm warming up to them. Can I ask you a question?"

"Of course, sweetheart." Her wrinkled hands made quick work of throwing together a ball of dough, and she kneaded it with surprising strength.

"What kind of magical creature are you? Ezra's Matruculan, Mariang's an Omen, the guys are Duwende. What about you?"

"I'm Matruculan, like Mason."

I eyed her bun curiously. "But your hair's been cut?"

Lynna smiled maternally at me. "Most of us have lost our strength. Ezra, as well."

"Do you miss it? Being stronger than everyone?"

She thought a moment before answering. "I learned long ago that I'm exactly who I want to be, and exactly where I want to be."

I chewed on her response, hoping that one day I could say the same. "You like it better Topside?"

She shuddered. "Much better. I used to live next door

to Ezra's parents, you know. I rescued him on the day he was born. I didn't need my Matruculan strength for that."

"I didn't know that. What did you rescue him from?"

"His father. Understand, it's quite difficult for Matruculan men to resist the lure of a pregnant woman. Otis tried. He was a good man. Wanted a son desperately. No one was more excited when Tilly got pregnant than he was. He resisted until she went into labor."

"Resisted what?"

"Eating the fetus." She spoke so clinically, my mouth twisted in time with my stomach. I vaguely remember being told the ins and outs of Mason's race, but I loved Mason, so I skipped over that whole eating babies part. "Otis snapped and tried to rip the fetus out of Tilly to eat it. I was the midwife on duty, and managed to escape with Tilly's son before it was too late. Tilly didn't survive, though." Lynna's glassy eyes were misting over, immune to my look of horror. "Months later, Otis was so ashamed that he took his own life. I took Ezra into my home and raised him as my own." A soft smile played on her lips, and I guessed she was picturing Ezra as a baby. "'Ezra' means help. I thought I would be the one helping by raising him, but over the years he's been a greater help to me."

"I had no idea. I'm... that's terrible. I'm so glad he had you." I eyed her with new appreciation. "You saved a kingdom."

She chortled at my statement, as if I'd made a joke. "I saved a baby."

I shook my head. "No. You saved a boy who grew up to run an entire kingdom, who then had a girl the whole of Terraway depends on for survival. If not for you, Terraway wouldn't be here anymore. You saved the kingdom."

Lynna smiled at me in her usual kind way, and then kissed my cheek. Her hands were covered in flour, and there were stains on her apron, but to me, she was a vision of love, kindness, and everything that was right with the world. She personified a high level of dignity only seen on Mrs. Brady. "Be that as it may, saving that baby would have been enough for me."

"You're kind of amazing, you know."

Lynna laughed like I'd said something cute. "Run along, now. I'll be right in with the tea."

"How about I carry the tray for you? I can't imagine it'll be light."

She shook her head, punching out circles with the lip of a cup into the rolled-out dough. "Go on, sweetheart. If I need help, I'll ask Ezra. Thank you for getting the tea tray ready for me."

"Thank you, Lynna. Thank you for everything."

Lynna didn't say anything. She merely smiled at me with a maternal glow that made me feel warm inside, like I belonged here.

Like I was loved.

10

CALLING ALL VANDERSHOT BOYS

I made my way to the conference room just as Ezra was coming out of it. "There you are," he said with an expression that was a mix between glad to see me and total business. Though I wanted to hesitate, I knew it was now or never. It was just the two of us in the hallway when I threw my arms around Ezra's neck. "Ho! Steady, darling. Are you alright? What's wrong?"

I squeezed harder, nodding into his shoulder. "I'm just glad you're you. Grateful you're here. Even when I'm mad at you, I wouldn't have you any other way."

Ezra melted in my grip, his arms banding around my waist to gather me closer. "How did I get so lucky?"

And there was the crux of why Ezra was so amazing. He'd lost both his parents, left his homeland to live in a land that was nothing like it, got stuck corralling a world on the brink of collapse, sacrificed his daughter for Terraway, and got stuck with me – and yet he still counted himself lucky. "I can be better," I promised. "I can be a team player. No more surprises, okay? I won't sneak off anymore. I won't make you worry."

He exhaled and held onto me until finally I let go. His handkerchief found its way to the two tears I'd squeezed out of him. "Thank you, dear. Thank you for all of it. Thank you for being my daughter, and for working with me on this. We'll get Von back." His arm stayed around my shoulders to corral me into the conference room with the others. "Gentlemen, this is Lady October Grace, the new Omen who Von and Mason belong to."

They each stood, dipping their heads in my direction. Alton's eyes were wide with fear, which made me chuckle. I waved off their display of respect for my job. "Nice to meet you guys. Where are we on bringing everyone home?" I took the seat between Mason and Ollie at the table. Mariang was between Graham and Alton, giving Mason a break from pulling for the two of us.

"We're waiting on Finn to take Alton and Graham down to Lumipad," Mason informed me.

Ezra pointed to the twins, one of whom was studying me as if sizing up both my bra size and my weak points simultaneously. That one was clearly Boston. I decided the level of horn-dogness was how I'd be able to tell them apart. Easier to spot than a birthmark. "Boston and Bishop will go as soon as Prince Langgam sends word his spies have located Von."

"Just the two of them?" I asked in dismay. I gave Bishop a two-fingered wave to let him know I knew which one he was. Bishop grinned at me and dipped his head in return, glad that I remembered him from our phone conversations.

Boston stiffened, as if I'd insulted them both. He cracked his knuckles. "You don't need to worry about your Reaper, Cherry. We'll bring Von home, no problem. Git owes me twenty quid. You think I'd let him die before I get my money back?" He flashed me a wide grin, revealing a tooth to the top left that was slightly off kilter, though it didn't look like genetics played a roll in that. My guess was that Boston had been in a good number of fights. I don't know why this calmed me a little, but I sat back in my chair, avoiding their gazes as the four gawked at me.

"Good to hear you're motivated," I said, looking up when Lynna came in with the tea tray. I stood and helped Lynna with the enormous tray, but the four guys protested. Alton moved around the table to arrest the sugar bowl from my hands so he could help unload the tray instead of me. "I can get it, guys. It's no trouble."

Alton was ashen. "Forgive me, your highness. I didn't realize who you were when I asked you to bring me tea."

"I don't mind helping. Plus, now you get to go home and tell all your buddies that a real, live Omen waited on you. Now, if you can get a unicorn to shine your shoes, you'll really be the king."

Alton's face fell, and I swear his cheeks paled while his ears went pink. It was adorable. He was probably around twenty-six, but he looked like a little boy facing the principal's office. "I think I'm going to be sick. I never would've asked you to bring us tea if I knew who you were. A thousand apologies, your grace."

"I don't even need the one. You're too funny."

Boston chuckled at his brother. "You asked an Omen to fetch your tea?"

Alton was sweating now. "Well, how was I supposed to know? She's dressed like a common servant."

I looked down at my jeans and t-shirt, confused. I was dressed exactly like they were. Maybe they were expecting me to be wearing a pretty skirt like Mariang. Boy, were they in for a shock.

Ollie stood in my defense while Lynna chortled as she left the room. "You want to think that through, man? There's not a thing wrong with the way my sister dresses."

Alton spluttered as he sank deeper down into the hole he was digging himself. "I didn't mean anything foul by it. I only meant that she doesn't look like Mariang."

"And how does my other sister look?" Ollie spouted, his anger revving up. "Is there something off about Mariang, too?

Mariang sat a little straighter in her seat, clearly

pleased that Ollie claimed her so easily. "It's alright, Ollie. Alton's a good man."

"That good man just called my sister his servant. Not happening on my watch."

"It was an accident!" Alton pulled out his handkerchief and mopped the sweat from his forehead with stubbier fingers than the rest of the brothers.

I clapped my hands to stop the downward progression. "Alright, everyone. Relax your balls. Actual work needs to get done here."

Boston threw his head back and laughed with his whole body, his hand on his stomach. "Ho! That was priceless. I've never heard an Omen say 'balls' before." He turned to Mariang and begged. "Please say it, sis! Make it a double feature."

Mariang only blushed in response.

Ezra shot me a scolding look as he motioned for everyone to take their seats. "And I truly hope you never hear an Omen say that again. Let's focus, shall we?" Ezra started going through all we knew about Von's predicament, which wasn't much.

We stirred and sipped our teas as Lynna came back with biscuits and bowls of chili. Alton shot up out of his seat to help her, while Ezra started giving the guys a rundown of the chaos they might encounter in Lumipad.

Alton was nervous as he placed the bowl of chili in front of me, the edge of his stubby thumb catching on the lip of the bowl. The entire steaming pile tipped over onto my lap before I could right it. "Oh! That's hot." My instinct was to jump up at the burn that covered my lap, but I knew that would only fling the chili to the unmarked carpet. It would stain the nice room, and I couldn't stand for that.

Boston brayed like a jackass, clapping his hands at Alton, who was so horrified, his whole face flushed a deep red to match his ears. "I'm sorry. I'm so sorry, your majesty!" He grabbed my cloth napkin and started scooping the chili off my thighs.

"I've got it," I insisted. "It's fine, Alton. You're allowed a clumsy moment. No big deal."

Mason waved off Alton and handed me his napkin, knowing I'd prefer no one touched my lap but me. Mason's hand cupped my shoulder to pull the chagrin out of me. He tried unsuccessfully to hide his chuckle at Alton's bumbling. "You haven't poured hot tea on her head yet. You want to give that a try?" Mason kidded.

"I can't believe I did that! How can I apologize, your grace?"

"You already apologized. I'm not going to go all off-with-your-head or anything. You're fine. Honest mistake." When the chunks of chili were gone, I stood from the table. "I know you all can't get enough of how stylish this is, but I think I'm going to go change. Be back in a minute."

Boston was still laughing. "Oh, but why? I think you look smashing. Before you know it, all the Omens will be wanting that style. They'll call it dinner chic. Instead of 'who's she wearing' it'll be 'what flavor is she wearing.'"

Bishop clapped his hands, sniggering. "Brilliant! Does the outfit come in chipotle? Perhaps sour cream and onion?"

"Shut it, Boston," Alton cringed.

As I walked carefully up the stairs, I couldn't help but giggle at Alton, and the brothers who had flown across an ocean to save their Superman.

11

UNLEASHING THE WHALE

I searched for more jeans in the dresser that had been stocked for me, but found only various pairs of leggings in different patterns. No doubt Mariang owned limited jeans and shopped for me according to her tastes. I was just grateful Mariang and Ezra had stocked my dresser with clothes that fit me without too much hassle, though I usually didn't wear a ton of clothing that showed off my shape.

I changed my shirt into a fitted long-sleeved deep purple blouse that was light-years more elegant than what I was used to throwing on. It framed my breasts with gentle ruffles and showed off about an inch of cleavage, which was about three inches more than I ever displayed.

I pulled my hair up into a bun and checked myself in the mirror. I couldn't believe the transformation that happened when Mariang picked out my clothes. I went from looking like a college kid in resale digs to standing out like a legit woman. I could see every curve I usually tried to conceal for modesty's sake, and debated throwing on a sweatshirt so I didn't look so strange. Mariang's form-fitting clothes weren't nearly as scandalous because she was a dainty size two. I had a healthy portion of breasts and a lower half that had an obvious curve of I'm-not-a-teenager-anymore to it. I bit my lip and decided to scrap the whole outfit. I didn't like the idea of showing strangers the shape of my body, and I could see every curve in the black leggings that were meant to be stared at. I was the dude friend, but now I looked like the girl you hold doors open for.

"October Grace, Captain Finn is here," Ezra called up the stairs.

I didn't have time to second-guess the outfit anymore, and jogged down the stairs in my bare feet to greet Finn and see Alton and Graham off.

Finn gave me a smile that had a hint of charm to it. "Lady October. You're looking lovely as always." His eyes fell to my legs and I saw the familiar flare of lust rising in them. His job was overseeing the Mermaid harem for the King of Dagat. The only female legs he saw were when the jackhole King Banak used his enchanted conch shell to give the Mermaid he chose to defile for the night legs. Finn mentioned the Mermaid's legs were apparently lifeless, useless, green and misshapen. Consequently, Finn had a bit of a foot fetish. I may or may not have let him suck on my toes and massage my legs a little in the privacy of our hotel room in Silo. Though I knew Finn was the one who signed Von into the harem as a slave for King Banak's son, we'd had a bit of a makeout and a few heated moments I'd decided to keep to myself.

Things were complicated.

"Hey, Finn. You ready to kick some Ekek and Manas butt?"

He lowered his voice, though the others had meandered back into the conference room. "I'm ready for whatever you need me to do."

My eyes darted around. "We don't need to talk about any of what didn't happen between us, do we?"

Finn cleared his throat when Ezra came around the corner. "I need to speak with the two of you in private before I go."

Ezra nodded in full business mode and led us upstairs to one of the many guest bedrooms I had yet to visit. He shut the door and turned to us, giving Finn the floor. "Whatever you've got, let's be quick about it. I don't fancy letting my fiancé and my son wander through Lumipad without ample protection a second longer than they have to."

Finn shot me a look of apology that made me panic at what was about to tumble out of his mouth. "Something happened to me, and you two are the only ones who will know it. My curse was broken. Completely severed. Banak doesn't know. No one knows except the two of you."

Ezra and I both gasped in unison. "That's amazing!" I was elated for him, so glad he didn't have to be ordered around by that pervert posing as a king.

"I'm keeping it secret because Banak trusts me to run his kingdom. Believe me, you don't want him in charge. The more he's distracted, the more I can do to keep Dagat afloat. I just wanted you to know in case there's anything you need done that Banak wouldn't approve of. I'm free now, and I'm pledging my allegiance to you, Ezra." He got down on his knee like he was about to be knighted, bowing his head to my dad. "Now I can confess things Banak ordered me to do and keep secret from you, Ezra. The human man murdered in the hospital? The note written in blood warning the Omens more humans would be killed if they didn't meet their quota? Banak ordered me to do that to inspire the Omens to work harder."

The muscles in Ezra's jaw tensed while my jaw dropped. Ezra was controlled in his response. "I suspected as much. It's nice to have it confirmed, though."

"You've always acted in the best interest of Terraway, so my sword belongs to you, if you'll have it."

Ezra blinked away his shock as best he could before he placed his hand on Finn's shoulder. "Captain, welcome home. How did you come about this miracle? I assumed your curse was permanent."

"So did I." Finn shot me a look of apology and lowered his head further, as if he was expecting Ezra to turn on a dime and cut it off his shoulders. "I kissed a fair maiden, and something happened to me. From that moment, I could feel the curse broken. I've tried in secret doing a few things Banak's always forbidden, and it worked. He's got stores of *buhay* shoots that grow in our land. He keeps cellars of it and shares only the bare minimum with his harem and the Kataw soldiers. I've started feeding some of the *buhay* to the starving civilians in secret, and that usual tug that's kept me from acting on my own is gone! My curse didn't stop me."

Ezra's happiness clashed with the blood that ran cold in my veins. "That's incredible! How free you must feel. Yes, we can keep your secret, even from the council. Tell me, who is this fair maiden who can break curses with a single kiss?"

Finn kept his head bowed and placed his hands on the carpet to kneel on all fours for mercy. "I kissed October, sir. It's what made me have that fit in her bedroom, and why I disappeared so quickly."

I groaned and covered my face with my hands. "Is that never talking about it again? That was private, Finn!"

"He needs to hear this, and so do you. Did you know you could do that?"

"Break curses? Of course not! You're like, the third guy I've ever kissed in my life, and as far as I know, Beto and Mason weren't cursed."

Ezra's look of shock took a few seconds to focus into disdain. His hand flung out and shoved Finn's head downward. He gripped the back of Finn's neck, slowly burying the military captain's face into the carpet. Though I was pretty sure Finn could win in a throwdown, he submitted to Ezra and let himself be lowered to the floor. Ezra's grip on the nape of Finn's neck was trembling with barely controlled rage. Trepidation made the hairs on the backs of my arms stand up as I covered my mouth. Ezra squeezed Finn's neck, speaking through gritted teeth in a low, angry voice I didn't recognize. "Glad as I am that you're free, my daughter is not yours for the taking. I know your quality on the battlefield, and that is the use you have for my family. Nothing else. You'll stay out of October's bedroom. Am I clear?"

"Yes, your majesty."

"You're free now, so I'll be watching to see who you really are. Choose wisely, Captain. You've been forced to carry out a great many sins in Banak's name. From here on out, any further transgressions will be on your head alone."

"Yes, your majesty."

"You have too much blood on your hands to kiss my daughter ever again. You'll stay away from October. Do you understand?"

My heart was pounding, my mouth dry and my palms sweaty.

Finn hesitated, and then answered with a steady, "No, Ezra. I can't promise you that."

I swore into my hands, backing up from the men who looked about a breath away from killing each other. Ezra's fingers shook on Finn's neck, his grip tightening around the gills. "You're trying my patience, Captain. I'm this close to transitioning, so I can tear your head clean off!" Ezra didn't look up at me when he worked out a low and deadly, "October Grace, go downstairs and wait for me there."

Having a dad was a bit more like getting a whale than having the pretty goldfish I'd been hoping for, and thought Ezra to be. "Ezra, it's alright. I can handle myself. You don't need to do this. It's really not all that big a deal."

"Go on, October," Finn urged, his face still buried in the carpet, his backside up in the air like a dog digging for a bone.

I started clawing at my hands, taking my anxiety out on my skin. "Ezra, please! Let him go. It was only those couple times, and that's it! It didn't go any farther than that." Finn most certainly didn't see me in a towel. I didn't let him suck on my toes, nor did I think about it in detail every now and then when I wished for just a little more time with him in Silo.

Ezra's head whipped toward me. "Couple of times? Not just the one that happened under my roof? Go downstairs!" he barked, making me jump.

Something in me rose up at being bossed for something I had every right to have done. "Let's all take a breath and be cool. I'm allowed to kiss a guy, Ezra. I'm even allowed to not have to explain myself. I'm twenty-two."

"Then you should know better. If you knew what he's

done, the role he's played in ruining Von's life, you wouldn't give him the time of day."

I kept my voice steady. "I know all about Von's time in the harem. I also know Finn couldn't refuse Banak when he was given an order, so I don't hold that against him. I saw who Finn was beneath the curse, and that's who I kissed." I shook my head in dismay. "Don't you want me to be the kind of woman who can see past the worst part of someone to who they really are? Isn't that exactly what you did with Bev? Are you really telling me not to be like you?"

Ezra's grip began to slacken, but he held his position of dominance as he mulled over my words. "I don't like it. He's not right for you, or any man's daughter."

"You don't even know who he is now. Neither of us do. And no offense to you, Finn, but I wasn't about to jump into anything serious anyway." I kept my words quiet to calm Ezra. "Finn and I haven't spoken since I apparently broke his curse. This is all an overreaction. How did it even happen?"

"It wasn't the first kiss, but the second one." He gripped the carpet as if preparing for the worst. "When your tongue touched mine, I felt the shift in me."

Ezra lowered his face to speak a low threat to Finn. "I would like nothing more than your head mounted on my wall right now. Don't test my patience. Despite what everyone may think, it has its limits."

I tried to keep my voice even. "Dad, I'm an adult, and I can kiss who I'd like."

Ezra narrowed his eyes at me. "Be that as it may, I'm allowed to protect my household. I don't want you alone with him. He's yet to prove his quality."

I held up my hands. "Fine by me. If it'll get you to let him up off the floor, then I can deal with that. Mason's my shadow anyway, and I promised I wouldn't run off without him anymore. Built-in chaperone."

Ezra backed away, but Finn only rose to sitting, leaning back to perch on his heels with his head down. "Very well, dear. Finn, you have much to prove, and make no mistake, I'll be watching." Ezra opened the door and snapped his fingers for Finn to move it.

"Yes, your majesty." Finn stood, keeping his chin lowered to give me a secret wink on his way out.

12

KABAYO'S TOKEN

Alton stood when I entered the conference room, his ears turning pink again. "Lady October, there aren't enough apologies for my behavior. I'm so very sorry."

I was so turned around that I couldn't remember what his apology was for. "Huh? Oh, right. The chili thing." I waved off his sincerity. "It's fine. No big deal."

Mariang's smile brightened when she saw that I was wearing one of the more feminine outfits she'd bought me. "You look lovely."

"Thanks. Where are we with Lumipad?"

Ezra took the floor, his spine stiff with concealed anger. "Alton, Graham, you haven't been back to Terraway in a while, so prepare yourself for a change. The famine's deadly in Lumipad, so make sure you fill your packs with food and eat well before you go. Captain Finn can refill your canteens as needed."

Ezra motioned to Finn, who shook hands with Graham and Alton over the table, but disregarded his chair and stood behind mine as a sentry of sorts. I didn't know what to make of that, but I guessed it might keep any more food from spilling on me at random, so I was grateful.

Ezra was not. He pointed to the far corner contemptuously. "You'll stand right there, where I can keep an eye on you. Not an inch closer, or your king will be hearing from me on your disobedience."

Mason raised an eyebrow to Ezra, but said nothing to the sharpness radiating from the usually composed man.

Finn obeyed, and I prayed everyone else in the room wouldn't read my blush for the crime it was.

Ezra continued on with a tightness to his jaw and an edge to his tone. "My hope is that Captain Finn can get you through Lumipad without incident. They'll recognize him, and hopefully won't attack you on your journey. But just in case, make sure you're heavily armed. You know where Danny keeps the weapons. Stock up before you leave." While Ezra was speaking, the back of his hand started glowing in the shape of a blackish-blue X, letting him know he was getting a summons. "Excuse me." He pointed to Mason, who straightened. "October's not to be out of your sight. Not even for a second. Understand?"

Mason examined me curiously, wondering what it was I'd done this time. "Of course."

Finn started giving the guys instructions on which parts of Lumipad they were going to travel through, letting them know that most of the journey would be spent jogging to make up for lost time.

A burn started making my right arm itch. I scratched the sting, but Mason quickly scooped up my hand to keep from letting my secret shame be made known to the room. "Something's itching me," I explained, though this did not force Mason to let go of my hand. "Oh, ow! Mason, it's burning!" The fire twisted around my right forearm, drawing on my skin like a pen fueled by lightning. "Help!"

Ollie tore back my sleeve, letting out a noise of alarm. Finn crossed the room in a few steps, and pinned my shoulders to the back of my chair. They revealed the marks I'd given myself, sure, but beneath those were Kabayo's loopy scar he'd given me when he'd wrapped a thick braid of his hair around my forearm. The design was an X on the inside of my forearm and one on the outside that were connected at the tops and bottoms. Usually the scar was a faded pink, but my eyes bulged when I saw it was black now with a blue glow on the edges of the design. The heat filled my arm as I squirmed.

Mason slammed my forearm on the table to show the brothers and Mariang, who all gasped. "King Kabayo's token!" he shouted to the others. "They're in danger. We've run out of time! Get your things and go!"

"This is good," Finn said, staring with too much focus at my arm. "I can use her active link to Kabayo to locate him. Without that, we'll be wandering around for who knows how long trying to find them." He looked to the brothers. "You heard Mason. Get your things and meet me at the front door."

"It's burning! My arm feels like it's on fire! Someone do something!" The room before me seemed to vanish, and all I saw was Kabayo with his sword and dagger, swinging at what seemed be a never-ending swarm of ravenously hungry Ekeks. Their yellowed elongated teeth were gnashing and their sharp claws were tearing at Kabayo's arms. They had bird-like features and stood on painfully thin legs that didn't seem to slow them down at all.

I saw Danny fighting next to him. He was glorying in the fight as he finally put muscles to use that had been fetching tea for Mariang for far too long. They were sweating and grunting as they fought, with Bev nowhere in sight. "Danny! Watch behind you!" I shouted.

Then Mason shook my shoulders, and the fight gave way to the conference room. The violence vanished as quickly as it came, though my arm still burned. "Danny's in trouble! They're fighting, and completely outnumbered."

Mason's voice was level but stern, carrying the authority of a man who had once run an entire country. "Ollie, go help the guys get packed. Mariang, tell Ezra we're not to be disturbed."

Mariang flew to me, gripping my face so I saw only her. "Is he alive? Is he safe? Where is he?"

I wanted to lie to her, but my mouth produced the truth without filter. "He's alive, but he's not safe."

Mason gave Ollie a nod, and Ollie extracted Mariang from me and escorted her out of the room with the others, shutting me in the conference room with Mason and Finn.

"What's happening to me? Was that real, what I saw?" My head whipped from Mason to Finn, taking in their dutiful looks that made it feel like the air was harder to breathe.

"It was real, yes." Mason pointed to the floor behind the table. "Lie down here. This is going to hurt, and I don't want you hitting your head on a chair or something if you pass out."

"Pass out?"

Mason lowered me to the ground on my back and Finn rolled up his sleeves, looking down on me with a closed expression. In that moment, I saw why people feared his cold nature. Mason's voice was gentle as he pressed my hands into the carpet on either side of my head, pinning me down slowly, so as not to spook me. "Your mark ties you and Kabayo together. When you're in danger, he can see you, find you so he can help. It works the other way, too. That's why Ezra hasn't been as frantic. We would've known if something had gone south."

"Well, it's going south now, so hurry!"

"Shh. We will. You've never been to Lumipad, so Finn's going to try and look through your eyes so he can use the landmarks to find Kabayo's exact location. Then they can make a beeline for him to help."

"Well, do it then! There were so many Ekeks. Do it, Finn!"

Finn locked the conference room door with an air of awful finality. "This is going to hurt, *hani*."

13

A PLACE TO TORMENT ME

"This is going to hurt" is something I told inmates when I was resetting a broken bone. I wasn't lying, and neither was Finn when he warned me. He stared down at me with determination, kneeling over my torso with his knees on the outside of my legs, pinning my thighs together. "Try to be still," Finn said, looking at my face with something akin to affection mixed with resolve.

"Why can't I stand up for this?" I started to get impatient and a little scared. I didn't much like the idea of men pinning me down, even if it was Mason and Finn. "Get off me, Finn. Let me up, Mason."

Mason ignored me. "Go ahead, Finn. Once Ezra hears her screaming, he'll try to intervene."

"What? Guys, what are you doing? I don't like this!"

Finn leaned down and kissed my cheek, drawing a territorial hiss from Mason. "I'm sorry, *kendi*."

"She's not your *kendi*!" Mason barked.

Finn smirked at Mason. "She's not yours, either."

"Pee on me later, guys. My arm hurts like it's on fire, and like most sane women, I don't do well being pinned to the ground with a man atop me! Let me up!"

Finn stroked the curve of my cheek tenderly, his thumb tracing the crest of my lip. "Trust me to get the job done. We're the same person in that respect. You'll do whatever it takes, and so will I, even if it hurts someone I..." Finn cleared his throat, swallowing as he pried his gaze from my lips.

"I swear to you, I'll stab you straight in your stupid gills if you don't keep it together, Finn. Go back to your king's harem and look for legs in there with Banak's conch shell. October doesn't belong to you."

"Finn?" I whimpered, begging him with my eyes for the fire in my arm to go away. A panic not from me welled up in my guts, turning my pleas frantic. "Kabayo's hurt! You have to save him!"

"Hold still. I'll take care of everything, *sinta*."

Mason growled, "You'll especially not call her that. Not ever. She'll never be your *sinta*."

Finn paid Mason no mind as he closed his eyes and started murmuring an incantation in a language I didn't know. I fruitlessly struggled beneath both men, trying not to lose myself to Kabayo's alarm.

"Now, Finn!" Mason commanded, scaring me with the ominous sound of his voice.

Finn exhaled through pursed lips over my face, confusing me and making the muscles in my cheeks ache out of nowhere. Then lightning suddenly shot through my arm and into my chest, pushing a scream from my lungs that was so terrifying, I didn't know my mouth was capable of such an awful sound. Light and heat filled my body as I convulsed beneath Finn, who pressed me down with his significant weight into the carpet. My arm was on fire, I was sure of it. My toes rang with horror and agony as I thrashed without purpose or hope of victory. The only thing I could think to ask for was the only thing that always came through for me when life seemed to go up in flames. "Ollie!" I yelled, my back arching as Finn continued murmuring in his guttural language.

Mason's hand clamped over my mouth after stretching both my arms over my head to pin them down with one of his larger mitts. "Shh. It'll be over soon."

But it wasn't. I don't know if Mason was just lying, or if time had ceased all meaning for me. The fire burned my body without destroying, so it would always have a place to torment me.

Finally, *finally* I heard a fist banging on the door. Then a few fists. "October? Open this door! Ezra, help me!" Ollie called, frantic. He slammed his body against the solid wood, but it didn't budge.

Finn pulled his face back from mine. The only thing

that distracted me from the white hot pain were his eyes. They were black now, instead of a clear green. The same glowing dark blue X that emanated from my forearm was mirrored in his eyes, like an eyeball tattoo or something. The blue X-shaped glow trailed off from the edges of his irises, making him look like a space monster or something equally freakish. I screamed in fear as well as agony this time, and finally, Ollie and Ezra broke the sturdy double doors open, stumbling into the room.

"I got it!" Finn cried out as Ollie jumped him from behind.

That was the last thing I saw before the pain flowed out of me, leaving me a limp noodle on the floor as the room faded from my vision.

14

NOT SO DIFFERENT

I was still on the floor when I came to in fragments and pieces. I stared up at the ceiling and listened to Ollie yell at Mason while Mason tried to answer for himself calmly. Mariang was on the floor near my head with one of the twins, who was dabbing at my forehead with a cold, wet rag. I hoped it wasn't Boston.

"It's still smoking," the twin informed Mariang, who had tears in her eyes as she stroked my cheek. "And what are these marks? This is from Kabayo's token, but these claw marks on her arms? How does the Omen with two Reapers get into an animal fight like this?"

Mariang swept Bishop's hand from my arm, shushing him. "It's not worth mentioning. Von and Mason do a fine job. Some things can't be helped."

"What happened?" I rasped, feeling about a hundred years old when Ollie forsook his fight with Mason to kneel next to me. He encircled his arms around my upper half so he could slowly lift me off the ground.

"Get something to wrap her arm with!" he barked to Mason. "Why is her arm smoking?"

"It's what I've been trying to explain to you. Finn used her link to locate Kabayo. The mark lit itself on fire, but we put it out. It's okay, Ollie."

"You lit my sister on fire!" Ollie roared.

"To find your mother!" Mason countered.

"Screw Bev! I won't throw October under a bus to save your stupid world! I won't let you hurt her to save a woman who never lifted a finger for us!"

Ollie kicked the door all the way open and carried me to the kitchen, sitting me on the counter and running my arm under cold water in the deep sink. The cool stream hit me like a snake bite, reminding me of the fire afresh. "Ow! Oh, it's burning!"

"I know, hun. I know."

Mason and one of the twins followed us into the kitchen. Mason came right up to me and held my good hand so he could pull some of the anxiety from me. It wasn't a huge help. He was the thing that gave me a ton of stress, so as fast as he was pulling, more kept building up. "I'm sorry, *hani*. But you letting Finn do that might've saved their lives."

I nodded, biting my lip through the burn that felt never ending, even under the cold water. Ezra pushed his way to me, taking me from Ollie's embrace and holding me tight so my head could rest on his chest. The pretty purple shirt that made me actually look and feel like a true grown woman was singed on the sleeve now. That felt like a double punch to the gut. It was like the outfit knew I had no business wearing it, so it decided to light itself on fire just to get away from me.

Ezra smoothed my loose wisps of hair away from my forehead, tucking my head beneath his chin. I was holding it together until he started slowly rocking me, forcing embarrassing tears to form in the corners of my eyes. "Mason," Ezra barked, snapping his fingers and pointing to the spot next to him. "Let her squeeze your hand when the pain gets unbearable. You'll get far worse from me later, but we'll start here."

One of the twins rubbed some ointment on my hand, and I sucked the scream into my mouth, gripping Mason's hand beyond what he could fend off his wince through. Ollie was fumbling with the bandage, so Ezra turned my head away from the blackened linking mark and the scorching my arm had undergone. Ezra dabbed at my cheeks with his handkerchief while the other twin hugged the sobbing Mariang in the middle of the kitchen.

"You're finished. You're done," Ollie spouted, livid. "If this is the way my sister's protected, she's going to need protection from her guard detail. Ezra, I want him gone. He lit my sister on fire."

"It's not as simple as firing him, Ollie, though I'm

certain he deserves exactly that. She's bound to him and to Von. There's no undoing it."

"Then this is on you, Ezra. This burn? If you keep letting this guy around her, he's going to get her killed. He doesn't give a crap about her. I'm telling you right now, I wouldn't trust him to watch a log."

"Thank you for your advice," Ezra said, listening but not. He rocked me as his stomach growled. "Excuse me."

I gritted my teeth through a scream I tried to mute when the bandage moved along my burn too quickly, tearing at what I could feel was crispy skin beneath the ointment.

"Careful, Bishop!" Mason barked.

"Really, mate? *You're* the one telling me to be careful?" Bishop gripped my hand and gave it a reassuring squeeze. "It's all wrapped, love. Apologies for the pain." I felt him pull a little of my stress away and was grateful for the help before I reached a full-blown public breakdown.

The back of Ezra's hand started glowing, and I could feel his frustration. "This had better be good news," he grumbled as his stomach rumbled again. "Pardon me."

Ezra left me to Ollie's embrace, which was laced with anger I knew wouldn't abate with a simple conversation. "Listen up and listen good, guys. Just because my sister doesn't value her own life doesn't mean you all get to put her through the ringer. Without her, your world dies, so be better at protecting her than this one," he said, jerking his chin toward Mason.

Mason took the admonition with grace and didn't argue, which was probably best. Ollie was in no mood. "If we made the wrong call, I'll take responsibility. I don't want to hurt October, Ollie. I couldn't think of another way to help your mother."

"You don't want to hurt her? Every time I turn around, either you or Von is making a mess of things. I'll make it simple for you: if it's not good for her, don't do it. Even if it'll save your whole kingdom by setting her on fire, still no. You have one job, and it's to protect her. Not all of Terraway, just her. Let Ezra and the council worry about the rest." He glowered at Mason. "And holding a woman down while she's screaming for you to let her go? Again? No man should ever have to hear his sister go through that."

Mason paled at the insinuation. "Ollie, this was different. No one kissed her."

"And yet? Not so different." Ollie glared at Mason as he pointed out the tears on my cheeks. "Come on, kid. Let's do some recoup upstairs so your protector doesn't help you off a cliff."

Bishop and Boston looked to Mason and then to me, trying to catch up with everything their two brothers clearly hadn't filled them in on.

Before they could connect all the psychic, shapeshifter and vampire dots, Ezra ran back into the kitchen with new light in his eyes. "Prince Langgam's spies found Von! We've got an address! Move, boys!"

15

OLLIE'S SECRET

Mason's stomach growled as he sat with Mariang in the living room while I paced the floor. He was in the process of consuming a bowl of lamb and apricot stew, so I didn't bother to ask if I could get him something. I actually hadn't spoken in an hour, knowing that the slightest peep might set Ollie off. In truth, my arm was screaming at me, begging me to ask for more ointment that seemed to have a lifespan of twenty stinking minutes. I knew if I let myself need more of the cooling sensation I craved, Ollie would start a fight with Mason again, and as much of a Superman my brother was to me, Mason was just plain bigger. His muscles were earned the old-fashioned way – fighting zombies, just like Bruce Campbell.

Mariang stared at her phone, too tense for words. Ezra was in the conference room by himself, making calls and fielding who knows what. Lynna alternated between crying in the kitchen and bringing more food to Mason, who couldn't eat enough. Ezra's appetite was almost as strong, which struck me as strange, but not strange enough to warrant a conversation when everything was so tense.

Ollie stared at the movie that played on the screen, seeing but not absorbing. Being in the room with us, but not really. I knew that face; he was planning something, and I knew I wouldn't like it. The curtains were closed all over the house, ensuring no one could peek in and see me, informing the jackhole kidnapping Ekeks that I wasn't in Lumipad after all. It made for a pretty dreary day. I couldn't scrape at my arms anymore, so I settled for pinching my thigh, which helped a little and kept everyone off my back about the whole self-mutilation thing. Sheesh.

"I feel like Alton and Graham should've been back by now," Mariang fretted, tucking a lock of black hair that had strayed from her tight bun back behind her ear. "They were supposed to help and come back when things were settled. Where are they?"

Mason patted her back as they sat together on the couch, looking like a giant next to her dainty form. I knew he was doing his best to pull for both of us, and was probably grateful Ollie wouldn't let him near me so he only had to stay on top of Mariang. Girlfriend looked like she was about to fall to pieces. "They might not come back right after," Mason reasoned, stirring a chunk of hard bread into his stew and ladling the thick broth over the crust. "They'll most likely stay on to help your mom get to the main well. Then they'll be back, no problem. Come on, Mariang. It's Danny. Since when has he ever let you down?"

"It's not just that. It's Bev, too. I finally get a mother, and after everything, she gets herself back, and then this? I lose her without a say in things?" She leaned into Mason's one-armed embrace, which meant he had to pause from wolfing down his bowl of stew. He eyed it longingly as he held Mariang, so she had a solid refuge to rest her weary head on. Mason was good at that; he'd been my safe place for a brief period, too.

I moved into the kitchen to grab myself a bowl of stew, the scent having taunted me for ten minutes already. I ate in silence, unaccompanied in a clean kitchen, and for the first time even that wasn't enough to calm my heart. I'd been stuck with two guys and unexpected houseguests for months. Now that I actually had a bit of breathing room, I couldn't enjoy it. That breathing room came at a heavy price.

I realized that my relationship radar might be permanently busted after the whole Mason debacle. You think a guy's available, and then you come to find he's using you to see his dead wife. I mean, if this happens again with another guy, I'm really going to start getting a complex. I made a mental note to ask Von point blank if he'd been married before. Things you don't think you have to ask a guy when you're only twenty-two.

Of course, all that might be moot if Bishop and Boston didn't bust Von out in time.

I ate my stew and then a second bowl, filling up on the comfort food and hoping it did its job of giving me that warm and fuzzy feeling I always got when I ate delicious soup.

"Is the stew as good as it smells?" Ollie asked as he strolled into the kitchen, sniffing the pot Lynna had left out on the stove.

"Better, if you can imagine it. Have some. Then come sit and be fun with me. I need a little fun, and so do you. You're starting to get old man lines on the sides of your eyes. Gabby's not going to like that."

Ollie ladled a princely portion for himself, and grabbed a few inches of the long, crusty baguette. He sat on the stool next to me at the kitchen's island, resting his bowl on the marble. "I don't think Gabby's going to care what I look like in ten years."

"Ten years? That's a generous assessment. If you don't start sleeping better and stop throwing fits about things you can't control, you'll get wrinkles in a few weeks."

He rolled his eyes at me and dipped his bread into the thick broth. "Ha, ha. I meant about Gabby being around in ten years. This Terraway world is a little all-consuming. I can't imagine having a relationship with her that actually goes anywhere. Not if I have to keep her in the dark about our childhood *and* this."

"No one's making you keep our childhood secret from

her," I reminded Ollie quietly. "You're imposing that rule on yourself, isolating when you don't have to."

His elbow jutted into my ribs. "Hey. Stop being wiser than me. I need something to do with all this book learning I've got up in here. Don't tell me you've mastered relationships before I have."

"Not mastered, just found that it wasn't so horrible telling the guys bits and pieces about growing up. It was like running my fingers down a cheese grater the first few times, but now it's not as bad. Gabby loves you, Ollie. Maybe you should let her decide if you're too much a mess to stay with, instead of making that call without her knowing it." I jabbed my spoon in his direction. "Controlling."

"Stop therapisting me. It's therapissing me off."

"You're going to therapiss yourself when you try your stew. Reminds me of the kind Allie used to make whenever it rained. Remember that?"

Ollie chuckled, but it didn't touch his eyes. He stirred the stew, staring into the bowl as if he wanted to crawl inside of it. "I have to tell you something."

"Crap," I said in a gusty exhale, dropping the spoon into my bowl. "Whenever you say that, it's something terrible." I rubbed my hands down my thighs over and over while Ollie worked his way up to spitting it out. "Hit me with it."

He swallowed and cleared his throat about seven times

before words started to form. "I think... I can't be certain, but I think Allie might be dead."

I'm pretty sure things happened around me, words were said and the world somehow turned on its axis, but the bomb that crashed over my head and punched me in the face was the only thing in my universe. I gawked at Ollie, emotion rising in my voice when I finally spoke. "How could you say something so horrible to me? What would make you think that? Do you know something I don't?"

"Don't hate me," he warned, addressing his stew. "I have a phone number. A break glass in case of emergency kind of thing that she gave me if something terrible ever happened to you. I wasn't supposed to use it except for that. She was very clear when she left us. I couldn't give you the number, or you might call her when it wasn't dire and spook her. It was the only tether I had to her." He leaned his elbows on the counter and spoke into his hands. "I called her! I called her when I found out about Terraway and everything. I wanted her to come home. I thought maybe the three of us could figure this new world out together." Now it was Ollie's turn to get choked up. "But she didn't answer. I called again when Bev went to Lumi-pad, and still nothing. We had a deal! She'd leave us, and I'd get to keep a lifeline. She promised she wouldn't leave without a tether. She wouldn't... So I know something horrible happened. The only reason she wouldn't answer

that number is if she couldn't. It's been too long to ratio-
nalize it away."

It was a multi-tiered bomb that kept exploding. Ollie
had a way to contact Allie. *Boom!* Allie left a lifeline with
Ollie and not me. *Boom!* Allie wasn't answering, the only
logical reason being that she couldn't. *Boom!*

Only there was another logical reason she wasn't answering. Allie hadn't wanted us to contact her. Even with the
secret lifeline, she had specified no contact without a life-
threatening emergency. The part of me that didn't believe in
Santa Claus was certain that she wasn't picking up because
she didn't love us anymore. She'd been through enough, and
I was the beacon for it all. I was the reason she'd sacrificed. It
was because of me she worked after school to earn the
money for food, clothes and the mortgage while her friends
were blowing their paychecks at the mall on cute shoes and
designer coffee drinks. She'd given up too much. As much as
it hurt me beyond all the damage I could stuff down and still
be somewhat functional, I understood. I'd taken her youth.
I'd forced her to be a mama before she'd hit puberty.

There really wasn't forgiveness for that.

Neither of my mamas wanted me, and that's the name
of that tune.

I didn't know what to do or say to comfort Ollie, who
was holding onto the brink before tipping over the edge
into grieving. I stuck with the standard, "I'm here for you,"
but Ollie was past the point of that making a drop of differ-

ence. In true Reese fashion, Ollie reached out when it was already too late. I wrapped my arms around my brother, his shoulders and forearms tensing and relaxing in spasms as he wrestled with his urge to cry.

"I failed her," he choked out. "I should've..."

I shushed Ollie, only silencing his feelings when they were self-destructive. "No, no. You didn't fail anyone. You drove her to the shrink. You made sure she ate. You were always, always, always good to us."

"I let her carry too much of the responsibilities."

I brought his head to rest on my shoulder, wishing not for the first time, that Ollie could be a child for once in his life. That he could rest without worry. "You took on too much for any sane human to make it through, and yet you did. There was nothing you could've done better. Allie isn't dead, Ollie." *She just doesn't want me.*

"It's the only explanation," he argued, pulling away, lest he never be able to sit up on his own ever again. I knew that struggle well, and was grateful for Mason and Von, who broke me out of that bad habit of perpetual distance you get from growing up Reese. "Sorry. I'm alright," he assured me, rubbing his hand over his face to rid himself of the anxiety that never fully left us. "You get to be the broken mess next, okay? It's your turn," he joked, reaching for humor to keep the softness in his heart far away from fresh air and daylight.

I kissed his temple. "Okay, Ollie." I patted his back and

walked into the living room, my soul hollow and my voice expressionless. "Mason, Ollie needs you."

Mason sighed. "I'm not interested in more accusations from him. I apologized too many times just to shut him up."

I couldn't argue with that, but I didn't have the words to explain all the brokenness that was going on inside of Ollie. I didn't want to tell him about the shattering agony that was tearing me up. I tried to compartmentalize and shove the bad things into a drawer in my mind where they couldn't taunt me with their harsh reality.

I'd had too much hard truth in my life. I wanted whipped cream now. Whipped cream and no problems. I wanted lies. To be told it would all be okay, and for a harbor of a moment, let myself believe the beautiful blessing that was the lie. I couldn't make Mason understand. "Ollie needs a good pulling. He needs a Duwende. It's bad, and I can't fix it."

Mason considered my countenance and stood, giving Mariang a decent pull before leaving her to stare at her phone as she waited on word from the twins. "Alright. If that's what you want, I can do it."

"That's what I need. I need you to take care of Ollie."

Mason wrapped his arm around my shoulder, bringing me tight to his side. He kissed my forehead while we walked in step. "I can feel this. Whatever it is that's worse than it was when you went into the kitchen? It's pretty bleak, *hani*. Anything I can do?"

"Just take care of Ollie. That's what you can do for me." I paused in the hallway, the weight of Allie's absence crushing me afresh. *Allie didn't want me.*

My knees buckled, and luckily Mason caught me before I tripped too unforgivably.

"Whoa! Hey, take a break. What happened? What's wrong? I mean, other than the obvious. You left for the kitchen and hit a new low?"

I gripped Mason, letting him hold me, despite all the mistrust between us. I looked up into his slate eyes, unable to communicate with words the despair that dragged me under when the reality hit me that my mamas didn't love me. For years I'd had no one to talk to about my weird boy issues, no one to help me pick out the right hairstyle, no one to ask if I was alright in that special mom way.

So I just learned to be alright, and when I wasn't, I faked it well enough. But this was crap on top of too much garbage. Always too much garbage. Bev was in the middle of a cannibal war, Von was kidnapped, and Allie was gone, possibly forever.

Ollie had kept a secret. I don't know why, but somehow that felt like the worst part of the things that were staring me in the face with their too many eyes and monster tentacles that grabbed at my moxie to crush what was left of me.

Mason held me, and in the quiet of the hallway, I learned to let him.

16

VON, UNHINGED

The crash of bodies through the front door brought me to my feet and my heart into my throat. Boston, Bishop and Von – beautiful Von – were a mess of bloody limbs and torn clothing. Boston and Bishop deposited Von on the floor of the foyer, giving me a glimpse of Von's bindings. His wrists were tied behind his back and his legs were fused together with rows and rows of thick rope. Von's eyes were filled with malice, his fangs bared as he gnashed his teeth to get at the blood his brothers were dripping all over the foyer. Von inhaled, his head whipping at me. He roared to get at us, but I ignored his need and the fear I tried not to feel. Mason hefted Von up and carried him to the basement, where the vampire cage was.

I bolted to the kitchen and grabbed a few blood bags. Then I flew down the stairs and handed them to Mason, who was a little frazzled. "I don't want to keep him bound while he's in the cage, but I can't get his ties off without maybe accidentally setting him loose. I'm going to have to feed the blood bags to him." He looked down at his stomach that rumbled again, frustrated. "Let me grab a roll or two first. Be right back, Von. Hang in there, brother."

Mason ran up the stairs, leaving me to stare helplessly at my BFF. Von thrashed around on the floor, growling and dripping with venom as he howled his pain. Slowly I walked to the cage, taking a deep breath before I opened it. Von was bound, but I was still careful to keep my distance as I knelt down a couple feet from his head. I screwed off the cap to the plastic pouch, showing him the contraband and hoping the promise of relief would soothe his nerves.

Even when he was a monster, snapping at me to tear into my skin and break me, I still loved him.

"Here you go, sweetie," I cooed, careful as I brought the mouth of the pouch to his lips.

The sweet and sensual noises Von made as he drank from the blood bag were fascinating. I couldn't look away from the yearning, the fear of the need in his eyes as he sucked like a starving and dehydrated man getting his first taste of water. I didn't mean to run my fingers through his hair, but they found their way into the filthy black tresses easily enough. Von guzzled the blood, making gratuitous guttural noises that sounded like desire and felt like pain. I didn't like when Von was in pain. "It's alright, honey. I'm here. You're safe now. I'll watch you. I'll make sure no one kidnaps you ever again."

I didn't like the feeling of the cage, having spent so much time around men who'd been confined to them. But I would walk straight into the prison for Von, whether it was a good idea or not.

Mason was clomping down the wooden steps when Von drained the last of the pouch, his tongue reaching to sweep up every last drop so none went to waste. "What are you doing? I said I'd be right back! Get out of there!" Mason ran to me, his hands under my armpits as he dragged me out and slammed the door with a loud clang. "Do you have a death wish? I knew I shouldn't have left you unchecked."

I shook his hands off me. "Oh, brother. So dramatic. Von's tied up. It's not like he can attack me really. He was starving, so I gave him a bag of blood."

Mason looked up as if to communicate with God what a pain I was being. "It'll be dumb luck if you live through this whole thing. You keep throwing yourself headfirst into danger. I was gone all of two minutes! It's dangerous for Von, too, you know. The more he's around you when he's like this, the more chances he'll be able to drink enough of your blood to complete the transformation. Then he'll be lost to you for good. Is that what you want?"

"Of course not! I was careful. He didn't even nick me."

"Next time you go playing with a tiger and excuse it all

by saying 'I was careful,' don't be surprised when that tiger breaks loose and attacks."

"Message received. Now help him!" I lobbed the other blood bag to Mason, standing so I could watch every move.

"I will. You go upstairs and patch up his brothers. They're bleeding all over the place. See how much danger we're still in."

I ran up the stairs, trying to block Von's frustrated roars out of my head.

17

VANDERSHOT 101

I snatched up the first aid kit from the hallway bathroom under the sink and clicked my fingers to the guys, motioning for them to follow me to the bathroom. "Have a seat," I said to the twin who had more bumps and burgeoning bruises than scrapes. "Which one are you?" I asked of the bloodier one.

"I'm whichever one you want, love." He leered at me, which let me know exactly which twin I was talking to.

I closed the lid of the toilet and sat him down atop it. "Alright, Boston. I don't have any local anesthetic, so we're just going to have to sew this gash here up without it. Can you handle that, or do you want me to take you to the hospital?"

Boston scoffed, his bravado in full swing. "Do it up. A little needle doesn't bother me."

"Glad to hear it." I set to work getting the wound

cleaned, wishing for better lighting as I tried to assess which of his cuts needed stitches. "How do people normally tell you apart?"

"My dick's far bigger," Boston answered, not missing a pervy beat.

I threw my "do no harm" vow out the window and stabbed into the tender part of his arm with the needle. "Knock it off, jackweed."

"Boston's front tooth is crooked," Bishop offered from his position in the doorway.

"Are these three the only gashes? Are you hurt anywhere else?"

"I could use a physical," Boston teased, pulling his bloodied black t-shirt over his head to reveal his sculpted torso. He beamed with pride at the state of his well-earned physique, watching my face to catch me in an ogle.

I kept my examination of him clinical. "How was the retrieval? Did you kill them all?"

Bishop answered, since it seemed Boston was stuck on perv mode and might be incapable of normal conversation. "We killed seven Ekeks and salted one Manas. I don't know if we got them all, to be honest. I didn't see anyone escape, but it was pretty chaotic. Can't be positive."

"I did," Boston said, his voice grave. "I saw two Ekeks escape. A blond bloke and a ginger."

Bishop reeled back to gawk at his brother. "Why didn't you say something?"

"Because I was more concerned with getting Von out

alive. They were beaten decently bad, but they limped out through the backdoor before I could take them out."

Bishop shook his head. "We have to go back."

I turned and pressed my hand to Bishop's chest to slow down his fight. "You'll do no such thing. They're most likely long gone by now anyways."

"But they might come back for Von! If it worked once to manipulate an Omen by kidnapping her Reaper, they'll try it again the next time they want something."

I nodded at the logic. "When you're done in here, go back out to Ezra and ask him to get Lang to send his minions out to search for the two Ekeks." I opted for a change of subject. "How was Von when you found him?"

Boston kept quiet at this, and both twins avoided my gaze, looking far off as they pictured the thing they had never wanted to see their big brother go through. Bishop cleared his throat. "He's alright now. That's the important thing."

"They bled him," Boston explained. "He's not Von right now. Ezra's got blood on hand, yeah?" He looked down and cleared his throat, lowering his voice. "If he doesn't, Von can have some of mine. As much as he needs."

"Mine, too. Between the two of us, I'm sure we've got enough to bring him back."

I softened my grudge against Boston at the self-sacrificial offer. "Ezra's got blood in the fridge. Enough to bring Von back to normal. It usually takes a while to get into his system, though."

"He was chained to a post in the basement when we found him," Bishop said, looking into the distance, picturing the horror afresh. "Like he was their dog or something."

Boston winced as I pierced his bicep with the needle. "We made them pay, mate. It's over. Von's safe now. Can't keep a Vandershot boy down."

Bishop nodded, swallowing a lump in his throat as he rubbed a sore spot on his wrist. He was still coming down from the fight they should've had more backup on. "I've never seen Von like that. I mean, I've only seen him a few times since he was bitten. Danny never went into much detail what happened when he didn't get enough blood. I barely recognized him."

"I know. He's completely animal right now. I wonder if he could even recognize us." Boston looked down at where I was stitching to watch the needle weaving in and out of his skin. "We left him tied up, just in case. He snapped at Bish," Boston explained of Bishop's haunted look. He clicked his fingers at his brother to jerk Bishop out of the funk he was settling into. "Hey, he's not Von yet. He won't even remember you punching him to get him off of you."

I recalled when Mason pinned me down to kiss me. Even through his bloodthirsty fog, Von managed to call out for Danny to come save me. "Von understands that we have to use any means necessary to keep us and him safe. He doesn't want to hurt anyone, so he won't be pissed you had to defend yourself. He's usually only mad at himself." I looked at the two, feeling strange that I was instructing them on how to take care of their own brother. "So when he comes back to his senses, don't rag on him about any of it. He gets real upset with himself, and he doesn't need to feel that." I didn't look up, but I could feel their eyes on me. "Let's practice." I put on my best English accent, which didn't mix seamlessly with my occasional southern lilt. 'Hey mates, when I was out of my mind in some godforsaken basement, did I try to hurt either one of you?'" I shot them a look of warning to play their parts.

"Of course not," Bishop answered. "We know you'd never hurt your family."

Boston mirrored the sentiment, taking in my instructions with a curious tilt of his head. "You're awfully protective of our big brother."

"Of course I am. I'm protective of both my Reapers. They do handy things, like keeping me alive." I fixed my eyes on the task at hand, tying off the suture and bandaging up the rest of the abrasions. "Von's saved my life a couple times now, and never held it over my head. He can't control this, but he thinks he might someday be able to. So be cool and let him deal."

"Anything you say, love," Boston said as he tugged his shirt back over his head. "Looks like Von found himself a sweet little cherry to take up his mantle."

I glowered up at Boston, tempted to stab him in the arm with the needle again just to knock the suggestive smile off his smug face. Stupid Hippocratic Oath. Boston had a wide, sleazy smile aimed at me. "Something tells me I'm really going to hate you, and I'm not the first girl to say that to your face the first day meeting you."

"You haven't slapped him," Bishop pointed out, waving his brother out of the bathroom and closing the door to shut out the antagonistic twin's leering lips. "Well done. Not many pretty women have made it through the whole first day of meeting Boston without a good wallop to his mug."

I straightened that Bishop called me pretty, which was a far sight better than being called cherry.

"Well, the day's not over yet. Where does it hurt?"

Bishop shot me an apologetic look and peeled off his sweat-soaked shirt, turning to show me his back. There were several slashes across the taut muscles, stretching from his shoulder all the way down, vanishing below his jeans. "I got a little roughed up while Boston got Von out."

"I can see that. Can you move alright? Do you think anything's broken?"

"Nah. I'm fine. I more just came in here so Boston wouldn't hit on you too badly. He has a certain charm about him that some women find..." He cast around for the right word.

"Repulsive?" I guessed. "Yeah, I can see that. But since you're here, might as well patch these up." I set about cleaning his scrapes, which went pretty deep, the one on his low back needing stitches. "I'm sorry. I'm going to have to ask you to lower your pants just a little so I can suture the end of this slice."

Bishop unbuttoned his pants and slid them down the necessary two inches. He leaned over the sink and covered his eyes with his hand to keep from seeing the whole scene in the mirror. "This is so embarrassing! I meet the new Omen, and instead of bowing, I drop my pants for her."

I chuckled softly at his chagrin. "Don't worry about it. Mariang's the impressive Omen you bow to. I'm really a nurse. That's what I did before this gig, so just think of this as a visit to the doctor's. Save the bowing for the cool kids."

"My doctor's balding and has a mole the size of Big Ben on the end of his nose. Not quite the same thing."

"I'll take that as a compliment." I worked as quickly as possible to save him more embarrassment, his face flushed as he tried to hold still. "Do you think Von's hurt? Mason wouldn't let me near enough to give him a thorough examination."

"That's probably best. It wouldn't do any good for him to snap at you. Omens are part human, yeah?"

"Yup."

"Right, so your blood might send him over the edge." He shook his head, determined. "We can't have that. I've never heard of a half-vamp pulling for an Omen. Not to scare you, but I can't imagine life expectancy's all that long for this kind of situation."

"That's not supposed to scare me?"

"I worry, is all. The state of Terraway rests on the

Omens being able to function. I know from Von and Danny's letters and calls home that Mariang's not always at the top of her game."

I swallowed as I tied off the suture, placing a bandage over the line so the stitches didn't snag on his jeans as he pulled them up. "I can handle myself. And now that there's two of us, Mariang's doing a lot better. Plus, Mason's my other Reaper. If Von's not firing on all cylinders, Mason's got a handle on it."

"I guess that does make things better." He shook his head, turning to face me. "You should've seen him. I didn't know Von would get like that. Danny's pretty tight-lipped about Von's condition. Von didn't live in London after he was bitten; he was too afraid to see any of us. Afraid he'd bite us. It was dreadful to think of him out here alone and dealing with fending off a vampire transition. Then when he did finally come home to visit, he wouldn't stay at any of our flats. He rented a room to make sure he didn't bite any of us. It was awful."

"Well, you'd be proud of how far he's come. Von's a great Reaper. One of the best. He's starting to seem not so scared of himself most days." I searched Bishop's face for a friend and found one easily. "Danny wasn't too thrilled in the beginning, but it's working out. He's growing into his job."

A flicker of a haunted look crossed over Bishop's face. "Von doesn't need to grow up. Had a terror of a time when we were younger. He deserves a little irresponsibility.

Danny's too harsh with him. Expects him to be our father when that was never Von's role."

I crossed my arms over my chest and decided to let the façade of distance down. "You won't get any arguments here. I just meant that the things Von's had to make peace with? As much as anyone can, it seems like he's moving in that direction. It's good for him."

"Sounds like *you're* good for him. That's what Danny's been saying, anyway."

My eyebrows lifted. "Seriously? Danny hates me. I can't believe he said anything complimentary about me."

"Aw, that's just Danny. His way of caring about someone is barking at them to make sure they brush their teeth. That one took me a while to figure out, but it's there."

"Sounds like you're the person to see if I need a Vandershot family cheat sheet."

Bishop leaned his butt on the sink, crossing his arms and smiling. "Only if you want the truth."

"Hit me with it. Vandershot 101."

"Alright. Mum raised us. Dad split when Danny and Von were kids. He'd come back every couple years to knock up mum, eat pot roast and leave. Von was the man of the house early on, and when he dropped the ball, as most children tend to do, Danny reamed him for it." Bishop lowered his voice and leaned in conspiratorially. "Von sends us all postcards from Dad every Christmas. No one else knows they're really from Von, but I found them in his drawer one year." Bishop brushed his hands down his chest over and over one at a time until words surfaced. "You should read them. Apparently Dad's on a whaling boat that only docks once a year, and he can't control the port they land on. It's why Dad's been MIA since we were kids. Each postcard's filled with all the things you always want your dad to say to you, the things you need to hear."

My hand flew to my swelling heart. "Oh my goodness. That's too wonderful. Too precious. He really did that?"

"Still does." Bishop nodded. "To see him tied to a post, beaten and bled, snapping his fangs to get at us?" He shook his head. I wasn't sure how Bishop and I got to the place of such unabashed honesty, but suddenly we were there. "Von's my hero. Broke me a little bit to see him so bested."

I turned my head slowly from side to side, and no words came to me for a solid fifteen seconds. "That's the worst and sweetest thing I've heard in a long time."

"I can see he's in good hands with you. I worry sometimes that he's over here with only Danny. Danny's great, but..."

"But Danny's a raging butthole?"

Bishop sniggered. "I was going to say that Danny's great, but he's not so great to Von. Blames Von for Dad leaving."

My nose crinkled. "How'd he work that one out?"

"Because Von beat up Dad the last time he came around. I was only a baby at the time, but Alton can tell you the details. Dad was slapping Mum around, so Von broke Dad's arm and leg with a baseball bat. Told him if he ever came back, he'd break the other side of his body. So Dad never came back, and no one hit my Mum ever again."

My mouth had fallen open. "I can't believe Danny would be upset about a guy like that leaving. I can't believe he'd blame Von."

"I don't think he looks at the wound too closely. He just knows that Von's the reason he doesn't have a dad. So Von sends Danny Christmas postcards from Dad every year. The only way Danny hears the things he needs to is if he thinks it's coming from Dad."

"That's terrible. I mean, really. I think I'll need to mull over all that for a while."

Bishop and I looked at each other with new appreciation. He didn't have to be so worried about Von, and I had an ally.

18

SLUMBER PARTY

It was a long night of waiting out Von's anguished cries while the blood took its sweet time working its way through him. I let the others talk nonstop about if they should send down another team to help out Danny, Bev and Kabayo or not, while I stayed in the basement with Mason. He was reticent to leave my side when I was near the gnashing vampire. Mason brought down a couple sleeping bags and pillows, though I knew he wished for the comfort of our bed upstairs. I was a couple of feet from the cell, my knees clutched to my chest as I watched my BFF devolve while my heart broke for him.

By midnight, Von had quieted enough to let Mason pull out some of his stress through the bars. He lay asleep on the cold floor of the cell, twitching every so often as saliva trickled out of the corner of his mouth.

"He's alright," Mason assured me. "Come to bed, *hani*."

I nodded, releasing my grip on my knees and crawling to the sleeping bag as footsteps descended the stairs. "Hey, Bishop. You need something?"

"No. Just thought I'd sleep down here. I see I'm not the only one who had that idea. Sorry. Is it weird if I join you?"

"Of course not. Why would it be weird? He's your brother." I patted the empty space near my head. I didn't want him blocking my view of Von. The second he was himself, I wanted to bust him out of that cage. I didn't like Von in a cage. He was so much better freed.

Mason gave a heavy sigh. "He means were we planning on having sex tonight. No, Bishop. October and I are just friends."

I narrowed my eyes at Mason. "Don't say that like being my friend's the lame consolation prize. I'm a good friend."

"Of course you are. I didn't mean it like that."

Boston clomped down the steps. "He meant that he'd much prefer being your naked friend, Cherry."

"Boston!" Mariang admonished him, flitting down the stairs without making a single step creak.

My nose crinkled. "Oh. Well, no can do on that front." I craned my neck up to Boston. "And you shut up about it. Shouldn't you be out hitting on some underaged girls at a club somewhere?"

Boston threw down a sleeping bag near my head, with Bishop taking the spot between Von and me, blocking my view of the cell. "Nah. Doesn't feel right going out when

Von's not himself yet. After that, I'll be sure to take him out to hit on plenty of eager women. Looks like you get me for the night, Cherry."

I cast a baleful look at Mason, who shrugged. "Von's their brother. They're just as concerned as we are. Lay back down. It'll be fine."

Mariang laid down on Mason's other side, looking like a dainty angel atop her rolled out pink down comforter. She tucked her body under a fuzzy cream blanket. "Mason? Do you mind if I..."

"Of course." Mason shifted onto his back and clasped his hand with Mariang's, pulling so she could calm down enough to sleep. Mason's stomach rumbled, so I scampered up the steps to retrieve some food for him, knowing he'd soon be ravenous, even though he'd just eaten. I brought him down a few sandwiches, and he thanked me with a tender look in his eyes that made my stomach feel strange.

"Come here," he said, pulling me down by the hem of my shirt to hover over him. Mariang was already asleep by his side. He leaned up and pressed a kiss to my cheek before lowering me down to his other side so he could whisper in my ear. "You are a good friend. If that's all you can give me, it's enough."

I kissed his cheek and sat up. "Thanks. How about I cut you a break tonight so you don't have double the duties? I don't need you to pull from me right now. I'm not all that tired anyways. Get some sleep."

"You sure?"

"Yeah. I can hear your stomach rumbling a mile away. You're getting overloaded. It's not fair to you."

"We can help," Bishop offered. "Our family's Duwende, you know. It won't be as good as your Reaper, but it's better than nothing."

"Thanks, but I'm cool. Normal people go through stressful stuff all the time without a Duwende."

Mason cleared his throat, but still whispered so as not to wake Mariang. "No. You need a Duwende. If you cut your scars open in the night, it'll drive Von mad. It's painful for him when you bleed, *hani*."

I shot him a "dude, shut up about it in mixed company" look, which Mason only shrugged at. "Fine. But I'm not tired yet, so you're off the hook for a while, Bishop. That is, if you're still up for pulling." I crawled over to the cage, stopping a healthy two feet from the bars so I could watch Von sleep.

Bishop nodded, hand to his chest. "I'd be honored."

Boston moved his sleeping bag between mine and Mason's. "I notice you didn't ask me for help, even though I'm far better at pulling than Bish is."

"There's a reason for that," I groused. "Get some sleep, guys. Who knows what's going to happen tomorrow."

~

My dream was sucky, and I couldn't find Von in it. I dreamt I was throwing up, which made me feel like brushing my teeth when I finally woke. I'd fallen asleep in front of Von's cage, worried that he'd wake up in his right mind and panic at still being bound. I felt my body being jostled, and opened my eyes in confusion. "Sorry. I'm getting tired, and I don't like you so close to the cage." I was in Bishop's arms, and he laid me gently atop my opened sleeping bag, carefully zipping me inside. I couldn't believe a near stranger was carrying me like a baby and I wasn't protesting. I blame it on the puking dream exhausting me beyond my normal threshold. "You're cold. Do you want me to get you another blanket?"

"No, no. Thanks, though. Get some sleep." I was all set to nod off, but my eyes flew open when Bishop held my hand. I recoiled, suddenly awake.

"I'm sorry. How should I pull from you?"

"Oh, right. Um, I'm not one for hand-holding." I tried to think through the logistics of separate sleeping bags and how to make physical contact through so many layers.

"I promise I'm not trying anything ungentlemanly. I can't pull without contact, and holding hands seems the least intrusive way."

I covered my face with my palms and sighed, glad that everyone else was asleep. "I have a thing about people touching my hands. I know it's weird. It's not you. I'm just a freak." I felt suddenly defeated at the admission, wishing it didn't define so many of my moments. My shoulders slumped, and I couldn't look at him. I wished for the gloves Von had bought me, but they were upstairs.

Bishop studied my face, seeing the shame I wished I didn't have to admit to him. "You're not a freak. I'm practically a stranger."

"Any other suggestions?" I asked as I shivered in the cold basement.

Bishop looked guilty at his suggestion. "We could share a sleeping bag. I promise not to hold your hands."

I unzipped my sleeping bag without a word and motioned for him to come inside. He nodded and got out of his sack, crawling with a determined look on his face as he tucked himself into mine. I was too tired to evaluate how weird this all was, or that it didn't feel strange at all to let Bishop into my personal space. Now that we had a secret about Von, I felt I could trust him a little. At least enough to share a sleeping bag.

The space was snug with his larger body squished to mine, but I didn't mind it. The tight compression actually relaxed me, and whether it was the pulling or just Bishop's calming presence, my hand found its way to his chest. He reached behind me and picked up Boston's lifeless wrist as his brother snored softly, placing it on my shoulder so I could get a double pulling while I slept.

"Thank you," I whispered, snuggling into his body without the hesitation two strangers should have.

"No problem, sister."

19

MY NAME IS OCTOBER

I awoke to being the ham in the twin sandwich. Boston's arm wrapped around me like he was holding a teddy bear, and Bishop's arm was looped around my hips as our stomachs pressed together.

From behind Bishop, I heard my name whispered, and it jerked me awake. My head lifted, but it didn't have far to go. I was pretty glued to Bishop. "October?" I heard again, this time with more clarity.

"Von? Von!" I tried to scramble out of the sleeping bag, but ended up waking Bishop to a faceful of my breasts, for which I couldn't stop apologizing for.

"Help me!" Von whined, and I could hear the pain in his voice.

Bishop sat up once I extracted myself from the sleeping bag, taking in the darkness that was difficult to see through. "Von?"

"I can't feel my arms! My shoulders are burning. Why am I still tied up?"

"They couldn't get the ropes off without you biting them. Are you seriously yourself already? How are you forming whole sentences?"

Bishop grabbed at my leg to stop me. "Wait! I'll open the cage. If he's going to attack someone, it shouldn't be you."

"He's not going to... It's clearly Von!" I waved my hand to the cage, noticing the others stirring at the commotion.

"Bishop?" Von's voice quaked with self-loathing. "Oh, bollocks. You've all seen me like this?"

Bishop closed his eyes. "Nope. I see nothing but a bloke with too much pride."

Von let out a frustrated growl. "Well, apparently I've got no pride left now. I promise not to bite anyone. Just undo the bindings! It hurts too much."

Mason stretched and stood, moving in front to guard me. "Go ahead. I've got her." He called over his shoulder, "Mariang? Could you run upstairs and grab Von another blood bag?"

"Of course," she said through her yawn. Bishop waited until she scampered up the steps before opening the cell door.

Boston cracked his neck twice as he stood with Mason between me and Von, his fists raised in preparation. I didn't like any of this one bit. "Von? It's alright. Bishop's going to cut you loose. How are you feeling?"

"Like I've been tied up for half a week. Oh! Careful, Bish. I can't really move." I watched with longing as Bishop pulled a knife from his discarded boots and cut Von's legs loose. When Bishop severed the tie on his arms, Von's hands didn't budge from their position. It looked like he was too sore to move on his own. He let out a frustrated moan of pain and humiliation.

"Help him!" I cried, frustrated that I couldn't be of any use. Mason was a wall in front of me with Boston. Boston looked like he wanted to run to his big brother, but knew he couldn't just yet.

Mariang came down the stairs with a blood bag, and Von's nose twitched as a flash of something sinister flared in his eyes. "Keep the girls away!" Von yelled. He couldn't stand, but his body tried to inch toward the blood Mariang handed to Mason. "Don't let me hurt them!"

"We've got you, mate. Not to worry." Boston herded Mariang and me toward the far wall while I tucked Mariang behind my back, shielding her from any impending attack. Boston's muscles were tensed as his arm looped behind him to rest on my hip. "If I say so, I need you to take Mariang and run upstairs."

"Don't let anyone hurt Von," I begged.

"He's our brother. Of course we won't hurt him. But we have to keep him from injuring himself, or you two."

We watched the scene as Mason took the cap off the blood bag, knelt down and fed it to Von. Bishop started rubbing feeling back into his brother's arms. Von was breathing heavily to the point of a feral snort as he sucked down more and more blood. Bishop pointed his finger at me, his eyes flashing with fear. "Run! Lock yourselves in a room and wait until we say it's okay."

Mariang grabbed my shirt sleeve, obeying faster than I intended. She all but yanked me up the stairs and pushed me into the conference room where Ezra was already working. The light from the windows on the way there told me it was barely dawn, probably no later than five o'clock.

Von had been bled dry. There's no way he was himself already. Yet he'd spoken. He was coherent, though not totally out of the woods yet. It made no sense.

Ezra put his phone down, standing when we entered so he could lock the double doors behind us. "Good morning, girls. Did you sleep well?"

"Von's coming out of it, but they're not sure how stable he is, so we're waiting with you until they get him under control. Where's Lynna?" Mariang asked. "Call her and tell her to lock herself in a room. Ollie, too."

Ezra obeyed without hesitation, and we all breathed a little easier when we heard the bathroom door outside the kitchen slam shut, along with the ding of Ollie's text of confirmation.

The relief was short-lived. I heard one of the twins cry out in pain, and the angry clang of the cell door accompanying the shouting that rose up the stairs and wafted in under the door. Mariang was in her father's arms. He was her safe place.

I looked back at him from my spot near the doors, my chest heaving when he opened his other arm and waved me to him, inviting me to hide for a while until the storm passed. I had a handful of reasons to hesitate, but I ignored them all and ran to him, crashing into his embrace that held me tight. Ezra had his faults, but even when his engagement to Bev imploded, he hadn't turned his back on Ollie or me. "It'll be alright, darlings," Ezra said, his cadence calming.

"I know," Mariang said, gripping her father and me with all her dainty might.

I'd never met my birth father, and clung to Ezra more than either of us expected me to. I couldn't let go; I'd kept my chin up for too long, and it needed a safe place to rest. Ezra was that harbor, that lighthouse in the hurricane that held me tight until the monsters went away. Or more realistically, drank enough blood to turn back into themselves again. "I'm here," he promised. "I'm always ever here."

I bunched his shirt with my fist and clung tighter to him. It wasn't that I was afraid of Von, or that the guys couldn't contain him. I'm sure everything was under control already. It was that Von had to be locked up in the first place. It was the whole sloppy mess of a life that I was smack in the middle of, and wasn't quite sure how I'd gotten there. Ezra was cooing soothing words to me, but I couldn't hear them. When he asked if I was alright, I couldn't open my mouth to tell him that no, I wasn't alright, and most likely wouldn't be for a long time.

My name is October, and I have a problem. I don't have the healthy fear of monsters most people have engrained in them. I'd chosen to work at the prison. I'd chosen to visit Bev once a week to make sure she was alright. I'd slept next to a wolf and pretended he was my innocent puppy. I'd made out with a widower and was shocked to learn he had issues. I'd made out with a slave trader and killed zombies alongside him. I was now psychically linked to a reverse centaur with an attitude. And Exhibit A was gnashing his teeth in the cell as I remained locked away from him. Every kiss we shared was, in reality, a danger. One nick of his fangs could pierce my skin and turn his bloodthirst crank to the point of no return.

And yet I'd chosen all these things.

Yes. My name is October, and I have a problem.

20

BARFING IN THE BATHROOM WITH THE BOYS

Ollie and Ezra were firm that Von should stay locked up a full twenty-four hours after becoming sentient again to make sure he wouldn't hurt anyone. Von agreed.

I did not.

Unfortunately, no one gave two rips what I thought. Now Ollie and Ezra seemed to be in cahoots, with Ollie taking Ezra's side in little things, like me not going to work that day.

That debate didn't last long. Numbers didn't lie, and that's why I loved them. I laid out the math, reasoning that we needed to keep ahead of the reaping count to make sure the famine didn't kill more people while help was still in transit. In truth, I couldn't stand seeing Von locked in a cage like an inmate, and he wasn't too thrilled about any of us seeing him like that, either. I spent a fair amount of time in the garage, detailing Terence my Taurus and making sure there were no blood stains from the fight with the Ekeks. People underestimate how calming it is to clean.

I started up my car, loving the feel of the purr that connected me to Terence the Taurus. Mason rode shotgun while Tweedle-Dumbass and Tweedle-Not-So-Bad occupied the backseat. The guys made small talk while I drove in the direction of the nearest hospital.

"It's alright, kid. He'll be good as new when we get back."

Mason was sweet, but I didn't need it. "Thanks. I'm more in a fake-a-smile-till-it's-over kinda mood right now, but I'll let you know when I'm up for a pep talk I might actually believe."

Boston chuckled and leaned forward between our seats to crank up the radio. I swatted at his hand and turned the volume back down to a respectable level. When I parked on the third floor of the structure, Mason was still running through the list of the job responsibilities with the twins, down to the last "clear every corner before she goes down it" that made me internally roll my eyes. "I'm not a fan of the high-stakes, always looking over your shoulder kind of thing. Makes me paranoid after a while."

"Paranoid Omens live longer," Mason pointed out as he exited the car, stretching his arms over his head. He wore a dark green polo that made his eyes look even grayer, along with jeans that made him look a little too handsome for his own good. The haircut that removed his seven dreads had been cruel, but it certainly made him fit into my world a whole lot easier. Mason reached out his hand to grab mine, linking our fingers and walking with me in the direction of the hospital. Bishop walked ahead of us and Boston behind, keeping us safe and making me a little jumpy. I didn't like Boston where I couldn't see him.

We strolled through the glass tunnel that led to the main building, and as we walked, I noticed our reflection in the window that stretched from the floor to far over our heads. "Wait a second. I want to see something." I pulled Mason over and looked at our reflection, noting with a frown the stark differences between us. Mason was tall, broad and ruggedly handsome. I was far shorter, dressed like a teenager going to the resale shop and looked decidedly less attractive than he did.

"Whatcha looking at?" He stared beyond us to the people below.

"Us. We don't look right. I look like your sister or your kid or something."

Boston laughed while Bishop and Mason smiled. "You don't look like my kid. I'm only nine years older than you."

"I love that you say 'only', like almost a decade isn't totally weird."

"You didn't mind so much when we were together," he said, clearly miffed, his nose in the air.

"Minding something and acknowledging it's weird are two different things."

"Okay. Weird, yes. But it doesn't make me old enough

to be your father. Here," he said, pulling me into the kind of embrace that makes a woman suck her stomach in while her heart flutters. He grinned down at me with a devious and dashing smile, knowing exactly the effect he had on a girl. "*Now* take a look."

I glanced at the window-wall again, seeing a different image. I was less a teenager in this pose, and more a woman out for an afternoon of flirty fun with her guy. "Oh, that's much better. You look way less like you could be my dad now."

Mason's smile fell into a grimace as he released me. "Oh! Is that what this was? When we were together, were you trying to fulfill some childhood daddy issues?"

"No!" I was indignant, hoping none of that was true. "And where did you even hear talk like that? That's Topsider shrink nonsense."

Mason shrugged. "Mariang and I were watching TV, and there was a man on giving people advice."

"Well, his advice doesn't apply to us. We didn't get together because I don't have a dad. Forget I said anything. Let's move."

Boston sniggered behind us, while Bishop tried to conceal his grin at my discomfort. Boston made a few crass comments before I turned around and gave him a good shove to shut him up. "Knock it off. I'm working, here."

"Of course, your majesty," Boston said with a sweeping bow.

My gut led us to radiology where I pretended to be lost

until I reaped a tall, thin man with a limp that I walked past. He didn't even notice more than a brush of my arm to his, but I sure did. Out of nowhere, my stomach roiled, making me belch. Mason reaped the soul almost as quickly as it came into me, but my stomach was still throwing a tantrum, tiny fists pounding on the lining as the moshers threw a party on my gag reflex. I keeled over, unable to contain my discomfort. "Oh! Something's wrong. Bathroom, guys. I think I'm going to be sick."

Bishop located the nearest bathroom and cleared the way for me, my knees quaking and my forehead sweating with every step. I barely made it inside the one-person handicap-accessible room before the chunks started coming up. I didn't have a choice; I had to hold onto the toilet seat to steady myself as I threw up my breakfast. My eyes squinched shut as the fecal germs and who knew what else crawled all over my hands, making me emotional as I puked. "You should go," I eked out between heaves. I was grateful Bishop and Boston were safely in the hallway. "You don't want to be here for this."

"I'm exactly where I want to be." A tear jerked out of me when Mason pulled my hair away from my face and rubbed my back. "What's going on? Are you coming down with something?" he asked when I stopped vomiting long enough to hear him.

"No. I don't know. I was fine until I reaped that guy, and now it's all coming up. I don't know what's wrong with me."

"Take a breather. Hey." He looked surprised when he saw my compulsory vomit-induced tears. "It's alright. Just a little setback. We'll go home and let you get some rest. You'll feel better tomorrow."

"No," I flushed the toilet and stood slowly to start the lengthy process of washing my hands, wrists, the unbandaged inches of my arms, my face and anywhere else that irked me. "We'll finish out the day."

Mason's stomach growled as I finished cleaning up, probably taking far longer than a normal person would've. "If you're sick, we should go home."

"You're sweet, but you're going soft on me because we're close. The famine doesn't care if I'm sick. It's going to kill people, and I'm the only one who can stop it."

He ran his hand over his face. "If you say so, but only the bare minimum. There are four lands left who need the stone, plus one to keep everything going. So we've got four reaps left, and we're going home."

"Roger that." I reached for the knob with a shaking hand, but Mason got the door for me.

Boston handed me a stick of gum while Bishop cast me a sympathetic look. "This way," I instructed, not wanting a pity party or a discussion about us going home versus finishing the job. My queasy gut led us to another wing where there were lots of rooms with doors left open, which suited me just fine. I wandered in with Mason and Bishop, while Boston flirted with the nurses at the station to distract them. Or disgust them. I honestly couldn't tell with that guy.

The sixty-something woman with salt and pepper hair asked me to change the channel for her, since she couldn't figure out the remote control that was in the bedframe itself. I politely showed her how to operate the TV using the buttons on the side of her bed, gently reaping her without her knowledge.

My stomach rebelled as the waves of nausea rose up in me, taking me down with the slightest provocation. I was barely able to excuse myself before I ran to her bathroom and vomited again, now certain that the spontaneous flu I was undergoing was related to the reaping. I didn't understand why, but somehow when I reaped today, I puked.

I really missed my old job.

I was a mess by the time we got four reapings under our belts. I knew I needed one more, but I was so weak, I couldn't hold my head up. I didn't have the gumption to protest when Bishop scraped me off the floor of the fourth bathroom I'd barfed in that day.

I would not cry. I would not cry.

Bishop was gentle as he carried me through the hospital and to the car, insisting Boston drive if he could manage not to take any hard turns on the way back to Ezra's.

Mason was chewing on his hand, his stomach growling as he began panting his discomfort. "I'm going to shift soon if I don't get food, guys, and it's not going to be pretty.

Turn off at the first sign of anything I can eat. I'm not picky. Anything at all."

Bishop had stolen a bedside barfing tray for me just in case for the drive home, but luckily I passed out a few minutes after Boston drove us out of the parking lot.

The stink of the fast food revived me and made me want to ralph all over again, but nothing was in my stomach. When we finally reached the mansion, the sun was starting to set. Bishop roused me gently, pulling a modicum of stress from me. He walked around the car and opened my door, knowing I was too beat to move on my own. "Easy, now. Let me help you."

I looked up into Bishop's eyes and saw only kindness there. My hand was unsteady and trembled as I reached for his, but before I could grasp him, Bishop cried out in pain, knocked forward into the car.

I looked past him but saw nothing. And just like that, the invisible something lifted him ten feet off the driveway and launched him onto the front lawn.

INVISIBLE ATTACK

"**M**anas!" Boston cried. "Stay inside, kid!" He flung himself out of the car and ran toward his brother, getting caught in a fight with an invisible foe along the way. "I'm coming, Bish!"

Mason ran full blast at the force Boston was dueling and grabbed it around the... throat? Torso? Arm? It was anybody's guess. Boston whipped his blade around and stabbed it forward. He ripped upward, making me scream when it looked like he was gutting Mason. I exhaled when the invisible enemy began to bleed, and Mason's struggle with it died down. Boston hadn't gutted Mason, but the thing they were fighting. I remembered being told Lumipad was filled with Ekeks and Manas. I'd seen a few of the male bird-like Ekeks, but hadn't encountered many Manas yet, other than Sylvia, who'd been cool enough. I remembered Danny telling me that Manas were the women of Lumipad, and they could detach their top halves from their bottom halves. They sent their winged tops out to hunt for meat, usually invisible, to gain the best sneak and attack on their mobile meals.

As the invisible enemy who was oozing blood stopped struggling in Mason's arms, I started to see her features as she materialized before me. She had black hair that flowed to the end of her half-body. Her face was stunning: full, red lips, pointed ears almost like a fairy, rosy cheeks, and a giant pair of black bat wings. The leathery webbed wings slumped as she fought her last, and I guessed her wingspan to be just a little longer than Mason's arm-length. Her breasts and ribs were dressed in crimson leather to match her lipstick, and beneath the bottom of her shirt I counted two ribs before random intestines dangled from where her torso was severed from her lower half. Totally gross.

Ezra stormed out of the house in his suit, gun in hand and malice on his face. He stomped with purpose, calling out the Manas with a command in his tone I didn't recognize. Ezra with a gun was a fearsome, glorious sight.

I was already pretty well freaking out, but I screamed when the car door opened. A hand cupped my mouth and jerked me backwards. "Not a sound, little Omen. You have no idea how many of us are watching. I'll send them down on your men in a heartbeat if you try to escape."

I struggled, but I was so worn out from my random

puke-fest that I was ashamed at how ineffectual my fight was. When nothing broke me free, I thrashed around as best I could just to make it clear that I wouldn't go quietly. I knew what happened to girls who went quietly. I treated the men who took them to their graves. I grabbed her head and bashed it to the window, jarring her hand loose. I turned in my seat and punched her across the face, wishing I had more room or more oomph. Or that I could, you know, see her.

I bolted out of the backseat and ran toward Ezra, my legs weak, but knowing they had no other choice. "Ezra! Get in the house! She said there's more! Too many more! Go!"

"Get in the house, October." Ezra pointed his gun into the sky, aimed at nothing with a lot of precision and pulled the trigger, dropping the half body that materialized out of thin air and thudded onto the front lawn. Boston was charging from behind, it sounded like to tackle me, but at the last second, he rushed a Manas who had almost snatched me up.

I didn't join the fight because I knew I wouldn't be of any use in the state I was in. I ran to the front door, but just as I made to twist the handle, someone invisible grabbed my wrist and jerked it to the side. Before I could figure out which way was up, the world was upside-down. I was flung over the Manas' shoulder seconds before her wings fluttered outward like so many bats taking flight. I screamed and fought as I levitated, elbowing and punching the back of her head until she finally dropped me from a height of only seven feet in the air. Boston stabbed her in the next heartbeat with his blade, giving me exactly one breath of relief before more descended on the both of us.

I couldn't count how many hands were on me, tearing at my hair, clothes and skin. Sharp talon-like nails dug into me, drawing blood and slicing too deep to muscle my way through. I screamed and flailed, punching at random as the frenzy continued. It felt like I was being pecked to death by razor claws.

I hadn't seen Mason wolf out, but he dove into the mix, tearing as much as they did like the true guard dog he was. His gray fur was soon matted with streaks of blood, but he didn't seem to feel it. He bit down hard and tossed bodies with a flip of his overlarge head before moving onto the next.

Bishop and Boston were a powerhouse team, punching, stabbing and outright throwing as many as they could get their hands on.

I don't know how it wasn't enough, but even Ezra's gun and rolled-up sleeves didn't keep the Manas from lifting my bloody and torn body off the ground. Despite my fear of falling, I thrashed mid-air as one pinned my arms down around my torso and the other grabbed my feet, smashing my ankles together. All I could do was try and twist around in their grip as they flew upward and east.

I heard Ezra's gun, but knew it was no use. They took

me higher and higher until shooting them down would be detrimental if I fell.

I heard a second set of grunts I couldn't do a thing to help soothe. Bishop was being carried by a separate group of Manas, his fight no match for their numbers.

THE QUEEN OF LUMIPAD

I cannot describe what it felt like to fly above the world at too high an altitude for proper breath for so long. The world felt like it was moving at a different pace than it actually was, and I didn't know what to make of it. I'd never been flying before, and guessed that now I most likely never would. The Manas knew what they were doing, flying us too high for us to maintain our fight with so little oxygen, but not so high that we died.

When we finally descended more than half an hour later, I was lightheaded from the altitude and weak from all the vomiting. I couldn't feel my fingertips, and my lips felt fuzzy.

The house we were flown into was an abandoned colonial on a dead-end street. There were rose-colored shutters framing the windows that had the curtains drawn inside. There was a mailbox I stared at, imprinting the address in my mind. Of course, I didn't know what street we were on, but numbers had to narrow it down a little. We were flown in limp to the house, but I stiffened at the sight that greeted us – a row of at least forty bottom halves. From the waist down, standing in lines like soldiers in black leather pants were the butts and legs of the Manas who'd attacked us. I watched with horror as one by one, the Manas materialized when they plopped their invisible upper halves down onto their legs. It made a slurpy sound that ended in a loud bone pop as they fused with their lower halves enough to walk around. Their overlarge batwings tucked inward, folding like origami to make what could be mistaken for a leathery black backpack if you weren't too close up.

I would not freak out. I would not freak out.

Bishop crawled over to me, covering me with his body as I collapsed to the wood floor. "Do what you want to me, but let her go. You hurt her, and the whole of Terraway dies, including all of you."

A woman with black lipstick on her too large lips leaned over, her long bangs hanging down a centimeter past her eyebrows as she flipped her waist-length raven hair over her shoulder. "Oh, puppy. What we won't do to you." She chuckled darkly and clicked her fingers. "Show our guests the best room in the house," she ordered, her voice simultaneously cold and amused. With the way the others obeyed without hesitation, I could tell Black Lipstick was the one in charge.

Bishop made a show of holding his hands up to indicate we would cooperate, but the Manas didn't care about that. They jerked him up, giving him a few gut punches and knees to the groin before dragging him down the stairs.

I was stepped on a few times, lightly kicked just so I knew who was boss, and dragged by my hair down the uneven wooden steps after Bishop. We were thrown into the dank, cold basement. When the horrible monsters left up the stairs, they shut us in the dark, alone with only each other, our battle wounds and our fear.

"Bishop?" I whispered, not sure how much blood either of us had lost at this point. I knew my face and arms were gouged up pretty bad by their razor-like claws. The cold, stale air stung the long rips in my thighs and calfs. I wanted to cover the deep cuts, but I knew they'd only sting more if I touched them. My voice sounded painfully fearful, and I worried what that said about our chances of escaping. If I was afraid, then part of the battle was already lost. I cleared my throat and tried again. "Where are you?"

Bishop groaned a few feet away, so I crawled over to the sound, collapsing next to him on the freezing concrete. I could smell dust and decay of some sort, and winced at my many injuries that I knew needed bandages or stitches. As soon as my arm touched Bishop's, he exhaled and pulled me into his side, wincing at the simple contact. "Are you alright? I mean, you're in one piece?"

"Nothing's broken," I hoped. "Barely a scratch on me. It's like they want us to escape."

Bishop let out a one-noted laugh at my attempt at humor. "Wusses."

"Can I help? What hurts?"

"Only all of me. It's a chore to breathe. Do you think they cracked my ribs?"

I pressed my fingers to his side, waiting for the telltale howl that didn't come. "I don't think so, but if they're bruised, it might still feel like they're broken. Try not to move. Rest while you can."

"No time for that. They're building their game plan up there. Can you see a way out?"

"I can't see anything! I don't think there are windows down here, and neither of us are in any position to fight our way past them."

Bishop held me tight. "If they want information from you about the stone, where it's hidden and whatnot, then they'll use me to get you to talk." He shook his head. "No matter what, you can't give them anything. Not a word. Don't answer when they speak."

"Use you?" I knew what that meant and gulped audibly. "I don't like this. What can we do?"

"Hold out as long as we can, yeah? Hope that the guys find us. Boston can always find me. Twin thing."

"Let's hope that happens in the next five seconds."

Bishop squeezed my hand as a wave of pain hit him. "Talk to me, October. Distract me from it all."

I cast around for anything. "Um, I um, Ollie's probably freaking out. And did you see Ezra's face? I've never seen him so scary. He was amazing. All of you were."

"Why were you throwing up today? Danny made it seem like Mariang only gets sick if she reaps too much. But you were sick after your first one." He paused. "Are you pregnant?"

Well, that was a good distraction from the pain and terror. "No! Of course not. I'm the furthest thing from pregnant a girl can get."

"Okay, okay. Help me to sit up. I don't want to be totally defenseless when they come back for us. Let's see what we can find to use as weapons, yeah? They nicked my knife."

"Lousy knife nickers," I groused, slowly helping Bishop to his unsteady feet. "Use the wall for support. Feel your way around the perimeter and see what you find."

"Yes, ma'am. Bossy little Omen, you are."

"Little? You're twenty-three. I'm only a year younger than you."

"But I'm so much cooler."

I was grateful for the slight chuckle Bishop gave us both. The banter was important; it kept us from crazying up the place even more with blind terror.

Without lifting up my shoes, I shuffled my feet across the basement, reaching out in the pitch black that was so stifling, I could feel the oppression pressing in on me from all sides. I tripped twice over the toe of my shoe, banged into a hard, flat object that felt like a sled or something, and found a collection of paint cans that were a third of the way empty. "I've got paint cans," I whispered to him. "They're not all that heavy, but maybe we can do something with them."

I could hear the smile in Bishop's voice, making his sneaky tone sound more like Boston's than anything else. "Oh, good find. Well done, little sister."

We shuffled around, collecting rags, cups, a few old knickknacks I couldn't make heads or tails of, and the odd broomstick that felt like it had been used on every room in the world except for this cobwebby hole. Bishop and I met in the middle of the basement, foregoing the fact that we barely knew each other and indulging in a gentle hug as we tried not to hurt the other's many wounds. Bishop's voice was gentle enough to soothe me. "You should lie down. Von would tell you to conserve your strength. You really had the crap end of it today, yeah?" We inched over to the far corner and lowered ourselves to the cold floor, huddling together like the scared children we were.

I evaluated our options, coming up with no way out, and too many to fight against who were far better equipped than we were for a takedown. I said the thing neither of us wanted to admit aloud. "We're going to die down here, aren't we." It wasn't despair; it was fact.

"Shh, there's no use talking like that, love. Let's give Ezra some time to find us, yeah? And Mason's a decent tracker. He won't abandon his charge so easily."

"We were flown here. There's no trail to track," I pointed out.

Bishop squeezed my hand. "I need a smidge of hope, yeah? Not even a whole handful of it. Just a smidge to make it through. I need to get out and back to my family. My brothers need me, and Terraway needs you." He shook his head. "Boston must be in a right state."

"Boston's our hope in this?" I asked, dubious.

Bishop chuckled and then inhaled sharply at the sting in his ribs. "Yes, Boston's sometimes unfocused. But he's also fearless. No one I'd want fighting by my side more than him and Von."

"Jury's still out on my end. Boston might be good with fighting, but he's not so great with talking to women."

"Ah, well everyone has their flaws. Boston's never been one for serious conversations or even the bare minimum of normalcy when a pretty girl's in the room." He nudged my side as if to tease me.

"Ha, ha."

We sat in silence a few minutes before the fear started creeping up on me. "Your turn to pick a topic. I'm starting to freak out, so distract me with something."

"I notice you're more comfortable with Mason now. That's good." He'd caught wind of our distance on one of our many phone chats.

"Mason's great. I imagine he'd be able to make anyone comfortable. He's got that way about him."

"I didn't think he'd ever move on from Kara. It's good to see the way he looks at you. Keep Von on his toes."

"Mason doesn't look at me like anything. And he's not moved on from Kara. It's complicated." I fished for a change of subject. "If you were back home, what would you be doing for fun right now?"

"I'd probably be playing the piano at the pub in town. Nothing amazing, but well enough for the people who pay me in pints."

"Huh. That's neat." I'd almost distracted myself from the awful doom, but cruel laughter reached us from upstairs, making my blood run cold. I held tighter to Bishop, and he squeezed my hand.

"Now, now. Let's not let them smell our fear, yeah? Manas are plenty strong, fast and smart. This won't be an easy out. Best save the real fear for the end, or perhaps not even then." He leaned his cheek to the top of my head. "Remember, don't tell them anything. They stole us; they don't get to steal information, too."

The door at the top of the steps opened, and we stood to face the oncoming danger. The woman with black lipstick moved slowly down the steps. She was a cat approaching the flirtation with her mouse before she devoured the rodent whole. She wore black combat boots that laced up over her calf muscle. Her tight black leather outfit made me shrink inside my long-sleeved t-shirt and jeans as I held tight to Bishop.

"Well, well, which one of you can tell me what

happened to my sagrado stone? I thought I sent a clear enough message by stealing your vampy Reaper. If you don't give the stone to Lumipad, you'll lose the people you love." She pouted out her lower lip, her face illuminated by the foot of light filtering in from the top of the steps. "Maybe you don't care about your Reaper, but you might care about this one. This is your boyfriend, right?"

Neither of us answered her, but Bishop stood in front of me, his chest barreled as much as he could. "Serena, you're daft to think you can manipulate an Omen. What do you even want out of this? To find the stone and… what? Give it to your land? The council's already doing that."

Serena hissed at Bishop. "I want the whole sagrado stone, and I want Dagat to die, wishing they could have a taste of it. They sat back and watched while we wasted away, while our crops died and our animals fled. I want them to waste away now. The drought hit us too, you know. They didn't lift a finger to help."

"You know the Omen can't act without council approval, and they haven't been able to meet to discuss moving Lumipad up on the list."

Serena looked up at the ceiling in thought. "I wonder why that is. Could it be because they can't find Queen Sylvia? Where on earth could she be?" Serena was pleased with her game, her fingers splayed out in dramatic flair to her question. "Could it be that she's tied up right now? A little busy?" Her eyes clouded over with a sinister glare that pierced Bishop and worried me. "Dear old Sylvia's dead. I make the decisions now."

Bishop scoffed, which I'm guessing wasn't his best move. "What're you on about? You're the military commander. There are like, three people ahead of you who would inherit the crown first. You're batty, love."

Serena's bat wings fluttered in response at her sides, the leathery tips dangling near her fingers. "Maybe so, but wouldn't you know it? None of those three want to stand up to me. Two are in hiding, and the other will be killed off when we return home. Funny how sometimes things just work themselves out."

"That's quite the plan. Too bad the council won't recognize you as the queen."

Serena's nostrils flared and she straightened, her fists clenched at her sides. "I'd like to see you take the crown only *I* wanted enough to fight for. Sylvia was running our land into the ground. I can only sit back and watch my people starve for so long before I step up and do something. She let us starve, but sure, *I'm* the tyrant."

"Whatever helps you sleep at night, princess."

"I won't sleep until your little girlfriend tells me where the stone is. Do you want to make me hurt you? Is that what you want?"

He didn't speak, but the message was clear. She would have to go through him to get at me.

This didn't seem to bother her one bit. She cleared the distance and scraped him clear across the cheek with her claws, making him wince and drawing out his fight. Bishop lunged for her, and the two scrapped for a total of two horrible minutes as I tried to be useful, throwing in the occasional punch before she called for backup. Bishop knocked her head to the side with one blow from his heavy fist.

Serena seethed in my direction as she spat blood. "I didn't think you'd make me hurt him, but now I'm going to have to."

A handful of Manas leaped down the stairs at her command, pinning all four of Bishop's limbs down to the ground so they could take turns kicking him. "Stop! Stop it! Let him up!" I punched the nearest one, knocking her off Bishop's arm so he could at least have one limb free. I picked up a paint can and knocked another of the Manas unconscious, stomping on her face with the heel of my shoe when she hit the ground.

Bishop was able to struggle with the two left, gaining enough ground so he could sit up, but Serena called for reinforcements before Bishop could stand. Serena ripped me from the fight as more assailants descended on Bishop, and pinned me to the wall. "I want you to watch while we break your boyfriend's kneecaps."

"No! Stop! I'll tell you anything! I'll tell you about the stone!"

"No, October! Not a word!" Bishop cried between blows. There were six vicious women on him now, each one trained for combat and killing.

Serena held up her hand, and the women resumed their restraining positions. "Tell me, little Omen. Tell me all about my stone."

"It's already in Lumipad. It's on its way to your well now, if it's not there already. All this is for nothing. You're getting your portion, like we promised. I can't help the whole Dagat getting a piece of it thing. It's not my decision. I have very little to do with any of it."

Serena slammed me into the wall over and over again, my teeth rattling. "Do you think lying to me is a good idea? Break his kneecaps!" she ordered as I screamed.

"But I'm telling you the truth!"

"I know you're the only one who can touch the stone, and I have you here! It couldn't possibly be in Lumipad on the way to the well. Lies!"

The women dragged Bishop upstairs where I could hear him undergoing who knows what kind of trauma. He howled over and over as something hard brought him to a new level of agony. I was frantic, clawing at Serena and the two lackeys who stayed behind with her so I couldn't get to Bishop. "No! No!"

Serena was much bigger than me, but I didn't go down without knocking the wind from her a few times. She had to call for yet more backup, and it took four of her crazy batwomen on steroids to lower me to the ground. My stomach pressed against the cold concrete as they ripped my shirt up my back and over my head, cackling like the evil villains they were. I writhed and fought with every-thing in me.

"Now I can't kill you, but I can make life miserable for you. How would you feel about a scar right here?" She drew the outline of something wide and rectangular over my bare back with her pointy fingernail, laughing at the goosebumps that erupted on my back. "I think that would look pretty. Then you'll always know who you belong to."

"Screw you! I told you everything I know!"

"Except for the truth. Tell me where the stone is!"

"It's in Lumipad!"

I thrashed around as best I could, but there were five of them. My bra was cut open and my screams operatic as a knife sharper than anything I could picture cut into my skin, taking its time as the artist made me her bloody canvas.

BISHOP, BLOOD AND BLISS

I don't know how long I chewed on my knuckle as the pain washed over me in unforgiving waves of horror and regret. Bishop's cries of agony plagued me. I knew a decent kneecapping didn't take all that long; it was one of Darius' favorite ways to keep his dealers in line. I wasn't sure what else the Manas were doing to inflict judgment on Bishop to make him talk.

Only I *had* talked. I'd told them the truth, and none of it mattered. I hadn't saved Bishop, and now my back was scarred most likely beyond repair. The knife had cut deep around the edges of my back, going long and wide to cover the span of me. I was afraid to move, hoping the gouges would start to scab so I could shift without my epidermis peeling off. My whole body was sticky with too much blood spilling over onto the concrete from all angles. I let myself break down in silent tears in the pitch black of the freezing basement. They'd taken my shirt and bra with them, and I couldn't really move much without ripping the cuts even more. So I laid with my stomach to the angry cold of the concrete, embarrassed and wishing I could enact some sort of Biblical vengeance.

When Bishop was finally brought down, he was unconscious and drooling, beaten to the point of incapacitation. Serena came down with the women who deposited him, her smug smile too much for me to take. "If only I had salt to pour in your wounds," she mused. "I guess I'll just settle for this to give you a good taste of what's to come tomorrow." With that, she stomped her heavy boot on my shoulder where the incisions were still clotting, laughing at my bitten-off scream. "You'll make for a delicious little treat when my boys come around tomorrow." Then she bent down and spanked my butt before turning on her heels with the others to go upstairs and leave us in the dark.

"Bishop? Honey? Talk to me," I whispered, afraid when he didn't answer. "Bishop?"

"Ekeks," he moaned, and I could tell he'd been hit in the mouth one too many times. "Ekeks are coming tomorrow. They won't kill you, but you'll wish you were dead after they get through with you."

"What?"

"You're a very pretty girl, and they take what they want." Bishop left his implication in the air for me to fill in the gaps. He was a pile of limbs next to me, but he reached out and found my hand. "I need to bliss you out. I don't want you awake through any of this, yeah?"

I swallowed, afraid to go to sleep and even more afraid to stay awake. "No way. I want to be with you. I won't leave you alone down here. Talk to me. I'm here for you."

Bishop's voice had a note of kindness to it. "No. I won't let you be in pain just to lessen mine. Have sweet dreams, little sister."

I tried to remove my hand from his, but it was no use. My struggle was ineffectual as the dark world started to swirl with brushes of pinks and reds, taking me further down in its abyss.

24

KISSING AND PUNCHING

I wasn't in the basement, but was instead transported through space and time to a beautiful park that was decorated with leaves of every color of the rainbow. A handful of purple and pink leaves let go of their tree and dropped slowly, dancing on my skin as they brushed my arms with a delicate grace. I'd gone from terror to bliss in the span of a few heartbeats, and didn't know what to make of it. I half expected Serena to fly out from behind one of the trees and carve up the rest of me. I looked down and saw that I wasn't naked on top anymore, nor was my back burning. I had a cute white V-neck on with jeans that hugged my hips. I was barefoot, and had no qualms about stepping on anything sharp. This was my dream, and I owned all the rocks here.

"Boy, are you a sight for these bloody sore eyes."

It was the best thing I could hear in my happy place,

and when I turned, I was greeted by the most amazing sight. "Von!" I ran to him, unhampered by hunger, injuries or fear. I jumped up into his arms, wrapping all four of my limbs around him. I attacked his face with kisses to make sure we didn't slip away from each other. "It's you? It's really you?"

Von laughed, and I nearly cried at the sound of his happiness. His blue and gold eyes danced with new life I hadn't seen in him for days. "Of course it's me. I've been asleep for hours, hanging around here and looking like a bum, begging for loose nickels. Where've you been? Where are you?"

I recited the string of numbers I was being held at. "I don't know the name of the street, but it's on a dead-end road. The house has pink shutters and a tilted mailbox. Took us about half an hour to get here flying east. Send an army, Von. There're at least forty Manas I counted, and Ekeks are on the way. They might already be here, and Bishop's barely alive."

"Bishop's alive?" Hope soared in Von's voice as he squeezed me through a choked sob he muffled in the crook of my neck. He tore his face away and I saw moisture glassing his eyes. "We've been going mad trying to find his body. We knew they'd keep you alive, but we didn't know about him."

"He's only barely alive. They're torturing him to get information out of me. He needs a doctor, Von. I told them the truth about the stone, but they don't believe me! They don't think more than just me can touch it, so they're hurting him over and over so I'll give them the stone. You have to hurry!"

"We'll find you. Now that we're narrowed down a bit, we'll be there in a couple hours." Von kissed my lips, squeezing my butt before he set me down to get a good look at me. His hands ghosted over my shoulders, rubbing downward until his fingers linked through mine. "Beautiful. I'm just glad they haven't hurt you."

I shook my head, my eyes serious with warning. "You can't be in the search party to come find me."

His perfect lips soured. "I'd like to see anyone try and stop me. Mason and I are your Reapers. We're leading the party with guns blazing. Real action hero-type stuff."

"I know I look fine here, but I'm all ripped up in real life." I swallowed the emotion down like a bitter pill the size of an elephant. I would not spend this time crying. I had Von at my fingertips.

Von spoke slowly, his chin turning to the side as he stared me down. "All ripped up? How do you mean?"

My voice broke as the reality of my dire situation acted as a fog around us, pushing out the beautiful colors I needed so I could draw a proper breath. Now the world was gray. Gray trees with gray leaves. "Serena pinned me down and carved up my back with a knife. I'll live, but it's bad. You can't come find me because I'm a bloody mess. You'll get a whiff of me and attack."

"I can handle a little blood," Von said, posturing. "I've

been feeling far more in control since I got back." He held up his hand. "Honest. When I'm not bled dry, it's not as bad as it was, and I even bounced back from that in only a few hours. I don't understand it, but I've only needed one blood bag all day, and I haven't wanted to bite into Mariang at all. I promise, *hani*, I can handle a little blood."

I paused, looking up into his eyes and wishing for an eternity of anything but this kind of talk. "It's not a little blood, Von."

A fierce protectiveness flared in Von's eyes. His chest puffed anew as he pulled me in for a hug I only wanted more of. "How much blood?"

"Too much."

"I'll take care of it," Von vowed, solemn in his devotion to me. "They won't kill you, love. They need you alive."

Von smelled like mints, his sweet cologne and cigar smoke. After the day I'd had, he was utter perfection. "I'm scared," I admitted. "I need you to tell the others to come get me. Bishop's not going to last much longer."

Von squeezed me tight and nodded into my hair as he inhaled the scent of me. Slowly the colors around us came back. Gentle hues of blue and violet crept into the tips of the leaves, bleeding into the centers and brightening the whole world. That was the magic of Von. "You need to wake me up," Von instructed.

"Um, I don't know how to do that."

Von bit his lip. "Um, maybe try hitting me? It might jerk me awake."

"I can't hit you."

"What if I told you I sometimes tune out when you're talking because I'm thinking about your breasts?"

I lightly shoved him. "I do the same thing. You're all 'Let's talk about life,' and I'm like, 'Whatever gets you naked faster, buddy.'"

Von's mouth dropped open. "Probably not a good time to tell you that's the hottest thing you could've said just then."

"Oh, it's always a good time for that."

Von kissed me, sucking on my lower lip. My heart leapt at the thing I didn't think we were going to be doing. He'd wanted to cool things down, but we were all too good at heating things up. "You're making it harder for me to anger you, love. Right now all I want is a repeat of our honeymoon." He pulled me flush to him, making me gulp as I remembered all too well the details of our sheet-tangled tryst.

I pulled back and looked up to study his face, surprised at his phrasing. "Is that what we're calling it?"

Von grimaced. "Oo, probably not. My mistake."

He kissed me, and I couldn't keep the two worlds straight. In one we'd been married and had a honeymoon. In real life, he wasn't ready to be exclusive or call me his girlfriend. I pulled away. "I... we... um... You're making things confusing on purpose. You're not ready to be with me, so you probably shouldn't jerk me around."

"Right. I'm trying to get you to hit me, not hit *on* me.

Distinction." He tipped his head to me. He stepped back and rubbed his palms together. "Alright. Focus, Von. How about I tell you I thought about you naked the first day I met you?"

"I'd just call you a tool."

Von looked up as if searching for something bad enough to get him punched. "I yelled at Ollie earlier. To be fair, he started yelling first. He's got a temper. Turns out he doesn't like being called Buttercup. Can't figure out why. You seem to like it well enough."

"Don't piss Ollie off. I'm all he's got, and I'm missing. Be nice."

Von harrumphed. "Just hit me, Peach. It's to help you. I can't get to you if I don't wake up in time. Take a swing for the greater good. Come on, love. It's your one free shot."

When I didn't move fast enough, Von looked up, exasperated. He thought I was chickening out, but really I was just waiting for the element of surprise. As his chin lowered, I cocked my fist and took a swing, knocking him across the jaw.

I heard him cry out in shock and pain, and then he disappeared. I took a few breaths and tried to absolve myself of assaulting my boyfriend. I walked to the nearest tree, sitting down at the base and tangling my toes in the grass, trying to make the green rub off on my heels. There weren't any germs in our special place, so I could relax while I waited out the clock for Von to find us.

25

CHAOS IN THE KINGDOM

I had hoped to be jerked awake by Ezra or Mason, but instead it was Serena's boot to my back that woke me screaming. My scabs ripped open and started bleeding afresh. "Good morning, Sunshine. How was your break? Did it loosen your tongue at all?"

"I already told you everything I know."

"Aw, and that's the wrong answer again." She motioned to the women to grab Bishop, who reached for me I assume to bliss me out again, but he was jerked away from me before he made contact.

He cried out through gritted teeth, growling through his pain. He couldn't walk, and they weren't gentle as they dragged him up the steps, banging his busted kneecaps on each stair along the way. I sat up, scared of the ripping feeling on my back as I moved carefully. I covered my breasts and shouted, "I'm sorry, Bishop! I'm sorry! I'm so sorry!"

Serena seemed irritated, her fists clenched and her jaw set in a rigid line. "Maybe this time he'll sing for us." I could tell she wasn't gracious when she didn't get her way.

I tried to maintain some semblance of calm, knowing that the more worked up I got, the more she would need to punish me. I kept my head down and said, "He can't give you information he doesn't have. He's not my Reaper or my boyfriend. We just met in person for the first time a few days ago."

She let out a heavy sigh, her shoulders slumping now that it was just us. Serena cocked her head to the side and took in my anxiety. "You really are telling the truth, aren't you?"

"Yes! Let him go."

Serena clicked her tongue to scold me, turning vindictive instead of flying off the handle. I couldn't decide which version of her was more dangerous. "And stop the fun? I don't think so. I like to let the girls play every now and then. Sharpens their senses, gets the spirits up. Good all around for morale."

"He's done nothing to you. Let him go," I said, keeping my desperation to a mere reprimand. I tried to speak to her like an adult, and not as if I was the hostage. "If you're really going to rule, then this is beneath you."

Since there was no one to posture for, Serena had a

little less bravado. "You know nothing about Lumipad, or what it takes to lead a people."

"I know that every time some dictator's tried something like this in my world, it always blows up in their face. This is just lusting for violence. You can't build a kingdom on that. Chaos, sure, but not a kingdom. What you need is loyalty."

She scoffed, motioning to the upstairs as Bishop started howling. "I have an army of loyal soldiers."

I tried not to panic, but rather strategize. "For now. What happens when one of them thinks they can do a better job? If it can happen to Sylvia, then it can sure as Sunday happen to you." If I couldn't get them to stop torturing Bishop, then I would at least plant the seed of paranoia in her mind. One way or another, crazy bat lady was going down. So much the better if it was by her own hands. "How many bruises did you order on Bishop, and how many more do you see? They're getting carried away with their bloodlust. That's the thing about stuff like this. They'll only want more and more. They're not stopping now when you're in the house to ask how much you want done. They're already going off-book, writing their own script."

Serena looked up the steps with a hint of worry pushing her overly plucked eyebrows together. "No, I didn't give specifics."

"A loyal soldier doesn't move without them."

Bishop's cries hit a new high, and I knew something

had gone horribly wrong. Serena bolted up the steps and locked me in the basement, keeping me in the dark as she shouted incoherently to her vicious monsters. I was afraid to hope she'd put a stop to the beatings, afraid to hold on to the truth that the guys were coming, and we had only to keep ourselves alive until then.

When the door opened too many long minutes later, Bishop wasn't dragged down the stairs, but rather carried down and laid before me like an offering. Serena ordered the others up the steps, and they seemed contrite, their bat wings drooping.

Serena's voice was cold and precise. "It seems you were right on this one. They got carried away." She pointed to Bishop's bare chest that had blood blooming like a chocolate fountain. "I'll do you the courtesy of saying goodbye to your boyfriend. Remember this kindness."

Bishop's breaths were choked, raspy and wet sounding, and I knew Serena was right; there was no fixing this. Even if I had all my tools with Doctor Brenden right there, we wouldn't be able to save him. Agony shot through me at my own uselessness. I had a degree to help me heal people. I'd saved many an inmate who didn't deserve to draw another breath. Bishop had done nothing but be a good man to me, and I was powerless to save him.

Bishop was trying to say something, so I lifted his upper half and pulled his torso onto my lap, not caring about our partial nudity as I cradled him in my arms, my tears falling as I tried to keep him calm. I couldn't give him another day palling around with Boston. I couldn't give him a friggin' Tylenol. I couldn't give him anything but me, and I'd lost myself a long time ago.

"I'm right here, Bishop," I cooed, my tears wetting his face. His nose was inches from mine, and as I rocked him gently, he gripped my hand as he tried to eke out his last words.

"Tell Boston…" He tried to suck in a wet breath, but there were precious few left. "Tell him to stay strong." Then he let go of my hand and tapped his bloody chest with a shaking and rigid finger, indicating his heart.

"I'm so sorry," I whispered, only noticing Serena had left by the complete darkness that encased us. Being deprived of any light somehow made every rasp of Bishop's struggle to breathe that much more horribly audible, his pain palpable. I sobbed over him, holding his shivering body tight. "I'm so sorry, Bishop. What can I do?"

"Von," he whispered. "Take care of Von. And don't give up on Danny."

I let loose a sob. "Stop being so damn unselfish! I need to help you, to do something for *you*!" I fished around in my brain, and the solution came to me like a letter from Heaven. "I can show you colors, Bish. Those beautiful paints that Von uses to make the pictures you love. Think about the paintings. Go to that happy place." It was a decision I didn't have time to debate. I lowered my face the few inches to his, muscling through the agony of a few scabs on my back ripping open again and bleeding afresh. Slowly and carefully, I kissed Bishop's lips.

I couldn't give him another day with his family, but I could fill his last moment with the beauty he needed. His lips kissed mine on reflex, and it was enough to pull both of us out of the basement, out of the dark and into a consciousness where there was no pain, and no more black. We were encased in swirling colors of pink and yellow that danced for us. He gasped into my mouth, and I tasted his blood.

We didn't see visions of course, but as my breasts brushed against his sticky chest, we saw a beauty that gave Bishop peace as he breathed his last.

26

FINN AND THE FLAMES

I don't know how long I cried as I lay slumped over Bishop's dead body. His blood had long since stopped pouring out of him, and he only had my body heat to keep him from turning unforgivably cold. I didn't care that I was topless, or that my back was probably getting infected the longer it went without proper care. Bishop was dead. He was my responsibility, and he was dead.

Von would never forgive me. *I* would never forgive me. I'd ruined his family forever.

I slowly went through the painful steps of trying to say a peaceful goodbye to my non-relationship with Von. Though I wanted to run to him more than ever, I knew this was something that would keep us broken.

I cried quietly in the dark until I passed out on Bishop's bare chest, sticking us to each other with his blood and my filthiness. I hadn't eaten or drank anything in who knows how long, and I'd lost too much blood to do anything more than rest atop Bishop. When I rested, I didn't dream, and I guessed that Von wasn't asleep. It was just as well. I didn't want to do a surreal showdown. Von deserved the chance to yell at me out loud and to my face.

I heard the occasional shouting squabble upstairs, but I didn't so much as lift my head to try and decipher what was going on. I didn't care. If they were going to kill me, then I guess that's how it would end.

The squabbling picked up after a while, and then I heard the bang of a door, followed by several screams, things knocking around the room and something that sounded like a roar from a tidal wave. Then the screams really picked up.

The Manas were in pain, and aside from my heartrate picking up, I didn't have an ounce of sympathy for them. I clung to Bishop, guarding the body I lay atop with a vicious protectiveness. He was mine now. They wouldn't pry his body from my fingers. I had something left in me. It wasn't much, but the Manas couldn't have it.

The door flung open and heavy footsteps rained down the wooden staircase. "No! No! Don't be dead! You can't be dead!" I looked up and saw Finn, wild eyed and charging for me. His hands reached for me, but retracted, and I saw the fear as he took in my state. "What did they do to you?"

I wanted to answer, but I was so confused at seeing his

face that I merely gawked up at him like my IQ had dropped a significant amount. "Finn?"

He was gentle as he reached down to feel for Bishop's pulse, his jaw tightening. "Let's get you out of here, *sinta*."

"Finn?" I repeated, the world moving slower than I knew it was supposed to as the screams rose impossibly higher up the stairs. "You're here?"

He brushed his fingertips lightly over my cheek, and I felt them tremble. "Of course I'm here. Where else would I be? I'll always come for you."

The promise hit me at just the right angle, but I had no more tears. "Take me home," I begged.

"As you like it, sweetheart." He tried lifting me from Bishop, but he was afraid to pry me from my treasure. "I don't know how to move you out of here without hurting you." His eyes raked over my back, dread crossing his features.

"Take Bishop first."

"He's dead, October."

"Take him or leave me." I was firm on that.

Finn stared at the resolve in my eyes and nodded. He stood and ran up the stairs, coming back down half a minute later with Lang, who did a similar freak-out until Finn talked him down. "I can move her, but I need you to take the body out."

Lang nodded, afraid to touch me. "Hurry. The smoke's going to be hard to move through."

Finn didn't hurry. He was careful as he pried my fingers

from Bishop. Then he slowly wrapped my arm across his chest as he slid me off the body, my skin making a horrible squishing sound as my bare torso unstuck from Bishop's. I kept my mouth closed through a scream as Finn pulled me up so I could cling to his chest instead of the corpse's. When he stood in a fluid motion, his arm banded around the back of my hips, pressing me tight to him so my breasts were nuzzled to his t-shirt and hidden from public view. My legs were too tired to wrap around his waist, but they tried, just to give the appearance of being a team player. Finn's other hand cupped the back of my head, securing my face to his shoulder. I could hear his quickened heartbeat thrumming through his body. "It's over now," he said to me as he climbed the stairs, careful not to jostle me too hard.

We went into a thick fog of unbearably hot, black smoke, and Finn broke out into a run through the house, dodging enormous bat wings and keeping his eyes on the exit. "Hold onto me!" He removed his hand from my head and drew a long knife from his belt while I clung to him with weak arms. I bit my lip through a scream as he sliced through the upper half of a Manas that tried to impede our escape.

I saw Mason as a wolf, teeth bared and growling as he ripped into an enemy he showed no mercy to. I saw Kabayo fling a legit mace over his head and knock a Manas out of the air, along with several pieces of the ceiling that rained down. Ezra had a blowtorch and a can of gas, standing at the entrance with a look of pure malice mingled with utter disappointment. He gave the torch another shot at doing away with the enemy, ignoring the screams for mercy as bat women flew up into the sky in unquenchable flames. They burned as the wind encouraged the fire to finish them off mid-flight, their ashes descending like autumn leaves to the ground.

Ezra cried out when he saw Finn holding the bloody mass that was me, but Finn didn't stop. "I'm taking her to Dagat until these Manas are all dead! Until the threat on her life is gone!"

"No!" Ezra shouted in a rage.

Finn ignored Ezra and ran me out the front door. He murmured a few words, and just like that, the world in all of its chaotic ugliness disappeared.

BARE BREASTS AND BANAK

I clung to Finn as the greens and browns of Terraway materialized before my eyes. Dagat wasn't muddy like Sakuna, nor was it dry and dusty like Silo. The lush world was filled with greenery that had blue wet vines looping throughout the landscape. I heard a waterfall nearby, but I didn't lift my head to investigate. I clung to Finn, afraid and in far too much pain from being jostled.

Finn ran us to a grouping of trees that were several stories tall, but were completely flat and marshy on top, with blue vines dangling like party streamers. He kissed my face over and over as he lowered me to sit on the earth. Finn wasted not a second as he dug around like a madman at the base of the tree for a few *baga* roots. He all but crammed one down my throat, making me cry out as I choked, my ribs pulling painfully. He cupped his trembling hand to my face so I could drink the water that surfaced in the well of his palm. The water tasted like sunshine and healed the desert in my mouth, doing wonders as the fountain from Finn trickled through my body. I didn't care that my breasts were exposed; I greedily tipped his palm with my hands so I could get more, not fussing over the fact that I could taste blood, and I didn't know for sure who it belonged to.

He gripped the back of my head with his other hand, and I could feel the fear in how tensed his fingers were on my scalp. "You can breathe now. I'm here, and I'll take care of everything." He met my eyes with intensity that made me rally, which I didn't think was possible. His voice was scared through his pep talk, higher pitched than usual, and with too much urgency. "It's not as bad as you're thinking it is. I can fix this. I can fix it all."

I nodded as my lower lip quivered. I didn't think there was anything anyone could do to take care of me at this point. I could barely move without the skin on my back ripping.

"Say, 'I believe you, Finn.'"

I swallowed another mouthful of water that felt like the best thing in the world to my insides, barely choking out an, "I believe you, Finn." I sucked down all the water I could before my walking well started to dry. "More?" I begged. "Please. I'm so thirsty. It's been days."

"You can have anything you want, only drink quickly. You're still bleeding, sweetheart. How did you get so banged up? Why would they do this to an Omen?" His voice was sad and genuinely perplexed.

"Hide me, Finn." My voice rang with fear, and I hated the sound of it. I was small, and that feeling had never sat well with me.

"You're safe with me, *sinta*. But we have to move. Careful now. Up we get." Though Finn was gentle, there was no amount of movement cautious enough to keep me from trembling with too much pain. He ran me forward, not slowing for the voices that called to him or the many three-tailed monkeys that dropped down from their blue and dark green trees to chitter at him. Finn bolted alongside the river, drawing the eye of quite a few women who were swimming along the shore. I could only see their top halves, and idly wondered if they were Mermaids. They had seashells cupping their buoyant breasts, just like in the movies.

I don't understand how Finn ran for that long without stopping for a breath. When we finally reached our destination, Finn didn't slow. He ran up gilded steps that led into a palace of pure, sparkling gold. "Stand down! King Banak. I need to see King Banak!" Finn shouted, and the guards fell away at the level of clout Finn possessed. It was kind of crazy that he could run into the palace with a bloody woman and demand to see the king with no prior notice.

"The king's in the Hari room," one of them told Finn.

As we rushed through the palace, I noticed there was a

canal that ran through the left side of the rooms Finn bolted through. Occasionally a woman's head would pop up from the still water's surface. More strangely, a man's torso and shoulders supporting a guppy-lipped green-tinged fish head also watched us with his glassy fishy eyes. I caught sight of both their large, jade and iridescent scaled fins as they swam away from the grotesque sight that I was. It felt like I was in a surrealist painting. Everything that should have been normal was slightly off, making the whole world seem about seven inches away from being a cartoon I was bleeding my way through.

I clung so tight to Finn; I knew I was going to leave claw marks. "I need a h-hospital," I whispered into his ear. I rested my weary head back on his shoulder, my nose nuzzled against his gills that simultaneously freaked me out and fascinated me.

"I know, sweetheart. First things first." He ran without stopping through a series of winding hallways that were decked in gold opulence with seafoam green sconces. The window dressings hung in satin waves to the shimmering floor, looking like the ocean itself had been called upon to frame the windows of the palace.

Finn yelled at the guards to move away from the door, and like the subordinates they were, the two obeyed. They opened the heavy gold-plated doors before Finn had a mind to kick them down. "I need access to the healing waters!" Finn demanded without preamble, once the doors to the Hari room closed behind us.

I didn't look up, but buried my face in Finn's shoulder, hoping he was taking me somewhere safe. I don't know if it was the psychotic bat girls or the bug people or the zombies that gave me a healthy distrust of Terraway and all of its magics, but I decided to let Finn handle this one with no involvement from me.

I heard a man's deep voice bark, "What do you mean, barging in here like this when I'm clearly with a *kendi*? You know what this room's for."

I heard a woman's scared whimper and cringed. This was the bedroom for the king to use with his harem. Finn had brought me beaten and bloody straight into the harem he oversaw for the jackfish King of Dagat.

"King Banak, I need your help. This is the new Omen, and she's damaged, maybe beyond repair if we don't get her into the healing waters."

I heard the springs on the bed shift as the king got off the bed to face Finn. "You know the waters are kept secret to outsiders. I trusted you to guard them because I thought you understood that they can't be used by the other kingdoms."

Healing waters? Ezra never mentioned those.

"The Omen belongs to all of our kingdoms. If she dies, we all die!"

Banak answered with a curt, "Our kingdom's plenty safe. Let the other countries help her."

"It's safe for now. The water level's holding *for now*. Without her, we'll run out of food to feed the Merpeople."

Banak blew a loud raspberry, and though I still couldn't see his face, I wanted to punch him clear across the mouth. "Dagat's fine. If the famine gets much worse, we can always take Sama's rations. I don't know why you're always fending off the inevitable."

Finn shouted as he clutched me tight, his fingers digging into my scalp and butt. "You'll grant me this favor because it's my job to keep our land from war! How do you think it'll look if we could've saved the Omen, but didn't? We can be the heroes of Terraway if we put her back together! Imagine the songs they'll write about you."

Banak paused, curious. "Songs, eh?"

Oh, I hated him already. Before I even saw Banak's face, I hated him with a burning passion that could tear mountains and jackholes down with my fury. If only I could do more than barely lift my head.

"Songs about how King Banak saved all of Terraway in a single day." Finn's tone turned steely. "You'll do this for me, Banak. You trust me to keep you from war. Let me do my job."

King Banak waved his hand to Finn. "Very well, but the healing waters stay secret. If she breathes a word of this to Ezra, I'll cut her tongue out. You hear that, *kendi*? You can still reap without a tongue, you know." He chuckled when I only clung tighter to Finn. "Wash her up and then bring her to me. I haven't seen a real pair of legs in ages."

I was half-naked and knew I couldn't fight my way out of a guarded palace. I could barely stand. I pressed my bare breasts tighter to Finn's chest, hoping he would protect my body when I couldn't. I gripped Finn around the neck, my heart pounding as Finn laid down the law. "You've got a whole harem to play in. She's an Omen, not your *kendi*. The other kings hear about you forcing her into your bed, and they'll have something to say about it. You'll risk her going on strike and not reaping another day of her life." He held me protectively, angling me away from the king with a scowl. "You might not care about the safety of Terraway, but I'm running out of allies on the outside. You like the silks that come from Lumipad, don't you? You do this, and we're on our own."

The king sighed, the bed shifted, and I heard a horrible wrenched scream from the woman on the mattress. I shut my eyes and let out a quiet whine of distress into Finn's gills. "Fine. Take her to the waters and be done with it. And don't barge in here again unless you've got a pair of legs I can keep."

"Yes, your majesty." Finn's arms were trembling with barely controlled rage as he marched us through the room and out the second door at the back.

THE HEALING WATERS

"I'm sorry," he said through gritted teeth as we passed through a dim hallway. This passageway was not bedecked in gold, but the moldings instead were lined with large oval rubies. "You'll never see that room again, so help me. If there was any other way to get you to the waters, I wouldn't have taken you there."

"Hurry," I pleaded, every part of my body aching and burning as he carried me into a small room. It was serene and quiet inside, and when he closed the door behind us, I heard none of the bustle through the castle.

There was a trickling fountain dripping into a small wading pool in the ground that looked like it was built for about three people. There were no windows, so Finn lit the room with the tips of his fingers, giving us just enough light to see a foot or two in front of us.

I sniffled into his soft gills. "You let him take that

woman. You let him take her into that room. You're just as much responsible for that awful place, now that you can act on your own will."

"I know." He squeezed the back of my head and gently lowered my feet so I could stand. I swayed where I stood, covering my bloody breasts with filthy and trembling hands as Finn reached for my jeans and gently tugged at the button. When I shirked away from his touch, he held up his hands. "Just so you can bathe in the waters. You're covered in blood, sweetheart. I'll get you clean clothes after this, I promise."

My lower lip quivered as he slowly rolled my pants down my legs, his nose brushing my quaking knee on the way down. Though it was cozy and warm in the small room, I shivered as I stood in only my underwear. "I j-just want to go h-home."

"You can go back as soon as your home's safe, *sinta*." Finn stood and removed his clothing with deliberate eye contact, stripping down to his black briefs and revealing too many lacerations on his muscular form. He had bruises peppering his torso, and a large, fresh, angry slice on his thigh that drew my eye.

My mouth fell open when he turned and I caught a glimpse of a series of angry crisscrosses on his back. "What happened to you?"

"I'm captain of an army." He glanced over his shoulder and raised an eyebrow at me. "I've been fighting Manas and Ekeks in Lumipad so we could get the sagrado stone to their well. You fought with me against Sama's army. Remember that? It's a lifetime of battles," he said, motioning to his scarred body.

I didn't want to ask what weighed on my heart, but knew he would tell me the truth. Finn wasn't the type to sugarcoat things. "Is Bev... Is she alright?"

Finn nodded once. "She's not right in the head, but she's well enough to carry the stone from one place to the other. They should reach the well today, if there are no further attacks on the stone. Danny's still with her." His eyes steeled as he reached for my elbow. "You'll probably hear it from Danny, but I struck your mother."

I gasped, my eyebrows bunching together before words could form.

Finn pulled me closer, palming my chin in his free hand so I was looking up at him, my cheeks glowing with warm light from his fingertips. "She has a habit of running her mouth about you. I won't look the other way on that. I don't care if she's your mother or not. You're not stupid, and you're not ugly."

My eyes shut to fend off the hurt I tried not to feel. "Bev has the stone on her, so she's becoming the person I know again. It's the stone. I guess it's warping her mind."

"I don't care. You... You're important to me." He cleared his throat and dropped his hand. "You're important to all of Terraway. No one would dare talk like that about Mari-ang. I won't let your mother, of all people, tear you down while I'm in earshot."

I nodded, wishing I wasn't standing in front of him in only my underwear, covering my breasts with my arms. "Thank you." I turned to stare at the water that was only just barely visible in the dim light. "So how does this work?"

Finn sat down, dangling his legs in before sliding off the smooth rock-lined edge and immersing himself in the waters. I heard him howl from under the surface and covered my mouth, not sure how to be helpful while he thrashed under the water, as if fighting an invisible sea monster. It was a whole minute before he emerged, chest heaving not from near suffocation, but from enduring physical torture at the water's hands.

He looked like he was coming up from a deep sea dive or something, his face glowing like he'd undergone a religious experience. "I've needed that for a long time." He glanced down at his torso that moments ago had been laced with abrasions. Now there were faint pink marks instead of angry black bruises, and most of the cuts were completely gone. He leaned his elbows on the edge at my feet, scooping up a handful of the water and drinking it down, making a face at the burn that looked more akin to whiskey than water. "The water rebuilds as it heals. It won't fix everything, but it'll give you a far better recovery time. Gets rid of infection, and helps mend internal fissures and sickness in your bones. It hurts," he admitted, "but the longer you can endure it, the more it will do to heal you."

I was hesitant as he held his arms up to me, though I was about two minutes from passing out. "I can't hold my breath underwater," I admitted, my inhalations ragged each time my ribs contracted.

"I can help with that." The corner of Finn's lips lifted in a sexy smile I tried not to focus on. "Come here, *sinta*. I can fix it all."

It was such a beautiful promise. There was so much that was broken about me. I wondered if it could fix the emptiness, the pain that gnawed at my insides, and all the other things that haunted me. The waters were magical, so I decided to gamble on them, knowing I couldn't get much worse at this point. "Close your eyes. I don't want you to see me."

Finn chuckled in his deep, sensual way. "It'd be just like you to tease me with your breasts pressed against me all this time and then not let me see them. Come here. I won't look."

I hung my head as I fought off a heavy swoon that nearly made my knees succumb to gravity. "Um, this is almost as embarrassing as me being mostly naked right now, but I can't swim, and it looks like it might be over my head." I watched the surface of the water lap at his collarbone in dismay.

"You can't swim?"

I scratched at the filthy bandage on my right forearm. "Look, the things I didn't have the luxury of growing up could pile a mile high. I'm just telling you so you don't leave me in here to drown."

"I won't let you drown. I'm the best thing to have in the water if you can't swim." He met my eyes with a promise beaming through. "I'm perfect for you."

I swallowed hard, still nervous for too many reasons. I reached as far down as I could toward his arms until the horrible scabs on my back started opening again. I bit my lip as I let myself fall into Finn's embrace, leaving behind my former self as the water started boiling on my skin. I began to panic as my arms wrapped around his neck. "Ah! Ow! It's burning me! Let me out!"

Finn pinched the bridge of my nose and dipped me under the surface, immersing me in the water that only seemed to want to stab me deeper the more it got of me. His lips pressed to mine at an angle, but instead of kissing me, he started breathing for me, pushing air into my lungs as I screamed into his mouth. I felt a bubbling all over my skin, as if the impurities inside were trying to squeeze themselves out through my pores. The heat filtered into my mouth, my screams doubling when an invisible dentist straightened two of my molars without anesthesia.

I thrashed in Finn's grip as injuries that were years old started reminding me of the pain they'd caused when they first made themselves a permanent part of my body. I rubbed my thighs together as the scar on the inside of my left thigh burned like I was being stabbed all over again. The wound ran deep, so the medicine of the water went just as far, feeling like it was attacking my whole leg. I kicked and jerked around in the water that felt impossibly deep, despite the fact that Finn was anchored to the bottom. He worked off the bandage on my arm with one hand, and I screamed anew as the water got to the crusty skin, healing the burn he'd accidentally made happen. I felt the stab wound on my bicep crackle and pop as it was cleaned deep down to the bone.

Finn brought my head up to part the surface of the water, letting me breathe on my own. "Drink some of the water. You need it."

I obeyed, breathing through my teeth as the burning rippled through my insides. Something in my gut felt like it was repairing and rebuilding, making me worry at what could possibly have been wrong in my abdomen that I hadn't realized. Then I felt something in my head twinge and pop, making me terrified that I might be having a stroke. I was far from any sort of hospital.

Slowly, in tiny caresses of mercy, the agony began to subside into mere ripples of torture. My torn muscles repaired themselves with gentle licks at my skin that warmed my insides without burning them. I began to relax into Finn, slumping in his arms like a limp noodle in the almost darkness. I whimpered in his embrace, letting him hold me in the aftermath of the water's brutal ravaging. I was left breathless, and my already roughed-up body was overly exhausted.

"Just relax." Finn brushed his fingers through my wet tangles, his palm trailing down over my back and cupping my butt in a way that was positively covetous. He laced light kisses down my exposed neck, his lips puckering on my shoulder and lingering far too long for me to not have pushed him away.

"I'm seeing someone," I said quietly, but unapologetic. Someone who couldn't commit to me. Someone who had tried to bed my friend a week ago.

"How would you feel if he accidentally fell off a cliff?"

I pulled back, frowning. "Don't joke like that. I love him."

"A strange thing to say when you're a scrap of clothing away from being naked in my arms." He gripped my thigh, tracing up and down as he relished the feel of my legs wrapped around his waist, my body needing his to stay afloat.

Hopefully that was the only reason my body needed his.

"I didn't hide my own clothes from myself, you know. You could've just as easily given me your shirt to wear."

"You have no idea the state your back was in. It looked like Serena was one step away from peeling your skin clean off. A shirt would only have hurt you more when we had to rip it off you later."

The only way to hide my body from his sight was to keep it pressed against him under the water, which didn't seem like the right option. "I'm too naked. I feel like we should talk about something boring, like grocery shopping or the price of gas or something."

"I don't have much to say on either of those topics. And I think you're the exact right amount of naked, with one exception." His finger traced the edge of my underwear, treating me to a shiver I was embarrassed by.

"We definitely need a change of subject. Can I get out yet?"

"Give the water a few more minutes. You don't know if you'll ever be granted this privilege again. Only a handful ever have been. You have no idea how many injuries I've needed the healing waters for, and Banak wouldn't even share it with me, his number two. This is just as good for me as it is for you."

I tried to turn my head and look at what was left of the damage on my back. "Did it work? I can move a whole lot better." I wriggled my shoulders to test my scabs, but stopped when Finn let out a low, lusty moan as he wet his lips. "Is my back still torn up?"

As if he was blind and needed to read the braille on my spine, Finn's fingers ghosted over the slight curve of my back, teasing the line of my underwear again just like he knew he shouldn't. "I can see scarring, but it's healed as much as it can. You won't suffer infection, and you don't need stitches or bandages anymore." He peered over my shoulder, his sharp intake of breath alerting me that something was very wrong.

"What? What are you looking at?"

"Nothing. It's just the scarring. It looks like... I mean, from this angle at least it looks like you were cut in the exact shape of two bat wings spread across your back and shoulders." He held me unselfishly as I buried my nose in his gills again, the supple skin feathering over my face. His grip tightened protectively. "What did they do to you?"

"They wanted to know where the stone was. I told them it was already in Lumipad, but they didn't believe me. They still think only I can carry it, so they thought I was lying. They tortured Bishop for so long, Finn!" I finally had the required moisture in my body to make tears with. They fell with a grateful release, sliding down Finn's muscular back in a slow trickle. My grief mingled in with the healing waters, and I prayed there would be restoration granted to my internal agony. "They assumed Bishop was my boyfriend, but when tearing him apart didn't get a different answer out of me, Serena took my clothes, held me down and carved that into my skin with her knife. Said I could still reap, but I'd never forget who owned me."

Finn lifted me higher on his body so he could look me in the eye. "I'll fix it."

"You already did. I can move now without my back skin ripping off. Well done on the whole healing waters thing. If only the spas and doctors back home knew about this. You could make the medical profession a thing of the past."

"Let me rephrase. I'll take care of *her* for you. No one marks up my... No one marks you up and lives to brag about it. If Ezra and the guys haven't already killed her, I'll bring you her head so you know she's not going to come after you again. I don't want you losing sleep thinking she's still coming for you."

I grimaced. My fingers found their way into his hair to give it a slight scolding tug. "Ick! I don't need her head. Thanks for the bloody vengeance and all, but I think you've earned your gold star just by getting me out of there and bringing me here. Thank you. It's more than I could've hoped for."

Finn pressed his cheek to mine, his stubble scratching my jaw and exciting nerve endings in places I wished weren't pressed up against him at that exact moment. "I need you safe." His tongue reached out and licked my earlobe, as if I was his tasty treat. His words sent shivers through me, and in the dim light with no witnesses, I clung to my beacon of safety.

A CABIN ON THE BEACH

"I need you to cool down." I jerked my head to the side. "I told you I'm seeing someone, and I'm not sure how much of this whole thing I can honestly pass off as being for the greater good."

"Tell me his name."

"No."

"Tell me anything about him."

"Why? He's seeing someone, you know. If you're looking for me to set you up with a guy, you'll have to look elsewhere."

Finn breathed heavily in my ear. "I don't like you with someone else."

"Then get used to disappointment, because it's already done. I'm happy, Finn," I lied. The truth was, I couldn't be further than happy with the non-arrangement I had with Von. "And honestly, we're too different. You live here, and I can't even swim! We'd be a disaster together." My eyes locked with his. "And you're still letting women sell themselves for food to your jackwagon of a king. You've got to know I can't be with someone who does that."

Finn's eyes steeled when he stared into mine, both of our ingrained defiance rising a moderate amount. "I don't make them do that. I just do what the king asks of me. It's called a job."

"I'm familiar with the inner workings of a... What did you call it again? A *job*? But your conscience is off the map on this. Where does it end? What if I was toe up and wanted to sell my body to Banak in all of his disgustington glory? What then?"

Finn sneered at me, knowing I was being ridiculous to prove a point. "You wouldn't do that. No matter how desperate things got, you wouldn't do that."

"Would you let me? Would you take me back to his sex dungeon and close the door with a shrug?"

His eyes bored into mine with fiery determination. His hand slipped from my hip downward, gripping my butt with a hard squeeze. "That would kill me, and you know it. I wouldn't let that happen."

"What if it was my only option?"

"I'd offer myself, my home as a better option." The conversation took a left turn, and I found myself lost in the mess I'd thought I had a handle on. Finn was serious, and I was getting nervous. I debated which fart joke I should tell to divert the topic when Finn's lips grazed mine. He puckered my lower lip so he could suck on it like a tantalizing piece of candy he knew he shouldn't have, but slid into his pocket like a greedy child anyway.

The room and the whole palace slipped away from us, replaced by lightbulb flashes of green and silver that shocked me and drew me in for more. I fell down the rabbit hole with a gluttonous groan that fueled his passion, igniting mine in the same breath.

Finn's other hand slid down my body, ghosting over my legs and gripping my feet that he loved to treat himself to. The massage was deep, and filled with too many things both of us loved. His movements grew rough the more excited he became, and I slowly began to see past the brushes of color and music. I heard a slow-building cacophony of trumpets that should have been alarm bells to warn me away.

"I'm seeing someone!" I protested, but it was too late. The colors were swirling around me like a tornado. Music in the form of trumpets of every shape and size started playing, drowning out splashes of the water as the kiss took on a mind of its own. I gasped into Finn's mouth as the kiss mutated into a frenzy neither of us had any control over. There was need, there was biting, there was sucking and plenty of writhing. We couldn't stop the addiction that only grew with each forbidden hit. We toppled over the precipice of restraint so we could completely possess the madness that engulfed us whenever we finally let our guards down.

The music was enchanting, bewitching us in our cozy borrowed haven as a few misplaced seconds turned into whole minutes of regret. "No!" I cried the moment I managed to pry my lips off of Finn's. I jerked myself backwards, slipping out of his arms and flailing as I sunk below the surface of the water, kicking at random and waving my arms in the water like I'd seen swimmers do in movies. They made it look so effortless. I started swallowing water, taking a portion into my lungs as Finn came to his senses and yanked me up. He tipped my top half over his forearm to push any water out of me that burned as it healed things I didn't realize were still wrong inside my body.

He was out of breath, though it had nothing to do with the water. His eyes were unfocused, his fingers clumsy and his lips parted as he steadied us both against the side of the pool. "What w-was that?" he stammered. "Did you see that?"

"The colors? I know. Pretty, but we can't do that again. It was an accident, and we have to be more careful."

Finn's head snapped toward me. "I didn't accidentally kiss you. I meant every second of that. I wasn't talking about that, though. The cabin."

"The what?"

"Did you see it? There was a cabin set on a white-sanded beach. We were picking mangoes and *buhay* off our property and feeding them to each other." His gaze slid downward, biting his lower lip in obvious lust. "We were slightly less naked than we are now. Beautiful. You really didn't see any of that?"

My pounding heart plummeted, and despite the fact that I would be completely exposed, I pulled myself out of the water so we didn't fall into the trap again. I crossed my quaking arms over my chest as I stood, finally feeling taller than him. "I need a towel and some clothes, please, if you can scrounge any up."

"You don't need a towel. I can suck the water off of you just by touching your skin."

I narrowed my eyes at him. "A towel, please."

"What's wrong?"

"So many things. But I don't want to walk around mostly naked. That problem's fixable." I harrumphed, frustrated at both of us. "I told you I was seeing someone. You shouldn't have kissed me. And don't tell anyone about the vision. Put it out of your mind as best you can."

Finn hefted himself up out of the water and stood dripping before me, making me the shortest person in the room again. I turned my back to him to shield my body, my cheeks burning. "I'm not putting anything out of my mind. Is that normal? Is that what happens when you kiss an Omen in the water or something?"

"I don't want to talk about it!"

"Fine!" Finn stomped off, moved down the hallway, barked out of the Hari room to the guards, and waited a minute before two blanket-sized cream-colored fluffy towels were presented to him. Clothes were ordered for us, but those would take a bit longer.

Finn wrapped his towel around his shoulders and held mine out for me to cuddle my body into. I breathed a little easier now that I was covered. I peeled off my underwear and cast it into the pile of clothes that were so filthy, they were only fit for the garbage can.

Finn watched me avoid his eyes. "What does it mean that I saw a vision? Will that happen every time from now on?"

"There won't be any more times," I corrected him. "That was the last one, and I didn't mean for it to happen."

"I know, but it still did." He dropped his note of aggression and rubbed my arms through the towel. "What does it mean? Will that come true? Will we get a cabin in your world someday?" His voice lowered. "Will I get to run away with you?"

The dream of hope in his voice pinged at my heart, and I wished I had better news for him. "No. All it means is that you're in love with me." I couldn't look at him, but instead stared at the edge of my towel. I clutched the terrycloth like it was my saving grace, though we both knew I was beyond salvation. "When we kissed before, we weren't in love. That's why it was all abstract. Colors and music, but no images. You're in love now, so you saw things that kissing me makes you want." My eyes slowly climbed to his as I swallowed down my shame at letting things get so out of hand. "But it's not real, Finn. It'll never be real. I didn't have a vision. In fact, I just started having them with someone else."

Pain hit Finn, contorting his mouth and nose to a grimace that was hard for me to watch. I resisted the urge to comfort him, to tell him it would be alright and that I was there in his moment of hope lost. I knew I couldn't. It would be nothing but bad for the both of us if I didn't rip the Band-Aid off so he could bleed and then start to heal. His words were quiet when they finally came to him. "Who is he?"

"It doesn't matter."

"It's not Mason, is it?"

"No. Stop guessing. You're going to leave my guy alone because you love me. Love can't be selfish. You have to want what's best for me, even if it isn't you."

Finn's full lips soured. "I *am* what's best for you."

"You know that's not true."

"I saved you in there! *I* went down to the basement through the fire to find you. Me! Where was your guy then?"

"I know, and I'm so grateful you did." I raked at the flesh on my arm again, surprised when I didn't feel the ridges from all my previous fits. "I don't want to hurt you. I actually like you some of the time, so don't make me do this! I didn't mean for us to kiss. I didn't mean to be so naked. I... I... I was just abducted and my clothes were stolen from me! I just held a guy while he died in my arms! I haven't eaten in days, and I've been beaten up too many times! I'm not at my best right now, so give a girl a break!"

Finn's arms wrapped around me, tucking me into the fortress of his opened towel. He warmed me as best he could until the knock on the door interrupted whatever it was he'd been gearing up to say.

The soldier apologized to Finn for something before Finn shut the door and handed me a pile of clothes. "We don't have any women with legs, so these shorts are for a teen Kataw boy."

"It's fine. Thanks. And I'm sorry, Finn. You rescued me, and I'm hurting you all over the place. I didn't mean for this to blow up."

He waved off my apology, chagrin settling over him. "I've only ever been in love with Dyesebel. I didn't think I'd feel this again, especially for someone so different. I mean, you're not even of my species."

I stammered more apologies, feeling the lowest of the low. He forgave me, which somehow made it all feel worse. He should've been yelling, cussing me out for letting him touch my feet that first time it all went south. I should've turned away from the kiss that sucked me in and made me want only more of the luscious luxury

There were a lot of things I should've done different.

ATTACHED AT THE MOUTH

Finn had sent word to Ezra through their elite council communication channel that he would bring me back to the surface once the Topsider team had captured all the Manas and the Ekeks.

Apparently that was going to take more than a couple days.

"You'll stay with me," Finn offered as we stood on the shore that separated the king's fertile island from the rest of the mostly underwater country. The city in the distance was filled with half-submerged houses that butted up to a long peninsula. It was attached to a piece of land that looked like one long marsh. Finn's arms were banded over his chest, and I could tell by his limited movements that he was still sore from the work the healing waters had done on us. My back was so stiff, I could barely move my muscles without wincing. But I wasn't bleeding anymore, so you know, bonus.

Finn stepped into the water, the blue going up to his knees as he stood in black pants and nothing else. He had a backpack fitted to him I hoped he could swim with. "I'll have to work during the day, but so long as you stay locked inside my home, you should be safe."

"Thanks. So long as Ezra knows where I'm at, that's cool."

"He knows. He's not happy about it, but you're safer here than with Manas flying around, trying to pick off you and your team at random. It's temporary," he assured me. "Come on."

"Uh, Finn? Is there a boat or something?" I looked to the sea, the waves large enough to make my stomach churn. I'd never seen an ocean in person before, and the village of homes looked so very far away. "You know I can't swim."

Finn smirked at me, tilting his head to the side as he reached for my hand. He tugged me forward so my bare feet were cooled from the hot sand in the water. The ocean was warm, like bath water. "I know, little fish. I'll take you. The only people who use boats are outsiders who come to visit. It draws attention, and I'd rather keep your time here as secret as possible."

"I don't like how often I have to push my limits and just trust you."

He palmed my chin and looked down into my eyes with gentle but stern authority. "Hey, I saved your life back there. Don't forget it's me who got you into the healing waters. Then I kept you from Banak's bedchambers. My men told me he demanded to have you again while we were in the waters. I may push your limits, but I'll keep you safe."

"What's Banak's deal? He's got a whole harem. Why me? Not to talk myself down, but I'm pretty normal looking. Compared to legit Mermaids? I can't imagine why he's interested."

Finn touched his toe to mine under the water. "We don't get many legs in here. The only people with legs are the Kataw like me, and we're all men. We have to travel to different countries to have sex at all. It's... frustrating. I've had my fair share of women outside of Dagat. The Mermen and the Mermaids can procreate just fine, but for us? We're starved for a good pair of legs. And yours?" He looked down at my body in a way that wouldn't do either of us any good. "I wouldn't have to be starved for legs to see the appeal of yours."

I gave him a light shove to keep things platonic, though I worried that ship had sailed. "Alright, alright. Knock it off. I get it now. Let's get going. Why are there hardly any people around?"

Finn tapped his toe to the water. "Most of them are underwater, or in their homes way over there in the village." He tugged on my hand, leading me deeper until I sucked my stomach in as the water climbed up my body. "Finn? I don't know about this."

No sooner had I squeezed the words out did Finn pull my front flush to him and duck down under the surface, his mouth latching to mine. I screamed into his mouth at the speed at which he was torpedoing us through the water. Every second, he seemed to build up our pace, swimming far faster than I'd seen the athletes do on the Olympics. His eyes were open as we shot forward, his head tilted so he could direct our warp speed. I was clinging to him as I hung off his body, my back facing the abyss below. My arms and legs squeezed him like a vice as I whimpered into his mouth, wishing I could tell him to slow down.

Though we were moving crazy fast through the water, it took us a long time to cross to where the village was. I started to panic when Finn pulled his mouth from mine after blowing a long almost sensual puff into my lungs for me to hold onto. "This is the grotto," he explained, and though we were under the water, I could hear him as if he was speaking through a glass. I wondered if being able to talk clearly underwater was one of their many gifts. He pointed in the distance to a pink and gold coral maze. It was busy with movement, green fish tails flipping out, casting bubbles as we stayed on the periphery.

"Are those Mermaids?" I asked in wonder, not sure if he could hear me without my fishy enhancements.

Finn chuckled, his chest moving against mine. "Your voice sounds funny under here. Like a child's. It's been awhile since I've heard an outsider's voice that wasn't screaming for help from drowning or something."

"Screaming and drowning? Save some sexy talk for later," I joked, probably inappropriately.

Finn laughed, tracing my leg with his thumb. "Will do. That place they're going into over there? That's the market." Then his mouth was on mine, and my body reacted with too much desire before I remembered he was just blowing more air into my lungs for me. He groaned, pressing me tighter to him. "Oh, you're driving me crazy."

When he pulled his mouth away, I tried to appear contrite, which was hard to do so out of my element as I was. "Sorry about that. I got confused for a second."

He looked deep into my eyes as we continued to shoot forward. "I'm not confused." The water whipped at us, feeling tepid on impact, but the friction left us with traces of true heat. The enclosed feeling was claustrophobic, but somehow comforting with the space it seemed to give us from the rest of the world. They were far away, and we were hidden from eyes that would make us examine the things I didn't want to look at too closely.

Finn continued to breathe for me as we raced through the sea. It was a battle not to kiss him. His lips were full and beautiful, but I knew we were too much on the edge already. He was in love with me, and I was in love with Von. Von was in love with me, but was scared of promising me a life he couldn't deliver on. The whole thing was just swell. And yes, I'd like some kind of prize for not kissing a hot guy whose mouth I was currently attached to. A big friggin' prize.

Finn swam us like a well-aimed missile to a lone house far away from the village of Merpeople under the water. The village seemed to be a surreal series of apartments all attached like a gigantic honeycomb for Merpeople to pop in and out of. The water was perfectly clear, lit by glowing yellow and rose puffer-sized fish that had been caught and were swimming in bored circles inside of glass balls. The makeshift fishy lanterns hung on posts jutting out of the football field-sized aquatic honeycomb apartment complex. The yellow and pink glow filtered through the clear blue water, but Finn angled me away from view, distant as we were from the village.

A SAFE PLACE TO BREATHE

Finn's house was separate and far from any other home or piece of land. I wasn't sure if that gave me peace or pause. I needed fresh air soon, and knew I was breathing in too much CO_2. When we stopped in front of a building the size and shape of a home that was partially underwater, I was worried about being stuck to his mouth much longer. Finn gave me more air to hold in my lungs and fumbled with his keys as if he was nervous letting me so deeply into his private abode. The door opened, revealing a submerged home with a mossy couch in the corner and a table anchored to the concrete floor. He lit the way with his fingertips and swam me through the home, and then up a ramp instead of a staircase.

The second my head broke the surface on the second floor, I cried out in relief at the fresh sea air that didn't come from a man's mouth. "There you go. See? I told you I'd take care of you. The Manas can't fly out this far, and the Ekeks don't swim."

"I just… Breathing like that is…" My chest heaved as I sucked in too much oxygen, making me slightly light-headed while I drooped in Finn's arms. There was that, plus the whole being beaten and starved thing, and then torpedoing through the water. I was actually pretty proud of myself that I was still conscious. *October Grace, the Incredible Conscious Girl!* Watch me keep my eyes open like a boss.

"Relax, *sinta*. I told you I'd take care of things. There's no place safer than with me." He lifted me up and carried me like a bride through his home to what I can only assume was his bedroom. He gently sat me on a circle-shaped bed that was fluffy, despite being inside a house in the middle of the ocean. He popped open his window that was a few feet away, making me cry out in relief as more fresh air wafted over me. I was cold, but I didn't care. I rubbed the goosebumps that broke out on my arms, but couldn't take my eyes off the blue out the window that I swear had sparkles dancing on the surface. I watched as a Mermaid's head poked through the waves in the far distance, and then did a dive, flipping her tail up almost in welcome.

Finn ran his hands through my hair as he knelt next to me on the bed. He watched me look out the window as I relished the freedom of breathing on my own. I didn't realize it until the fifth swipe, but with every pass his fingers made through my tangles, the moisture left it in degrees until my hair was completely dry, and his fingers remained just to play.

"Finn," I cautioned, but before I could admonish him on all the things we couldn't do, his hand breezed over my arm, drying my sleeve and giving my goosebumps a new guilty purpose.

"Let me dry you off. I don't want you to catch a cold."

Then I did the worst thing I could've done in that moment; I let Finn dry me. His strong and capable hands ghosted over my body, warming me in my cold places and relaxing me deep down. I inhaled sharply when he gripped my thighs harder than I was expecting, our eyes meeting in a warning to behave. He dropped my legs and stood, rubbing a sore muscle in his arm. He watched me, debating something that made me feel very small in his far larger presence.

"I'm seeing someone," I reminded us both. "Someone I love. So don't let either of us get the wrong idea."

The corner of his mouth twitched upward, and he turned on his heel out of the room, coming back a few minutes later with a plate of food. "I brought you something to eat in my backpack. I'm guessing you don't have a need for *buhay*, like we do."

"You guess right. Really? You have legit food here?"

"For Duwendes and half-humans who travel through our country."

My stomach nearly clawed its way out of my body and leapt at the feast of crusty bread, hard cheese with a pink rind on it, a few small fish that looked like they'd been freshly caught, and a dollop of greenish mustard... for the bread? To make a cheese and mustard sandwich? A dip for the fish? I had no idea, but I wasn't above trying whatever was put in front of me. "Thank you, Finn. I don't know how long it's been."

"Eat up. I didn't think it was possible for you to get thinner." He reclined on the bed next to where I sat, his hand finding my back while the other unfurled a scroll on some sort of waterproof parchment. "The joys of being gone a few days. I come back to grim status reports."

"Because you're so very important?" I teased. "Only Captain Finn can Superman away the problems of tomorrow, today?"

His finger tickled up my side like a spider, making me squirm. "You joke, but yes. My lieutenant wants to make plans to wage war on Hayop. He says it's for them violating our trade agreement, but I drink pints with him. Lieutenant Emil just wants to go to war to get away from his nagging wife. Not that I blame him. Frida's a pill."

"Remind me why you're single again? You seem like such a romantic. Tell me more sweet nothings like 'nagging wife'." I wolfed down the bread and cheese, only pausing to chew the minimal amount.

"I'm single because I'm always gone. I'm always working. If I'm not keeping the harem in line, I'm keeping my men straight so they enforce the peace among the people. When I'm not doing that, I'm Banak's ambassador to the Topside, helping Ezra with whatever he needs so we're seen as team players."

"Sounds like three people's jobs you're doing."

"Hence the paperwork." He held up the scroll as evidence. "I've got a man in charge of the harem while I'm gone. My lieutenant organizes the guards on my orders while I'm away."

"You're helping Ezra, helping bring the stone to Silo, helped lock Geon up, helped save my life. That's a lot of helping you're doing."

"Favors are like cash. You give it when you have it, and when you need it, you can ask for it in spades if you've given your favors to the right people."

"That feels off. You should give because you have and other people need, not because you're keeping track of favors."

Finn chortled at me and resumed rubbing my back. "That's very sweet. What a nice worldview. Spoken like someone who's only responsible for their own household, not tens of thousands."

"Shut up. Good men don't give things to get stuff later."

"Good military men do."

I turned to look at him over my shoulder. "Is that satisfying to you? Is that the only kind of good you want to be? Good at your job, but not good in your heart?"

Finn quieted, lowering his scroll as he met my eyes. "It's the only kind of good I know how to be, and I'm the best there is at it. A lot of people are still alive because of me giving to get. I've done everything I could to keep our people off of Sama's rations, and so far it's worked." He went back to his paperwork and muttered without looking up, "I sure hope your new boyfriend can jump high on that white horse you've got him on."

I sighed heavily, the exhaustion dawning on me afresh. "He's not my actual boyfriend. He's not ready to settle down with only me yet."

Finn's hand stilled on my back. "You're putting me on hold for a guy who's putting you on hold?" Then he surprised me by chuckling slowly. "I'm sure I should be upset, but I can only feel sorry for the poor, stupid soul who thinks there's anyone out there better than you."

I broke off a piece of cheese and fed it to Finn. I'd seen him eat food Topside, but knew it didn't sustain him. He survived on *buhay*, like most of Terraway. Food to him was more like chewing gum. Nice, but you can't live off of it. "We were talking about your world, not mine."

His eyebrows danced up and down twice as he chewed. "Right, you were telling me how very moral you think I should be."

I examined the piece of cheese, turning the chunk over

in my hand. "I guess I don't know your world well enough to judge. I just think you're better than that."

"Better than what?"

"Better than the bare minimum of kindness and strategic goodness."

"And what kind of goodness are you doing that you don't get anything in return for?" he challenged.

"Um, other than saving a world that's only tried to kill me, abduct me, and starve me? Not too much lately other than the whole Omen thing."

"I believe the job pays well enough for you to live comfortably."

I raised my eyebrow at him. "Would you call Mariang comfortable? I bet she'd trade that mansion and a whole pot of leprechaun gold for one more year with Danny."

"Fair enough."

We stared at each other for a hot minute before he jerked his chin toward the plate and opened his mouth. I fought off my blush as long as I could, but when his lips touched my fingers, I knew the flaming pink had found my cheeks. We finished off the rest of the meal like that, his hand on my back as he reclined next to where I sat on the bed, and me feeding him the occasional bite. My days of anxiety slowly came to a halt in our little island haven, giving me an adrenaline crash that made me yawn. "Lie down," he offered, patting the spot next to him. "I know you're exhausted."

I set the empty plate on his brownish orange coral

nightstand. Part of me wished there was a guest bed to sleep on, but the guilty side of me was glad there wasn't. I'd been abducted too many times to feel safe going off on my own, even if it was just to another room in Finn's house. I touched his arm as my nerves built, pushing out my fear in a nervous, insecure ramble of, "Will you stay with me?" Then I shook my head. "Never mind. I know you're busy with your paperwork and stuff. Forget I asked. Go do your thing."

My words tapped into something precious inside of Finn, his gaze saying too many things before his mouth opened. "Of course I'll stay with you."

I gusted out a breath of pure nerves. "Thank you. I'm usually not such a wuss, I promise. It's the whole abduction thing. It's messing with my head. We're safe here? You're not leaving right away?"

He sat up and kissed my cheek. "If I'm around, you're safe."

I draped my arms around his shoulders in a hug of gratitude for the friendship I needed in my vulnerable moment. My chin rested on his shoulder, and for the briefest of minutes, I let myself breathe. In a world of catching my breath and always looking over my shoulder, Finn gave me a safe place to exhale. It was a luxury I didn't take for granted.

Finn pressed his lips to my ear, and then stood up on his knees to tug the hanging fabric behind him that stretched from ceiling to floor around the edge of the large circular bed. The red velvet draped us in darkness and probably too much secrecy. My mouth went dry as it dawned on me that I was completely stranded on a figurative desert island with Von's arch nemesis, who was pulling me down next to him in the soft, concealed enclosure of his bed.

"Of all the women I've had that wander into our land to see the beautiful Mermaids, I've never brought one to my bed before. I usually rent a room near the palace on the land." He pointed in the direction of where we'd just swam from with his lit fingers. The gentle light fell on our faces, illuminating only the most prominent features useful for highlighting conversation.

"Would you rather I slept on the floor? Because I'm cool with that. I totally get it if you don't want me in your space."

Von had taken up space in my bed, but it was the space in his future he had a problem with me being so permanently in.

Finn rolled me over to face him and stroked the outer curve of my leg, pulling my knee to sandwich between his. "If I had my way, you'd sleep in my arms every night. Then I'd know you were safe. Your Duwendes are careless if you've been snatched at this many times."

I frowned at this. "Well, then when we get back, could you teach us how to do it better? I don't want to get taken again, and they're good guys. But we're all new at this."

Finn considered this, nodding. "I can do that for you.

But part of it can't be taught. It's earned. People fear me, as they should. Some dismiss Mason, and the other one's a joke."

"Von's not a joke. It's a crappy time for all of this – to break in a new Omen. This stone business is making everyone crazy."

"Those are excuses for a job poorly done. No one would lay a finger on you if you were mine."

I don't know why that struck a chord with me, but I couldn't look away from his earnest green eyes. They drew me in with the promise of never getting my back sliced up again like it had been. Though Finn was a monster to many, he'd saved me, healed me, and was looking down on me with tender affection. He soothed the fear I worried might never stop clawing at me. "Don't say nice things like that. I want to hear them too badly."

The guilt acted like an aphrodisiac, making me want things I knew I wouldn't dream of in the daylight. My safest bet was to fall asleep as quick as possible and run to Von, if he would still have me after getting his brother murdered.

The corner of Finn's full lips twitched upward, his glowing fingertips cupping my cheek with hands that I was surprised knew how to be gentle. "I'll teach you to swim, and you can teach me all your silly ideals, and everything you think I need to become." He grinned at my frown, and I noted his use of "I will" instead of "I would". Things were getting too serious, and I wasn't sure how to derail the train that part of me very much wanted to be on. "You'll stay here and let your mother take the stone to the well in Lumipad, if it's not there already. She can take it to the other lands, too. Let her loud mouth keep the warfare away."

I shook my head. "She doesn't know what she's gotten herself into. I won't have her risk her neck when she's just barely started to get her head on straight. She's not built for it. She gets upset when she has to work five minutes past closing at her receptionist job. It's not fair that I'm here, and she's doing my job."

Finn's eyes glinted at me as if he had a thousand angry things to say on the subject, but wouldn't because it didn't play into his master plan. "She can sacrifice herself to make up for how horrible she is. You should've seen the fit she threw when she found out we would have to sleep out in the woods."

I chuckled at the image of Bev camping. "It's not her. The stone warps her mind."

"I don't care how warped a person is. I won't let anyone talk about you like that."

I swallowed hard, my gaze breaking from his. "If there's more she said, I don't want to know. It doesn't matter how she talks about me. I know who I am."

As lost as I was in our own little desert island, that night I closed my eyes treasuring the time I could take in Finn's arms to breathe. Of all the things I'd lost, I still had bits of myself. Terraway hadn't managed to cut it all out of me, though Serena had tried. Terraway hadn't starved it out of me, beat it out of me or scared it out of me completely.

Beneath all the craziness of both worlds, I was me. And that night, it was just enough to get me through.

32

PLAYING HOUSE WITH FINN

I suppose it was too much to hope I saw Von in my dreams. I couldn't imagine him sleeping much, what with funeral arrangements being made for Bishop and whatnot. I couldn't imagine sleeping ever again if anything horrible happened to Ollie. I spent my dream with Philip, eating and making love with my imaginary prince. He even held me while I confessed all the horrible things Serena had done. He promised to avenge me like the knight in shining armor my pretend man was to me.

A few times in the night, I'd woken in a blind panic. Once was when thoughts of Serena infiltrated my dreams of Philip. A bleat of distress had woken me when I recalled the bite of her blade cutting up my back. Later in the night, Finn shook me awake from a nightmare I was having about hundreds of little children in Terraway. They were sobbing that they were hungry, and calling me "Bev" because I had the ability to feed them, but wasn't.

Finn was a gentleman and held me through the worst of it, the first time assuring me that no one was going to carve me up or abduct me here. The second time, he didn't know what to do with me. "You can't keep children from starving, sweetheart. There's literally nothing you can do from here. That's not on you; that's on Lumipad for not monitoring their people. You can go back to work as soon as it's safe up there."

I was barely lucid as I sobbed in his arms. "Mariang's probably reaping herself haggard every day. What if she dies before I get back? What if I could've saved her, but I'm busy being lazy and laying around here? I can't let her die, Finn. I've got one sister who left me; I couldn't take it if my only sister left up and died!"

Finn got up and brought me a tissue, and then held me while I sobbed incoherently about all the people in Terraway I couldn't save, and the guilt that weighed on my heart. Von and Mason usually pulled the baser emotions from me so I didn't have to dwell in this dark place. I was without them now, and my aching conscience tormented me in my sleep, and then bled into my wakefulness.

"Okay, I can't even understand you anymore. You have to calm down. You're not responsible for the mess Terraway or Mariang are buried in. You're one person, and we were broken long before you came into the picture."

My face was wet from tears as I sobbed and hiccupped

disjointedly until the words couldn't stay in me any longer. The thing that haunted me since I first kissed Finn bubbled to the surface. "If I don't leave you and go back Topside to reap, you'll die. To keep you, I have to leave you."

It was like I'd slapped Finn with the harshness of the obvious truth. The stung look on his face mutated to anger, then pain as it dawned on him there was no escaping that reality. "Let's not talk about it anymore. We're together now, and that's what matters. Be with me while you have me. Everything else is a problem for another day."

His lips pressed on my cheek after he pulled me back down and slid the blanket up over us. He cradled me in his arms until my sobs turned to pathetic whimpers, my eyelids drooping as exhaustion claimed me. I treasured the tenderness he exuded that only I got to see. His arms stayed wrapped around me until I drifted back to sleep.

I'd felt Finn shift to wakefulness before the sun came up, kissing my lower lip before I was aware enough to protest. The colors flooded me, and I could barely piece together enough of reality to tell Finn that a kiss was certainly not kosher (which he already knew, the sneak). "Finn, we can't," I murmured through my green and silver-smeared haze, batting at him and missing as the curtains around us slowly began to materialize through my blur.

Finn buried his head next to mine, panting from the simple one-way kiss that made him see things I was certain I didn't want to know about. His hard gasps of breath in my ear made me feel things I knew I shouldn't and couldn't, but somehow did. "Beautiful," he whispered in wonder. "I don't get a lot of beautiful in my life. I get an ocean of ugly." His emotions were raw and uncensored when he came out of the vision, and I didn't ask him what he saw. The wonder on his face hit a decrescendo as he looked down on my nervous expression, taking in the apology that didn't match his own elation. "Sorry about that. I didn't mean to, but I couldn't... It won't happen again."

"Finn, I'm sorry!" I was barely lucid, but I knew I'd hurt him before I'd even set foot out of the bed.

"Don't worry about it. It was my fault." He shuddered as a residual high rippled through him. He collapsed onto me, panting anew.

I didn't know what to do. I mean, dude was wrecked from something I hadn't even meant to participate in. His head migrated to my chest, his ear tuning into my heart-beat. I tried my best to calm him down by running my fingers through his short brownish-blond hair. His cheek nuzzled my breasts as if *I* was *his* safe haven, instead of the other way around. He was big and scary outside of his home, but here in my arms, he was a kitten. I didn't take the gift lightly that I got to see him so unraveled, so without the right words and without the angry wrinkle between his eyes.

I fished for a change of topic so we didn't say things we shouldn't while we waited for his heartrate to slow. "How did you start working for Banak?" I asked, my fingers doing their best to relax him as they brushed down his stubbled cheek.

He paused, and I could tell he was debating between the PG version of his beginning, and the real-life HBO edition. "My parents didn't know what to do with me. They're both Merpeople. My race is an anomaly, which is why there aren't as many Kataw. The Mer call us Kataw 'sandwalkers'. Most sandwalkers are given to the Academy to be looked after. See, we can stay underwater for hours, but we can't live there. And Merpeople can breathe fine above water, but they can't walk on land, obviously."

A frown pronounced itself on my lips at the thought of being separated from your parents just because of a flip of the genetic pool. "That must've been hard for you. And for them, actually. How terrible not to be able to live with your baby."

"They kept me as long as they could. Then when I got to be school aged, they gave me to the Kataw Academy. Well, it's an academy now. Back then, learning wasn't the primary goal. We were trained to be soldiers, to do what the king needed without pause. I went through my classes and graduated at the top. I wanted to run the Academy. That was my goal. To teach kids about our people, our history. To take a kid that's been given up and give him purpose." He reached down and picked up my foot. My knee bent up, and he kissed it while he rubbed the sole of my foot with perfect pressure to relax me as he spoke. "Purpose is a powerful thing. Kids tend to drift without it.

Adults, too. That's one of the things I like about you. You have such a strong sense of purpose."

"Whatever. You like me for my big toe," I teased, trying to lighten the mood.

Finn tickled the bottom of my foot only enough to make me squirm, and then worked his fingers around each toe. He took his time with the tenderness he doled out only behind a closed curtain. "The Kataw Academy's all about churning out soldiers, which we need, make no mistake, but I don't like the way it's done."

"How's it done?"

He was quiet a moment, as if seeing a memory he didn't care to describe in detail. "A few of my scars that healed in the waters last night were from the beatings I got when I didn't perform as I needed to."

My face twisted in horror. "Your teachers hit you? Hit you hard enough to leave scars? What kind of a crap school is this Academy?"

"The kind you're lucky to only get scars from. There are many of my classmates who didn't make it out at all. If you survive the Academy, you deserve to get to keep your life."

My arms tightened around him. "Shut that nonsense down, Finn. I'm serious. Kids shouldn't have to go through that. Is that what the Duwende Academy's like?"

Finn let out a light scoff. "Not even close. Duwendes are kind of a joke in our country. Our army's terrifying. Duwendes don't even have an army. They're spread out all through Terraway and the Topside. They make us feel better and really are mostly useful to Omens. Their Academy's like a Topsider school, with a bit more physical training added in. I ordered one for you while you're staying here."

"Huh? Ordered one what?"

"A Duwende. He should be here soon. That's why I was getting up. I've got to go get him from the shore."

"For what?"

Finn rubbed a spot behind my ankle that made my whole leg feel like it was one long noodle in his capable hands. "For pulling. You get a little high-strung without your Reapers. I just got those scars off your arms; I won't see your skin marked up the very next day. Those claw marks kill me. It looks like you've been attacked by a wild animal."

"I don't need a Puller who I don't know. I can handle myself," I said, though we both knew I was lying. I was several days without my medication. If Bishop hadn't blissed me out before he died, I would've been rocking and counting things for sure. Though, I was surprised how even-keeled I felt. I wondered if that pop in my brain I experienced when I went into the healing waters did something to balance whatever was chemically wrong in me. I closed my eyes, praying that was true.

"I'm sure you can handle yourself just fine. But I promised Ezra I'd look after you. Those pills you take. Are they important?"

Now it was my turn to debate between the PG version

and the uncut one not suitable for people you didn't want to look at you like you'd gone insane. "Your Duwende can't cure that, but it would help. Thank you."

"What are the pills for?"

I hated the direct questions that hit right where I couldn't take it. "Nothing you have here. I get a little messed up in the head sometimes, and they help me think straight. I start to disappear without them. Bishop blissed me out, and was pulling regularly while we were locked up. Then I'm guessing the healing waters helped me over the hump, but I don't last long as me without them." I shrugged, as if none of that made me sad at all.

"Do you start to become like Bev?"

"No." I gulped, knowing nothing would turn a man off more than the brutal truth. "And I don't need to talk any more about it. I'll be fine." I secretly worried if that was true. "You saved the day again, getting another Puller. Thanks for that, by the way. Super awesome of you to look ahead for the potholes. You're like, King of the Ocean or something."

"That's me. Super awesome." He mocked my intonation and made me sound like a valley girl. I forgave him the insult because he rubbed my feet like a practiced masseur. "And I'm second in command of our land, which is mostly ocean, so I'll take the title of 'King of the Ocean', since Banak's screwed his way into uselessness."

"Yeeshk. He seems like a giant child. Not sure why you work for him."

"It's what I was bred for, *hani*. Not many other options for sandwalkers."

"What about being a teacher at the Academy? Or running the Academy? If you think it's being run wrong, do something about it."

He scoffed, and then seemed to consider it, his mouth drawing to the side. "I don't have the patience for children. And sandwalkers? We're a troubled bunch. It does something to you, being taken from parents who don't know what to do with you. Being put in with a bunch of other boys with issues that most of them only know how to fight about, and you've got a recipe for disaster. I wouldn't know the first thing about how to handle a kid like me."

"I think you turned out alright. But usually if something bothers you, like how the Academy gets under your skin, it means you might need to look into finding the solution yourself. Anything less will just make you feel... less."

Finn switched to rubbing my other foot, turning me into a pile of mush. "No one talks to me like you do."

"No one calls you King of the Ocean? I think you might need to off-with-your-heads a few people to make them fall in line." I smiled at his chuckle that flowed easily in our enclosure. "Did you get to see your parents much after you graduated from the Academy?"

Finn's smile died, his eyes glazed over with duty I wanted to scrub away from him, shield him from and somehow make less painful. "My dad isn't worth mentioning. I ran into my mom a few times. Last year she wanted to sell herself into the harem for food, but I turned her away."

My mouth fell open, and my hand stilled on his cheek. "Are you joking? Please tell me you have a horrible sense of humor."

"I don't think she even knew I was her son. She hadn't seen me since I was three."

My heart tugged in my chest, leaping out at him as I hugged his head tight to me, kissing his hair and wishing I could actually help him somehow. The healing waters only went so deep. Would that there was a soul cleansing that might wipe away the stain something like that would leave on a man's psyche.

I didn't realize there'd be more. Once Finn opened his locked vault, too many secrets spilled out. It's like he'd been waiting for a friend, someone to share his life with, and that person just so happened to be holding him in the comfort of his bed. "It gets worse. When she was begging for a place in the harem, she said she would be willing to bear the king's child. Give him another heir." He breathed through the emotional pain. "It was all just to make sure she stayed fed. Banak wouldn't starve the mother of his child. It was a smart move on her part." He let out a humorless snort. "At least I know where I get my ability to make a solid plan from."

"Holy birth control, Batman. Are you serious? How would that even work?" But as I asked, the image came to me. "Oh, he can get a Mermaid pregnant using the conch shell." I held him tighter, my heart breaking inside my ribs. His mother had unwittingly gone to her son so she could ask him to help her get used for her body, all so she could have another son. One that she wouldn't have to give away.

Finn patted my hand that was probably holding him too tight. "Banak's sterile, so it wouldn't have worked anyway."

"What? But he's got a son. What about Prince Julius, that vicious blowhole who took Von?"

"I forgot Von told you about that. Well, Banak's sterile as of the last five years. Banak doesn't know he's sterile though."

"Are you serious? How do you know he's sterile, but he doesn't?"

Finn's voice lowered, and he stopped massaging me to hold my foot. "Because I ground up the *kutad* root myself and fed it to him without his knowledge. I sterilized him one day while bringing him his wine." He sniffed. "I graduated top of the Academy, am second in command of Dagat, but he had me bringing his wine. When he started demanding more Mermaids and more, I knew I had to do something. I couldn't feed his spawn as well as the harem. Plus, at the rate he was going, we'd have a sea of half-siblings, which would be a nightmare when they all grew up and tried to have their deformed and weird children. Banak doesn't think long-term. It's my job to think about our country."

"I really hate that guy."

"I'm just trying to make it so he doesn't destroy us. So I let him screw himself into the ground while I take care of the things that need fixing. With him nice and distracted by the women I feed him, I can rebuild homes, my men can keep the peace, and I can make sure the things that need to get done are being seen to."

I didn't know what to say to that. "There's still no excuse for having a harem, Finn. I think you're amazing for doing all that you do, for helping where you can, but you're throwing a bunch of women under the bus in the process. There's got to be a better way."

"The women volunteer themselves," he spouted, miffed. "I need Banak happy and distracted. Otherwise my people, my land, we won't make it. I do what I have to. I don't expect you to understand that."

"I understand it all just fine. I've treated my fair share of pimps. But there's a reason you wouldn't let your mother join the harem, and a reason you wouldn't let Banak take me in that sex dungeon. You know it's wrong."

A veil of you-went-too-far fell over Finn's expression. Finn dropped my leg and knelt over me, inching toward the edge of the round bed. "I've got to go. Stay here and don't go near the door, no matter who knocks. Don't open it for anyone, understood?"

"Finn, I'm sorry. I pushed too hard. I pissed you off."

"It's fine. Your new Duwende's probably waiting, so I've got to go pick him up from the shore. I'm locking you in, so don't trust anyone on the other side but me, and I've got the only key."

"Please, Finn. I didn't mean to upset you. You're right. A harem's the most logical option." Logical, yes. Right? No. "I just think you're smarter than this."

His eyes sharpened. "You think you're so clever. You're responsible for you, and that's all."

"Are you kidding me?" At this, I knelt on the bed before him just so I didn't feel so small. This didn't totally remedy that, but my fire came back a little, so that was something. "Everything rests on me! I can't go to my regular job or have any kind of a life. Some days I can't even eat! Everyone needs me to give up my life so Terraway can survive. Don't tell me about responsibility. You have one country to answer to. One. I have all of them! You have choices, Finn. You can think of a way that doesn't throw your mom into Banak's bed. You're second in command because you're smart and capable, not because you take the easy way out. With your curse gone, you finally got your conscience back. Friggin' use it."

Finn's mouth dropped open at clearly being bested, chastised and complimented all at once. "I don't know what to say to that."

I was angry, my logical argument shifting to indignation as I started talking animatedly with my hands. "Don't say anything. Don't do anything different. Let your women be miserable and scared. Women can live like that forever, right? We can take it. You're not creating a powder keg of garbage that's going to explode in your face the second they get themselves organized. You're not a sitting duck staring down the barrel of oh-holy-crap."

"You don't know what you're talking about. I'm in control of it. There won't be any uprising."

My finger flew in his face as I thought about Von being pimped out to Banak's son. "You're destroying Dagat just as much as Banak is."

Okay, in hindsight, not the best thing to say to a military captain.

In a move so quick, I couldn't brace myself for it, Finn swiped at the backs of my thighs from where I knelt facing him. He pulled my thighs forward and up, upending me and landing me with an "oof!" on my back. Finn hovered over me, nostrils flared, and I watched him debate just how angry he'd allow himself to get with me. "Your mouth's run its course."

Then he got up, tore open the curtains and pulled a shirt over his head, dressing for the day in angry, jerky movements accompanied by an unforgiving sneer.

Well, that's one way to solve the problem of Finn being in love with me.

33

KEEPING BUSY WITH EUSTACE

With Finn gone, I was free to move around his home and explore. I hadn't had many days off, and even fewer were spent alone. I relished the luxury of the quiet, my ocean view the perfect setting for reading a good book, or just sitting quietly with my breakfast.

I knew I was hungry, but the second the cheese hit my mouth, my stomach was immediately up in arms, forcing the food out of me and into the toilet. "What the crap?!" I exclaimed to no one, angry that even with no reaping and nothing to keep me from eating, I still couldn't choke down much food. After about half an hour of putting my frustration to use cleaning Finn's already decently clean bathroom from top to bottom, I managed to stomach a few pieces of plain bread. That perked me up enough to fish through Finn's bookshelf for something to read.

That's when I learned that the residents of Dagat had their own written language. While we spoke the same, we didn't write the same, which was a bummer. I opened each of his books, smiling when I finally found a text with English on one side and the Mer equivalent on the other. It was like figuring out a code, which was a game I was totally up for.

I opened the bed curtains all the way and made myself a cozy reading nook with the pillows atop the soft bed. Everything smelled like Finn. Finn smelled like ocean and aftershave, which as it turns out is a very delicious combination. I tucked in with my book, which wasn't anything particularly gripping. It was an account of how the Academy was founded, and the history surrounding the school. It was all told in boring, stuffy textbook language, which I didn't mind too much. I sifted through as many chapters as I could, scribbling on the backside of Finn's parchment the words I picked up as I learned them by process of elimination and a little guesswork.

The Academy was founded by some jag named Eustace Degault, who thought that boys needed the childishness beaten out of them with a thick reed for the younger ones, and a legit cane for the older ones. There was a whole section on the legislation for discipline, which was more archaic than actually helpful in raising children to be good men. Finn's violent swings began to make more sense. I chewed on my bottom lip as I thought on the many angry crisscrosses I'd seen on his back before he'd dipped in the pool.

Good old terrible Eustace Degault lasted me a couple hours until I was hungry again, and this time ate without barfing. It's a little sad when a good day is one spent only partially over the toilet. After that, I cleaned Finn's dining room, organizing a few haphazard items, but his stuff was, for the most part, in order.

My hands started to itch, so I put them to work again, this time cleaning his living room – dusting, polishing, mopping, straightening and doing anything else to keep myself from gouging up my freshly healed hands. I checked them over and over, making sure they were still amazing looking. I couldn't even remember what they looked like not marked up; it had been so long. I wanted to be different now. This was my second chance, and I was bent on making my undamaged skin last.

My muscles were sore from the healing waters cleaning out my wounds and rebuilding what was broken in my body, but I managed well enough. I scrubbed every surface, and when I was finished, stuck my palms to the concrete floor, breathing in guttural snorts like a bison so I didn't start scratching my arms or counting random objects. I didn't want the numbers to comfort me. I didn't deserve comfort. I'd gotten Bishop killed. I bathed in the feeling of loss, of guilt and every other bad thing so Von would know he didn't have to start from scratch if he felt like laying into me. I'd wrecked his favorite brothers, getting one killed and leaving the other without his twin match.

When I finally got my neurosis under control with a lot of deep breathing, I went back to my cheat sheet and selected another book, since I'd had my fill of Eustace Degault, the lousy crackhole. The books Finn had were printed on vellum, which I'm guessing had a fair amount of waterproofness to it, since it survived in here. The series of carats, squiggles and foreign symbols were slowly developing a system in my mind, giving my need to put things in order a purpose. I would learn the language, so help me. I wouldn't be totally dependent on Finn. Reading was power. That had been drilled into me by Judge and Allie from a very young age.

Allie, who didn't want me. Allie, who left us because we were too much to handle. Because *I* was too much. My heart ached for Ollie, knowing that he would be freaking out until I was home safe. I felt bad for Ezra, who no doubt was trying to keep Ollie together, manage a funeral for a family member of two of his three Reapers, and protect his fading daughter, who was shouldering the brunt of Omen duties. I felt like such a tool for making a sick woman work, and by proxy, a man who'd just lost his brother, but there was literally nothing I could do about it. It wasn't like me to run when there was work to be done, but it wasn't like I could swim back to remedy the problem.

From what I could tell, the second book was a collection of poetry about the sea, though because the language was new to me, nothing rhymed and there was no meter. I liked meter and predictability, so these took some getting used to. They were pretty all the same, telling stories about the roughness of the waves and comparing that to a tryst with a grateful lover. I got the shivers a few times. I missed Von terribly, though I tried not to expect anything would be the same between us.

I hadn't been able to visit him in my dream. That either meant that we hadn't been asleep at the same time, or more realistically that he wasn't in love with me anymore. My anxiety was running high, surrounded by the ocean I couldn't swim through. I was trapped in a safe house so flying bat women didn't come and snatch me up into the sky to carve up my body just for kicks.

I totally remember when my worst fears were of getting stabbed in the prison triage.

I made myself another cheese sandwich, selecting a piece of fruit to round out my meal. I was determined not to get sick this time. My stomach wasn't nearly as sensitive anymore, but I paced myself as I migrated to Finn's soft bed. I chewed slowly while I read to keep my mind occupied, so I didn't slip into destructive patterns.

I fell asleep after I finished my sandwich, curled around my book and the language key I'd been cracking away at all afternoon. I hoped to find Von, but knew better than to count on it.

34

FINN'S PROVISION

I awoke to lips on my cheek, warming me to the sensation of being loved and feeling that rare thing called "safe". Safety had for so long been elusive to me, so my body cried out for it even before I was fully awake. I kissed the cheek that brushed up against mine, wrapping my arms around the glow I needed while I was so completely lost. "Hey," came the voice that was certainly not Von's. "I missed you, too."

The bliss started to crumble the second I dared believe it was real. Von wasn't here, nor had he come to me in my dream, the details of which I couldn't remember anyway. I slowly released Finn, who looked radiant at the warmth of my greeting. I felt awful that I'd made him so happy by accident. I managed a wan smile as he gazed down at me, his hand palming my chin in that oddly possessive way he had. His thumb dragged on my jawline as I tried to form a coherent sentence. "Sorry. I must've dozed off."

"I was gone longer than I expected. Business to see to for Banak. Then Garrick wasn't keen on me breathing for him, so I had to secure us a boat."

"Garrick?" My eyebrows pulled together in confusion.

"Garrick's the Duwende I hired to pull for you until we can get you home." Finn lifted me up gently, as if I was as fragile as Mariang and needed the coddling. I appreciated the gesture, but didn't linger in his arms. "What's all this?" Finn asked of the book and parchment that shifted as I sat on the edge of the bed next to him. "You can't read my books."

"Oh, I'm sorry. Were they off limits or something? I didn't realize. I can keep my hands off your stuff from now on."

"No, of course I don't care about that. It's just that they're written in Mer, which I'm guessing isn't a language they teach in your schools."

"I'm trying to figure out your language, but it's a slow go. I don't mind, though. It's kind of fun decoding it all."

"Decoding?" He picked up the parchment, his eyes widening. "You wrote these? This is a key?"

"Well, yeah. I had to make a master list of the basic alphabet. It's too many weird characters to remember without writing it all down. After that, it got a bit easier." I picked up the book of poetry. "I've been entertaining myself with your collection of sexy sea poems. Never pegged you as the romantic limerick type, but you surprised me with all this flipper flapping foreplay and seashell sexiness."

Finn took the book from my hands and blushed – actually blushed that I'd found his tender spot beneath the healed scars and armor he generally used for killing off zombies and whatnot. "Alright, alright. I've got other books you can read. I don't know how this got here. I think it was a gift or something."

I grinned at his mortification, elbowing his side. "Aw! You're actually embarrassed I found your saucy poetry book?"

"Well, I never let anyone into my space, and I didn't expect you, of all people, to be able to read Mer in less than a day. How'd you even manage that?"

"I didn't. I mean, I'm still learning. Maybe you could teach me?"

Finn looked at me, amused at my eager desire to understand part of his culture. "I guess that'd be okay. Later tonight, though. We have a guest." He glanced down at my arms, running his finger over the skin that used to be scarred. "Still smooth? I was worried you'd undo the healing waters with an afternoon left unchecked."

My nails dug into the bed to keep my hands from acting out on my skin. "I'm dealing, and I don't need a babysitter."

Finn overlooked my sass. "I see you did some cleaning while I was gone."

"It helps if I have something to do with my hands." I stood when I sensed things were taking a turn to the off-limits topic. "So where's the new guy?"

"He can wait. I brought you new clothes. Figured you might want something clean." He motioned to a plastic-wrapped package on the nightstand.

"Speaking of clean, do I have time to jump in the shower? I'm a little gross." I stood and took the package from his hands, accidentally brushing his knuckle with the tips of my fingers. The simplest touches set off too many sparks; I needed to get ahold of my crush before I threw him down on the bed and kissed him right good.

"Of course you can use the shower. My house is your house." By his raised eyebrows that followed his declaration, I could tell he was just as surprised as I was that the words flowed out of him so easily. He reached out and fingered a curl that had fallen loose from my ponytail. "I want you to feel at home here. If you need anything, write it down and I'll send for it."

"You don't have to do that. I'm more than grateful for the new clothes and the shower and books. It's incredibly generous, Finn." I thought of something I actually did want, but didn't think it appropriate to ask.

"What?"

"Nothing."

He stood before me, massaging down my arms and lifting the hem on the back of my shirt so he could trace a sensitive line across the small of my back. "Tell me what you need."

"I mean, I don't *need* need it, so if it's a big deal, don't think twice, okay?" When he responded only with a sideways tilt of his chin, I sighed. "My stomach's been bugging me. I got sick this morning. I know it's all the drama of being beaten and starved and all that, but if you have medicine that can keep me from barfing up my breakfast, that would be like, nine kinds of helpful. I hate that you went to the trouble of scrounging up human food, and I can't even keep it down."

"Nine kinds, eh? I think I can manage that." His arms encircled me as he looked down at my upturned face, debating something I couldn't decipher. His expression vacillated from amused to protective to frustrated. "Now when you come out, be nice to the new guy."

"When am I not nice?"

"I know you. You hate the idea of needing anything, and a Puller is a definite need."

"Oh, you think you're so smart. I'll be good."

35

VETTING GARRICK

I came out of the shower wearing the shortest skirt of my life, which I never would've bought myself in a million years. It was a black slippery material that hugged my shape at the waist and flared out at the hips, almost like a tennis skirt. The sexy thing ventured only about four inches past my butt. I'd seen Gabby in similar wear and never thought twice. That was Gabby, though. She liked when guys checked out her legs. Me? Not so much. Something about getting hit on by sex offenders even through the armor of baggy hospital scrubs makes a girl not too keen on showing off her goods. Add the nickname Bait to that, and I was surprised I ever wore anything besides baggy old sweats.

I wasn't totally shocked to find that the light green silk blouse Finn got me was form-fitting and showed off a line of belly if I lifted my arms too high. I'd had my bare breasts pressed to him for the better part of yesterday, so we didn't really have the illusion of secrets in that department. He knew the shape and size of my curves well, and I couldn't decide if that was a good thing, or a very bad one.

I came out tugging my skirt and shirt downward to attempt modesty for the newcomer, but knew I was probably overreacting. My girlfriends wore short skirts all the time. Instead of going out into the living room, I went back to the bedroom that was joined to the bathroom. Normally I wasn't the type to take things without asking, but I knew I couldn't meet a new coworker looking like a girl fresh off her shift from Hooters. I fished around in Finn's drawers, finding a button-down shirt that looked like a dress on me.

Finn's brows pushed together when I came out, my outfit concealed and my hair up in a messy bun. I waved to the new guy – a mid-twenties Nordic model, complete with blond hair and shiny white teeth. "Hey, man. I'm October. Nice to meet you."

He had a slim but muscular build, leaner than Von's. He wasn't quite as tall as Von, standing a mere four inches higher than me. "Pleased to meet you, Lady October. Garrick Keener, at your service." He wore slacks and a dress shirt, looking like he was ready for a day in an office, not a seaworthy adventure to a secluded home in the middle of the ocean. He had a British accent that made me miss Ezra, Mariang and the Vandershots.

Finn frowned. "Why are you wearing my shirt?"

"Because the outfit you brought me is very nice, but I think it's a little too small."

"Let me see. I tried to describe you to the women in the palace. Did I get it wrong? Because they're working on a whole wardrobe for you, and I don't want the whole thing to be too small."

"You don't need to see. You just need to be a gentleman and let me borrow your shirt. Is that a problem? Are you a gentleman?" I challenged.

Finn rolled his eyes and stepped toward me. "You can have whatever you want that's in my drawers." His unintended double meaning made his eyebrow raise up in time with the corner of his lips. "Let me see." He unbuttoned the top button, frowning when I lightly swatted him away.

"Back up," I warned, ignoring Garrick's intake of breath. "I can do it myself." I undid the rest of the shirt and opened it so he could see the outfit was very nice, but just too small. I angled my body away from Garrick, shooting him an apologetic look over my shoulder. "See?"

"What's wrong with it? It fits you perfect. You're just not used to nice clothes. Your Reapers don't present you as you should be seen."

"That's the thing. I don't want to be seen."

"The clothes fit you well."

I looked up at the ceiling and prayed for patience, bravery, and I don't know, a handful of Oompa-Loompas to Wonka me out of the uncomfortable situation. "Oh, fine. Here, you big baby." I took off his shirt and handed it to him, crossing my arms over my breasts to ensure my lack of a bra didn't get noticed by my new colleague. "Sorry about this," I said to Garrick, who watched our exchange with a note of trepidation in his eyes. "You alright?"

Garrick swallowed. "Of course, milady. I've just never seen anyone swat at Captain Finn and live to call him a 'big baby'. I'm trying to catch up so I know how to do my job accurately."

When Finn turned to Garrick, his sneer was fixed firmly in place. "I'm every bit the same man who killed Wesley of the West Hills, freed Stephen from Lumipad's dungeons, and helped put King Geon in Kabayo's prison. She can call me what she likes behind closed doors. Don't forget that she's an Omen. She's irreplaceable. You are not."

"Yes, Captain," Garrick said, his arms behind his back, chest puffed and eyes forward like a well-trained soldier. "Forgive me."

I slapped at Finn's arm as he sat down in his beige recliner in the open living room. "Knock it off. Garrick's allowed to ask questions. Now you really are acting like a big old baby." I sighed, motioning for Garrick to sit down in the living room on the brown sofa. "Relax a little. Tell me about yourself. I'm thinking you're the same Garrick who was in line to be the next Reaper before Von and Mason were at the right place at the right time. Graduated top of your class. Friends with the infamous Danny." I was stalling. I didn't want some stranger pulling from me. I'd been incapacitated too many times to blindly trust a new guy.

I stood on the opposite side of the room next to Finn, who leaned forward in his recliner, elbows on his knees. I was good at conversation, but too scared to go near Garrick and let him actually do his job. I was punking out, and we all knew it.

We exchanged a few pleasantries, with me being evasive about my backstory, and keeping everything as light as I could. As it turned out, Danny had been Garrick's big brother-style mentor at the Academy, which was why Danny was so bummed when Von slid into the position before his protégé could.

Finn looked up at me in the middle of our polite conversation, exasperated. "I know you're trying to put this off. I didn't bring him here so you could talk about the Duwende Academy. I brought him here to guard the house while I'm gone. He's supposed to pull from you while Ezra takes his sweet time getting rid of the Manas."

I didn't want to expose my nerves, but I couldn't help the uncertainty in my voice when I finally owned up to my reasons for staying away from Garrick. I mean, dude seemed perfectly professional and nice; I was just being a chicken. "I'm a little on edge about all this," I admitted, my hands finding my arms and raking down the flesh. "It took me a long time to trust Von and Mason. Even Danny. I've been blissed out by Pullers before, and I didn't like it. I...

You trust him?" I asked Finn, insecure and more than a little scared.

Finn stood, wrapping me in his arms, despite our company. "It's good that you're cautious. I respect that." He squeezed me, claiming me in front of Garrick in a way that actually made me feel safer, instead of peed on. There was the implication that if anything did go south, Finn would send a swift reckoning. I exhaled and let my body lean into his embrace, trusting him to keep me from anyone who wasn't above reproach. Finn kissed my cheek. "I trust him on Danny's recommendation, the Academy's, and the fact that I've had someone watching him since we got back from Silo."

"Huh?" I asked.

Garrick's ears perked up at this new information. He nervously brushed the front of his shirt.

"I was concerned you weren't well-protected, so I started at the top, researching Garrick and putting a tail on him so I knew for sure he was good enough for me to trust with your safety. Von didn't graduate, and after Mason's hair got cut off, I worried you'd be left vulnerable."

"I'm glad I passed your test, Captain," Garrick said in his crisp British accent. His mouth was set in a stiff line, though his tone betrayed none of his visible irritation.

"I'm glad you did, too. I had a few untrustworthy candidates eliminated before I landed on you."

"Eliminated?" I inquired, my stomach queasy. "I don't like the sound of that."

Finn took his thumb and drew a line across his throat. "Eliminated. They were confirmed moles for Sama." His eyes hardened when he observed my disapproval. "I won't take chances with the main supplier of souls. And now that I know you? Now that you live here with me? After everything, my standards for your protection are even higher."

"I don't need you offing people in my name."

"It's no trouble," Finn said with a casual wave of his hand, as if he was doing me some big favor. "You can trust Garrick. He's never been arrested for anything, volunteers at his local foodbank to pull from the more depressed rung of society while he stocks shelves. His fiancé Hamish is set to marry him in the spring, so we've got him for a few months, at least."

I tipped my head to Garrick, who clearly didn't like his business, nor his sexual orientation discussed so casually. "Congratulations on your engagement," I offered, apologetic at how awkward this whole thing was.

"Thank you." Garrick nodded stiffly, his lips pursed to keep whatever he had to say locked tight inside. Dude really was a professional.

And I wouldn't shut up and just let him do his job.

Finn wrapped his arm around my hips and drew me to the middle of the room, motioning for Garrick to meet us there. "I'm right here, okay? You're going to let him pull from you, and I promise I won't let anything bad happen. One wrong move, and they'll never find his body."

"Jeez! You don't have to threaten him like that. Now he's probably just as jumpy as I am."

Garrick held up his hands. "It's alright, Lady October. Captain Finn's spot on; pulling is a grave responsibility, and those who misuse it should be dealt with. I've never blissed anyone out, which you should know after having me followed, Captain. That's why I was reluctant to take the job when you called me about it. I thought you were trying to hire me to work in your harem, bliss out your girls so your king could..."

"That's enough," Finn snapped, his tone sharp, like the crack of a whip.

"I told you I wouldn't be taking the job if it was for that." Garrick turned to address only me. "I promise, I'm only here to help keep you safe. So much rides on the Omens. It would be an honor to make your burden lighter."

My finger flew in Finn's face. "You and I are gonna have words about the whole Duwendes in your harem thing later. Like, buckets and buckets of words."

"Quit stalling. Honestly, I'm doing the right thing here, and you're being difficult."

I knew he was right, but I was too uneasy to be reasonable. I backed up, meeting the resistance of Finn's arm clutching my hips to keep me in place. "I'm not ready," I squeaked, panicking when Finn drew me toward Garrick against my will. "Stop!"

"It's fine!" Finn growled, moving me closer to Garrick

as my whole body arched away, squirming to get just a few more minutes.

"I can handle it! I can deal on my own! I don't need help! I'm fine, Finn! Promise!" When that didn't work, the panic inside of me built to a breaking point. I ducked under his arm and flew to the corner of the room, knowing there was no way out. The wall pressed up against my back, so I knew no one could push me into something I didn't want.

Finn gawked at my brawl-ready fists in dismay. With his hands raised, he stopped his advance when I positioned myself to pop him one. "Are you really fighting me on this? This, of all things? I'm trying to help you."

"I don't need help! I'm fine! I can handle myself without drugs, without a Puller and without anyone!"

"For how long? You were just abducted. Your whole back was nearly skinned!"

"And look at me. I'm standing right here, just fine!"

"Fine? Really?"

Garrick was unsure of my mental state, so he stayed back, the smarty. Finn moved toward me, and I shouted, "Take one more step, and so help me, I'll knock you flat out, Finn!"

Finn was neither amused nor afraid. "You want me to hurt you? Fine! You cried in your sleep last night. Actual tears, October. I held you while you cried for Ollie, stone asleep. And that's after two nightmares I had to wake you from."

"Shut up!" I barked, livid he'd bring up something so embarrassing. "I did not!"

"You told him not to get on the plane. You begged him not to leave you. Do you really want me to go on?" His voice calmed when my fists lowered, losing a little of their purpose. "I'm not trying to hurt you. I promised Ezra I'd keep you safe. This is part of that. It's the bare minimum, actually."

"That wasn't meant for you to hear," I choked out, fists clenched at my sides.

"I know. You trusted me to get you through Silo. You trusted me to fix your back. Trust me in this. You need a Puller, *sinta*."

Garrick's intake of breath told me Finn had just said something weird, though I didn't know what it was.

My head whipped from Finn to Garrick. "What does that mean? That word you just said."

Finn's eyes narrowed at Garrick in a silent threat. "It's a word I like, and it suits you. It's for me to call you, and no one else. If anyone else calls you *sinta*, I want you to punch them on the spot."

"Huh?"

"It's my word for you, and no one else's. That's all you need to know about it."

Garrick cleared his throat and held out his hand, though we were still several feet from being able to touch. "On my honor, I'll only pull the slightest amount to help you get ready to go back to work when it's safe. You tell me if you need more, and I'll oblige. Otherwise I'll do the bare minimum."

Finn growled at Garrick, "I didn't call you here to do your smallest effort. I called you here because you're supposed to be the best there is."

Garrick met Finn's glare with a defiance of his own, his stubborn rounded chin jutting out as he shed his bland, professional demeanor. "Then trust me to do my job. If you want me to help her, I will. I'm honored to. But we start slow. It's a long road, building a relationship between an Omen and her Puller. If I go in guns blazing, I'll do exactly what she's afraid of and pull too hard. She has to be ready to trust me, and she's clearly not. Why should she? I'm an utter stranger to her." He turned his gaze to me. "If anything, she's showing the proper amount of caution, which will get her far in the long run."

Finn ran his tongue over his teeth, visibly seething. "I'm this close to chucking you into the ocean and seeing if that Academy taught you how to swim."

Garrick ignored Finn, which I actually found kind of amusing. "I'm going to stand right here and wait for you to come to me. I'm not going to attack you or pull if you're not ready. That's how this is going to work. You need pulling? Then monitor yourself. You don't want us hovering? Then come to me when you know you should, yeah?"

I watched him not move, taking in his caution and nonthreatening demeanor with a skeptical eye. "I can work with that. Sometimes the guards Ezra hires to help out pull from me without asking. Andy used to do that a lot. I don't like being pawed at."

"I can't imagine many do. It's a shame about Andy. I didn't know him well, but I had a few classes with him. We had the same teachers, but I guess we got very different things out of our education." He showed me his hands again. "I'm not Andy. I'm also not Von or Mason. I don't know you, and if you don't want me to, that's fine. I'll be here when you're ready."

"This is pointless," Finn complained. "Just pull from her already!"

Garrick shot Finn a dirty look. "I'd never question you on matters of running Dagat for King Banak. You've no need to question me about this. You had me vetted, and I passed your tests. You've no cause to distrust me now."

I took a small step forward, banding my arms around my stomach. "I don't like people touching my hands," I admitted, working my way up to being cool with this whole thing.

"Elbow?" Garrick suggested.

I nodded gratefully, taking another step, hoping I wasn't walking smack into a trap. "I'm sorry I'm making a big deal about this. I've had a hard time with the whole pulling thing in general. I gave Mason and Von a rough time in the beginning too, if it makes you feel any better."

Garrick managed half a smile. "I know. You forget, Danny and I are friends. We keep in touch. And I knew Von when he was in school for a brief period, too."

"Danny was pissed when Von took the job. He wanted you to be my Reaper."

Garrick shrugged. "It worked out for the best. It would be difficult to get married if I was a Reaper for an Omen. I'm happy. Von's more capable than people give him credit for. And Mason? I've never met the bloke, but if half the stories about him are true, you shouldn't have any trouble feeling safe at night after this is all over."

I met his eyes, allowing a portion of my hopelessness to flicker through. "You really think the stone business will end someday?"

Garrick's shoulders lowered two inches as his eyes softened. "Oh, sweet girl. I have no doubt. That's what we're doing this for, yeah? One day soon, all the countries will have a portion of the sagrado stone. Then you can stay Topside and stick to reaping, which won't even be all that big a job when the suns have the fuel they need from the stone."

I took another step toward him, knowing Finn's patience was reaching its limit. "You really think I can have a normal life after this?"

Garrick managed an amiable chuckle that touched his green eyes, endearing me to him a little. "You've got Von as your Reaper, which I can't imagine will ever give you a mundane life. He snuck me into a club once a few years ago. I've never seen someone charm a bouncer so fast and so effortlessly. And I see the mark of King Kabayo's token on your arm," he said, pointing to the pink, loopy X that ran on the inside and outside of my forearm. "Normal people don't get protection like that. You work for the ruler of the Topside, and if even half Danny's stories are true, that sounds like the best place for anyone to work." He motioned to Finn, who stiffened. "And you've managed to befriend the Great Captain Finn, which I'm sure no one thought possible. So, normal? I don't think normal's in the cards for you." His green eyes twinkled with the mischief of someone who knew how to judge the good from the bad in life. "Extraordinary might be your only option, your grace."

I returned his smile, closing the gap between us with my heart pounding as I fought through the impulse to run. I planted my feet firmly in front of Garrick, slowly extending my arm to him so he could do his thing.

"May I?" he asked, reaching for my branded tattoo from Kabayo. I nodded, and watched as he carefully traced the pink Xs that stretched from my wrist to my elbow. "Wicked," he breathed, entranced at the design and the implications that I had a direct link to one of the kings. He shed his professional demeanor and turned my arm over with all the fascination of a young boy poking at a frog to see if he could make it hop.

I didn't even realize he was pulling until my smile didn't feel forced anymore. He accidentally brushed my hand with his arm, and I didn't even cringe. "You're good," I said of his occupational prowess. "I didn't even feel you pulling until just now."

He cast me a sideways smile. "I didn't get to be top of my class by being bad at my job."

"Finally," Finn exhaled dramatically. "I can see you relaxing." Then he said to Garrick, "I didn't want to have to kill you."

Garrick gave Finn a shrug and a grunt. Only I could see the slight tremble in Garrick's finger as he continued to trace my scar.

RICARDO AND LISSIMA

As it turns out, Garrick wasn't too bad a guy. Once we got used to each other, I was cool with Finn leaving me alone with him. Finn was able to go back to work during the day, returning each night more troubled than the last. He didn't tell me what was bothering him, only that work was stressful.

I'd taken to barfing at least once after breakfast, but was fine by midmorning. I couldn't tell if it was perpetual seasickness, or if I was allergic to one of the foreign pieces of food I was given to eat.

Finn and I started to develop a routine where we would read to each other in bed before we went to sleep. He brought from the shore a series of books about a Mermaid falling in love with a sandwalker, and the harrowing journey their forbidden love took them on. He told me it was a recommendation from a few of the girls in his harem.

Finn was patient with me as I struggled to translate the sections. He lazily rubbed my feet while I puzzled through, teaching myself Mer one weird rune at a time. When my brain grew tired of translating, Finn took over, reading fluidly and making the story come to life. He added just the right amount of passion into his voice, making me swoon at all the right parts.

Finn looked at me over the top of his book, pausing the story at the good part. "You're getting all worked up again."

"Am not. I just want to know if she leaves her parents' place or not." I cast him a look of mild frustration. "I'm exactly the right amount of worked up for this part. I feel like she's going to chicken out and stay at home. She should go with Ricardo."

Finn smiled at me with no hint of aggression. He jerked his chin to the spot on the round bed next to him, sighing contentedly when I curled up to his side, propped up against our nest of pillows. I wanted to scratch at my arms, but knew I couldn't give in to that. I wanted to count the folds in the curtain, my OCD flaring, as it always did in the evening when Garrick was in the other room, too far away to pull from me.

My arm snaked around Finn's stomach. My thumb brushed lightly up and down over his navel under his shirt, with my head resting in the crook of his firm shoulder. I shut my eyes to keep from counting.

Finn warmed to the cuddle with a grin. "No, you're not worked up at all. Maybe I should stop reading for the night."

"Don't you dare. We're like, fifteen pages from the end of book one. I have to know how it turns out." I adjusted his overlarge shirt that I wore as a nightgown. Finn had brought me a couple nightgowns to wear that he'd had made for me. We will not discuss the amounts of alcohol I would need to consume to put on one of those lacy scraps of sheerness. His old shirts worked just fine.

"You realize this is an eight-book series, right? This is still the first book. Lots more ground to cover before you learn how it all turns out." When my expression didn't change, he consented, wrapping an arm around me as he continued reading. "'Lissima was beside herself with worry at leaving the home she'd always known, but Ricardo wasn't willing to give her up to the fears that held her in place. She was afraid of change, of leaving her reef, but most of all she worried that she wasn't afraid enough to turn Ricardo's offer away, and what that said about the kind of Mermaid she was. Ricardo begged her for days to come with him, but on this last September's Sunday, he found he didn't have the words. Instead of asking her to run away with him again, he simply stroked her cheek. 'If you can live without this, then you should stay.' Her breathless reply was barely audible. 'But you can't breathe under the water. We'll never last.'"

Finn sunk down a little to kiss my neck before he continued to read. "'Lissima, don't you know by now? If you live, then I breathe.'" Finn stroked the skin of my cheek, melting me and keeping me with Lissima in the moment. "'Ricardo then tasted her lips. 'If you can kiss another man without thinking of me, then you should stay.'"

Finn's thumb dragged across my lower lip, making my breath hitch. He rested the book on the bed so he could run his hand over my naked knee. "Run away with me," he whispered in a quiet plea. I didn't know if he was still reading the book, or going off-script. This would usually be the point in our evening routine where I pushed him away, but that night I was feeling far different after a day of Garrick pulling. That, and Von wasn't in love with me anymore. It had been several days of not being able to reach him in my dreams. Earlier that morning, I tried to make my peace with moving on from the man who had told me over and over again how unavailable he was.

"Could you do me a favor?" I asked, my lashes fluttering shut when Finn's hand gripped my thigh possessively.

"Please tell me it involves working my shirt off of you."

I chuckled. "Actually, I was going to ask you to take your shirt off. Nothing kinky; I just wanted to check something on your back."

Finn quirked an eyebrow at me and was half naked in

the next blink. "As you like it." He bent over me on all fours, burying his lips in the crook of my neck – otherwise known as the danger zone. My back arched of its own volition, my knees falling open to allow Finn's body into my space. Finn knew the buttons to push to get my body to sing for him. He was passionate and gave me no misconceptions that he wanted to be gentle with me. In the same token, his hands were steady, a solid promise that they wouldn't break what they craved.

His hand trailed further up my thigh, alighting on the edge of no return. I gasped like I was being dunked underwater, the pleasure too much for my brain to hold onto its morals, when all it wanted to do was send up the white flag. I wanted to surrender to Finn's experience, his hard, muscular body. I wanted to be the sensuous woman I felt like when he looked at me like that. I knew that if he kissed my lips, there would be no question to how much I would give up to him and regret in the morning.

I didn't want to regret Finn. So few people knew he had this side to him – the passionate man who held me while I slept, who read romantic adventure stories to me, who bought me clothes and provided for me when I actually needed the help. I wanted to treasure him, to savor him. I wrapped my arms and legs around Finn, securing his body to mine, but also making sure the sheets didn't tangle any further. I locked him in place until our breathing slowed.

Finn finally rested in my arms, temporarily surrendering his fight to make me see what we truly were to each other. I brushed my fingers over his shoulder as he rested his cheek to my breasts. "Yeah, that one's on me. I actually wanted to see your back to check something. Sorry I started things up."

"Don't be sorry. Just let me stay here a little while longer. I hate that the memory I have of your breasts are when they were all bloody and you were inches from death." He cupped the outer swells of my breasts, gathering me to him so he could kiss his favorite parts of me through his shirt, making my breath catch in a throaty gasp. "Tell me they're perfect again. Tell me the healing waters kept them soft for me."

I looked down on him with unmasked affection. He wasn't ogling my body with teenager horniness; he was cherishing me. I got a solid amount of unwanted ogling at my old job. This was different. "They're good as new." I ran my hand over his stubble, stroking his cheek to keep him close. "I wanted to check your back, though. Is that okay?"

Finn sat up, chuckling as he gazed down into my eyes. He looked so much younger when it was just us. Freer somehow. "I'm making myself a home out of your breasts, and you're asking permission to look at my back? *Sinta*, my body's yours. You can have whatever part of me pleases you."

His words were like a slap to my nervous system. I'd been waiting for a guy who wouldn't even call me his girl-friend, passing up on a man who had no problem pledging his whole self to me. Finn anticipated my needs and met them without being asked. It's a rare man who does that.

I swallowed hard. "You fed me." I'd spent so many years going hungry, that when I became an adult, I vowed I would never let myself rely on anyone else for food ever again. Here in this foreign land, I'd needed someone to find food for me, to care if I starved. Finn had cared without being asked, thus I didn't have to worry about where my next meal was coming from. People take things like that for granted, but not me.

Finn quirked his eyebrow. "Of course I fed you. What were you expecting?"

I couldn't voice the big, fat nothing I expected life to hand me. Finn had even stored up a jar of *baga* roots in the kitchen, so I never had a chance of going without breathable oxygen. My heart started to beat unevenly as I took in the scope of his love. "You clothed me."

Finn picked up his head an inch more to stare at me curiously. "Of course I brought you clothes. Do you really think so low of me that I wouldn't provide the basic necessities for you to live here?"

I was afraid that if I opened my mouth, my entire childhood would come tumbling out all over the place. My lower lip quivered as I gazed into his green pools of sincerity and protection. "I used to go dumpster diving," I confessed in a low voice. I looked around to the nothing that surrounded us inside of his bedroom, making sure no one heard the scandal. "Bev didn't buy us clothes or much food, so when things got real dire, Ollie, Allie and me would go dumpster diving."

Finn's eyebrows crinkled. "I don't know what that means."

"Dumpsters are these giant metal boxes that people from all over throw their trash inside. When things were real bad, we would dig through the trash to see if we could find food scraps people had thrown away. Restaurant dumpsters were the best ones." A tear escaped the corner of my eye in time with a filthy swear escaping from my lips when the chagrin hit me. "I don't forget the people who feed me when I can't get food for myself. That you feed me here?" I shook my head, struggling to find the right words. "I know goodness when I see it. You're a good man to bring me food every day, like you do."

Finn leaned on his elbows, placing them on either side of my head so he could stare down at me. He smelled like the ocean, and I wanted to bathe in his scent. "You went inside the trash bin? Like, inside with the garbage? To find food, you had to dig it out of a trash can?"

I nodded, scared that my filthy secret would make me repulsive to someone so wonderful. "Not all the time. Just when things got desperate."

Since I was opening the tightly locked Pandora's box, I decided I might as well dive on into the muck headfirst. "There was this one time that Ollie was sick, so Allie and I were going to go diving and surprise him by bringing him home some food to make him feel better. I think I was probably like eight or so at the time. I went in, and Allie kept a lookout. After I handed her enough salvageable food, I couldn't climb my way out. The dumpster wasn't full enough for me to climb on top of the trash to hoist myself out, and the inside was coated with something slimy and slick. I was stuck there while Allie sobbed, trying to get me out. She's always been rail thin, so she wasn't all that strong. Had to call our friends Darius and Terence to fish me out." I shuddered. "Sometimes I still have nightmares about the garbage I couldn't get out of."

Finn's mouth popped open with the horror I knew was coming. "Tell me you're lying. Tell me that's a Topsider joke I'll never understand." When I didn't take it all back as the worst joke in history, Finn closed his eyes. "No wonder you like things clean. Oh, *hani*." I could see him mulling my confession over for a few beats. "I have a net outside I can keep our trash in. That way you don't have to be in the same building as the garbage. Would that be better?"

My intake of breath was all I could muster. Anything more, and the dam would break. "You still want me here?"

Finn's thumb traced the outline of my face. "I want you here forever."

"I'm not... I'm not gross to you now?"

In answer to the question of my fragile heart, Finn leaned down and lightly nipped my lips. The kiss was gentle, tender, and soft. He reached down and hitched my leg to wrap around him. "Never gross. Always beautiful."

"I don't deserve you," I said in wonder, staring up at him with my mouth open.

His body was heavy atop mine, but I didn't dare move. "You deserve to have whatever you want. Tell me, *hani*, how much of me do you want right now?"

I was transfixed as I stared at his full lips. "Too much. More than I can handle. You shouldn't..." I cleared my throat, lest I kiss him and make a mess of the whole thing. Von being frustrating wasn't the only reason I couldn't act on my very carnal desires. Finn was in love with me, and I couldn't return the affection to that degree. As much as I wanted him in every sense of the word, I cared about Finn enough to know I wasn't good for him. I couldn't stay. At the end of our hiding out, I would have to leave him regardless to go back to the job. "Let me see your back."

He slowly kissed my cheek. "As you like it." Then he turned away from me, sitting cross-legged on his mattress while I opened the bed curtains so I could get a better look.

My fingers were gentle as they traced along his ribs, seeking out the crisscrosses that had been there in spades. "The healing waters really did a number on you. You can barely even see your old scars." I traced a line from memory that wasn't there anymore. "What was this one from?"

Finn shrugged like it was no big thing. "Childish behavior."

I lowered my voice and rested my chin on his shoulder. "It's from the switch they used in the Academy, isn't it?"

Finn's chin dipped. "Yes. Switches for lesser offenses, canes for the more stubborn sins. Most of them were from childhood."

I wrapped my arms around him from behind. "I'm sorry your childhood left too many scars. They shouldn't have hit you like that."

"It's alright, you softy. I was a willful child, if you can believe it. Gave the headmaster the worst time before they broke me in. He hasn't lost a bit of his strength in his old age. Still runs the Academy with an iron fist."

"What's his name? The guy who beat you, who is he?"

Finn looked sideways at me. "What does it matter? I'm grown now. No one takes a cane to me anymore." He said it like a promise to himself I wanted to help him keep.

"Give me a name, Finn."

"He was doing his job. I've outgrown the pain of it all."

"I want his name. If he's hurting kids, if he hurt you, I want his job on a silver platter. I mean it. I want him dethroned, fired, ousted – all of it."

Finn shook his head at me like I was trying to be cute or something. "None of it matters anymore, though I appreciate you fighting for me."

I crawled around so I was sitting in front of him on the bed. Cupping his cheeks, I stared him down so he could see I meant business. "It all matters. *You* matter, Finn. If he's beating children who've already been ripped away from their parents, he deserves a cage, not a paycheck. I'm serious. I'll talk to Banak myself and see that this is taken care of."

He searched my eyes for something he could latch onto. "You can't say things like that and expect me to believe you don't love me." He pulled me closer so I was straddling his lap. *Platonic friends do that, right?* "You'll stay far away from Banak. Do you understand that? If he's in the palace, you're in my home. I want you miles away from him."

"I'm an Omen, right? That holds some kind of clout?"

He chuckled as he trailed his fingers up my thighs. "You're about as powerful as Ezra. You can demand whatever you like of me or any of the lands."

"Your old headmaster, he's still running the Academy, beating the children like this?" I reached around him and traced a scar I remembered on his body that was no longer there.

"Of course. If it works, why would they change the system?

"In the morning, I want you to give me the name of a soldier you trust. Someone who can raise the Kataw boys to be good men, not just obedient soldiers of death. I want that jag replaced, Finn. I mean it. Tomorrow the regime changes." I took a chance and brushed my lips against his when I couldn't resist his allure any longer, flirting with certain disaster. "People know you as Banak's number two, but I want them to know you as a man who ends an administration of abuse. I want people to see you like I do. Save those boys from this, Finn. Let that be your legacy."

This was either the wrong thing to say, or the very right thing. Either way, Finn closed the gap between us, that wasn't much of a gap at all. His lips tugged on mine, and mine devoured his. I wanted, and he gave it in spades.

The colors slammed into me, the green and silver explosions demanding to know exactly what I thought I was doing. I ignored them with a flip of my hand, being careless as my need drove my tongue to wander into Finn's mouth. The trumpets yelled at me to stop what I was doing, to think about Finn in all of this, but I was selfish and thought only of sating my own needs that had grown wanton and completely out of control.

I didn't want complicated. I didn't want kisses that were all or nothing. I wanted something beautiful, and Finn was very much that. His body was firm, but his will was pliable in my gentle hands.

Only I didn't want to be gentle.

I pushed Finn backwards onto his mattress, locking his body underneath mine so I could peruse the parts that had been tempting me most. He let me steer the passion, which was completely out of my control when he offered up a helpless whimper that told me I was taking things way too far.

But still I wanted more.

I kissed him, sucking on his lower lip to draw out his moan. I pressed my body down atop his, letting him feel the curves that I tried to keep off the map. He hiked the nightshirt I wore up over my backside so he could squeeze and lightly slap the parts of me that teased him without mercy. I wasn't in the mood to be merciful; I wanted more of him, always more.

It wasn't until a well-timed knock on the door brought me out of my indulgence that the colors started to fade to reason. I wanted the colors. I wanted the music. I wanted to be swept away.

Just not all the way away, as Finn clearly was. His lidded eyes saw me in his hallucination, and mine saw only his bedroom bedecked in shimmering green and silver. "Just a second," I answered the knock, standing up from the bed Finn was sprawled out on. I situated the shirt that fell to mid-thigh and cracked the door. "Hey, Garrick. What's up?"

"I heard noise from in there and wondered if you needed another pull before I turned in for the night."

"Oh, right. Thanks. That would be nice." I let him do his job and felt a modest portion of the creeping anxiety slide out of me. "Have a good night."

He bowed his head to me, which I would never stop finding totally strange. "Goodnight, Lady October." Then he mouthed, *Be careful.*

I nodded, realizing I was going off into an abyss I might not find my way out of. Von had asked me to wait for him, to give him time. I'm not sure making out with Finn constituted as waiting. What's more, I wasn't sure I wanted to wait for someone I was in love with to decide when he'd be able to work a relationship with me into his schedule. I knew it was more complicated than that, but none of Von's many reasons for keeping me on hold made life any easier to accept.

I bid Garrick goodnight again and sank down onto the floor, my back resting on the door. Too many things reminded me that I didn't have a life that welcomed a burgeoning relationship. Danger seemed to stalk me, and I didn't want that for Finn.

"You're doing it again. Have Garrick pull a little harder."

"Doing what?"

Finn pointed to my arms. "You're scratching your hands. What's got you so on edge?"

"Other than my Reaper's brother dying in my arms? Other than getting kidnapped, stripped down and carved up? Other than being without my Pullers?" I paused, considering his question and just how honest I wanted to be with the man I was sharing sheets with. "I'm more than a week off my meds, Finn. Those healing waters really did a number on me. Without that, I would be rocking in the corner, tearing my skin and counting things until I drove myself crazy. Actually crazy. I'm doing a lot better than I would've been without a Puller and the healing waters, but some things about me can't be fixed."

"What can I do? Do you want me to let Garrick sleep in

here?" His expression twisted with disdain at sharing our alone time with another man.

"No, no. It's fine. Or it's not fine, but it's certainly not fixable. I need to keep my hands busy, or I'll start scratching them again." I admired my skin that was smooth and looked brand new. "They're so pretty now. I don't want it to all fall apart." I eyed him and twirled my finger toward the bed. "Lie face-down. Would it be okay if I rubbed your back?"

His eyebrow raised like I'd just asked him if he enjoyed surfing. "Of course. I already told you; my body belongs to you – especially if you want to massage it. You don't have to, though." I could tell by the new light in his green eyes that he was very much looking forward to it.

"It'll keep me from accidentally kissing you. Bad habit I seem to've picked up. Plus, you work hard. It's not good for you to carry around so much stress." I lifted the bottle of oil from the nightstand that he used when he massaged my feet every night. I drizzled a little onto my hands to warm it. I talked myself through the germs I knew would coat my hands, and waited for Finn to lie down. "Tell me about work."

I hadn't given a whole lot of massages, so I took my time on Finn, kneading and rubbing where his groans of pleasure and want led me. He had a fair amount of knots in his back, and I was determined to get each one out.

"I had another run-in with Atius of the Western Waves. I'm this close to just gutting him to be done with his attempts at an uprising. He wants to start a war against the throne for taking their women."

"Can't say I blame the guy for that."

"Well, many of the women I took into the harem left to escape him and his men. He doesn't so much take no for an answer. At least Banak feeds his women."

"Ick. Why are there always sex offenders?"

"Oh, right there," he moaned when I dug into a knot near his scapula. "Atius has these tattoos of waves on his face that stretch all the way back over his bald head. The Mermaids are terrified of him, but he's managed to bring in the most *buhay* for the kingdom, so Banak won't let me kill him or lock him up. Plus, the danger Atius presents chases the women right into the harem, so win-win for Banak."

"Have I mentioned how much I hate that guy?"

I tended to Finn's back for nearly half an hour, repaying him for all the things he'd done to make my life better. I'm sure it was madness that drove me to plant small kisses on the back of his neck. I watched his body coil and stretch through his growing attraction.

When I was finally tired enough to sleep, Finn was a puddle of clumsy limbs he could barely lift without concerted effort. I kissed his temple and covered him with the blanket, sliding in beside him. "You saved my life back there from the Manas," I whispered. "Thank you, Finn."

"Don't you know?" he mumbled, his eyes closed. "'If you live, then I breathe.'"

I melted when he quoted the book to me, and wondered if anyone else knew the romantic Finn was at heart. "Goodnight, honey."

"Run away with me," he begged, just as Ricardo had done to Lissima in the book. Then Finn drew me closer so he could kiss my lips once more before he drifted off.

37

FINN'S DOWNWARD TURN

I loved living with Finn. I'd put a kibosh on any further kissing, and the line was holding, however grudgingly. The uneventful evenings were followed by flirty foot and back massages while we read to each other the adventures of Ricardo and Lissima. Then we wrapped around each other to sleep.

The no kissing rule was a safeguard so Finn didn't fall further in love with me, and so I could attempt to wait for my own self to get a clue and stop being so hung up on things I couldn't have – a concept that was never appealing, but quite necessary.

Philip kept me company in my dreams while I waited for something real to come along. My dream guy was very concerned about my health. He was far more careful with me than he'd ever been. Though, he was my fake dream prince, so I suppose that's how I wanted him to be – how I hoped to be treated while I came down from Serena and that whole mess.

A few nights I'd been entertaining Philip in my dreams, but as the days added up, Philip began to disappear. Then I was stuck reliving Bishop dying in my arms, our bodies bathed in blood and basement germs. Finn had shaken me awake those nights, holding me and not saying a word to damage my pride as I wept in the safety of his arms. I slept only because Finn was strong, and I knew in his home, I was safe. I hadn't been safe in so very long.

Though Finn was a harbor for me, it wasn't so much the case for our roommate. He didn't speak kindly to Garrick, instead clicking his fingers when the stress got to be too much for me to handle. Garrick and I would mute our lively stories about clubs, cute boys and our various life adventures when Finn came home, making sure not to grin too loudly so as not to piss Finn off.

After two more weeks of the same routine, I'd had enough of Finn's attitude when he barked at Garrick for chewing too loudly at the dinner table. "Dude, check your attitude. He's allowed to eat," I snapped, finally speaking up at Finn's increasing black cloud.

"Eating is different than chomping like a Tikbalang."

"Behaving like a child is different than conversing like an adult."

Finn glared at me. "And how would you know? You're nearly a decade younger than I am."

I swallowed my fish uncomfortably at that blatant

truth. "Then you should know better," I countered, unfazed by his aggressive fork-holding. I waved off the anger that seemed to emanate off of him. "Relax your butthole, Finn. If work's getting to you, don't take it out on us."

"You tell me to talk like an adult, but you say things like 'relax your butthole'? What do you care about the state of my butthole?"

I choked on my wine, trying not to laugh while Garrick kept his eyes averted so as not to crack a smile. "I'm sure you have a beautiful butthole, Finn. But you're acting like an ass. Just calm down."

"I'm out," Garrick ruled, unable to keep his high-pitched giggle to himself. He had a normal guy voice, but when he really got to laughing, this girly giggle bubbled out of him, which always made me chuckle. He all but ran to the bathroom to escape Finn's wrath that lately was always just under the surface. What angered Finn most was my blasé attitude about the whole thing every time he lost his temper. He was used to people cowering, which I refused to do in the place I rested my head.

"Don't tell me how to be or pretend you know a thing about my world. It's because of you my job's been uphill. It's listening to you that's made things awful. Don't know what I was thinking, but it's too late to back out now."

"What are you talking about? I've been holed up in here for weeks! How could I possibly have ruined your life so dramatically from in here? You're being a brat, and you were totally rude to Garrick, who's been nothing but nice. I mean, seriously. Chewing? You need to try meditation."

"Enough!" Finn pounded his fist on the table, making me jump. Garrick thrust himself out of the bathroom, his fight face on to match Finn's as the great captain stood to tower over me. "Get out," he seethed at Garrick.

"You know I can't do that. You brought me here to make sure she was taken care of. If you're the threat, I can't leave you alone with her."

"Oh, you can't?" Finn's eyes lit with a burning ember of cat-and-mouse, and I didn't like it one bit. "Who are you to stand up to me?"

"I'm her Duwende," Garrick challenged, rolling up his sleeves as he positioned himself between Finn and me.

"Garrick? Maybe you should give us a minute." I worried about the unpredictable nature of Finn's growing temper the last two weeks. I'd seen Finn in action on the battlefield. I wouldn't let him unleash on Garrick, who promised to introduce me to Hamish and their two dogs if I ever visited him in London.

"Get out," Finn snarled, chest puffed. He held his superior height and muscle mass as leverage over Garrick.

"You know I can't do that. Not until you calm down."

I saw the shift only seconds before it happened, which wasn't enough time to move Garrick to safety. "Run!" I cried, trying to shove myself between the two just as Finn lunged for him. Finn accidentally knocked me sideways in his attempt to throttle Garrick. The regret on his face was obvious, and I debated letting out a scared scream so he could see the monster he was in that moment.

But see, I'd dealt with my fair share of monsters. When my scream stayed tucked inside me, my fist compensated by punching Finn in the kidney.

Garrick remained in control when Finn's hands wrapped around his throat, choking him so hard his eyes bulged. I don't know how Garrick had the fortitude to remember to pull when he was inches away from death, but that's exactly what he did. Slowly, Finn's grip loosened as reason reentered his brain. Garrick croaked for me to lock myself in the bedroom, but I think we both knew I wasn't having any of that. "You think you can try to kill me with no repercussions?" Garrick yelled, kicking Finn in the side for good measure when he collapsed onto all fours. "Now you get to watch while I take your girlfriend and run her right back to Ezra, where she belongs."

Finn tried to fight through the relaxation that had been shot into him against his will. "You take her, and it'll be the last thing you do. I'll kill Hamish without a blink, and make you watch while he bleeds out all over your perfect life."

Garrick kicked Finn again, and I decided I'd had just about enough. "Stop it! It's enough, Finn! What's gotten into you? You know you can't go attacking my Duwende like that. He didn't even do anything wrong!" I watched physical pain mutate to emotional agony so quick, I dropped to my knees to get a better look at the waves of too much that crashed over him.

"Get in the bedroom, October," Garrick cautioned as I took a chance and wrapped my arms around Finn, lifting his upper half so I could hold him through his torment. "I'm serious. He just threw you across the room. He's not safe."

"That door won't keep me safe if Finn's determined." I held Finn tight, letting him know that even though the burdens he shouldered were heavy, that I was strong enough to carry a few of them for him. "I'm here," I assured him softly, turning the horrific scene into something tender I knew he wouldn't want to shatter by shouting. I kissed his cheek, melting my sea monster into something more pliable as he came down from the aggression others had feared him for. "What's got you so twisted?" I asked, my breath against his ear.

And just like that, Finn slumped in my arms, going from homicidal loon to broken puppy in the span of a sentence. "I tried! I tried to dismantle the harem. I tried to reason with Banak and tell him he only needed a few girls, the willing ones who didn't want to leave and had nowhere else to go, but he wouldn't have it."

He sat up straighter, tugging me onto his lap when I refused to let go of him. I knew if I did, he might forget to be gentle and go after Garrick again. I wrapped both my arms and both legs around him, encircling him in the warmth of my body and the treasure of our odd friendship. "I didn't know you did that. I'm so proud of you."

"Yeah? Well, don't be," Finn said bitterly, returning my embrace with weakened arms, due to Garrick's stellar pulling. "I've been sneaking women out of the harem for two weeks now, and he must've caught on." He gripped me tighter, so tight I almost protested at the creak of my ribs as he fought off Garrick's hard pull. "He took her! He took my mother into his bed. He sent out a guard, brought her in and roughed her up in his bedchamber. All week I've been listening to her screams filling the hallways of the palace." He let out a strangled cry into my shoulder. "I can't take it! I can't take it! Banak's torturing me for letting some of the women go! It's what he did to Dyesebel when I wanted to leave the palace to go off and marry her. I know his game. I know it, and I can't take it!"

I had no words that were the right ones, only jaw-dropping horror that made me squeeze Finn tighter. I was surprised to find that Garrick had the peace of mind to speak sense into the madness Finn howled into my hair. He touched Finn's shoulder, gently giving him a pull to dull the never-ending awful that would no doubt haunt him for too many years. "I can help you," Garrick promised. "You're not alone in this."

"Yes, I am. It all falls on me. It always falls on me."

"Tell me who's next in line to rule after Banak."

Finn scoffed. "Julius, who's every bit as bent as his father. Only he prefers men in his bed." He cast me an apologetic look through the anxiety that had overtaken his stoicism. "Prince Julius wanted Von, so I had him watched, brought in when his brother's gambling debt grew high enough. Then I gave him to Julius to work off his brother's debt in the royal bedchambers."

"Hush, now," I warned, wishing Garrick wasn't there to hear Von's darkest secrets. Garrick gasped, and I shot him a deadly look. "You didn't hear that. Not a word of it."

Garrick's hand went over his mouth, horrified. "I had no idea. Danny mentioned Von was a prostitute. Made it sound like Von wasted his life on purpose. He didn't mention him taking his brother's place. Is that what Danny was on about? Because he's a foul git for looking down his nose on Von and talking about him like he does."

I gritted my teeth, hating myself for talking about the thing I'd just said we couldn't discuss. "Von plays it off like it was his choice, having sex with wealthy women for money. It was very much against his will, and only with Julius. Danny sees what he wants to see, and you'll let him. It's Von's business, not yours."

"That's awful. Which brother did he take the rap for?"

"It doesn't matter. It was Von's choice to save his brother, and he doesn't want Danny or anybody to know. It was a dark time for him."

Finn leaned back a few inches, his arm still around me. He touched his knuckle to my abdomen, his expression fearful. "I hurt you. I didn't mean to knock you out of the way. I'm so sorry. Is everything... Are you alright?"

"I'm fine, but just so we're clear, I'm not sorry I punched you." I lowered my voice to a threat and moved his chin so he could see my sincerity. "Come at me or Garrick again, and I'll knock your kidney even harder next time. You don't get to solve your problems like that. I came here to escape getting knocked around. I know you didn't mean to get me, but if it happens again, Garrick's taking me back to shore, whether or not Ezra's cleared the Topside of the Ekeks and Manas. You promised me a safe house, and that wasn't safe at all."

Finn held my gaze, and then nodded. "That's fair. I am sorry I hurt you."

"I know, honey. I know."

Garrick waited a few beats and cleared his throat. "Okay, then. Who's in line for the throne after Julius?" Garrick asked, trying to focus.

Finn shrugged, holding onto me through the up and down of his shoulders. "Mathias of the Green Lakes, who's so old, he wouldn't be in power for long."

"But he'd give you a year maybe? Two? We need just enough time to scrape together a decent leader who can actually rule without pushing it all off onto you."

"I guess. I mean, I know a few who'd be great at it. They've fought alongside me and know what's important. But what's the plan? Banak barely leaves the castle. He's happy with the Mermaids and doesn't bother with war or his people or anything like that."

Garrick stood. "I think it's time October's Duwendes

come to get her. It's about to get bloody, and I won't be able to help you and keep her safe at the same time."

"Help me?" Finn questioned, finally looking up at Garrick with something other than loathing.

My mouth fell open when I heard Garrick say, "I think it's time Banak was relieved of his throne."

38

BAKING BREAD

I sat on my hands so I didn't scrape the skin off my arms while I listened to the two plot out the murder of the king and his son. "It's got to look like a family feud, or it'll set the next rule on a bloody course. The people will see how to dethrone a king, and everyone will try it when they're the least bit unhappy. That's how Lumipad devolved into the mess they're in now. Our monarchy's untouchable, but theirs wasn't after that first murder of their queen a couple years ago." Finn thought aloud as he paced the kitchen with Garrick. I sat on the couch, trying to stay out of the mutiny planning.

Garrick touched his rounded chin when he was deep in thought. "Von's the best ticket for that. When he comes to get October to bring her home, tell him the plan. Let him go back to Prince Julius and sell himself back into the harem. Only give him a knife this time and tell him to kill the bastard. Von's deadly when he needs to be."

"No!" I cried, horrified.

Finn acted as if I hadn't spoken. "I can switch out the normal guards for two that I trust with something like this. They can sneak Von out and let Julius 'sleep it off' for a few hours." I could almost see the wheels turning in his mind. "I can do the same with one of the women in the harem for Banak. There's no shortage of Mermaids who'd jump at the chance to gut the king. I always frisk them, and they have no access to weapons anyway. I can slip Maleeah one. She'd be great for the job. She's a fighter, that one. Bit clean through Banak's earlobe her first time."

Garrick nodded appreciatively, but I was livid. "Do you hear yourselves? Von's not going back to that awful place. He won't set foot inside the palace. Do you get what you're asking him to do? You're asking him to take the fall for murdering the heir to the throne! How much diplomatic immunity do you think Ezra and I have up our sleeves? Not enough for this."

Finn waved off my concern. "We won't let Von take the fall for it. We can move the bodies after they're both dead into the throne room. We'll stage it so Banak and Julius look like they got in a fight and killed each other."

Garrick laughed, clapping his hands. "You're the master. That's it, right there. Exactly like that. Your two men, they're trustworthy with something like this, yeah?"

"The things they've kept secret would undo many a kingdom. They're good men."

"Hello! Doesn't anyone hear me? I won't let this happen. Von isn't going to go back to the man who raped him and hand himself over for more. I won't allow it."

"You won't allow it?" Finn chuckled. It just figured that something awful like this would finally put him in a good mood, the jerk. "And just how are you going to stop us?"

I hadn't seen Von in my dreams the entire time I was in Dagat, but I was determined to connect with him tonight, whether or not he'd fallen out of love with me. "Von's my Reaper. He's like my best friend. What you're asking him to do? It's cruel."

Finn sobered for a moment. "Von knows true cruelty, and this is his chance to end it."

Garrick finished the thought. "Don't you think he deserves justice for what Julius did to him?"

"What about you?" I asked, standing and staring down Finn. "You stood back and let it all happen. You let them take Von and who knows how many others. Does Von deserve justice on you, too?"

Finn's eyes steeled over as he met my glare with his own. "He's welcome to try. I was following orders, October."

"That's pathetic, and you know it. You've been operating on your own conscience for over a month now, maybe two. Take some responsibility."

Finn postured, his attitude flaring. "Men have been hanged for less. I'd watch yourself."

"Passing off blame like you're doing? It's weak. I'm glad you're righting the wrong and all, but if you're doling out justice to Banak and Julius like this, what makes you think you're exempt?"

Finn stared at me a moment and then blew out a loud raspberry. "You're just having mood swings. Von knows where to find me if he wants revenge."

"Mood swings?" I reared back, offended. "Because I'm a woman, my points are invalid when they clash with yours? You can write it all off as a mood swing and ignore me just because I have breasts? You're a jackwagon if I ever saw one." I stomped to the kitchen cabinet, yanking out the bucket and filling it with soapy water from the tap, splashing a rag inside. If no one would listen to me, I would take it out on the floors, cleaning until they shined for me. The floors would listen to me. They always did.

Garrick followed me to the kitchen and brushed his hand over my back, pulling a portion of anger from me. Lucky for me I had plenty to spare. "Leave me alone," I huffed. "I'm just as pissed at you as I am at Finn. Killing off a monarchy doesn't solve anything. Read a history book, you jags."

I went to the living room and rolled up the rug, getting down on my hands and knees as I took out the rag and started scrubbing the concrete floor. "Look at what's happened to Lumipad. Serena thought she could do a better job than Sylvia, so she killed her. Now the whole land's in an uproar. You people never learn."

Garrick threw out his hands. "That's why we're not making a big revolutionary scene of it. We're staging it as a family feud. No one's going to get it in their heads they can off the next ruler. There's no precedent. It's not the same thing. The people will mourn, protocol will be followed, the throne will go on to the proper person. Everyone wins."

"Fine, whatever. You both know best," I spouted, my words dripping with sarcasm as I wrung out the rag over the bucket, focusing on the floor.

I didn't expect Finn to shout in exasperation at me, so when he barked out a frustrated, "Would you get off the floor?" I tilted my head up to look at him.

"What's it to you if I clean the floors? I'm three weeks off my meds, Finn." *Thank God for those healing waters.* "This is the sanest I get at this point, and it's only because Garrick's been pulling all day long. You're lucky I'm not rocking myself in the corner, counting the ceiling tiles."

Eighty-eight. There were eighty-eight total. I knew because I'd counted the ceiling tiles every day for two weeks, checking the tiles eighty-eight times each day just for good measure. I fought the urge to look upward and check again.

"I don't mean that. I mean get off the floor. Come on. You know this isn't good for someone in your condition."

Finn walked over and helped me up, moving me to sit on the couch.

"Actually, this is the best thing for my condition. You said you didn't want me scratching up my arms. I have to do something with my hands, or I'll go back to that. I'm barely hanging on here, Finn. Don't act like you know all about OCD."

Finn shook his head, looking down on me with a hint of resentment in his eyes. "Not that. Your *condition*."

"OCD is my only condition, other than living with two homicidal maniacs."

"You're going to make me say it? You're really going to make me go there? Why are you pretending it's some big secret you're hiding from us? We've known for days."

"Huh?"

"I know you're pregnant! You throw up every morning, and you're moody as anything lately."

It was as if Finn had started talking gibberish. "Are you high? What are you talking about?"

"I know your secret boyfriend got you pregnant. I can't believe it's lasted through your kidnapping."

I stood, confused and indignant. "I'm not pregnant! I'm a virgin, you backwards jackfish. Just because a woman throws up while she's living at sea doesn't automatically mean her uterus is baking bread, alright? I'm seasick, is all."

Garrick tilted his head at me. "We know you're pregnant. It's okay, October. You don't have to pretend for us. We won't tell anyone."

"But I'm telling you the truth! I'm not pregnant, guys. Of all the things to say to me. Am I gaining weight or something? I gotta tell you, it's mean to assume a girl's knocked up because she's eating regularly."

Garrick's hand went to his heart. "No, sweetie. Nothing like that. I'm pulling for two when I touch you. I can tell the difference."

"Pulling for two what? Two Reapers?"

Garrick buried his head in his hands. "No, I'm pulling for two people. Do you really not know? How long's it been since your last..."

I shoved my fingers in my ears, not caring that I looked like a child. "I'm not discussing my body with you two! I'm not pregnant, and that's the size of it. You have to have sex to get pregnant, and I've never done that."

"Why are you lying to me?" Finn asked, a cloud of betrayal stinging his features.

I spun on my heel and marched into our bedroom. I slammed the door shut and locked them both out, staring down at my stomach in total confusion.

39

KNOWING NO BOUNDARIES

That night, Finn and Garrick tiptoed around while I pretended to be asleep in the bed. Garrick combed his fingers through my hair, pulling out a bit of stress before he went to sleep on the couch.

When it was just the two of us, Finn took off his shirt and kicked his pants to the ground, crawling into the bed behind me mostly naked, clad only in his black cotton briefs, as he always did these days. He rolled me onto my side and spooned me with his body wrapped around mine, just how he liked to sleep together. "I know you're awake," he accused, kissing my neck. When I didn't answer, he said, "You didn't snore when we were on the road in Silo, but you do now. Another reason I knew you were pregnant."

"I'm not pregnant, and I don't snore. Stop trying to freak me out."

"Who's the father?"

I scoffed as I rolled my eyes, frustrated that it had only taken a handful of sentences from him to piss me right off. Maybe I was a little moodier than usual. "You. You're the father, Finn. You got me pregnant one night. You were reading to me, and I got so turned on that I imagined having sex with you, and now have a hysterical pregnancy. My ovaries just can't get enough of your love juice. I'm thinking of naming the baby Leonard. Leonard Reese or Leonard Fredo? I can't decide." I palmed my stomach and frowned. It actually did feel a slight bit rounder. I cringed, miffed his teasing was getting to me. "Go to sleep."

Finn chuckled at my attitude, though I couldn't tell you why. "I'm sure I'll find out who the father is soon enough. Though if it were mine, I can tell you for sure he wouldn't be named Leonard. He'd be Finn Fredo, II. I don't know why you're lying to me. I already know."

I turned in his arms, scowling up at him. "For the last time. I've never had sex. I only just started seeing New Guy, and I've been either locked away in some lousy basement or locked away with you here. New Guy and I barely got in more than a handful of kisses before I was taken." I raised my palm and put my other on my heart. "I swear on all the seaweed and facial mud masks in this ocean."

Finn kissed my cheek, more amorous than usual now that he was in a better mood with their new (stupid) plan in motion. "You'll have to send Mason away when you get back. Maybe not right away, but at some point."

"Um, good luck with that. I've tried to fire both of them more than a few times, but it never took."

"For your safety. He's Matruculan."

"He's not a wild animal when he transforms. He's still Mason." I shrugged, picturing Mason's furry wolfy face.

"I know. You should see Ezra when he transforms." Finn shuddered. "Pacifist though he tries to be, Ezra has no control over himself when he turns. Mason's wolf is far more easily tamed."

"I like Mason as a wolf. Sometimes I like him better that way. Less bickering. Plus, I always wanted a dog of my own."

Finn huffed his frustration at my limited knowledge of unicorns and leprechauns. "Matruculans eat babies. He'll start getting hungrier and hungrier through your pregnancy until he can't control himself. When the mother's somewhere in her third trimester, that's when they snap. The more zealous Matruculans start gnawing on the woman while she's still pregnant. Best send him away until the baby's at least a month or two old. That's usually when the craze dies down."

"Do you hear yourself? Gross! Mason isn't going to try to eat me or my baby." I harrumphed and growled my frustration. "There's no baby! You're driving me up a wall, you jackballoon."

"I don't know why you're denying this so hard. You don't have to hide it anymore. Are you doing this to spare my feelings?" The edge in his voice died down to insecurity. "Because I know you're not in love with me. I get it, and I'm okay."

I softened, feeling horrible for the rough spot I'd unwittingly put him in, and how gracious he was being about the whole thing. "I'm sorry, Finn."

Finn's hand drifted down to shift me and wrap my leg around his waist. Our stomachs sealed together, giving him easy access to my feet. He wasted no time reaching his hand behind his back to massage my heel. "You like that?" he asked when my lashes fluttered shut, his voice husky with too much desire.

"You know I do. But don't get carried away."

He responded by rolling atop me and rocking his hips against mine in a PG-13 kind of way that was unsuitable for children, or women who were trying to get their life in some sort of adult order. "It's our last night together."

I pulled a fast one and rolled us so I was on top, my frown pronounced as I scolded him. "See? That's getting carried away. Exactly what I told you not to do. Don't make me go sleep on the couch with Garrick."

Finn gripped my hips, his eyes climbing slowly up my body and making me feel gloriously naked, though I was safely clad in the tank top and shorts he'd brought for me to sleep in. I didn't like how the branding of the bat scar Serena had carved into me was visible on my shoulders, and every now and then I caught the guys staring at the markings with sad eyes.

Finn sat up, massaging my thighs in a way we both

knew he shouldn't. His hands felt... and they made me want...

"I'll miss this. You in my bed. Us like this." He brushed his nose back and forth across mine. "This is how we should always be."

I harrumphed, climbing off of him. "See what you did? Now I have to go sleep on the couch." I stomped into the living room, waving Garrick back down when his head popped up from the arm of the couch. I couldn't imagine he was comfortable there, but he never complained. "Hey, roomie. It's a little crowded in Finn's room. Mind if I sleep out here?"

"Of course, October. Here. Take the couch. I can sleep on the floor."

"No, no. I call the floor."

"I'm not letting an Omen sleep on the floor, much less a pregnant one." Garrick stood, stretching and drawing me in for a hug I'd started softening into after the first few days of getting to know him. My eyelids drooped as he pulled a modest amount of stress from me, relaxing my rigid posture in his arms. Garrick was a love bug, and I was starting to trust him more every day we spent together.

Finn stomped out in black shorts for Garrick's sake. His fists were clenched with sheer irritation. "Get back to bed, October."

"I'm sleeping out here tonight. I told you to slow your roll, and your roll didn't slow one bit."

Finn cast his arms out, flustered. "You also told me to relax my butthole."

"Well, you're too relaxed in there with me. Boundaries, Finn. Don't confuse me."

Finn stopped short, his eyebrow raised. "You're capable of being confused about your ridiculous attachment to your stupid non-boyfriend?" He took a determined step toward me, reaching for my hand.

"No. That's not what I meant." Strands of my auburn waves had fallen out of my messy ponytail, dancing around my shoulders and the edges of my face, the slight tickle irritating me all the more. "Don't put words in my mouth. Whatever. I'm sleeping out here."

"You're not sleeping on the couch. It's not good for the baby."

My pitch climbed in exasperation. "Quit saying things like that! I'm not pregnant, you jackwagon. You have to have sex to get pregnant. I don't know what kind of flunky taught you sex education, but the basics are pretty non-negotiable." I blushed at how very almost naked he was. "And would you put on a shirt? Garrick's going to think we were... you know, doing things."

Garrick rubbed the flat of his palm to my back in a circular motion that soothed me. "Finn's right. You'll not sleep on the couch or on the floor. You'll sleep in the bed." He leveled his gaze to Finn. "Finn can flip me for the couch if he's misbehaving."

Finn's eyes widened at being kicked out of his own

room while I grinned. "Yes, he's misbehaving. Thank you, Garrick. And thank you, Finn. I'll be sure to mention to my non-boyfriend what a total gentleman you were, offering up your room so I could be comfortable with my imaginary fetus." I rubbed my belly, making a show of sticking out my usually flat stomach.

My hand stilled as my frown pulled down the corners of my mouth. The toned muscles I'd earned the old-fashioned way weren't nearly as defined. I palmed the lower half of my abdomen in confusion at the small swell between my hips. "Weird," I breathed before I remembered I wasn't alone in the room. I dropped my hand, raised my nose in the air and stomped into the bedroom. "Enjoy the floor, Finn," I called before slamming the door shut.

40

IF YOU LIVE, THEN I BREATHE

*W*hen it was just me alone in the darkness, I opened the curtain so the moon could shed light on my stomach. I lifted my tank top to observe the oddity more clearly. I traced back over every moment, knowing I wasn't pregnant, but feeling a childish confliction all the same. I was pissed at the guys for getting to me, and shoved the hem of my tank top down, feeling foolish that the moon watched me behave like an ignorant kid who didn't know where babies came from.

I climbed into the large round bed, stretching out in the center like a cat on her perch, sniggering that Finn had been dethroned to the floor. I missed Von and Mason terribly, missed my own bed, but Finn's mattress was a stellar second option. I closed the bed curtains, grateful for the pitch black. The darkness made it impossible to count the things that called out to me, or touch the objects that seemed to need fiddling with. Though the OCD never fully left me, I was proud of myself for making it so long without my medication. I hadn't suffered a breakdown, and though I couldn't stop counting things without concerted effort, I could tell that the healing waters and a steady dose of pulling were giving me a chance at a better life.

I concentrated on breathing, hoping to see Mason and Von the next day when Finn swam me to the shore to meet them. I worried for Mariang, knowing that me being stuck here meant she was carrying the weight of feeding Terraway on her own. I missed her gentle presence, and longed to take some of the burden off her frail shoulders.

I decided not to hesitate this time if Ezra opened his arms for a hug.

I wished again to connect with Von in my dream, but had lost hope that he still loved me. For surely if he did, he would've met me in my dreams by now. He couldn't go without sleep for three weeks. There was no explanation, other than that he'd fallen out of love with me as quickly as we'd fallen in step with each other. Our weird personalities somehow matched up in all the important ways they should, but now it was back to the friend zone. Do not pass Go. Do not collect $200. My stomach churned as I worried about seeing him again. I would have to face a relationship where I'd been head over heels, but he wasn't anymore, and maybe never really was more than those few moments. He'd warned me about his attention span and aversion to relationships. He'd said from the beginning that he was temporary. I don't know why I thought I'd be the difference to change it all. Yet another thing that made me feel like a childish idiot.

I drifted off to sleep, almost grateful I didn't see Von. Night after night not dreamwalking with him was serving as decent closure for the feelings that didn't do either of us any good. Instead of wishing I saw Von in the night, I didn't complain when my dream took me to watch a chicken strut around in a pigpen instead. I sighed dejectedly at the chicken, wondering how I got stuck in such a boring dream.

When the jostling on the mattress woke me some time in the night, I groaned and rolled onto my back. "What?"

"I'm not sleeping on the floor in my own house. Move over." Finn was resolute, and I knew better than to argue when I could barely form words through my sleepy haze.

"Fine. Whatever. Be a prince and let me sleep."

Finn scooted me to the left and flopped on the bed in his spot. He was much heavier than me, which made my body roll toward him, landing me in his arms. He let out a contented sigh as he drew his thick brown blanket up over us, his nose nuzzling me as he rested his forehead to mine. Our lips were inches apart as he held me, his hand cupping on my bare hip under the covers. "Much better." He started massaging my backside with his tired hand. "I don't like that you're leaving tomorrow. I don't want us to end."

I exhaled slowly, keeping my eyes closed so I didn't have to see his pained expression that most likely mirrored my own. "I know, but it's what I've been trying to tell you. I'm an Omen, Finn. I can't stay here. If I do, you'll eventually starve and die. If I want you to have a chance at surviving and finding good things out of life, you have to let me go."

He brushed a light kiss to my lips, inhaling the scent of my face. "You think about me when you're reaping?"

"I try not to. I try to think about all of Terraway. If I think about you too much, I..." My hand drifted to his waist, alighting on the band of his black cotton briefs. I wondered where his shorts had landed on his pathway to the bed. I didn't want to confess to Finn how often I thought of him. The non-platonic things I saw myself doing in this very bed taunted me with their utter impossibility. I swallowed, but my heart forced words out of my mouth I had no business uttering. "'If you live, then I breathe.' No matter how far away we are, I'll always know what I lost in leaving you." I stroked the side of his face with clumsy fingers, unable to keep my heart stony when we were so thoroughly tangled in each other. "I'll miss us."

Finn's whisper held so much pain, I had a hard time hearing the words that shook me. "I love you." He pressed his lips to mine, sealing his love inside of me to take with me while I reaped and carried on without him. "We don't have to say any more about it. Goodnight, *sinta*."

"'Night, Finn."

41

FIVE MORE MINUTES

Finn's face or palm always landed on my boobs by morning, and today was no exception. I awoke to his cheek on my chest as the suns' lights filtered in through a narrow slit in the bed curtains, rousing me gently as I combed my fingers through Finn's hair. No one got to see him like this, defenseless and precious. He was always so surly outside his house. I didn't take the privilege lightly that he trusted me in his vulnerable moments, sleeping with his guard down.

I smelled something sweet in the air, but wasn't awake enough to place it. My stomach was queasy before I even thought about sitting up. I tried to move to the edge of the bed without bothering Finn, but the second my breasts left him, he woke, wrapping his arms around me and anchoring me beside him. "Five more minutes," he mumbled through puffy lips.

"I'm getting up. You can sleep in, though."

"I don't like my bed without you in it. Just five more minutes." He spooned me and started kissing a line up the nape of my neck, making my back arch as my body responded before my brain could tell it not to.

"Knock it off, Finn. You know I'm still hung up on that other guy. You're making the boundaries confusing again."

He didn't listen, but sucked on the juncture between my neck and my shoulder, making my lashes flutter shut. I bit my lip against the temptation that was getting all too sparkly and beautiful. "Your non-boyfriend's not here."

I sat up, indignant as I shook off the waves of lust I tried not to feel. "But *I'm* here. I told you I was still hung up on my non-boyfriend, and great as you are, it's not the same as what I still feel for him. Why are you making me hurt you like this?" I shook my head, rubbing the sleep from my eyes as Finn sat up.

"Why do you want to be with someone who doesn't want to be with you? I wouldn't hesitate to make you mine. He doesn't love you, *sinta*."

Fair point. "Because I'm a masochist. I'm so over this conversation. Aren't you tired of it?"

"You let me kiss you in the waters," Finn reminded me, his voice low.

My cheeks flushed. "I pulled away. And I hardly think when I've been under that much duress that I can be on top of every rational decision. I was barely alive, Finn. You want to call a spade a spade? You saw your window and moved on it."

"I'll call a spade whatever I like." He pointed his finger to the mattress. "It doesn't change the fact that you've kissed me in this very bed nearly every night for three weeks now. Don't tell me you feel nothing."

I huffed. "We're not debating if I make great decisions. Of course I have feelings for you. That's not the point."

Finn scowled at me. "You know I'm in love with you, and if that other guy wasn't in the picture, you'd love me. I can see it in you."

I pulled my knees to my chest. "Don't make me lose you. Don't make me push you away. You're like, my last safe place." I hung my head. "Ugh. I'm sorry. This is all my fault. I clung too hard to you. I let it get confusing."

"I'd take care of you, you know." He glanced down at my stomach. "Even though it isn't mine, I would..." He left the implications of him raising my nonexistent baby with me.

Though there was no baby, the gesture was grand, hitting me in my tender spots. "Stop, Finn. That's maybe the nicest thing you've ever done for anybody, but you're wasting it on me. Save all this for the right girl. I care about you a great deal, but I'm not her. I'm sorry for making you think I was. If things were different, yeah, I'd stay here and never look back. But that's not my life, Finn."

"I know you want me. I see it in your eyes all the time."

I looked away. "A crush. That's all it is, Finn. A little crush. Of course I'm attracted to you. But I couldn't stay with you even if I wanted." The sweet smell that wafted in the air stung my nose, making my stomach churn. "Oh, I'm getting seasick again."

Finn watched my discomfort play out on my face. "Do you want me to get a bucket?"

"No. It'll pass."

Finn smoothed back his hair, his shoulders deflating their fight. "Alright. Sorry I made you uncomfortable. This is our last day together, and I know when you leave, things will be less... just less. I love you, *sinta*. I want you to stay. I'm better when you're here. Everything's better when you're here."

I gripped his hand. "I love you, too. Just not in the way that would make you kissing my neck something that led to more. Those few kisses we shared? It's all I can give you, so take it and run. I have to leave you to do my job. That song can't change, no matter how much both of us wish it could. I'm an Omen. If I want you to live, I have to leave you and go back to reaping." His lips brushed my cheek, and I gripped the back of his neck, wishing I could give him what he wanted, but knowing I couldn't.

He was a fish, and I couldn't swim, and there was the crux of it, the metaphor of why we would never work.

I pulled back the curtain, but before my toe could touch the rug, I gasped. The sweet smell manifested in the form of smoke coming from the tip of Von's cigar. He cast me a hard smile from his spot in a chair on the other side of the room. "Well, that saved us a few dodgy conversations. I feel like I'm all caught up."

42

REUNITED WITH TEAM TERRAWAY

I didn't ask how long Von had been there or exactly what he'd heard. I didn't care that he looked miffed or that I was climbing out of another man's bed. For the briefest of moments, I forgot that he wasn't in love with me anymore. I didn't ask questions, but ran to him, crashing into his arms as he stood. "You're here! How? I thought we were meeting you on the shore!"

"Clearly. I didn't want to wait. Thought I'd surprise you early. One point for me on the surprise part, though seeing you in here? In bed with the great Captain Finn? Quite the surprise I'm suffering myself. That's about fifty points for you. Maybe more when the shock finally wears off."

Finn climbed out of the bed in nothing but his briefs, which I'll admit was pretty damning. He pulled on a shirt and pants, grumbling about this being his space as he pushed past us to go to the bathroom.

"Those are some spectacular pajamas, Captain," Von jabbed loud enough to carry down the hall. There was a lightness in his tone that didn't match the anger in his eyes.

"I haven't been seeing you in my dreams," Von accused when the bedroom door closed the two of us inside. "Can I guess Finn's the reason why?"

My nose scrunched. "Finn's got nothing to do with it. I've been trying to find you in my dreams for weeks. It's not me who fell out of love, Von. Though, believe me, I've tried." I looked up at him, trying not to let my underbelly show.

He took a puff on his cigar, his eyes slits as he sized me up. "It's not me. I've been taking sleeping pills, trying to find you."

"Well, you found me." I didn't care that he was irritated and I was wounded. I cared that he was there.

"Is three weeks all it takes for you to forget whose bed you belong in? Shall I remind you?" The second the cigar left his mouth, he leaned down and kissed me. He tasted like love, and smelled like the sweet smoke I'd missed. His lips were warm and pliable, despite his attempt at stoicism. The colors started swirling, and that was all it took to sweep us away. Von groaned into my mouth as I bit his lower lip, drawing it out a little just how he liked it. He was a glow of blue and gold. Von was all the gold I needed.

The streaks of paint and swells of violins transported us to our park – the special place we shared when we hallucinated. We were a tumble of limbs that were frantic to get at each other. We rolled in the grass as our lips and hips stayed fused together, fighting for dominance as we flipped to him on top, then me, then him. It felt right, like comfort mingled with exhilarating danger.

I couldn't get close enough, couldn't make him understand with my lips and my body just how much I'd missed him, and needed to be with my best friend through the very low lows I'd endured.

"We weren't meant to be apart," Von said, pacing himself as his lips moved to my neck. "Let's never do that again."

"Never," I promised, seeking friction he was withholding just to make me crazy. "Closer," I begged. "I need you."

"It's all I can do not to tear your clothes off and make love to you right here."

"Do it," I taunted, working off his shirt so I could see and feel the wondrous body I adored.

"I'll not take your virginity in Finn's bedroom."

I opened my eyes and looked around at the surreal setting. The blue-painted trees with purple and pink leaves swayed slowly around us, bathing us in nature's confetti to celebrate our reunion. "We're not in Finn's bedroom; we're in our park. Make love to me again."

Von growled low and deep, his lips kissing me roughly with abandon. "I can't be sure I'm not doing this in real life. When you punched me last time to wake me out of our dream, I ended up with a bruise the next day. That's quite the left hook you've got."

"Huh?" The colors started vibrating, going from dull to super bright like a slow-moving strobe light. The sensory input was overloading me, making my stomach churn in ways I couldn't ignore. "Wait! Wait, stop!" I rolled away from him, his hair a perfect mess as we both blinked the blur of the park away and came back to the floor of Finn's room.

"What's wrong? Did I hurt you?"

"No, I'm going to be sick." I scrambled to my feet and stumbled to the bathroom, making it just in time to empty the meager contents of my stomach into the toilet. My only solace was that I'd managed to swing the door closed to limit an audience. I'd just cleaned the floor myself the day before, so there hopefully weren't too many germs sticking to my knees and hands.

Von let himself into the bathroom, his shirt tugged on in a hurry and his hair rumpled from our horizontal rumble. "Oh, bollocks! Are you alright?"

"'m fine. Go on out. You don't want to be here for this."

Von ignored me and gathered my hair into his fist, making me love him even more as another wave hit me all over again. I cringed as I gripped the toilet, holding on for dear life as I degraded myself in front of my non-boyfriend. "Did you eat some bad fish or something?"

"Ugh! Don't say fish." I braced myself for the next roil, but thankfully there was nothing in me left to throw up.

"So embarrassing. I can't believe you came in here, staying for the whole disgusting show."

"I'm not going to leave you when you need me most."

Yes, you will. I flushed the toilet and looked across the bowl at him, grateful for so many reasons, and he was at the top of that list. "You love me?"

"I think we proved that on the floor of Finn's bedroom. That's going on my top ten list of coolest places I've ever made out with a woman. Captain Finn's bedroom. How many people can say that?" He shook his head at himself. "I should've listened to Danny. He said he and Mariang couldn't find each other if either of them had been drinking. I didn't think it would apply to sleeping pills, but it was the only way I could sleep without you next to me. I was trying everything to reach you, but maybe I'm the reason we couldn't find each other. I'm sorry, darling." He frowned in concern. "Aw, you're white as a sheet." He felt my forehead for a temperature, pulling my stress over the bathroom germs that were now crawling all over me, and making me love him even more. "Come. Let's get you washed up, yeah?"

"Thanks." I leaned against the sink and Von as he helped me to stand so I could wash my hands up to my elbows. I brushed my teeth probably too many times, but, you know, barfing.

I looked up into his eyes when I finished rinsing my mouth the last time, noticing something slightly off. "Your gold eye. It's different. I mean, it's still gold, but there are flecks of blue in there now." I frowned. "It didn't used to be like that. Your one eye was completely gold. How'd that happen?"

Von shrugged. "I don't know. Worried me at first, but I've been feeling so much stronger in my resolve to stay human lately. I don't know what did it, but in the past month, I haven't been so bloodthirsty. I can get by on one blood bag a day. Sometimes less. When the Ekeks bled me dry, that was rough, but even that I bounced back from far quicker than usual." He shook his head. "I don't understand it, but I'm not about to question a little of life's mercy."

"Seriously? One blood bag a day?" My spirits lifted at the beautiful thought that perhaps Von would be able to control himself far easier – that he wouldn't be temporary, but a permanent fixture by my side. "Von, that's the best thing I've heard in a long time. See? I knew you could control your cravings."

"I'm working on it." His arm remained around my hips, his hand supporting me as I leaned into him when he led me out to the couch in the living room, setting me down gently. I would've told him not to baby me, but I'd spent too much time missing him and thinking he'd moved on to care about pride. "Easy, now. Do you want me to get you a trash bin in case you need to blow chunks again?"

Garrick brought me a piece of dry bread and a glass of water, as he always did after I barfed. "She should be alright. She usually only throws up once in the morning, then she's okay for the rest of the day."

I took the bread with gratitude, chewing slowly before testing my stomach with the water. "Thanks, Garrick."

"Usually?" Von asked in time with Mason, who came out of the kitchen with a sympathetic smile for me that was laced with concern.

"Mason!" I was slower to close the gap between us, pacing myself so I didn't throw up all over him. I squeezed him around the neck, glad that he was gentle when he hugged me. "I missed you." And I truly had. I missed the smile in his slate eyes that had no agenda, and finally, there it was.

"Oh, *hani*. Never again. This whole you getting kidnapped thing? It's not for me. Let's not have that happen again, alright?"

"Oh, fine. If you insist." I leaned up to kiss his cheek, but his lips met mine in a closed-mouth gesture of friend-ship that told me how scared he'd been, despite his efforts not to be outwardly emotional. In that simple kiss, I could feel us forgiving each other, moving from the rocky abyss to something more solid we could actually lean on without the foundation crumbling.

"What's this about you getting sick? Huh, even pulling from you, I feel something different." Mason asked as he led me back to the couch.

"It's nothing. Just a stomach bug."

Garrick waved off my answer and pursed his lips. "Yeah. It should go away in about nine months."

"Shut up, Garrick. Don't start with that nonsense again."

Von looked from me to Garrick in confusion. "What nonsense?"

"They don't know?" Garrick pointed to Von and Mason with a "you're busted" face.

"It's nothing. Finn and Garrick were teasing me earlier. Don't pay attention to them."

Finn came out from his bedroom, dressed and ready to go, his knife strapped to his thigh outside of his black pants. "We ready to talk about the plan?"

"Sure, but then we get her out of here. Ezra's anxious to have her back at the mansion. She's been in Dagat too long." Mason plopped down next to me on the couch, his stomach rumbling. "Forgot to give you these." He tugged my prescription bottle out of his pocket that was sealed in a Ziploc, and I nearly cried.

"Thank you! Poor Garrick does his pulling thing all day, and by morning, it's like he hasn't done a thing." I shook a small pill out into my hand, downing it quickly as the relief spread over me at finally being within arm's reach of not feeling so neurotic anymore. "Thanks, guys. That's exactly what I needed. Go Team Terraway."

Von sat down next to me, his arm draping around the back of the couch behind my shoulders casually after he relit his cigar and took a puff. I wanted to smell like Von, to bathe myself in his scent. With both of them actively pulling, I felt lighter than air, soaring away from my OCD, and not questioning my actions at all as I leaned my chin toward Von, silently asking him for a puff of the cigar I'd missed. He put the stick to my lips, both of us jumping when Finn barked, "What are you doing? You know you can't smoke when you're pregnant."

I choked on the mouthful of smoke I accidentally inhaled while both men flanking me on the couch went completely rigid. "Would you knock it off with that? They're going to think you're serious."

Finn threw his head back, pacing the living room. "I *am* serious! I know you're pregnant, you know you're pregnant, Mason's stomach probably already knows you're pregnant."

As if on cue, Mason's stomach rumbled.

Von shot up from the couch, livid. "Who've you had sex with?" He cast around the room for the culprit. "Was it Finn? Did you sleep with Finn while we were off burying my brother and killing all the Manas we could get our hands on so we could bring you home?"

Finn puffed out his chest. "She could do worse. What's it to you who she's having sex with?"

"Because she's my girlfriend!" Von shouted, aiming his anger anywhere and everywhere.

I scoffed, affronted. "Excuse me? I thought you were allergic to that word. Don't go throwing it around when it's convenient. It's either all in or all out, and you took your-self out."

Von winced. "Well, you're almost that. We were headed in that direction."

"Not good enough," I argued with a glower.

"You're the non-boyfriend? You're the one who kept her on hold? You?" Finn scoffed. Then he turned to me, indignant. "This clown? This is the love of your life? Give me a break!"

I leaned forward, my head in my hands as my elbows rested on my knees. "Oh, this is so out of hand. Seriously, I'm not pregnant. And Finn, I told you I was seeing some-one. Here he is, in the flesh. Someone. Von, calm down. I don't know why Garrick and Finn thought it'd be funny to tease me about being pregnant, but it's time for the joke to die. You guys, the astronauts in outer space, science, and the friggin' Easter bunny all know I'm a virgin."

"You didn't have sex with Finn?" Von challenged, waving his cigar in Finn's direction as he gestured with his hands.

"Of course not! I would never do that to you. Give me a break. Do you even hear yourself?" I lowered my eyes to the floor to muscle out the very private thing that was now public. "We've kissed, which I have every right to do, but nothing more."

Garrick held up his hands. "If she doesn't know, that's one thing. Mason, you'd be able to tell. You're Matruculan.

You know what the hunger's like around a fetus. Do you feel it?"

Mason showed me his hand before slowly moving it to my stomach, as if his palms had sonar or something to be able to detect a baby moving inside of me. His eyes widened as they met my confused ones. "Why didn't you tell me?"

Von jerked Mason up, not caring that Mason was bigger. "You knocked up my girlfriend? I stepped aside when you wanted to be with her, even though I knew we would be right together. How could you?" Then before anyone could stop him, Von took a swing at Mason, snapping his head to the side.

Mason's gaze slowly returned to Von, both men glaring with their nostrils flared and fists clenched. "You get one of those in your lifetime. I hope you enjoyed it."

I leapt up and shoved Von away from Mason. "Von, stop! I'm not having sex with Mason. Jeez, are you insane?" Then I turned, touching Mason's sore cheekbone. "Honey, are you okay?"

"I'm fine. A swat from a very stupid, reckless fly." Mason leaned into my palm while he glared at Von, choosing not to retaliate, thankfully. "Von, you're a fool if you think I'd try to mess October up any more than I already have. Even kissing her was too much for us to handle. Of course we haven't had sex." Then he lowered his face to look at me, his expression one of no negotiations. "But she is pregnant."

43

BRAWLING BULLS AND BREAKING CURSES

Von was livid, which didn't help the situation any, since it was a tossup which dude was angriest. I was at a loss as to why Mason would say I was pregnant when I knew I couldn't be. I tried to keep my head down and my mouth shut, since everyone else seemed to think arguing with each other and barking at me was a swell idea.

Garrick had to be the only adult in the room and took up the task of calming us all down so we could talk rationally. "Go to your corners! Everyone pick a spot and march." He pointed to the wall, lowering his arm only when we were all in our separate spaces. Mason was angry at Von, Finn was miffed at me and annoyed with Von, Von was mad at all of us, especially me. Me? I was just plain lost.

I'd gone from having one casual guy my whole life to

being in a room where it would be feasible for an outsider to think I'd been with any one of the three men who were now in my life. I didn't like how that felt one bit. I don't think Mrs. Brady ever had this problem.

When Garrick was satisfied no one would try to hit anyone else, he took the floor. "Alright. We're not discussing the pregnancy issue anymore, since clearly everyone's got their heads up their arses. Everyone assume October's pregnant, which means no fighting around her, got it?" When no one responded, Garrick clapped his hands together, his voice deepening and barking out at us. "I can't hear you, soldiers!"

We responded with various tones of "Sir, yes sir!"

"That's more like it. Now Finn and I've got a plan. He's been trying to disband the harem, but Banak's not pleased. It's time Banak and his son are taken off the throne. We all know it. Terraway knows he's a selfish pervert, and that Finn does everything the king should be doing for Dagat."

"I'll burn this place down before I see Finn on the throne in Banak's place," Von spat. "I'll not trade one bloody asshole for another."

Finn's eyes narrowed with too much attitude. "That's not how Dagat works, you idiot. There's a system in place. I wouldn't rule after Banak. If I could, do you think he'd still be alive?"

"You can't kill Banak. You're under his control." Von snarled at Finn, not bothering to hide his superior disgust.

Finn straightened, and I groaned, knowing the catastrophe that was going to tumble out of his mouth. "Actually, my curse was broken. It seems the woman who wasn't good enough to be your girlfriend has a little gift. October kissed me, and it broke my curse." He looked up at the ceiling as if in thought. "Not our first kiss, but the one where I sucked on her tongue. That's the one that did it. The ones after that were just for fun."

I kept my head down, moving my chin from side to side. "Oh, you are such a jerk."

All three men whipped their heads to gawk at Finn, then at me.

I thought Von would spout something cruel to either one of us, but he touched his lips as his eyes saw something in his memory. "That explains it. My bloodlust is far less. I used to need three blood bags a day, and even then I could smell October's blood when she walked into a room. But since we kissed... Yes. That makes sense. I'm down to one blood bag a day now, and I haven't felt the urge to tear into your neck for any nefarious reasons so far."

I met his eyes with unconcealed hope. "Do you think there's a chance? There's a chance you'll live a normal life-span? We get to keep you?"

Von softened at my words and returned my gaze with his own that was filled with affection. "It looks to be that way. I didn't know an Omen's kiss could break a curse." He pointed to the blue flecks polluting his gold eye. "That explains the discoloration. I'm still part vampire, but I'm at least more than half me now."

Finn was none too pleased with this conversation. "Could we get back on track?"

Von turned back to the room. "Where were we? Oh, right. Killing Banak, and why it's not been attempted before."

"No one's killed Banak because I protect him, and also his son's even worse." Finn's full lips twisted into an evil smile. "But you already know Prince Julius' dark side."

Von's fists tightened, and I saw the spring before it happened. Von lunged from across the room at Finn, and I stood back and let him. Von had been sold into sexual slavery to a very cruel man. Finn deserved what he got making cracks about it.

Garrick and Mason acted as referees and finally as restraints for the two while I remained in my corner with my arms crossed. "Look, it was a bad plan to begin with, guys. Kudos to you for trying, but we can't even work together to *discuss* a plan, much less execute it."

Garrick shot me a look of frustration for being unhelpful once the guys were back to their corners. "As I was saying, we need to take out Banak and his son to end the rule. After they're gone, the throne will fall to Mathias of the Green Lakes."

"Mathias? But he's at least eighty years old!" Mason protested.

"Exactly. He won't keep the harem, and it'll give Finn enough time to get someone suitable for ruling ready for the task. We've already discussed a few names. Any objections to Mathias of the Green Lakes? How about Henri Clearwater to replace him when he passes?"

Mason tilted his head from side to side, weighing the options while Von remained focused only on his fury. Mason finally nodded, his arms crossed. "I think that could work. Really, anyone's a better candidate than Banak's son. But how?"

Garrick addressed Mason, since he seemed to be the only rational one. "That's where you guys come in, or more specifically, this one," he said, pointing to Von.

"Me? For what? I'm not staying in Dagat a moment longer than I have to."

"You wouldn't stick around to kill Prince Julius?"

Von exchanged his fuming for intrigue as his ears perked up. "How's that, now?"

"We need to make it look like Banak and his son fought and killed each other. Otherwise we'll be in the same boat as Lumipad when civilians murdered Sylvia. We don't want to undermine the whole idea of the monarchy; we just want the poison replaced with an antidote," Finn explained, his anger cooling. "I'll pick one of the stronger, more prone to fight girls from the harem to give to Banak for the night. And if you're up for it, Von, I'll bring you in as a gambler with too much debt you can't pay, just like the last time. Only this time I'll make sure you're armed with a knife."

"Like *what* last time?" Mason asked, in the dark about the truth concerning Von's previous time in Dagat.

"No! Stop this right now!" I shouted, stomping my foot. Von quietly and succinctly explained his time in Dagat to Mason, who paled. I was livid that Von's private business was being spilled out for open dissection. "I already said last night that's not an option. Where do you get off asking Von to do something like that? Who do you think you are? I expected this from you, Finn, but Garrick? You're supposed to be a good guy."

Garrick leveled his gaze at me. "I am a good guy. I'm giving Von the opportunity for revenge, letting him be a key player in taking a corrupt monarchy down. There's not many who deserve to deliver the final blow more than him."

"You're horrible for asking Von to be in the same room as that criminal! I work with sex offenders. Most of them fake remorse when it suits them and go right back to their old habits as soon as no one's looking. Only this guy has no prison to be afraid of. Julius doesn't even have to fake giving up his disgustingness. I'll check myself into the harem and put an end to it all before I let Von volunteer himself again. I'm telling you right now, I won't have it. I won't let it happen."

Von broke our stick-to-your-corners rule and made a beeline for me, sweeping me up in a grand kiss that neither of us were prepared for the fallout of.

Kissing the love of your life, I've learned, can be problematic when you're trying to indulge in a grand union that spans more than one level of consciousness. On the first collision of our lips, the hallucination took us both under, ripping us from Finn's home and transporting us to our park where Von's tongue tied mine as he searched for a way to tell me without words that he appreciates me.

I appreciated the crap outta him, and wasted no time showing him just how much. "You love me," he whispered.

"Of course I do, you idiot."

His lips couldn't bear to be parted from mine for even a few seconds, so he spoke quickly. "I know the kind of love it takes to offer yourself up in someone's place."

"I won't let them take you."

When the kiss picked up the pace, Von slammed me against our tree, knocking the wind from me while simultaneously spurring me on for more. I always wanted more.

It wasn't until Von was ripped away from me that the beauty lost its gold and blue sparkle, crashing us back to Dagat where I tried to come down from the high gracefully. I reached for his outstretched arms that were trying to grab for me, but Mason and Finn held him back while Garrick restrained me. "Let me go!" I shouted. "Von! No! Don't take him!" I clawed at Garrick, unable to tear my eyes from Von.

"Give her back to me! We weren't meant to be apart." Von was just as desperate to get to me as he thrashed in Mason and Finn's grip. They were wild-eyed and looked a wash of confused and borderline scared at our ravenous hunger for each other.

I couldn't help it. I flipped a switch or something. I

mean, he was Mr. Brady, for crying out loud. Who could be demure around that kind of sex appeal?

"Get your bloody hands off her, Garrick! I'll kill you!"

Garrick jerked me backward, indignant. "Would you listen to yourself? Get a grip, Von! I'm not hurting her, but you will if you slam her up against the wall like that again. She's pregnant, mate! You have to be gentler. And maybe don't snog like rabbits when you've got a roomful of people watching."

"Huh?" Von slowed his struggle. "I didn't slam her against the wall. It was in the hallucination. And if she says she's not pregnant, then I believe her. November doesn't lie to me."

Garrick's grip slackened, the chump, and I broke free and ran to Von, crashing into his arms. The smell and the sight of him felt like the home I'd been ripped from too many times. "I'm not lying," I promised. "I've never had sex with anyone in real life. Only in my hallucinations."

Von rubbed my back, kissing every part of my face except my lips, for fear we'd slip into our craze again. "Since that first kiss, it's been only you for me. I tried everything to find you in my dreams, but I couldn't. Never again. We don't split up again. It killed me, not being able to go in and rescue you from that house Serena had you in. Killed me, Peach!" He gripped me hard, grinding his teeth. "I'll do whatever it takes to get my blood cravings under control. I'm nearly there as it is. I don't like having to stay away when you're bleeding. It was torture to know you were barely alive, and I couldn't do a thing to save you."

I squeezed him, disregarding the very intimate conversation we were having in full view of everyone. "I wasn't all that bad off. Everyone just overreacts because I'm the Omen. I'm good as new now. See?" I smiled up at him, looking into the pools of gold and blue I couldn't get enough of. Von had never looked at me like that before, with such unswerving devotion. I thought I understood loyalty and oaths, but the mere look in his eyes took my meager definition to the next level.

Finn cleared his throat. "She's lying, by the way. Buckets of lies. She *is* pregnant. And Serena carved her up with a knife. The skin was almost peeling clean off across her whole back. They'd beaten her so badly, there was more blood and bruises to her than regular skin. I found her holding a dead man, covered in blood from head to toe, her back almost skinned off, half naked, starved and probably a few hours away from death."

I cast Finn a baleful look as Von gripped me tighter. "Finn, he doesn't need to know that. I'm fine now. That's the important thing."

Von sunk down to his knees before me, hugging my butt and pressing my abdomen to his cheek. "No, no, no, no..."

Finn stood next to us, his arms crossed over his chest. "Point is, it was good you stayed back. As much as you're beating yourself up for it all now, you made the right call. I got her out and ported her right to the palace, ran her in and got her fixed up. It's the only reason she's alive now."

Von kissed my left hipbone and stood, slowly meeting Finn's eyes and extending the hand that wasn't wrapped around me. "Thank you for saving her."

I could see the amount of putting aside old horrors this took for Von, to shake hands and be grateful for the man who'd sold him into slavery to Julius. But Von was a bigger man than most gave him credit for. I clung to him as if I feared he might be ripped from my arms again. Which, given the state of the last month, wasn't too far a stretch.

Finn snarled at Von's offer of gratitude and bygones. "I didn't do it for you."

Von shrugged. "I'm still grateful." Von gripped Finn's hand, a hard line to his jaw. "This thing you want me to do? Sell me back to Prince Julius so I can gut him?"

"Yeah?" Finn had a challenge in his eyes as the brawling bulls clutched hands beyond a normal time limit.

"I'm in."

44

OWNING FINN

It was a long time of me pleading with no one who would listen, and Von going through the plan with Finn over and over. Mason eventually escorted me to the kitchen where he made us both a sandwich. I tried to fight off horrible mental images of unspeakable things happening to the man I loved. Mason tried consoling me, but I was numb to any kind of talk that led to Von handing himself over to his former tormenter.

When the time came to go, Finn pulled me into the bedroom while the others were readying themselves for the boat ride over. "Are you packed?" he asked, not meeting my eyes. He looked like he was building up to what he really wanted to say, which gave me no uncertain amount of discomfort.

"I didn't come here with anything, so there's nothing to

pack. I came here with barely the skin on my back." I slapped my knee at my terrible joke. "Sorry. Just a little torture humor."

Finn didn't crack a smile. "The clothes I gave you. Take them."

"Are you sure?"

Finn shrugged, his hands in his pockets. He looked younger when he did that, his insecurity somehow making him more impish than dominating. "What am I going to do with them?" His eyes combed my form that was clad in a too tight white t-shirt and yet another short skirt. This one was light green to match his eyes, and despite the fact that my legs were on display, I actually liked this skirt. "One favor? I know you weren't comfortable wearing the nightgowns around me that I brought for you, but it would rip my heart out if you wore them for Von."

I pursed my lips at the very adult conversation. I'd gone from kissing one casual boy my whole life to a legit man buying me sexy nightwear. It was a steep incline, and not one I was totally comfortable with. I banded my arms around my stomach. "I completely understand. And thank you for buying that stuff for me. The nightgowns really are beautiful."

Finn nodded in reply, but said nothing more on the subject.

"Thank you for putting me up here, and for getting me into the healing waters. I honestly would probably still be in the hospital if it weren't for you, if not, you know, six feet under."

He rubbed the back of his neck, still not looking at me. "Look, you told me you were with some guy, but I didn't know the level of... whatever that was between you two. I wouldn't have... Or maybe I would've tried even harder. I don't know. Point is, I shouldn't have pushed so hard. I'm sorry. I didn't get it, but I do now. Whatever Von's putting you on hold for? It won't last. He's smitten."

I nodded slowly. "Forgiven. I'm sorry, too. I let my crush on you get a little out of hand." I tilted my head to the side and gazed up at him in surprise. "That was nice of you. You're actually trying to be a good friend to me. I see it, and thank you."

"It's the only way I get to keep you in my life, so I'll take what I can get."

I tried to plead with him using my eyes, and when that didn't work, I resorted to more words I knew he wouldn't listen to. "I don't like this plan. You're handing Von over to that disgusting perv, using him as bait."

Finn held out his hand to me, motioning me to him. When I wrapped my arms around his middle, sinking into his embrace, we both sighed at the contact. Somewhere through the ups and downs, we'd become friends who could lean on each other. I knew that Finn didn't have many of those, so I gave him a reassuring squeeze. His voice was rough and laced with emotion. "I'll do what I can to make sure we get Von out. My guards will be posted outside the door. We can trust them, *sinta*. This is the best way."

"Who are you going to get to off Banak?"

"I've got a few solid options of women he hasn't sucked the will to live out of. I don't know them well, though. I'm worried I'll choose the wrong one, and he'll overpower them. Then we're really up a creek."

I shuddered. "For what it's worth, I'm proud of you for stopping it all. Not so much the murdering part, but the whole disbanding the harem thing. It was the right thing to do, and you're so strong to've done it." I rubbed my hand down his spine. "I'm sorry about your mama."

Finn stiffened, and then became pliable in my arms once more after the circles I rubbed into his back calmed him. He brushed his lips to mine, just lightly enough that we didn't take each other under. "You'll stay in the boat with Garrick and Mason. I don't want you anywhere near Banak ever again. He's got a thing for a pair of great legs. I almost snapped when he demanded to sleep with you. I need him to believe he still owns me, and that wouldn't have helped."

"Don't worry about me. Worry about Von. I mean it, Finn. He has to be okay. He has to. I need him to make it through this."

"You know I'll give you anything that's important to you." He cast me a wounded look. "You know you own me now." He leaned down and kissed my cheek, making me blush as I stepped away. I moved to the dresser to pack up my short skirts, form-fitting tops and lacy nightgowns he'd gotten me to wear. I didn't look at him again, closing my eyes and exhaling when he left for the living room.

45

MASON'S HAND ON MY BUTT

I came out a few minutes later, ready with a new "let's rethink this terrible plan" argument. I looked around, but didn't see my favorite vampire. "Where's Von?" I checked in the kitchen, calling to Mason. Dude was on the couch with his head laid back as he looked up at the ceiling.

"Finn took him. Left us with the boat."

"What?" I ran out to the living room, gaping at Garrick and Mason, who didn't look the least bit concerned at my burgeoning wrath. It was like they wanted me to sprout six heads and breathe fire down upon them, which is just about what I proceeded to do, if you can imagine it. "Which of you crackheads thought that was a good idea? Since when do we split up? Can we call them back?"

"Nope." Mason stood, cracking his neck and stretching

his arms over his head like we had all the time in the world to shrug through the upheaval. "We'll take the boat and meet them at the palace. Garrick and I are helping with the cleanup."

"Well, let's move!" When both of them reached for me to pull some of my fury, I snapped. "Don't you even think about it! I'm taking all this rage and using it for something good. Stand back if you know what's good for you."

Mason raised an eyebrow at me, and said nothing as he reached out and tweaked my nose, as if my fury was adorable. I slung my waterproof sack over my shoulder, shooting Mason a don't-mess-with-me glower. I was running out of time and options, still unwilling to let Von subject himself to the terrible plan.

"The boat's tied to the side of the house. I'll go out first, and Mason, you take the rear." Garrick shoved his socks and shoes in my pack to keep them dry, as did Mason.

"Um, problem. Do we have to swim to get in the boat?"

Garrick nodded, hand on the door. "Of course. Is that an issue?"

"Only inasmuch as I can't swim."

Mason sniggered under his breath, earning a light harrumph from me. "It's fine, *hani*. I'll take you." He nodded to Garrick, wrapping an arm around my waist as Garrick opened the door to the submerged basement. "Don't worry. It's a short swim to the boat. Just hold your breath. Maybe twenty seconds, and we're there."

The basement was pitch black without Finn's fingers to light the way. I didn't want the guys to know I was punking out, so I didn't ask Mason to light up his fingers for me. I was nervous stepping into the basement, something twisting in my gut to warn me away. "Twenty seconds?" I asked, clinging to Mason.

He chuckled and pecked my lips in that we've-been-married-for-decades kind of way I adored him for. "Twenty seconds, little chicken. I'm right here." He held me tight to his side, smiling through a dramatic big inhale we did in unison before he dunked us under the water.

Let me tell you a little story about holding your breath for twenty seconds. It might as well be a hundred years. I held tight to Mason, unable to see through the murky basement. I had to just trust he knew where he was going. He swam not as fast as Finn, but well enough to support two bodies. He gripped me tighter as he dragged us through the door, shutting it behind him. There was light now. The clear blue water guided us upward where I could see the bottom of the boat that was our destination. Garrick's legs disappeared from the water as he boarded, and my lungs felt like they might burst if we didn't reach him in the next handful of seconds. Mason pinched my side just to freak me out, grinning when our heads broke the surface.

The fresh air was a welcome relief, but I couldn't feel calm until I was in the boat. Something brushed against my thigh, making me squirm. "Knock it off, Mason. I'm freaked out enough as it is."

"Knock what off?"

Now there was a clear hand on my butt that swooped down the slope of my thigh. "Not cool, dude." I reached for Garrick, who leaned over the edge of the boat to pull me up.

"What are you talking about?"

"I can feel you grabbing my butt!"

"You're imagining things. Got her, Garrick?"

Garrick gripped my palm, but no sooner did he lift me two inches upward did something jerk me down, forcing a scream out of me. "Help!"

Mason kicked out, making contact with something that I could hear letting out a sound like a rippling growl. "Mermen! Get her in the boat!" He pushed me up while Garrick pulled, but the hand tugging on my ankle was determined. If this were a fight on land, I would've been more clearheaded about the whole thing, but the sea was completely out of my element. I panicked, screaming and kicking as I clung to Mason, who started grunting, livid at our unexpected foe. "Got her?" he called to Garrick.

"Kind of!"

That was all the assurance Mason needed to give up on being a human and transform into a wolf. I'd been holding onto him with one arm while Garrick secured my other hand, but Mason slipped out from my grip when the hair grew coarse, and his nose and mouth mutated into a wolf's snout. He dove down toward the hand that jerked on my leg, and pretty soon I felt two hands, then three, then five grabbing at me. It was too much for Garrick, who shouted as I slipped through his fingers. I gathered up one deep breath before the water closed over my head.

46

THE MADNESS OF MERMEN

’d seen a lot of craziness in my day, giving me no doubt at all why the Brady Bunch was my favorite show. The iconic housewife with the help of a maid, the loving father who always came home and never abandoned his kids, the kids whose biggest problems were usually of the variety that could be solved in half an hour. I knew with absolute certainty that not one of the Brady Bunch had ever been pulled under the water by a gang of tattooed fish Mermen mutants.

I say mutants because the Mermaids, from the distance I’d seen them at, were your typical Disney variety. The Mermen, or Siyokoy, as I recalled from Finn’s lessons, had the standard green and iridescent scaly fishtails, normal man torsos, but on top they weren’t the male counterpart of the pretty Mermaids. They had green tints to their skin, and their heads were mutated to look strikingly like a human mixed with a giant guppy. They had enormous mouths and lips, with tentacles stretching out from their elbows and faces. They had gills all the way up their necks and even peppering their ears like tiny slices from a razor. They were horrifying.

The ones that grabbed at me were tattooed with markings that looked like a bird in various stages of flight. It would've been poetic if they weren't grabbing at parts of me I tried to keep off the map, and pulling me down faster than I could struggle away.

I screamed into the clear blue abyss, not sure if I was grateful or more scared when one of them breathed air into my mouth as Finn had. It kept me alive, but for what? The Siyokoy whose mouth was on mine had too many sharp teeth, each one jutting out at janky angles like a shark in desperate need of braces. My wolf bit clean through the dude's ear, raking his teeth down his shoulder and chomping into his side, shaking his head with vigor as the Siyokoy howled his pain and dropped his grip on me.

Now there were only three of them, and from what I could tell, the leader was shouting out orders to take me deeper where Mason couldn't get at me after my wolf went back to the surface for a breath.

I thrashed as best I could, trying to strategize as my fear of drowning came full circle. I had no weapons, and my movements were labored and slow in the water, while the Siyokoy were quick. My scar from Kabayo glowed, drawing the eyes of the Merman who held me. I wanted Kabayo to somehow come to our rescue, but knew he was in a completely different country. And mighty as he was, I wasn't totally sure how stellar my favorite horse could swim in comparison to a fish.

My eyes locked in on the one who was calling the shots. He had a sinister smile that, as soon as I stopped panicking, I knew I'd be creeped out by. He had a flat nose like the others, but unlike his friends, he had a face tattoo of a wave that went straight up between his eyes and I'm guessing finished on the back of his bald head. It was him – the Merman Finn had too many run-ins with. Atius of the Western Waves. The facial tattoo was a dead giveaway, but so was the calculated malice in his glassy eyes.

"You're Finn's pair of legs. He's had enough luxuries," Atius ruled. Though we were underwater, he spoke clearly. "He took our wives and daughters into his harem? You're ours now." He turned to the Merman who restrained me from behind. "Go ahead and make good use of her legs, boys. Send Captain Finn her clothes as a souvenir."

I screamed, thrashing around so they couldn't make heads or tails of where they could grab me, though they hit their jackpots quite a few times, tearing my shirt in the process. Of all the things I'd survived, I vowed to myself I wouldn't go out like this, my life ending with a tragic barely-there splash. I'd worked too hard to die now. I had too much left to do, too many wrongs to right.

I reached into the mouth of the man who'd been breathing for me once he pulled away for a second. Without thinking it all the way through, I yanked on his slithery snake tongue, surprised I could wrap it around my wrist. His head flung back in pain. He could've easily bit down on my arm, but he hadn't counted on needing to defend himself against me – the girl who couldn't swim. I yanked on his tongue, pulling something that wasn't meant to be ripped so heartlessly. I sawed his long tongue against his upper row of teeth, shrieking when he tried to bite at me, but dude only managed to slice open his own tongue. I wasn't able to remove his tongue completely, but I'd done something that damaged him enough to render his mouth and his concentration useless. He fell away from me, hand over his mouth as he cried out in a deep howl. The pained sound had a simultaneous high-pitched screech to it that made me cringe.

Now the man who'd been breathing for me was temporarily down. I wasn't sure if I should rejoice about that one just yet.

Garrick was bleeding; I hadn't seen how he'd been hit, but it didn't seem to deter him. He swam with his knife clutched in his hand. He reached for Atius, brushing the Merman in charge with what I'm guessing was a bliss-level dose of pulling. I was fascinated and terrified all in one go.

Once the top Merman was subdued, Garrick stabbed him in the gut and ripped downward, cutting a slice from his belly button down to where his knees would be. Purple strings and slime bubbled out of the broken fishtail like the worst kind of carbonation. The others yelled and turned away from trying to rid me of my clothes so they could attack Garrick. Mason bit down into one of their tails, ripping off half the dude's flipper like the barbarian my wolf Viking was.

The Mermen were pissed and dropped me to converge on Garrick, who was going up to the surface for another breath. Just before he broke the surface, they yanked him under.

Mason swam to my flailing form, waiting until I grabbed onto his fur before he moved us upward. I knew he was struggling for air, but his slate eyes remained determined, never panicking as he remained ever my beacon of strength. He guided us through the water, leaving Garrick to fend them off as best he could.

When our heads broke the surface, Mason doggy-paddled me to the boat, nudging me up and giving me a look of almost satisfaction that I was safe before he disappeared below to go help out Garrick. I shivered in my shock and fright. The cool sea air hit me before the horrors of the traumatic happenings did. I screamed into my hand, counting the seconds Garrick went without oxygen. I rocked back and forth, trying to calm myself but knowing it was impossible at this point. Every breath that dragged in and out of my lungs was a blessing I didn't take for granted.

I held myself, realizing that my shirt was torn clear

open and my skirt had been hiked up around my ribs. I shuddered to think of the permanent damage that could've been done as I situated my clothing, holding my white t-shirt closed. I was shivering so hard, my muscles started convulsing. Tears fell down my cheeks as I wondered what they could possibly have wanted my legs for if they only had fins. They had a rapey M.O., but I couldn't puzzle through the mechanics of just what they expected they'd be able to do.

Fear. Curiosity. Insecurity. Torture. Same as every sex offender. They wanted to take Finn's prize and mangle it at the bottom of the sea. I'd never understood the minds of the rapists I'd patched up in prison, and as I shivered in the boat, clutching my shirt closed, the degradation made even less sense now.

Thirty seconds. Thirty seconds since I'd come into the boat. Surely it had to have been over a minute or even close to two since Garrick's last breath. The ocean was pissed beneath me as the fight below made waves. I held tight to the boat while all my fears smacked me in the face.

At forty seconds, I started hyperventilating, terrified for the brave men who'd tried to save me. I didn't know how to express how not worth the sacrifice I actually was.

Garrick's hand separated the small waves that rocked me, and I grabbed for it with so much zeal, I almost tipped the boat. I didn't expect Garrick to be so light, but the arm lifted from the ocean effortlessly.

I was crying with relief until I realized only his arm

came into the boat. The rest of Garrick was somewhere underneath still. Mason had pushed the arm up, his furry head just above the surface, howling out a warning I could barely hear above my unending scream.

47

A MOMENT OF SILENCE

I reached out and snatched at Mason, somehow pulling him up and over the edge of the rowboat without tipping us clean over. I kept my mouth closed through my noise of angst at the appendage and the impossibility it represented.

Garrick's arm survived, but not Garrick. "Is he... Did you see him?"

Mason nodded, nudging the paddle with his nose.

"I'm not leaving without Garrick! We have to go back down and find him! You don't know! Some people can hold their breath for minutes on end!" I was frantic for a way to undo the damage I'd somehow been part of.

Mason was at a loss for words, since he couldn't speak to me in his wolf form. He shook his fur and stretched out his neck, his gray wolfy hair disappearing as his body lengthened and became smooth. He snatched up the oars, sat his bare butt down on the bench and began paddling us toward the shore, which looked at least two miles away. "He's dead," Mason gusted out, eyes wide and muscles tensed as he rowed like a seasoned fisherman. "I saw them rip out his throat. I got his arm for his fiancé to bury, but that's all I could manage. We have to get out of here."

Mason had lost most of his supernatural strength when Geon had his hair cut, but even without the bulk of The Hulk, Mason was no one to be trifled with. His muscles bulged as he rowed us in long strokes, never stopping for a breath or looking behind him toward the shore to see if we were close.

He was naked and bleeding from his side, but didn't seem to feel any of it. He was a man on a mission, and anything outside of getting us to safety would have to be bothered with later.

I sobbed as I turned from him and fished through my pack, taking out a clean blue silk blouse and removing the ripped t-shirt that could no longer be classified as a garment. I shoved my arms through the undamaged blouse, my back to Mason as he gasped. "Is that the scar Serena left on you?"

"Oh, sorry," I answered through my tears. "I just didn't want to keep showing you my breasts. I forgot about my back. It's all healed, just a little marked up. No big deal."

He cursed under his breath as he rowed with renewed vigor. The reminder of the last time I'd been snatched away made him use everything in him to get us to safety.

Each pull of the oars caused his side to dribble with a little more fervency, his blood dripping and puddling on the floor of the boat.

I took my shredded shirt and knelt at Mason's feet, dabbing at the blood oozing from his side with trembling hands as I tried not to break down completely over the loss of Garrick. It was too sudden, too unreal. I fought with everything in me not to scream on repeat. The man who'd been telling me romantic stories about his upcoming nuptials just yesterday was now torn apart at the bottom of the sea.

Because of me. Because he'd been sent to help me.

I had to switch my focus, or I knew I'd be useless to the world. I would crawl into my den of self-loathing later, and heap the grieving and guilt atop me like a warm blanket.

Mason. He survived and no doubt needed help. His side looked like one of the Siyokoy had bit into him with his razor teeth, shredding as he gnawed. "I don't think he hit anything vital, but I need to get a closer look at this."

"It's fine. Take care of you first. Then we can worry about me," he worked out through gritted teeth as he put all his strength into rowing. He didn't stop until the boat hit the sand, gusting out a shudder of relief that we'd made it. Despite his nudity, he slid off the bench onto his knees, reached forward and grabbed me to him. Mason clutched me to his chest not to pull stress from me, but to alleviate some of his own anxiety.

I loved when he did that.

Holding each other gave us both a portion of peace and reminded us of our purpose. I hugged him back, burying my face in his neck as we shook through our adrenaline that didn't seem to see an end in sight. "Are you alright? I did everything I could, but I saw them grabbing at you, trying to take your clothes off. I'm sorry! I'm so sorry I wasn't fast enough."

"Shh. It's okay. You're safe. That's the important thing. I thought I lost you! You took so long coming back up. I thought for sure they'd... But you're here." I gripped him, unsure how we'd gotten to the point where I could hug his naked body and not feel weird about it. I suppose that's where we were in our no holds barred friendship. We knelt in the boat, sopping wet and shivering, grateful our strange partnership was solid enough to be able to give reassurance through a horrifying time in our lives.

"I'm here," he promised. "I'm sorry I couldn't save Garrick. I tried my best, but there were too many of them. Maybe if I hadn't been shaved I could've done something, but now?" He closed his eyes as he held me, ashamed. "I'm so sorry."

"Shh. It's not your fault. Hey, look at me." I angled his chin so he was staring into my eyes. "You're my hero. You saved my life, Mason. You're not responsible for saving everyone."

His hand migrated between us to my stomach, his knuckle brushing over my abdomen. "Do you think the baby's okay? I didn't see them punch you. Finn would never be the same if his baby was lost."

My nose crinkled as I brushed Mason's hand away. "I told you all, I'm not pregnant, least of all with Finn's baby. I've never had sex, Mason. Let it be."

He tilted his head to the side. "You're telling the truth, aren't you?"

"I've got no reason to lie about that."

Mason nuzzled his nose to mine, adding a touch of sweetness that increased my awareness of his nudity. "I believe you, then. But somehow, someway, make no mistake – you're pregnant, *hani*." His stomach growled. "I'm Matruculan. I can smell a fetus a mile away."

"I don't know what to tell you. You have to have sex to get pregnant, and I haven't." I kissed his cheek. We held each other tight and simply breathed, taking in the gift of oxygen with renewed appreciation. My eyes swept shut, clenching in pain. "Garrick," I whispered.

"I know. Let's take some time and just be sad for a moment."

I pressed my torn shirt into his wound while we held each other in the boat on the shore, the waves lapping and mocking us with how peaceful they sounded. The silence between us fell softly, knitting together a little of the tearing our hearts suffered at the loss of one of our teammates.

The longer we clung to each other, the more I began to see things with a sliver of clarity I'd been missing, giving my feet new purpose. "I think we should go to the palace and meet up with the others. See if they need help."

Mason released me after pressing a quick kiss to my lips. He looked down at his physique that would make any bodybuilder jealous, and gave his chest a rub before bending over on all fours. His back sprouted gray hair and his body transformed back into the wolf I loved.

I wrapped Garrick's arm in my torn and bloody t-shirt, tucked it under the bench of the boat, and ran with my backpack and my wolf toward the trees. I stumbled in the sand as my movements grew desperate and uncalculated through the trauma and exhaustion that was still hitting us in waves.

Mason howled at me to slow down, but I knew what I had to do. In the wake of Garrick's horrific death, I knew I couldn't let anyone else do dirty work I was equipped for. I wouldn't let anyone else risk their life when mine was at my disposal. A plan began to form in my mind, my fists clenching as the details cemented, giving me a clear picture of what must be done.

48

MEETING FINN'S FAMILY

I hadn't had the chance to properly appreciate the grand nature of the palace my first time there, what with me being a bloody mess on the brink of death and all. This time around, I requested to see Finn when the guard stopped me at the gate. I insisted I was the new Omen, but apparently that was something that needed to be verified by the up and ups.

Finn ran to the gate, barking that I was who I claimed to be. I ran to Finn, crashing into his arms that were stiff upon my welcome, but melded easily with my body after a few seconds. The half dozen guards with gills like his turned to gape at their fearsome captain, who was fawning over my minor abrasions. "Why are you shaking? What happened to you?"

Mason growled while I explained as best I could. "The face tattoo guy, Atius! He was waiting for us outside your house. Mason and Garrick fought them off, but they got him, Finn! They killed Garrick! They killed Garrick, cut up Mason and tried to..." I gulped, unable to work out the rest.

"What? Why?" Finn gripped my arms as if gearing up to pounce. "How'd they even know you were there? Don't they know who you are, what attacking you would do to Terraway?"

I shook my head, holding tight to Finn's shirt as he clutched me to him. "I don't think they know I'm the Omen. All they knew was that I was with you. They're pissed about the harem, so they were going to take me to hurt you."

"Take you?" he inquired, searching for the thing I didn't want to say aloud. When I stepped back and clutched my silky blue blouse to my chest and wouldn't meet his eyes, he seemed to understand for what purpose they dragged me under. Finn postured, his arm banding around me as he clicked his fingers to the guards. "You heard her. An attack was made on the Omen, which is to be treated as an attack on our soil and on the whole of Terraway. Find Atius and his men, and bring me their fins."

"Garrick and Mason killed Atius, I think, but he had four other guys with him – all Mermen."

"I'll take care of it. Don't worry about a thing. I can fix this." Finn nodded to a soldier, who was armed with a triton, a knife and a scaly breastplate. The man saluted

Finn and led a battalion of two dozen out into the water to finish the fight. "You're trembling." He ran his fingers through my hair, massaging and drying as he kissed my face. "Come in and sit down. You too, Mason."

"N-need to talk to Banak," I insisted.

"About what? No, *sinta*. You've just been through it out there. Rest a minute."

"Banak," I insisted, knowing I had a small window before my adrenaline ebbed.

Finn sighed, offering me his arm to lean on as he led Mason and me further into the palace, my pack slung over his shoulder. "You can't see him right now. He's occupied. He's been occupied with my mother since this morning before we got here." The grave note in his voice told me Banak was in his sex room making a perfect mess of the poor Mermaid's psyche. It also informed me that Banak wasn't even close to being offed, since Finn hadn't been able to swap out the victim for someone who was secretly armed.

"It's important."

Mason looked up at me with a curious tilt to his head. I was grateful he didn't have the words to ask what the crap I was doing. Finn led us down a series of corridors, my plan pushing out my panic over Garrick or the fact that Von was nowhere in sight. Finn frowned at my request. "What do you need Banak for? We're not to interrupt him unless it's a national emergency."

"This qualifies," I ruled, frustrated when Finn didn't

take me at my word. "Look, this is the only way I can bust your mother out of there. Let me help you. I can interrupt them with some Topsider crisis, and you can get your mother out of there."

Finn's eyes looked hopeful for a moment, but then crashed. "No. I'll not trade you for anyone. You'll not take her place in Banak's bed."

"Of course I won't. Let me try, Finn. This is the only way."

"No. I won't stand for his eyes on you."

"Do you think my title's for show?" I cried, pulling the I'm-a-tool card just to get him to go along with whatever I said. "If I say I need to see your king, I'm pretty sure you're not allowed to refuse me."

"So that's how it is?" Finn's jaw tightened as he nodded. "Right this way, *Lady* October."

I pinched the bridge of my nose. "That's not how it is really. I need to talk to Banak, and I can't stand here while your mother's in there. It's killing you, and I won't sit around and do nothing when I could help."

Finn's gaze softened. "You love me," he marveled.

"Please let me do this for you. I'll only be talking politics with him while you get your mother out of there."

He kissed my lips once, eliciting a low growl from Mason. "Thank you, *sinta*."

My bare feet stumbled along as we walked past light green floating tapestries on gold floors. When we stopped at the door, I took my pack from Finn, casting up a reassuring smile as I stroked his bicep, putting just enough pressure there for him not to notice me sliding out his knife from his belt. Then I gently shoved him toward the door, tucking the knife into my pack without him seeing it.

Mason saw it, though. He glanced curiously from me to the pack, silently asking why I'd pickpocketed Finn for a knife, of all things. I winked at him and nodded, hoping he understood the universal "be cool".

Finn marched through the door, which I realized was part one of two barriers that kept Banak from being disturbed. The second set of doors was flanked by two guards, who looked surprised to see their Captain accompanied by a girl and her wolf.

"Step aside," Finn ordered. "It's an emergency." I saw in the way the men bowed their heads that though Banak wore the crown, Finn was the man in charge. "This is the new Omen. Whatever she wants, see to it she gets it."

"Yes, Captain," they answered in unison, opening the door for us.

I knew I should've been prepared for the scene I walked in on, but I shrieked when I saw the mangled green and scaly legs of the midfifties-aged nude Mermaid sprawled out on the lavish bed.

I'm sure there were far better ways for me to meet Finn's mom for the first time, but there she was, unconscious and naked on the bed. There were bruises peppering her neck and body, and one eye completely swollen shut with a purple shiner. I could see a slight resemblance – the dark blonde hair, the fuller lips, and other small genetic traits that drew a clear line from mother to son.

I cringed when the king roared his frustration at being interrupted. "I'm not to be disturbed in here, Finn!"

Finn's voice was tight. "The new Omen insisted she speak with you. It's an emergency, your highness."

"Very well," Banak grumbled. "Call in the guards. I tired of this one hours ago." He motioned to Finn's mom's limp body as Finn turned away. Finn called to the guards in a pinched tone that belied only a fraction of the horror that was no doubt ripping him up inside.

The two soldiers came in, trying unsuccessfully to rouse the woman. The taller soldier pressed two fingers to her neck. "She's dead, your majesty." There was no note of accusation in his tone, only a resigned sigh that something like this had happened again.

Finn let out a choked cry I wanted to hold him through, but knew I couldn't without forfeiting my window of opportunity. "Go with him," I urged Mason, hoping he could at least give him a solid pull until I was finished with Banak.

Mason didn't listen, but planted himself at my feet, knowing I was up to something. I gripped my bag and gently moved Finn out of the room. "Go say your good-byes. I'll be there in a minute to help you bury her."

Finn's hand trembled as he gripped my arm, swallowing as the shock rippled through him in waves. "K-keep Mason with you."

"He'll be right outside the door. Just a quick conversation about empire logistics, and I'll be back by your side."

Finn looked a mixture of nauseous, shocked and defeated. The defeat part left me with a sour taste in my mouth. Finn wasn't meant for a white flag. He was strong, fierce, and had more power than he realized. He had me. He had me in his arms, on his side and by his side. He was ever the professional as he walked away, his head bent as the soldiers tried to be respectful. They carried his mother's body wrapped in the comforter down the hall toward the outside sunshine.

BAIT

I'd known quite a few sociopaths in my day, and the one thing they all had in common was the fact that they didn't like being seen as sociopaths until after they revealed their true nature. They wanted to feel sneaky, to take in their prey and go for the kill when their victim started to feel safe. There was a certain glory to the "I fooled you" surprise that they reveled in.

I knelt down and hugged my wolf, leaning in to whisper, "Stay right here outside the door. If I scream, come in and get me."

He whined, and I knew he was wishing he could talk me out of whatever it was I was up to, but ultimately, he obeyed.

Banak pulled a robe on over his enormous belly that was covered in oil and sweat, though I'd already seen him completely naked by this point. He had black cropped

Julius Caesar hair that was unflattering on pretty much everyone except old Caesar himself. He had gills, like Finn, but there was a greenish tinge to his, making them look dirty, like he hadn't showered in days. The room stank of sex and excrement, though I tried not to notice. His pig nose and round face were sweaty, his eyes leering as he took in the scope of me, noting with pleasure that we were alone. "Excuse the mess. Have a seat, milady." He made a sweeping gesture toward a gold chair in the corner.

Ollie's voice wafted in my psyche, though I'm positive his brotherly advice hadn't been meant for situations like this one. *Keep your chin up, take it slow.*

I swallowed down my flaring germ phobia as I sat down. My imagination didn't have to work too hard to conjure up what kind of filth made my butt feel like it stuck a little to the chair. "Thank you, your majesty. You've got a lovely palace."

I let Banak lock the door, his creepy smile telling me how sneaky he thought he was being, separating me from my wolf, who I could hear growling on the other side. Getting me alone in his sex room, away from Finn and the guards who were occupied burying his last conquest was a feat I could tell he was proud of himself for executing. "I assume you've come here to observe more than just my palace. What can I do for you?"

I gulped, knowing it was now or never. My nickname Bait had never been more true than it was about to be. I warned myself to breathe evenly as I undid a button on my blue silk blouse, giving Banak my best you-know-what-I'm-really-here-for eyes. I felt like a complete kid trying to seduce an old man who'd seen and had just about everything.

Everything except for legs, and I had those in spades.

"Captain Finn told me I needed to come up with a way to thank you for letting me use your healing waters before I left your land. I hope you don't mind me getting creative." I lifted my leg, extending it between us as I rubbed a muscle on my calf. "My toes are wet. Dry them for me?"

Banak's eyes widened, looking like he'd just won the lottery. It would've been flattering if the whole thing didn't wreak of ick. I was part of the ick in this scenario. I'd just sat in it, and was about to create a whole lot more cringe-worthy nonsense for what I hoped would be the greater good.

This wasn't about the kingdom anymore. This was for Finn. For Finn's mother. Whatever hesitation I'd been harboring, I knew this was my chance to stop the torture of hundreds of women and even some men who'd submitted to degradation no one should have to endure.

Banak knelt down before me. His smile showed me that though he knew he was a sociopath, he had no idea that I was perhaps a bigger one. *I* was the danger. I don't know how long the psycho in me had lain dormant, waiting for the right trigger, but Banak had tipped my sanity to the breaking point. I tripped straight into his web, letting him think I was a dainty fly, when really, I was the scorpion.

He slowly rubbed my toes, his eyes taking their time undressing me in preparation for the real show. I tried to keep my scream in my throat as Banak started licking my toes with his stubby tongue, sucking on each one as I put on the fakest smile of my life.

"Perfect." He stroked my calf, giving me the creeps. "Young and soft." He traced the inside of my knee, and I knew I was just about out of time. "We're going to have some fun, child. What a tasty treat you are."

"Let me slip into something more comfortable. I have a feeling I'll be extra grateful to you for a good long time in here." My backpack was at my feet, and I opened my knees as I slid it onto my lap, inviting him in, but not as close as he wanted to be. I cast him a coy smile, hating myself and him. Every heartbeat that banged in my chest screamed that it was now or never. I reached into my pack as he moved between my legs, his breath stinking like he hadn't bothered with hygiene for days. He gripped my thighs roughly, lifting my knees up so my pelvis was angled and exposed.

He expected me to pull out a sexy outfit to entertain him with.

The widening of his eyes before his choked cry told me he hadn't been expecting the knife that slashed across his throat before he could register what it was.

I counted on Finn to keep his knives sharp, but I'd not

done a ton of throat-slitting (some, but not a ton), much less to someone with gills as an alternative breathing apparatus. Banak's arms flung out, trying to get at me, but his hands were without direction. I tipped the chair over and ran to the other side of the room, gripping the knife and breathing through my fear of him and myself.

I didn't wait for Banak to see if he could right himself after he fell forward onto his face. He gurgled and tried to cry out for his guards, who were nowhere near, thanks to his appetite for things that didn't belong to him.

I pressed my lips together to muffle my noises of distress as I rolled him over and stabbed him through the chest, which is harder than it sounds. The first few times I hit bone, the knife not piercing its mark.

Banak's arms flailed to grab at my throat, but I shushed him. "Are we having fun yet?" I whispered. A cold note I didn't recognize from my psyche crept into my voice. Finally, Finn's knife found its new home. I felt the pop of a balloon, and Banak's arms slowly began to descend, though his mouth moved as he cursed me to the ever-loving place we don't mention in good company. "I know. I'm the bad guy," I admitted without regret. "I don't know how you got this way, but I won't let you hurt these people anymore. You let your son take Von!" I whispered, my voice shaking with rage I didn't often like to admit I was capable of. "Von could hurt a lot of people with the damage your family did to him, but he doesn't. He chose to rise above it, to let the damage stop with him. You didn't care who you hurt." I plunged the knife into his enormous gelatinous belly and slid it along the hemisphere for good measure. "Finn did everything you asked of him, and you murdered Dyesebel and his mother!" I shook my head, tears falling down my face. "How could you?"

I covered Banak with a blanket from his bed once his eyes glazed over with that awful look I'd seen after many a prison fight gone south. I clenched my fists and wished that, of all my shortcomings, I wasn't so very good at this.

WOUNDS AND WOUNDED PRIDE

I lost all sense of time until Mason whined at the door however long later. I wiped off my face and tried to calm my silent sobbing as I stood, cracking the door open and kneeling to whisper to my wolf. "Banak's dead now. Go get Finn in secret so you two can move the body to stage it for the big finale. I'll lock myself inside, so knock twice when you get back."

Mason looked from me to a space behind me where I knew he saw the sheet with one giant dead guy underneath. He let out a low growl that let me know he was medium pissed, but then rested his head on my shoulder for a brief moment of solidarity. He licked my face, trying to pull from me. "No," I ruled, backing away and closing the door. I pressed my hand to the surface and said to him through the gold-plated wood, "I deserve to feel this. Go quick, now."

Mason took my order to heart and returned not four minutes later with Finn, who scowled at me through his tears, fresh from burying his mother. "I see you did what you felt like without consulting us, as usual."

"Be as mad as you want later. Just get Banak out of here and help me clean the blood up." I caught Finn's arm. "And call Ezra. Tell him to bring Mariang down here right now. And I mean, right now."

"For what?"

"We have a small window where she can use the healing waters. I need her healthy, Finn. I can't let her die." I looked up into his glassy green eyes, unable to hide my sadness that read like exhaustion and felt like fear etched too deep to be real. "I can't do it all alone. I need help, and she deserves a full life that Terraway doesn't suck out of her."

Finn nodded as Mason trotted in, upright and clothed in black soldier's pants and a t-shirt. I didn't ask how he came into them; I was just grateful for the help. "I can do that. Thanks for finally cluing me in on a plan of yours. That's a good plan. This one?" He motioned to the sheet covering Banak on the floor. "This one was borderline suicide. We're going to have words about this after it's all over."

"Hopefully they're pretty words with plenty of prose, thanking me for doing the dirty work so you didn't have to. Just get your guys to move him. Mason? Come here."

Mason obeyed without question, for which I was grateful. I led him through the back door, giving Finn a nod to let him know we'd be back. Mason scratched a spot on his elbow. "What are we doing? Finn might need me."

"You need this more. Finn has his two guys to help move Banak." I held Mason's hand, our fingers slipping together like knots as I led him through the dark corridor. "Finger lights?" I requested, appreciative when he turned his on. We all but ran until we reached the door at the end, pushing through to the utopia of the small pool that was surrounded by beautiful rocks and jewels. "It's the healing waters. Banak's been hiding them the entire time. It's how I'm upright." I held myself through a shiver, though the room was warm and cozy. "You gave up your life for me. This is the most I can do to make up for that."

Mason's eyes went wide. "Are you serious?"

"We don't have much time. You have to get in now. And let me tell you, it hurts like your bones are being broken, and you have to keep quiet. Not a sound, Mason. Quick as you can." I turned away as he ripped his shirt and pants off. "Go all the way under. Drink some of the water, too." I bent down and scooped a handful of the water, drinking it down for good measure. I didn't know how deep the healing powers went, but if they could make me not so prone to homicide, I figured that would be a good thing for all involved.

I wasn't expecting the searing pain in my abdomen, but I gripped the edge of the pool as something hot rocketed through me. I closed my lips through my muted scream, not sure what could possibly have been damaged since the last time I'd dipped. Mason knelt beside me, holding me tight once again with no clothes on. He cupped my mouth as I grunted and howled into his hand, coming down slowly, and probably looking like a feral animal.

When the pain passed, I kissed his cheek, sweaty and worn out from just that one swallow. "Your turn. I'm going to go get Von. Just make sure you don't make too much noise." I glanced down when his stomach rumbled, blushing that he was naked again.

"Okay." He squeezed me before releasing me, his eyes on the pool. "I thought this was a myth. Thank you, *hani*. This? I'll never be able to repay you for this." Though he was naked, I didn't shirk away when he pulled me to him and pressed a closed-mouth kiss to my lips. I loved it when he did that.

"You're worth much more than this, but it's the best I can do right now."

"I love you, October."

"I love you, too, sweetie."

I DIDN'T IMAGINE BANAK'S SON WAS MORE VIOLENT THAN Banak, but when Finn made me turn around when he brought a limping Von into the secret room with the healing waters, I knew it had to be bad. "He doesn't want you to see him like this," Finn said quietly to me. "Let him keep a little of his dignity."

Finn's two trusted men moved Banak to the throne room where the dead version of Prince Julius was waiting for him. The weapons were staged to convince the country their family feud had turned fatal. Von had been waiting out the death of Banak with one dead Julius, patiently bleeding while Banak had taken his sweet time with Finn's mom.

Finn had marched Von the long way through the palace, taking circuitous routes so no one would see him walking around when he normally would've been escorted back to the harem and locked in with the other concubines.

I turned to peek as a naked Von was lowered slowly into the healing waters, his body oiled and his pride irreparably wounded. Mason dunked him under, holding him there while Von got out the brunt of his howling as the waters rebuilt him piece by piece. My heart broke for him while a raging fire of vengeance roiled inside of me, daring anyone to ever hurt him again.

When Mason finally let him up, Von was panting, revived and very much confused. He pulled on his t-shirt, boxer briefs and jeans that I'm guessing had been taken from him at some point upon his induction back into the harem. I waited until he was clothed and then ran to him, my body crashing into his. "I did it," he breathed. "I killed that snake. It's done. He'll not rape anyone now."

My arms couldn't wrap tight enough to hold him together as I knew he needed. "I'm so sorry you had to ever see his face again."

"It was worth it. Now no one else... It's over."

"Promise me that's true. That the worst of it's over."

Von cuddled me to his chest, and I could feel his love for me trumping his fear over all he'd confronted that day. "Oh, Peach. It's all smooth sailing from here."

Doubtful, I looked down at my feet at the edge of the pool, my eye catching on one of the rubies on the ledge that was completely broken off. My curious gaze was met by Mason, who was positively beaming.

THE BRADY BUNCH INCARNATE

I didn't want to be there for Mariang's screams when she dipped into the waters with Danny a couple hours later. The guards posted outside the throne room where the royal bodies were rotting still hadn't discovered the carnage inside, so we had a bit of time to make ourselves scarce.

We waited in silence in Banak's sex room until Danny joined us with Mariang. She had been carried inside, her skin almost completely translucent from three weeks of reaping for an entire kingdom with no backup. Now she was standing, looking very much alert with no hint of frailty. Her skin was normal now, if not a little pale. I'd never seen her with regular skin before, and the difference was shocking. She crashed into me with the most ferocious hug I'd ever received from the woman, thanking me in tearful whispers while Finn glared at us to shut up. Now she had a chance.

Now we both did.

Sneaking five people out of the palace was easier said than done, but Finn managed the feat with no hiccups, though Mason's stomach growled pretty much nonstop.

Finn brought us to Lang, who'd ported Danny and Mariang into Dagat. Lang had waited for us, hidden in the woods to the left so he wouldn't be associated with Banak's death.

Finn inclined his head to Von, who was attached to my side. "I need a word with her before she goes."

Von looked Finn over. "A word? Sure. But I don't port until she's safely on her way."

Lang jabbed me playfully with his elbow. "I see you've found yourself another husband or two while I was away."

"Oh, shut it."

Finn jerked his chin to the side, motioning for me to follow him out of earshot. Von had stellar half-vamp hearing, so I guessed we didn't have anything more than the illusion of privacy, which seemed to be what Finn needed. Finn lowered his head, speaking quietly to me. "I didn't know Atius would do what he did to you. That was about getting even with me, and I'm sorry you got caught up in it. You should know my men killed them all."

I don't know why that made me feel better, since I didn't plan on ever coming back here again, but somehow it did. "Thanks. And thank you for saving me."

Finn rubbed my cheek with his thumb, cupping my face. "I'm pretty sure you saved me."

I couldn't help but be transfixed by his pure green eyes, earnest as they were. I placed my hand over his to hold onto it one more time before we parted. "Be a good man, Finn. Be someone I'm proud of."

He smiled at me. "You'll be a good mother when this one comes out. Promise me that Von's a good guy."

"He's a good guy, and I'm not pregnant. For the millionth time, I'm not baking his bun in my oven."

His eyes shifted, remembering his frustration with me. "You shouldn't have gone up against Banak without us. No backup, no warning. It was stupid. You're lucky you didn't get yourself raped or killed."

"Oh, that reminds me." I reached down into my pack and pulled out his knife. "This is yours. Thanks for letting me borrow it. Security's kind of lax around here, don't you think?"

Finn grumbled and sheathed the knife on his belt. "You make me crazy."

"You make me laugh."

Finn's eyes moved on to that next emotion our friendship always pivoted on. "You make me happy. I haven't had a lot of that."

"You make me..." I swallowed. "Thanks for saving me."

"Anytime, *sinta*."

Von cleared his throat. "And that's the last time you call her that, yeah?" he shouted to Finn, who scowled at the eavesdropper. "You don't want to know me when I'm in a foul mood."

Finn snarled at Von, but cut the feud short when I jerked his chin back to me. "Knock it off. We're all one big happy family. We're the Brady Bunch incarnate. No one's fighting here."

Finn brushed my hair from my face, looking at me like I was more to him than anyone ever could be to a person as jaded as he was. "Be safe. That knife I gave you? Not the one you stole, but the one I actually gave you? Keep it close. It's the only way I can help keep you safe while I'm here and you're Topside." Then he leaned forward and kissed my cheek, gripping the nape of my neck in a way that reminded me of his constant need for control, for domination. Now his world was set tail-spinning, first with his mother dying so horribly, and then with the country on the brink of a change in monarchy. I was leaving right when he needed me.

"I'm sorry I'm splitting the second it's all hitting the fan." I watched as Lang ported Mariang and Danny, and knew our time was up. "Thank you for loving me so well," I whispered. I knew I could never say anything that would make him understand just how amazing it was to be loved by someone as incredibly fierce as him.

"Don't leave," he whispered with his eyes closed.

My hushed response wasn't thought out, but came from the depths of my heart without hesitation. "'If you live, then I breathe.'"

He kissed my lips just once, reminding us both of the connection that might always be there.

Slowly I migrated from Finn to Von, my hand resting in my best friend's. I couldn't help but sneak one last look, my heart pounding as I geared up to leave the man who'd given me his home and his arms to borrow as a safe haven. I looked over my shoulder to catch one last glimpse of the soldier I'd held to my breast when he'd been reduced to a lost child.

Finn kissed two fingers, looking at me with such unfathomable loss that I had to turn away, lest I run back to him.

Mason wrapped me in his embrace, kissing my temple as he held me, gearing up to zippity-doo-da Von and me out of Dagat.

LAYING IT ALL ON THE TABLE

I held on tight as a sucking sensation lifted the three of us from Dagat, straight to Ezra's front doorstep. My shoulders slumped. "Any chance I could get a one-way ticket to my house instead?"

Mason kept one arm around me. "Ezra was pretty specific."

"Sure. And thanks for the lift. King of Sombi being my chauffeur? You're spoiling me all over the place."

Ezra greeted us with open arms, messy hair and his shirt untucked, which told me things hadn't been smooth sailing Topside. "I'm so glad you're all home safe." He hugged Mariang in a bone-crushing embrace I could tell he'd been waiting to unleash on the girl who'd been so frail for too long. He kissed Danny and Von on the cheek and hugged Mason like a son. Before I could ask, Ezra held up his hand. "Oliver's helping Kabayo, Alton, Graham and your mother in Lumipad still. They're close to the well, but they needed a bit more manpower. I hope to have them back by morning."

"They're still there? But it's been weeks."

"Indeed, darling. Lumipad is in complete and total anarchy, which makes traveling problematic. They're hiding out until the opportunity presents itself to deliver the stone."

Ezra's face was streaked with tears, but he said nothing further, other than that he'd missed us. When the others made their way to the kitchen, he was reluctant to leave the foyer, needing an extra few seconds to get himself together.

"Ezra?" I inquired of his hesitance. "Are you alright?"

He shook his head, making me appreciate his honesty and the fact that it came with a small shadow of a forced smile. It was as if he didn't want to tell me the truth, but knew he couldn't very well lie to me about something I'd spotted outright. "I fear it might be a long time before I'm alright."

I softened, seeing the hurt boy behind the ruler. "I'm sorry I made you worry. I didn't mean to."

He didn't have words for this, but closed the gap between us as if I was cold, and needed him for shelter. His hug was tight and filled with emotion he didn't voice, worrying me as I kept my arms tight around him. "You belong here. You know that, yeah?"

"Thanks. Are you going to tell me what's wrong?"

"Nothing, dear."

I tilted my head at up at him. "I think I know you better than that by now."

"I guess you do." Ezra pulled away and braved a smile. "Nothing's wrong yet. There's still hope for now. I'm doing my best to hold tight to it, so it doesn't slip through my fingers." He held my arms and took a good look at me. "My, the last time I saw you, there was more blood than girl. Healing waters, indeed. I can't believe King Banak kept that from us this entire time." His tired eyes were lined at the corners, which for some reason drew me toward him. I let him hold me, since it seemed to give him a brief reprieve from his sadness.

As I pressed my nose into his shirt, I couldn't help but admit to myself that having a dad felt kind of nice. He worried about me, waited up for me, slayed dragons, Ekeks and Manas in my name. It took me a few seconds of muscling past my aversion to anything permanent as far as parental figures went, but eventually my gratitude couldn't be put off. "I'm sorry," I whispered, my fist bunching in his shirt.

"My darling. Whatever could you be sorry for?" His stomach growled, and he begged my pardon, as if that was something he could've controlled.

I wanted to tell him so many things, but I stuck with the most basic root of it all. "I kept pushing you away. Your life, all of it. I took my anger out on you. I was mad that everything got turned on its head, but it's not your fault." I swallowed, unable to look at him. "I shouldn't have treated you like it was."

"You can be mad at me." His voice sounded like his mind was talking about something else I didn't understand. "You can be very mad at me, and I'll have deserved it."

I looked up at him, confused. "That's my whole point. You didn't deserve it. I never had a... you know, a dad before. It's a steeper learning curve than I was ready for. But I'm ready now. I'll be better at this, at being your daughter."

I didn't anticipate this being the wrong thing to say, but apparently it was. Tears started forming in the corners of Ezra's eyes, one blink sending them over the edge as he dabbed at them with a handkerchief from his pocket, embarrassed. "I'm sorry. To hear you say such lovely things?" He cleared his throat and braved a smile. "It's a good day, then. No matter what, this is going down in the books as a good day."

I eyed his sadness with suspicion. "What aren't you telling me?"

"It's you that has the telling to do. You've been in Dagat for weeks! You dipped in the healing waters. Apparently you even made friends with Captain Finn, which I admit, I didn't think possible. I trust he was a gentleman?" he asked with the hint of a threat.

"Very much so."

Ezra's arm coiled around my shoulders and corralled

me to the dining room where the others had been shooed by Lynna. "I simply must hear everything."

Lynna broke out more food than I'd seen in a while. Mariang and I ate our fill while the guys glutted themselves on ham, mashed potatoes, vegetables and wine. I tried to always keep my mouth full so I couldn't respond when asked a direct question, but Ezra was wise to my game after the third shrug I tried to pass off as a response. "I've heard Danny and Mariang's account of the healing waters. You've heard how many Ekeks and Manas we've slaughtered with the help of Prince Langgam, Ruiz and Klark. You heard every detail of Bishop's funeral. Now it's your turn."

I pointed to my mouth again, which I'd just shoved a bite of mashed potatoes in, but Ezra folded his hands over his lap and waited, setting the precedent that all other conversation would cease until I complied.

Darn his good politics.

I took my time chewing, swallowing the lump in my throat as I offered up a simple smile. "So, you know, got abducted with Bishop, rescued by Finn, the healing waters, crashed at Finn's place, Banak's dead. And that's about it."

I didn't expect Von to be miffed at my non-explanation, but his was the first reply that came out with a note of irritation as he speared his Brussels sprouts next to me. "That's rubbish, and you know it. All Ezra knew was that Finn came flying out of the basement with you half dead and half naked in his arms. He mentioned something about getting you medicine or a healer or something, and that he'd bring you back once the Manas were destroyed. Fill in the blanks, or I'll draw all sorts of sordid conclusions."

Indignant that Von called me out on my evasiveness, I turned to him, arms folded across my chest and a defiant scowl on my face. "Did it ever occur to you all that I'm being succinct for your own good? Do you really want to hear all that Bishop went through down there?"

"I think I deserve to hear that much, yes. He's my brother."

I let out a steady exhale. "He was kneecapped, Von. He begged me not to tell Serena a thing about the stone, but I told them the exact truth, that it was on its way to Lumipad already. Serena didn't believe me because she assumed I was the only one who could touch the stone. She tortured Bishop because she thought he was my boyfriend. Is that what you want to hear?"

"It's a start." Von mirrored my body language, sitting back in his chair and staring me down. "We deserve to know what went down, even if it's ugly. Danny and I should know what happened to our brother. And Mason and I *need* to know what happened to you."

"You *need* to know that Bishop was so far gone by the end, he could barely speak through the pain? You *need* to know that they killed him by accident? That if they hadn't been careless with the torture, he'd still be here? He died in my arms, Von! Is that what you want to hear? They collapsed his lung. He'd lost too much blood by that point." I sucked in a deep breath and dove for the deeper waters. "I kissed Bishop while he died. I kissed your brother because he loved your paintings and wished he could see them again. He wanted you to paint more, so I kissed him to make him see the colors, to take away his pain as he died. My own way of blissing him out as best I could."

Von was patient while I got myself worked up, angry that he was making me talk about the trauma that never needed to see the light of day. "That's good, and right decent of you to ease his pain. There's nothing to be ashamed of in that."

"No shame? Are you flipping kidding me? He was captured and tortured because of me! Your brother's dead because of me!" I grimaced. "Nothing to be ashamed of? I'm surprised you can even look at my face!"

Danny spoke up, the anger in his eyes not directed at me. "Why are you making her do this, Von? It's not going to bring Bishop back."

"No, but it might bring Boston back. Boston's been a wreck. Not eating, barely sleeping. He deserves answers, and we haven't been able to give him any. And you didn't get Bish killed, Peach. Serena did. Don't forget that. They snatched up Bishop against his will and took him away. Blame yourself all you want, but no one else is. It could just as easily have been Mariang they kidnapped with Bishop. Would that have been her fault?"

I glanced over at Mariang, who was eating her dinner like a normal person, and not someone who looked like chewing the wrong way might make her faint from exhaustion. Through my frustration at the conversation, I was glad to see her so strong and alert.

Danny glared at me. "I'll answer that one for you: No. It wouldn't have been her fault, and it's not yours that they took you and Bish. Let the guilt rest with Serena."

"But I..."

Danny slammed his fork down. "Did you try to escape?"

"Well, yeah."

"Did you do everything you could to help get the two of you out?"

"Of course!"

"Then you have nothing to feel guilty about. And you even kissed him to ease his passing." He cleared his throat, gearing up to say something kind. "Thank you for doing that. It's nice to know his last moments weren't spent screaming for his life to end quicker."

Mariang put her hand on Danny's back, and for a minute, it almost looked like she was pulling the stress from him, instead of the other way around.

My mouth dropped open. "You're seriously letting me off the hook? Just like that?"

"What hook?" Danny's upper lip curled. "The only hook is the one you put yourself on. Move on to the next bit. How'd you get so bad off that Finn broke his guarded secret and took you to the healing waters? Mariang's been on the brink of her last breath for years, and Finn takes *you* there? How bad off were you?"

"Just a little banged up," I lied. It was all fixed now. There was no reason to invoke a freak-out amongst the ranks.

Ezra twiddled his thumbs in his lap. "She was a bloody mess. I barely understood it was her in Finn's arms before he vanished. We owe Finn a lot on this one. The whole kingdom does, actually. My girls are better than ever because of him." He leveled his gaze at the guys. "You'll not forget that." He cleared his throat and turned his attention back to me. "Can I assume the bulk of your injuries were Serena's handiwork?"

I nodded, my eyes on my plate. "They knocked me around a bit. Then Serena took my shirt and carved up my back pretty good with her knife." I shrugged at Von's widened eyes and Danny's dropped open mouth while Mason chewed without looking at me. "I survived, so it's fine." I scratched the nape of my neck. "The healing waters did their thing, but I guess it left a pretty big scar across my back. So, you know, be cool about it."

"You *guess* it left a scar?" Von inquired.

"Yeah. I can't actually see my own back. Finn told me."

"Finn saw your naked back?" Von was reaching his breaking point of how angry one man could be.

I took a drink of water. "He saw a whole lot more than that. Serena took my shirt."

"He should've given you his shirt."

I slammed my glass down, unhappy we were having this conversation at all. "Look, Serena was going to peel the skin clean off my back, Von. She drew the outline over and over. My back was literally peeling off every time I moved an inch. A shirt? Really?"

"You shouldn't have kept me away from the rescue team. I should never have listened to you."

"You would've killed me without a blink, Von. I was drenched in my blood and Bishop's. I hadn't eaten in days. You were on the mend yourself. I couldn't have fought you off. Be pissed all you want, but it is what it is. Maybe a lot of things could've been different, but I didn't ask to get scarred."

Von spoke through gritted teeth. "I would've controlled myself. Your kiss broke through a lot of my vampire curse. I'm not nearly as bloodthirsty as I was a month ago."

"You were being starved!"

"You should've had more faith in me."

Ezra tapped his fork to his wineglass. "That's neither here nor there. It was a pragmatic decision, Von. As her Reaper, you should be glad when your charge exercises caution." He nodded to me. "Do continue, dear."

"After the healing waters, Finn took me to his house where he brought in Garrick to pull for me." I let Mason explain Garrick's death, since I didn't have that many more horrible words in my soul that dared birth out of my mouth. After Mason finished, the conversation was handed to Von, who explained his role in taking down Banak's son.

Von traced the lip of his glass, speaking to it instead of the people who gawked at him. "Finn led me into the harem, checked me in using all the normal paperwork, oiled me up and brought me to Prince Julius' Hari room, which is more or less a dungeon with a bed." I stopped moving and probably breathing as Von explained what Ezra, Mason and I already knew – that Von was never a male escort for wealthy women, but a bedslave for Julius to work off Boston's debt.

Danny held his stomach. "I think I'm going to be sick. I can't hear this."

Von glared at his brother, for once not shrugging off Danny. "That's right. All those times you wrote me off and told people I was a prostitute, I was really paying off a stupid gambling debt the old-fashioned way. A debt that wasn't even mine. Finn caught me the first time and brought me in. I was Julius' slave for the worst three months of my life. You heard a rumor I was an escort and wrote me off. Never even bothered to ask. That's the kind of brother I get. I walked you to school every morning, packed your lunch, handled the blokes who bullied you, and you threw me under the bus over a rumor. I've always believed in you, and you jumped at any reason to be ashamed of me."

Danny's chin was low, and his spirits even lower while he shook his head, as if the slow side-to-side would make it all go away. "Why didn't you set me straight?"

"You never asked. You wanted me to be a screw-up, so that's what I was. You wonder why November and I are so close? Because she asked me what happened. You ever wonder why Ezra would hire a prostitute to help guard the mansion? Because he knew the real story. He gave me a chance to explain, and then helped me get back to normal. You?" He waved his hand to be done with it. "I already lost the brother who truly loved me, and Boston's a shell now because of it. Danny, you threw me away a long time ago. The prostitute label was just a nice little excuse for you to have no guilt at writing me off. If not that, you would've found another reason." He shook his head in disappointment. "And the sad part is, I never expected any different from you."

I buried my head in my hands when Danny abruptly stood and marched up the stairs. Mariang didn't run after Danny, but got up from the table and flung her arms around Von's neck. With tears in her eyes, she whispered, "I'm so sorry that happened to you."

Von kissed her cheek with a sad smile. "You're a good sister, you know. You loved me even when you thought I was a prostitute."

"I do love you, Von."

Ezra whipped out his phone and barked into it. "We haven't finished. You're not dismissed from the table just because you don't like something you heard. Come back down immediately." I kept my head downward as Danny skulked back to the dining room table and slumped in his chair, refusing to speak or look at anyone. Ezra straightened. "That's better. Von, you went to see Julius, and then what?"

"I don't think Danny can handle a play-by-play, but I got him to let his guard down. Finn had hidden a knife in the room for me. I grabbed it, we fought a bit, and finally I stabbed him. A few times, actually. Then I waited all afternoon for Finn to come and take the body. I'm not sure why it took so long for the other girl to off Banak, but there you have it. One foul monarchy gone in a day. Just how we like it." Von slid his hands together as if gearing up for delicious gossip none of us wanted a taste of. "Anyone hear details about Banak? Did the lass make him suffer?"

Mason opened his mouth, but I shot him a look to shut his donut hole. "Does it matter? Point is they're both dead, and that's that. Finn's plan is to put Mathias of the Green Lakes on the throne, since he's next in line with no heirs. That gives Finn a little time to get a good face in front of the people so that when time comes to choose a new ruler, they'll have a better one to follow. Harem's going to be disbanded immediately."

Ezra nodded. "Sounds good."

Mason sat back in his chair, glaring at me. "Really? You're going to sit on this one? Well, I'm not, and I don't know why you're keeping it a secret. This is the time to put it all out on the table, October."

I fought the urge to run and hide. "Fine. Tell them what you want. I'm tired."

I made to stand, but Ezra was unswerving. "Remain. Seated."

I reared back in my chair. "I'd like to know when you thought you could tell me what to do."

Ezra stood, his fists resting on the table. "If you want me to play the ruler card, I will. You and Mariang are Omens, which puts you under my jurisdiction. You'll sit and give a full account of things, young lady."

I directed my anger at Mason, who shrugged as if to ask me what I expected. "Fine. Von, it took so long to get a girl in to Banak because Banak had Finn's mom in his sex dungeon for days." I paused for the gasps. "That's right. None of this is my secret to tell, but you're making me lay out his garbage so you all can sift through it like scavengers. Finn was trying to disband the harem because I made him see how cracked it all was. Banak caught wind of it, and wanted to get back at Finn. He can't exactly fire Finn, since Finn does everything for him, so Banak took Finn's mother into the harem."

Ezra rested his hand on his head. "So Finn killed the king?"

I swallowed a lump in my throat as the backs of my hands started to itch. "No. When we made it to the palace, I found out Banak was still in there with Finn's mom, so I played my Omen card to interrupt them with a national emergency so Finn could get her out of there. Only I was too late." My voice quieted, and I kept my eyes on my plate. "Banak had already killed her."

Von hung his head, swearing. "Oh, bollocks. That's dreadful. Honestly, I didn't know about that. I wouldn't have given him such a hard time before we left."

"Finn was a mess, so while he and his men went out to bury her, I slipped into Banak's sex room."

"Locking me out, by the way," Mason interjected, clearly miffed.

"You're welcome. Did you really want to watch me seduce Banak? Trust me, no one needs a front seat to that noise."

Von gripped the table, eyes shining with horror and revulsion. "You did what?" he said in time with Ezra.

"I lifted Finn's knife when he was distracted, hid it in my backpack and, how did you put it so eloquently? Waited until Banak's guard was down." I drew my thumb across my throat. "He's got a thing for legs. And toes." I shuddered, and the ripple made its way across the table, hitting everyone like a punch to the gut. They no doubt wished they hadn't asked me for more details.

Mariang let out a horrified cry of distress into her hands.

"You shouldn't have done that," Von murmured. "How far did it go?"

"I'm still a virgin, if that's what you're asking."

Mason cast me a dubious look. "A pregnant virgin? Okay, October."

I ignored Mason as Ezra stiffened. "I did what needed to be done. I wasn't about to let Finn bring in a woman he's already dominated and terrorized to try her hand at killing him. Plus, I already knew Banak would be up for it. When Finn brought me in to get at the healing waters when I first got to Dagat, Banak told Finn to give me to him, even though I was almost dead."

Ezra rested his elbows on the table, looking disheveled, confused and completely lost. "Wait. First things first. You're pregnant?"

I threw out my hands. "I can't keep having this same conversation. I'm not pregnant. You have to have sex to get pregnant, and I've never done that, *Dad*." I said the last word like a dig, but Ezra took it as a compliment.

Ezra looked to Mason and Von. "Which one of you is it?"

Mason shook his head in time with Von. "Not mine," they said in unison, like they didn't want to get caught with the hot potato. If I had actually been pregnant, I'm pretty sure I could've been offended at that point.

"Why won't anyone listen to me? I'm not pregnant. This is so infuriating. Is this your circuitous way of telling me I've put on weight? Because it's mean."

Mason spoke up. "We're pulling for two, *hani*. We can tell just by touching you."

Mariang put her hands on the table to stop the back and forth. "There's a simple way to get to the bottom of this, you know. Just take a pregnancy test, October. I've got an extra one upstairs."

Danny and Ezra both clutched their chests like Mariang had issued them conjoined heart attacks. I rolled my eyes. "Fine by me. But I want each of you to have to do something equally degrading as peeing on a stick when it comes back that I'm not pregnant."

"Of course, dear. I think we'd all like to resolve this as quickly as possible."

As I stood and stomped toward the stairs, Mason called out, "I got most of my strength back, by the way. Thought you all should know the healing waters did a number on me. I'm good as new." He grinned as he snapped his knife in half using one hand, his thumb on the flat of the blade and a triumphant grin on his face.

53

FAILING THE TEST

I had never taken a pregnancy test before, and read the instructions over several times. When I finished, I came out of the bathroom, my brow wrinkled as I held it out to Mariang. "Something's wrong with this test."

The joy in Mariang's eyes told me she'd been hoping I was lying, but deflated when I showed her the stick. "It's supposed to have one pink line for not knocked up, and two pink lines for baby. This has the whole reading area fogged over to black. That can't be right. There's not even an option for that on the box."

Mariang frowned and pulled out her phone. "Danny, could you go get another test for October? This one's not working. Maybe it's expired." She hung up to cut off his gruff complaining and hugged me. "I know you don't want to hear this, but I do hope it's a girl. I'm so strong now; I'll be the best aunt in the world. You have no idea what this feels like. To go from not being able to go for a walk most days to being normal? Normal feels like Wonder Woman." She flexed her bicep and laughed. "If it's a girl, we can dress her up in ruffles and bows. Pink from head to toe. Danny and I can take her for weekends. I'll be Aunt Mariang. We can bake cupcakes!" She grinned at the sound of it.

I didn't have the heart to burst her bubble. "You know, if you want a kid this bad, it might be worth a conversation with Danny to look into getting a little crawler of your own."

Sadness passed over her eyes. "We want one, but it's not possible. I started reaping too young and it made me too weak to carry a baby." I tilted my head at her as the light dawned in her eyes, spreading through her body like honey that only glowed sweeter as the idea festered. "But I'm healthy now! Maybe, do you think I could..." The light fell again. "But no. I couldn't do that to the kingdom. It would put me out of commission for at least a few weeks, if not longer."

I waved off her concern. "Pfft. I've got you covered. No big deal. Plus, with the stone going out to the nations, we have to reap way less. If it's something you want, you should totally go for it."

Mariang's eyes glassed over. "I told Danny I wouldn't do that to him, saddle him with a sick person. It's why I told him no when he proposed."

I gaped at her, though I probably should've guessed as much. "Danny proposed? He actually got down on one knee and the whole nine yards?"

Mariang nodded. "Two years ago. I told him no. I wouldn't make him a widower so young. But now? Maybe now I can have that life. Maybe now I can have *a* life." Tears fell down her cheeks as I wrapped my arms around her, grateful that the sweetest, most unselfish girl I knew could finally have a few good things for herself. She waved her arms around. "Look at me. This is your special moment, and I'm making it the Mariang show. I'm sorry. It's all hitting me at once."

I laughed. "This isn't my special moment. It's barely a moment at all. Have at it. You deserve something good for a change."

We girl-talked about Danny's proposal and how she really wanted two children: a boy and a girl. She told me about her first time with Danny, which was also in her dreams, the way mine had been. She asked a good many questions about my dream honeymoon with Von, which I tried to answer in as few words as possible.

Danny knocked on the door, red-faced with a grocery bag clutched in his hand. "Never make me do that again."

"Thanks. You're the king of Mariang's dreams." I opened the bag and found a dozen tests inside, each a different brand. "How many times do you think I need to take this test?"

"I would've thought just the one, but apparently at least twice."

I fished through the bag and pulled out a bottle of water, a pack of condoms and some prenatal vitamins. "Are these supposed to be funny?"

"No. They're supposed to get me out of ever having to go buy those things for you again." He leaned in, conspiratorially. "Seriously, though. Whose is it? Did you take up with Finn or something?"

I answered by slamming the door in his face and chugging the water. I waited the necessary minutes and took another test, coming out equally baffled by the non-results. "Same thing. It's supposed to be one pink line."

"Or two," Mariang amended.

"But it's completely black and fogged over. What gives? You take one. Maybe I'm doing it wrong."

"You're a nurse. Is there more than one way to take these?"

"No, but I need a control to see if the whole pack's defective. Maybe because I'm an Omen they're turning out weird?"

Mariang and I took turns working our way through the packs, chugging water and comparing results, which I hope is the weirdest thing I've ever done with another woman. Hers all turned out normal, not pregnant, and mine were all defective. She got so frustrated that she asked to watch me take one of the tests, which *then* turned out to be the weirdest thing I'd ever done with another woman.

When we descended the stairs to a pacing Ezra, an impatient Danny and Mason, and Von smoking his cigar out on the porch, we had no new news to report. "I've called the family doctor. He's a Duwende," Ezra told me, apologetic. "I got worried when you didn't come down right away. If you'll consent to an exam, he can confirm everything right now. He's set up in one of the guest rooms upstairs."

"Oh, jeez. I'm not getting out of this, am I." When Ezra was resolute and Mason guarded the front door to ensure I didn't make a run for it, I huffed. "Fine, but when this all turns out that I'm not pregnant, you're all getting colonoscopies, do you hear me?"

Never mind that I had a general practitioner. Never mind that no one else was subjected to this kind of treatment. I jerked my head for Mariang to come with me, and like a good sister, she didn't bat an eye.

54

MY SURPRISE, AND DANNY'S DREAM

"I'm what?!" I shouted, unable to control the volume of my voice. We were all sitting in the living room with Doctor Henderson standing in the archway. Dude needed a bulletproof vest for all the ammo I was ready to fire at him. "I'd like to see your medical degree, sir."

"She needs to go off her meds immediately, as hers can cause birth defects for the baby in rare cases." He recommended a different brand that was apparently a little safer, though not without risk. His higher-pitched voice was matter-of-fact, and left us all with only more questions he didn't have the answers to. I heard precious little after that; it was all a blur of white noise and shock that just kept on coming.

Mason was in my face demanding answers. Mariang was bouncing on the balls of her feet with glee. Danny had his planning face on to account for the changes in security he insisted would need to happen before I ever left the house again. Ezra had his arms around me.

I didn't feel any of it. I only felt the nothing of shock and the confusion of biology – the subject I'd loved and excelled in – failing me just when I needed black and white to stay put. Now my uterus was a storm of gray I hadn't asked for, or even earned.

The worst was Von. He started yelling his confusion at me, accusing me of sleeping around. His hands were running through his hair until it completely stuck out in the back.

I hung my head, the world tilting at an odd angle that forced everything to fit into the wrong puzzle. I heard them all talking to each other around me, but none of it made sense. My ears filled with a buzzing that made it hard to breathe. My arms banded around my stomach as I rocked myself on the couch, hoping for anything to make sense. The only constant in the past year seemed to be that nothing ever did.

There was a bang of the front door, some yelling, but I couldn't decipher a word until Ezra knelt in front of me, putting himself in my line of vision that saw, but didn't interpret as fast as it should. "Sweetheart, you need to try breathing. Lynna's making you some tea."

"Ollie?" I asked, hoping saying his name would make my brother materialize.

Ezra closed his eyes. "No, dear. It's Ezra, your father. Ollie will hopefully be here tomorrow."

I looked up and saw that Von was gone. Just utterly and completely gone.

Doctor Henderson cleared his throat to regain the floor. "If you'll all let me finish, I can confirm both that October's pregnant, but that somehow she's still a virgin. Short of artificial insemination, I don't see how this happened."

I lifted my head in semi-vindication. I hadn't heard much that buzzed around me, but I sure as Sunday heard that. "I told you all I hadn't had sex with anyone!"

The questions fired at warp speed toward Doctor Henderson, who had no medical expertise to explain himself with, other than the conflicting facts no one could reconcile. Twenty minutes of that later, and Doctor Henderson bowed out, leaving the mansion with a fistful of cash and a serious questioning of the science behind the basics.

"How did this... How?"

Ezra's eyes were earnest and sincere. "I don't know. But I do know this is a good thing. A baby is a wonderful blessing. Don't lose sight of that."

I knew I was about six inches away from falling apart, and I didn't want to do that in public. "I want to go home."

"Then I'll take you." Ezra was unyielding, and I was too turned around to form a proper argument. "We think we killed all the Topside Manas and Ekeks, but we can't be sure, since we don't know how they got here in the first place. Your home's reinforced with warding charms, but I won't gamble losing you again." His voice lowered to a darker note. "Serena's dead, but we didn't get the chance to kill her. We found her body, tortured and carved up days after Finn took you to Dagat. We can't be sure it's not another turf war from yet more disgruntled Ekeks or Manas, vying for the throne."

I consented to whatever would get me out of there fastest, not sure where my keys were, my car or even my shoes. Mariang kissed me, congratulated me, hugged me and helped me put one foot in front of the other until I got to the opened front door. I looked up and saw Ezra walking to his car, with Mason behind me, giving me a reassuring smile.

"Von?" I called, my voice shaky. "Where's Von?"

Mariang and Mason exchanged worried looks before Mariang glossed over it with a vague, "He stepped out."

I knew what that meant. My dad had stepped out on Bev the night she'd gotten pregnant with me. I'd single-handedly ruined everything for Bev. And now I'd ruined my non-relationship without lifting a finger. The dysfunctional family that somehow managed to work when I needed it most had fallen apart, with me as the catalyst for the break. "Von left me?" I whispered, unable to put anything else in my life in proper order except for that.

Mason's hand on my shoulder steadied me. "We're

here, *hani*. Von's overwhelmed by it all. He'll come back. He always does."

That was the tipping point for it to all become too much. My knees buckled as the weight of just plain too much crashed down on me, pressing me toward the ground as I fought to stay conscious.

Mason caught me before I hit the floor, calling for Lynna to bring me some water. Of all people, Danny came along on my other side, letting me lean on him when I couldn't hold myself upright. "It'll be okay," he assured me, sounding nothing like himself. If shock made me nearly faint, it made Danny spontaneously nice. It was a pretty solid tradeoff, overall. "Come, now. Let's get you some tea, yeah?" Mason and Danny slowly led me back into the living room and lowered me to the couch. Danny slid a white leather ottoman under my feet while Mariang tucked a throw pillow behind my back. Danny gently took my shoes off, and I was so confused by the kindness, I temporarily forgot about my impromptu baby. "What?" he asked of my gaping.

"You're being nice to me."

"Who wouldn't be nice to you right now? You're a knocked-up virgin whose boyfriend just ran off the second he found out about the baby."

Mariang closed her eyes as if Danny's ignorance pained her. "Danny, please. Be sensitive."

"Oh, sorry. Was that not right?" Danny sat straighter. His monster of Frankenstein eyebrows pushed together as he tried to remember the steps he'd seen modeled around him of how to be a decent person. "How about food? I'm good with food. Do you want something to eat?"

I shook my head, my eyes tearing up. "I just want to be alone so I can figure this out. How?" I asked Danny. He was sitting on the edge of the ottoman directly in front of me, so he caught the brunt of my questions. "How am I pregnant? And with who? The only time I medium had sex was when Von and I first had that hallucination. We had sex in our minds, but that's not real."

Mariang's eyes widened. "Oh! Oh. Oh, oh, oh, oh." She covered her mouth as she stood, pacing the living room as Ezra came back inside.

"What?" Mason asked, sitting down on the couch next to me. He wrapped an arm around my shoulders and gave me a decent pull, which to be honest, was a drop in the bucket for what I needed.

"Danny, remember that time when we were rock climbing in our dreams, and you woke up with a scrape on your knee in the exact spot from when you slipped on the mountain?"

My eyes flew from Mariang to Danny, who shrugged. "Yeah. So?"

"And the time we were dreamwalking and I ate shellfish?" She turned to explain to me, "I'm allergic to shellfish. I woke up covered in hives."

Danny nodded, but it was too many details for my crowded brain to keep track of. It was Mason who jumped up off the couch, hand over his mouth as he locked eyes with Mariang. "You're not saying the baby's Von's, is it? Is that even possible?"

Danny grimaced. "No. I mean, those were such small things. And I could've been sleepwalking and banged my knee that way."

Mariang gesticulated wildly, looking a little like me when I got worked up. "Really? You think I ate a truckload of shellfish in my sleep? Lynna doesn't even keep them in the house."

"Then how come you and I've never gotten pregnant? We've had sex in our dreams loads of times." The second the words were out of his mouth, he ducked like a turtle trying to hide in his shell, not meaning to have blurted out those words in front of his girlfriend's father. "I'm sorry. That was out of line."

Ezra pinched the bridge of his nose. "Continue."

Mariang pulled her hair back. "I'm on the pill. I'm guessing October's not?"

I shook my head, my chin trembling. "Why would I need to be?" Tears that had been held at bay now let loose and trickled down my cheeks. "I didn't know we would hallucinate. I'd never done that before. I thought it was just a really, really good kiss. This is what I get for having fake sex? This sucks!" I waved the group away when my tears invoked pity from them. I didn't want pity. I wanted to cry in private, let my brain work its way around the edges of the gray mass of hysteria that was building inside of me.

Mason sat back down and leaned forward, his elbows on his knees while he stared at the carpet, confused as he tried to process the impossibility. Mariang kissed the top of my head and moved into the kitchen, I assume to get me the tea they'd each promised as the miracle cure for what ailed me. Danny held my foot, which was akin to a hug from him.

I looked up, utterly lost as I searched out truth in Ezra's eyes. They always seemed to have a note of compassion, even in the direst of circumstances. "Dad?" I whispered, my voice shaking. He looked at me, and I saw that same kindness I'd mistrusted too many times to have the right to call upon now. Yet somehow it was still there, an endless reserve of goodness for me to take whenever I needed a refill. "Please don't leave me," I begged, my lower lip quivering as I hugged myself on the couch, feeling utterly alone and without a prayer.

Ezra cleared the distance between us in the span of a breath, kneeling by my other side and holding my hands, clasping them together like we were praying the same prayer. "Never. You're my daughter, and this is my grandchild." He smiled at the word. "My grandchild."

Danny stood, suddenly pissed. "Where does Von get off getting a kid out of this? What did he do to deserve someone incredible, like October? How does Von get a child, and I get none? Where's the logic in that?" He didn't sound like a petulant brat; he was a brokenhearted man. He pounded his fist to his chest. "I've given everything to

Terraway! And they took everything from Mariang." He shook his head as Mariang came back into the room, her footsteps quiet and slow. "This thing that fell in your lap?" he said to me, a mixture of angry and hurt. "I'd kill for that kind of luck! And Von just runs out on it, like he always does when he gets scared."

Mason held up his hands. "Hey, Von doesn't know it's his."

"He still ran out on his charge. Any way you paint it, he's still a coward."

Mariang cleared her throat from the archway that separated the living room from the foyer. Her voice was quiet, making everyone calm down enough to be able to hear her. "We've already had our bit of luck. We dipped in the healing waters, Danny. I was talking to October about it earlier. If you'll still have me, then I might be able to give you everything you want." She swallowed, and I swear I could've heard a pin drop. "Maybe I can give you a child."

Danny turned, thunderstruck as what dawned on Mariang upstairs slowly began to trickle into his brain like a waterfall that just kept coming, building in its momentum as it crashed over the rocks he'd kept firmly in place to guard his heart. "Are you... Do you really think... But is it safe?"

Mariang nodded, grinning like a much younger girl. "If it's safe for October, I don't see why it wouldn't be for me, too. Don't I look healthy?"

It was just the right amount of sheer joy to distract

from the torrential storm raging inside of me. I watched with my mouth wide open as Danny scooped Mariang up in his arms. He kissed her without caring who was watching, or that we could see the stages of euphoria overtaking them before they broke away, chests heaving. "Wait here," he said, tearing up the stairs with the same vigor as when he'd chased down Ekeks.

When he came back, he barely made it to her before he got down on his knee. Danny opened a small square box that made Mariang burst into tears afresh. Ezra fell backward from his perch onto his butt, Lynna shrieked with glee, and Mason covered his mouth with his hand as we watched with baited breath.

"Mariang, will you marry me?" Danny asked, simple and succinct, which was true to form. It was the only thing Danny had ever wanted for himself. I couldn't believe the infinite patience he must've had to want to marry her for so long, only to have her turn him away for the greater good.

Mariang's response could scarcely be heard as she nodded through her tears. "Yes! Yes, Danny!" He slid the biggest diamond I'd ever seen in real life onto her trembling finger, and I could tell by the borderline high looks on their faces when they kissed, that they were in their happy place.

We took turns hugging the couple, Danny foregoing his stoicism to indulge in a tight embrace from everyone in the room. He let out a bray of elation in Ezra's arms, the two holding onto each other as Ezra cried and welcomed him to the family.

They were the picture of happiness, so I did my best representation of *Who cares that I got psychically knocked up? You're getting married!*

Lynna ran to the kitchen and came back with tea for everyone and champagne. I took a tall glass of bubbly fruitiness, but Mason absconded with it before it reached my lips. "Pregnant," he reminded me, downing my glass and his with an apologetic shrug.

I waited for the right opportunity to slip away, making my way up to my bedroom in the mansion and collapsing on the bed. Since I was alone, I let my tears loose, crying myself into exhaustion, and finally drifting off.

Mason slid in behind me some time in the night, rolling me on my side so he could spoon me. "Goodnight, *hani*. Whoa!" he said as he held me. "You're practically radiating. You should've called me up here if you were feeling this."

"I'm fine," I lied, my eyes puffy and my face lined with both wet and dried tears.

He ran his fingers through my hair, draping the tresses up over my pillow so he could nuzzle my neck. "I need you at zero. We have to go to work in the morning."

I don't know why this made me cry all over again, but it seemed that I had an endless supply of tears on tap. Usually when I had an audience, I covered my face or did my best to suck it up. But when Mason rolled me over to cradle me in his arms, my sobs turned audible. A horrible, wretched strangled sound rocketed out of me as I wailed my pain into Mason's chest.

"Let it out," he crooned between my sobs that choked me and made me cough. I fought to breathe in between my cries of unbearable emotional pain. I had no words for the anger I had at just plain life for giving me something, only to take something else I needed away. Mason's repeated promises of, "I'm here. I'm here," hit me like a punch in the gut, reminding me that Von wasn't here. That he'd split on me. That I was leave-able.

"Ollie," I blubbered. "I need my brother here! Please get my brother!"

"He's coming, sweetheart."

The absence of the one person who always managed to make everything better forced a cry out of me so loud and painful, Mason jumped.

I heard the door creak open, but couldn't see much through my puffy and bleary eyes. I heard Danny above my bawling. "I can do a double pull to calm her down. This can't be good for the baby."

I screamed at him, "I'm not pregnant! I'm not pregnant!"

"I brought you a few sandwiches from Lynna. If she's this worked up, you're going to be starved all night."

"Thanks, man. Yeah. Get on over here. She's losing it."

"I don't need you! I need Ollie! He'll fix it! He'll make it okay." I slapped at Danny as he climbed over Mason and me to get on the other side of the king-sized bed that was pushed up against the wall. Danny's face became more clearly lit by the sliver of hallway light that filtered in through the door he'd left ajar. I hated the pity in his eyes. "Go away! I don't need you!"

Danny knelt on the bed at my side and held my face, his thumbs pressing on my forehead and drawing out the pressure along my hairline. "It's okay, kid. It'll all be okay in a second." He glanced up at Mason. "Have the fetus cravings started?" he asked, reminding me that I was in bed with a man who would eventually want to eat my baby.

Mason nodded, ashamed. "Yeah, but I'm handling it. It's just making me extra hungry, so the sandwiches help. I'll be fine until she hits the third trimester."

"Get me out of here!" I screamed, in anguish that this was my life. This was my pregnancy.

I felt my anger begin to lessen, and though I was still upset, my tears stopped flowing as Danny cradled my face in his hands. "Okay, Danny," Mason warned. "That's enough."

Danny released me, confused. "Strange. I've never pulled for two before. I think I did it wrong. Sorry, kid. I didn't mean to pull that hard." He lightly slapped my cheek and earned himself a drunken punch to the arm, which he grinned at. "Yeah, she's okay. Call me if you need help with her again, yeah?"

"Screw you," I murmured, exhausted.

"Hey, watch the language," Danny teased. "That's my niece or nephew in there."

I flipped my middle finger to Danny, earning a chuckle from him. He surprised me when he leaned down and kissed my forehead before climbing back off the bed, leaving me to sleep in Mason's arms in the dark.

55

A GOOD MOM

I awoke to cries that weren't my own, and I didn't know whether to feel relieved that I hadn't been crying in my sleep, or if I should be upset that someone else was sad.

I tiptoed to the bathroom and took a quick shower, scrubbing the fear and freak-out off of me as best I could. When I came out in jeans and a jersey-style blue t-shirt, Mason was tugging on a shirt, his ear attuned to the crying downstairs. "Wait here," he warned. "I'll go see what's what."

I nodded, unable to make eye contact. "Sure. Hey, sorry I lost it last night. It just kind of hit me all at once."

Mason stood, lazily kissing my cheek as he inhaled the scent of my hair, his stomach growling. "It's no problem. You don't ever need to apologize for that to me, alright?"

I bit my lower lip. "Thanks for being there. Thanks for not splitting on me. You're a good friend. A good guy."

He stretched his arms over his head. "Not for nothing, but I've missed sleeping with you. Makes me feel almost human again." He lowered his hand between us and rubbed his knuckle over my stomach, making me jump back. He grinned at me. "You're pregnant. It's cute. Even though it's not mine, I still like thinking about you with a baby. You'll be a good mom."

I shook my head, not ready to venture that far into optimism just yet. "I can't believe you think I can do this. I don't even know any good moms anymore."

Mama McCray had been a good mom, but she'd been dead for years. I wondered if I could be as fun, kind and patient as she'd been with her boys, and with Ollie, Allie and me. Her wide, cheery smile made it look so effortless.

"I can't imagine you being bad at anything you put your mind to."

I tilted my head up at him, not sure at what point we became friends who honestly trusted each other. "You really believe the best in me, huh."

"Always and only."

I leaned up and pecked his cheek. "Thank you. Now go see what the newest drama is, and let me know when I can come down."

"You hungry?"

"Nah. My stomach's a little queasy."

The corner of Mason's mouth twitched upward.

"Morning sickness. See? It never stops being cute." He pecked my lips, looking at me with too much contentment. "I'll be back in a minute."

When Mason went downstairs, I took my time brushing my hair, afraid to look in the mirror. I didn't want to see what I looked like pregnant, even though part of me knew I probably looked the exact same.

When Mariang's crying was mingled with Ezra's howls, I burst out of the door, bolting down the stairs as I feared for the worst. I didn't have my knife from Finn in hand, but I could add a few well-aimed punches to the mix in a pinch. If an Ekek broke into the house, I wouldn't let him get at my family. Ezra and Mariang belonged to me, and I wasn't about to wait it out while they were in trouble.

When my foot hit the floor at the base of the stairs, Mariang shrieked, "October! Go upstairs! Don't look! Don't look!"

My eyes fell on a pool of blood in the foyer. My mouth dropped open when I saw a woman's hand lying lifeless on the floor, the nails chipped and crusted over with sores, dirt and dried blood. I heard my brother's sobs, and a thousand pounds of relief flooded over me. "Ollie? Ollie!" I ran to him, lightly shoving at Mason, who blocked me with his too strong body. "Move, Mason. Let me see Ollie."

Mason's face was pinched with anxiety. "Give him a minute. Go on upstairs, *hani*. You don't want to see this."

"See what? Ollie!"

"Get her out of here!" Ollie wailed, the sound of his voice scary and horrible.

Mason turned me toward the stairs, but not before I got a clear shot of the woman in Ollie's arms.

I thought I knew pain before that moment. I thought for sure I'd reached some sort of karmic agony threshold, maxing out my account for any future fatalities. But I saw her, and I lost a fair amount of myself in that simple glance. Face shredded by thick claws, mouth open and face devoid of color and life, I saw my mama.

I saw Bev lying dead in my brother's quaking arms as he howled decades of agony into her stringy blonde hair.

Love the book? Leave a review.

56

TEMPER

Enjoy a free preview of *Temper*,
book six in the Terraway series.

Two months was a long time to spend only working and going to sleep, but Ollie insisted I not be allowed back into Terraway in my current state: pregnant, father of the baby nowhere around, and newly orphaned. He worked with Finn to take the stone into Dagat, dropping it uneventfully into their main well. Just like that, Ollie brought calm waves, *buhay* and vitality back to the Merpeople, who were already so happy that their evil King Banak was dead, the whole land practically rolled out the red carpet for Ollie.

My brother had a good many dreamy-eyed stories

about Mermaids after that. He trailed off when I knew they hit the PG-13 realm I didn't need the details of. Ollie was good at talking. I was not.

I went reaping with Mason during the day. We teamed up with Danny and Mariang, who were so in love, I couldn't help but watch them with fascination as they bloomed for each other. Mariang was simply glowing, and Danny? Well, Danny smiled at least once a day since he'd popped the question, which had to be some kind of record. I knew from the shared bedroom wall that they were going at it like rabbits at night, making up for lost time when Mariang had been too sick and weak to do much of anything other than psychic lovemaking.

Speaking of psychic relationships, Von was still nowhere to be found. I saw him in my dreams at night, which hurt even more than not seeing him at all. He put a vast prairie between us, stretching our perfect park to a distance I couldn't reach him at if I ran all night long, which I had no intention of doing. I'd taken to napping as soon as we got home midday from reaping, sleeping until Von showed up in my dream at night, at which point, I woke myself up.

No, Von still didn't know that I'd kept the baby, that the baby was his, or that I was miserable without him. He wanted to be gone, and that was the thing that mattered. He'd found out that I was knocked up, and he ran. The only person I was more upset with than him was myself for still being in love with the guy. He hadn't just ditched me, he'd ducked out on Terraway. There were still Omen duties to be done, and Von dumped all the responsibility on Mason, assuming he would pick up the slack.

Ollie tried to be a good distraction, but I didn't have much to say. We'd had Bev cremated. The whole thing happened without ceremony, without debate, and without Allie. My sister remained gone, and while Ollie assumed her dead, I was certain she was very much alive and simply wanted nothing to do with us. The truth is, I couldn't really blame her, either. We were damaged. Some days it seemed the damage was beyond repair.

Ezra mourned in the traditional sense, wearing black and crying in private. He hovered around Ollie, Mariang and me more than usual as he dealt with losing his fiancée to the Ekeks and Manas she was trying to save.

Kabayo had explained it all to us in as clinical detail as possible. The group had been on the mission to take the sagrado stone to Lumipad, but in the wake of the political upheaval of their queen Sylvia getting shanked, the country shifted violently, making it a dangerous place for travelers passing through. The group moved through Lumipad with Bev fully affected by the stone, devolving back into the woman who'd thrown me away time after time. I understood that the stone poisoned her, but it didn't make her blatant hatred of me any easier to bear.

They'd made it almost to the well when a swarm of Manas swooped in, tearing Bev apart because they assumed she was me. It should've been me. Bev had stolen the stone and went in secret to save me from the danger when she'd been able to think clearly.

Somewhere buried underneath all the poison, my mama loved me, and gave her life up for mine.

I wasn't sure what to do with that, so I sat by the window in my bedroom at Ezra's mansion most nights, afraid to go to sleep and face that stupid prairie across the way from Von, who was there but not. When I was alone in my slumber because Von was awake doing whatever he did to avoid life, I had nightmares replaying the attack from the gang of Siyokoys. The wicked Mermen dragged me under the water, molesting me and trying to take me so Finn would have one more loss under his belt.

I stared out the window for hours on end, not sure how my life in the mansion made any sense at all. Every now and then Ezra would sit in a chair next to me, saying nothing, but staying with me through my silent pain. In those quiet moments that knit together over the weeks, I started to trust Ezra with my grief, occasionally answering hard to face questions when he asked. Did I miss Bev? Was I starting to feel anything for the baby growing inside me? Was I sleeping enough?

I wanted the answers to all his questions to be an easy yes, but Ezra stayed with me even when I wasn't sure. It's a good man, the one who waits for you to puzzle things out. Ezra never pushed; he simply sat by my side in his spare moments of free time. It's a good dad, the one who stays with you, even when you know deep down, you're utterly leave-able.

I was just beginning my second trimester. My stomach started to stick out a modest amount, no longer giving me the space for a healthy dose of denial. I wore baggy sweaters and felt like death warmed over. All the books Danny obsessively quoted at me said morning sickness was supposed to end in the first trimester. All I can tell you is that the books are a lie. A vicious, stupid lie to give pregnant women false hope that maybe tomorrow you won't barf until it hurts because someone mentioned the word "cracker".

I did my best to compose myself when Kabayo came to visit that evening. He played it off like it was a work call, but his purpose was only half for business. He requested I be brought in on the meeting he'd scheduled with Ezra, but Ezra excused himself to go see to getting us some tea before the meeting formally started. Kabayo sat across from me at the polished wooden oval table in the conference room. He waited until we were alone before he leaned his elbow on the surface and lowered his voice to speak to me. "I can feel this, you know."

My shoulders were hunched in and my arms banded around my baggy sweater. "Feel what?"

He displayed his forearm, showing me the same two Xs branded on his arm that matched the scarring on mine. It was our limited psychic link, letting him feel if I was in danger, or any significant shifts in me. He motioned to my closed expression. "This isn't you. You were funny and willful, if not annoying. You're sad all day now, and it's time you started pulling yourself out of it. I can feel it, you know. Even when things are going alright in my kingdom, there's always that depression that weighs it all down. It's starting to get irritating."

My eyebrows crinkled as I lifted my chin to stare at him in surprise. "First off, I didn't realize you could feel that. Second, I don't want to hear that my grief is inconvenient for you. My mama just died, my sister's MIA, I'm nine kinds of knocked up, I'm barfing all the time, I'm down a Reaper, and the father of the baby's nowhere in sight. I think I've earned the right to a little piece of sadness pot pie."

Oo, pie.

Kabayo jabbed his stubby human finger at me. "If you'd heard the things your mother was saying about you toward the end, you wouldn't be so sad to see her go. You're better off. I barely know you, and I can say that for sure."

"That's a cracked-out thing to say to me. I know who Bev was both on and off the stone. It warped her. She died to keep me from risking my life, taking the stone to Lumipad." I tucked a stray auburn curl behind my ear, my shoulders lowering as I exhaled. "I get that she's hard to love, but I'm pregnant, and I don't have a mama around to show me what's what. It's sad, Kabayo. Just let it all be sad."

He sighed heavily. "I really hate that you don't use my

title when you address me. Ezra's my equal, and even he uses our proper titles."

"Fine. I'll call you King Kabayo, but you have to call me October, Queen of the Dancing Fairies."

"There's no such thing as fairies."

I quirked my eyebrow at him. "I think you mean there's no such thing as Tikbalangs, you giant reverse centaur. I'd actually heard of fairies before Terraway. I'd never heard of anything like you before." I motioned to his black horse head, smirking as he snorted derisively. "You gave up on that awful quick. I think you like that I'm not afraid of you."

"Kings don't bargain with children."

"Whatever you say, Kabayo."

He grumbled under his breath as Ezra came in with the tea tray, giving me a cup that warmed my hands. "To what do I owe the pleasure?" Ezra asked Kabayo. He sat at the head of the table, his hands folded politely over his stomach.

"Something's off with my people. The rain's been enough to start to heal our land, which is great. There've been almost no deaths, and the suns are finally regulated."

"This all sounds like wonderful news." Ezra and I waited for the other shoe to drop. It always did.

Kabayo rubbed the back of his neck, gearing up for the big reveal. "When our land was on the brink of collapse, there was a steady trickle of bodies that died of dehydration or starvation mostly. If the bodies weren't buried properly, they'd reanimate and head east for Sombi, just like every other country's unburied dead." He stared into his tea, not drinking. "My people have stopped dying so often, but the pilgrimages to Sombi haven't stopped. In fact, I've found people who are still very much alive traveling there."

Ezra frowned. "Well, that's not too strange. Some go to Sombi to see if their loved ones are still roaming. Mason used to reside there to bury the dead. Now that he's working Topside, perhaps your people wish to take up his mantle. It's a noble cause."

Kabayo shook his head. "That's what I thought at first, but the Tikbalangs who are going to Sombi are nearly catatonic. They're unresponsive and focused only on getting to Sombi. My men have tried reasoning with them, but they're on a mission. They don't know why, and they can't converse much. It's like they're all touched in the head, but this should be the time we're getting back on our feet."

Ezra did not look as confused as I thought he should. "I was afraid you'd come to me with something like this. Prince Langgam's reported the same problem in his country. It's not all over, mind you, but in the western territory of Sakuna, the people seem to have a singular focus. They finally have the elements they need to rebuild their land, but they've given up in that sector. They're unable to do anything that isn't related to the pilgrimage to Sombi. I didn't know what to make of it, but now that it's happening in two countries, it's a definite problem."

"I'll make a point to talk with Prince Langgam, then. See what all lines up."

I spoke up, which neither man expected me to do. "You might get farther with Geon. He's still locked up in your dungeon awaiting execution, right?"

Kabayo leaned his elbow on his armrest, sitting back in his chair as he eyed me. "But Geon's been in my prison for months, long before this started happening. What light could he shed on it?"

I tapped my fingertips on the table, aiming my response into my teacup rather than across the table. "Maybe none. But if I had to put my money on it, I'd bet it had something to do with Sama."

Kabayo's eyes narrowed as his temper flared. "Sama's spirit and his army were chased out of our land. I would know if he was there, luring my people away."

"I remember the battle, dude. I fought it right alongside you. What I mean is that in Lang's country – you said it's the western territory that's migrating, right?"

Ezra's head bobbed up and down slowly. "That's correct. What's the significance of that?"

"They're the territory that was hit hardest by the famine in Sakuna. They're the only territory in Sakuna who took Sama's rations. What about your country? Where did they start taking rations first? And are they still taking them?"

"The fourth district, and of course. *Buhay* crops don't grow in full overnight. We've still got a long road ahead of us. The rations are supplementing the growing crops, seeing us through. We have a large store of them that'll last us until well after our *buhay* shoots grow back, and we're on our feet again."

I tried to cross my legs, but couldn't do it without my mid-sized belly getting in the way. I sat straighter, uncomfortable in the chair. "Don't you find that strange? I mean, I get why Sama tried to take the rock from me. It would make his rations unnecessary, right? Supply and demand."

"Well, yes. But it was never our plan to live off of rations forever."

"But then why doesn't he go after your stockpile of rations? Hit you where it hurts? It's like after that big battle on your land, Sama went completely off the radar. Not a peep. Don't you think that's weird?"

Kabayo postured. "We defeated his army. We took his muscle, so he has no way to fight us."

I cocked my head to the side, and I could see Kabayo's conviction failing him as the reality of my words sunk in. "Really? Are we just going to believe that Sama couldn't raise a whole other army of undead in a heartbeat? There's a ton of dead Terraway citizens who haven't been buried correctly. Mason's been up here. There's no one to stop Sama's spirit from coming into Sombi and raising up what he needs to take back all the rations without a blink."

"If it's as easy as you say, then why isn't Sama doing

exactly that?" Ezra asked, not so much challenging me as he was wondering.

"It's like he wants you to have the rations. Like it plays in his favor for you to keep giving them out. Now you've got live zombies making their way to Sombi? Bodies without decay that have no will? Sounds like a fantastic recipe for a new and improved soldier to me. I'd be careful, guys. If it was me, I'd stop the rations first thing."

"That wouldn't go over well. We don't have enough food to sustain us yet."

"You will soon, if your people keep deserting your country for Sombi. You'll have plenty of food and no citizens. I don't know what Sama needs live people for, but it looks like he's got them in spades now. And anything that Sama needs? My guess is we shouldn't give it to him, no matter how little we understand about how it all works."

Kabayo gave a half-hearted snort, as if he wanted to scoff at me, but couldn't fully dismiss my warning. Ezra's mouth was hanging open until he put all the pieces in order, snapping to attention. "I'll make some calls and warn the other heads of state."

Kabayo stood and rested his fist on the table, shaking out his mane as he stared down at me, hesitant. "If I didn't think we were equals before, I have no choice now." He bowed his head to me. "I'll have the rations boarded up until we get to the bottom of this."

"That might be a good idea for now. See if it puts a stop to the migrations." I shot him a sympathetic look, worried about the fallout of cutting off their steady food supply. "For what it's worth, I hope I'm wrong."

Kabayo moved around the table to stand next to my chair, extending his hand to me. Our scarred Xs brushed together as he gripped my forearm, forcing me to do the same to him. "Thank you, Queen of the Dancing Fairies."

Read *Temper* and continue with the next book in the *Terraway* series.

ABOUT THE AUTHOR

USA Today bestselling author Mary E. Twomey lives in Michigan with her three adorable children. She enjoys reading, writing, vegetarian cooking, and telling her children fantastic stories about wombats.

While she loves writing fantasy, dystopian, and paranormal tales for her readers, Mary also writes romance under the name Tuesday Embers, and cozy mysteries under the name Molly Maple.

Visit her online at www.maryetwomey.com, and sign up for her newsletter, so you never miss a new release.